*Praise for Tilly Bagshawe*

'A rollicking romp of a read ... Bagshawe has come up with a corker' *Glamour*

'A racy, pacy and very funny updating of Jilly Cooper set in the racing world on both sides of the Atlantic' *Observer*

'Who said hotel management wasn't glam? Honor Palmer would disagree, given the opulence that runs throughout this fun romp. *Do Not Disturb* is like *The OC* meets *Dynasty* – but with even more sex. What more could you wish for?'
*Heat*

'*The Horse Whisperer* and *National Velvet* meet Jackie Collins behind the barn' *Publishers Weekly*

'Hums with sex and glamour – the 1980s blockbuster with an ironic, 21st-century twist ... *Adored* ... will lead the field' *New Statesman*

'Fans of *The OC* will love this sex-scene-studded romp ... Excellent escapism' *Cosmopolitan*

'*Adored* is total self-indulgent, escapist pleasure, I adored it!' Sophie Kinsella

'*Adored* is an ambitious romp of a novel ... all the crucial ingredients are there – cads, gold-diggers, starlets, super-models and whores – in suitable slinky settings ... you'll find yourself getting wrapped up in the drama of Siena McMahon and her messed-up family' *Heat*

'A grand tale of a young girl born into a Hollywood dynasty ... that is so much fun you won't be able to put it down' *OK!*

Tilly Bagshawe is the bestselling author of three previous novels. At the age of seventeen, Tilly was expelled from school for getting pregnant. Undaunted, she gave birth to a beautiful daughter, who she took with her to university and brought up alone before fulfilling her dream of becoming a writer. Now a tired but happy mother of three, Tilly lives in London with her family. Visit her website at www.tillybagshawe.co.uk.

# FLAWLESS

## TILLY BAGSHAWE

An Orion paperback

First published in Great Britain in 2009
by Orion
This paperback edition published in 2010
by Orion Books Ltd,
Orion House, 5 Upper St Martin's Lane,
London WC2H 9EA

An Hachette UK company

3 5 7 9 10 8 6 4 2

Copyright © Tilly Bagshawe 2009

A CIP catalogue record for this book
is available from the British Library.

ISBN 978-1-4091-0328-8

Typeset by Deltatype Ltd, Birkenhead, Merseyside

Printed and bound in Great Britain by
Clays Ltd, St Ives plc

www.orionbooks.co.uk

This book is dedicated to Al Silfen, a true diamond.

# Acknowledgements

Many thanks to Kate Mills, Susan Lamb and everyone at Orion for all their help, advice and hard work. Also to my wonderful agents Tif Loehnis and Luke Janklow and all at Janklow & Nesbit. This book is dedicated to my dear friend Al Silfen (a young Paul Newman) who for the last eight years has been my sanity in LA and my first call when I get off the plane. Thanks to you Al, and to all my friends and family, especially my darling husband Robin and our children, Sefi, Zac and little Theo, who was born during the writing of this book.

TB

# One

'Jake, be careful! You'll lose the stones!'

The panic in Julia Brookstein's voice was unmistakable as she reached down the side of the bed, her long fingers searching blindly through the cream shag-pile carpeting for a missing pink diamond.

'Sweetheart,' Jake Meyer's gravelly, infinitely sexy North London accent whispered in her ear. 'I carried these stones across three continents. I ran checkpoints full of armed police in Chechnya, saw off bandits in the hills of Kazakhstan, and even made it through a knife fight with some particularly tricky Triads in dear old London before I got them this far. Trust me, I'm not going to lose the finest natural pinks I ever laid eyes on under a bed in Beverly Hills. Now come here.'

Pinning both her arms above her head in the soft, marshmallow mound of pillows behind them – how the fuck did she and Al sleep on so many pillows? They must get terrible neck ache – he ran his tongue slowly along the length of her collar bone, the stubble on his chin barely grazing the tops of her massive, perfectly spherical breasts. Scattered across the black satin counterpane were more glittering diamonds, each the same translucent pink of guava flesh. Scooping some up with his left hand, Jake began dropping them carelessly onto her naked body, smiling with satisfaction at the way they glowed against the smooth, bronzed skin of her belly and thighs.

'Oh, Jake!' she gasped, clutching wildly at his blonde hair as his tongue moved tantalisingly lower. Her legs had begun to twitch with excitement, and he could feel her toes stiffen and arch beneath him, a sure sign that she was close to a climax. 'Put one inside me! Please. I want to feel it inside me!'

Jake Meyer had slept with a lot of rich, married women like Julia. They were his bread and butter as a diamond dealer in Beverly Hills, and seducing them sexually went hand in hand with the job of seducing them with the gems he brought back from Russia and Africa. Or in this case, from a little known facility in New Jersey that made some of the best simulants – fake diamonds – in the world. The little pink stones that Julia had so admired were in fact man-made garnets – gadolinium gallium garnets to be precise, known in the trade as GGG – and were almost completely worthless. But they looked the part, every bit as brilliant and dispersive as the real thing, as long as you didn't scratch them. Jake was betting that neither Julia nor her husband Al, a fearsomely powerful studio boss, would know the difference. Julia, a woman for whom size clearly mattered, would be delighted with the necklace and matching bracelet he'd have made up for her. Her old man would be convinced he'd beaten Jake down to a bargain basement price. And Jake would walk away with a very tidy profit. Everyone's a winner!

At thirty-five, Jake and his twin brother Danny were well on their way to becoming the most successful independent diamond dealers in the US. A pair of Jewish wide boys from North London, and the third generation of Meyers in the diamond trade, they had moved to America in their late teens to set up the now hugely profitable Solomon Stones, with Danny working the East Coast market and Jake responsible for LA and the West. Their father, Rudy, had been a world-renowned cutter, as well as a part-time smuggler in his younger days, working the dangerous but lucrative market of Zaire. Ironically, their grandfather, Isaac, had spent most of his adult life working for the CSO, the De Beers cartel in London set up to limit the supply of diamonds to the market and capture illegally smuggled stones, in an attempt to keep prices both constant and high. To say diamonds ran in the Meyer blood would be an understatement. But neither Isaac nor Rudy had had the gift of the gab, that innate talent for salesmanship so powerful it becomes more of a compulsion than a skill, that the twins were both born with. By the age of ten, Jake and Danny already had a lucrative playground business at St Michael's Primary School, Primrose Hill, selling cigarettes and liquor that they'd painstakingly decanted into sweet packets and bottles of Panda Cola respectively. Three expulsions and a smattering of O-levels later, they left school to work as full-time apprentices to their father. It soon became apparent to Rudy that neither boy had the patience or the temperament to make a master cutter. When he caught Jake trying to sell bags of worthless shavings from his workshop at Camden Market as 'genuine diamond dust' – not just trying but succeeding, and at quite a price too – he bowed to the inevitable. Two years later he agreed to provide his sons with the seed capital to start Solomon Stones, buying them each a one-way ticket to America.

Success was by no means instant. Diamond dealing is a tough game, fraught with dangers at all levels, both physical and economic. The Meyer brothers were fast talkers and had an instinctive feel for a good deal and a kosher stone, but they lacked vital experience. Even professional jewellers with years in the business are often unable to tell the difference between a rough diamond and a skilfully cut and coated piece of glass. At the end of their first year, having worked like dogs to build up a nascent client base and generate some savings, Jake and Danny lost everything on a single shipment of stones from a supposedly reliable cutting centre in Israel. Like every other rookie dealer, they learned the hard way that there is no comeback with diamonds, no sale or return, no redress. It's still a handshake business, a closed and uniquely male club. By virtue of their birth, the Meyer boys were members of that club, but that wasn't protection enough. After all, the value of a handshake depends on whose hand it is you're shaking. From that point on, they never wholly trusted anyone except each other. And they made a vow to stick to what they knew, never getting greedy, keeping their operation small and focused and, crucially, well below the radar of the big cartels and established, gang-funded dealerships.

As the years passed their mistakes grew fewer, their client base expanded, and they woke up one morning to find themselves small but established players in the biggest market for polished diamonds in the world. If their family name and good instincts helped them with suppliers, it was their looks and charm that made them favourites with clients. Although twins, they weren't identical. Danny was a good inch shorter than Jake and more stockily built, and although they had the same, unnervingly intense violet-blue eyes and thick, dirty blonde hair, Jake was undoubtedly the more classically good looking of the two. With his long, straight nose, arrogantly curling upper lip and growling, bear-like voice that reduced women to quivering mounds of desire whenever he opened his mouth, he was a natural choice for the looks-obsessed Hollywood market. Danny was handsome too but in a softer, more understated way that played well with the more sophisticated and conservative New York women whom it was his job to impress. Both brothers were possessed of the sort of untiring libidos usually associated with basketball players or porn stars. The first time Jake bedded Julia Brookstein, she'd told him it felt like being ravished by a death-row prisoner on day release. He was renowned amongst the diamond-buying wives of Los Angeles for fucking every beautiful woman like she might be his last.

Sliding further down the bed till his feet touched the padded satin footboard and his head was positioned perfectly above Julia's billiard-ball-smooth waxed pussy, he slipped the largest of the pink stones into his mouth. Grinning as her butterscotch thighs parted like the Red Sea to receive him, he gently pulled apart her glistening pink labia and, using his tongue, pushed the 'diamond' high up into the hot, wet tunnel of her vagina.

'Hmmm.' She moaned with pleasure, clamping her legs tightly around him, and he glanced up just long enough to see the lust dilating her pupils and her lips open expectantly before returning his attention to her clitoris. Flicking his tongue across it as lightly as a dying butterfly fluttering its wings, he mentally counted to three. Right on cue Julia came, stifling her cries with a pillow as her body shuddered with spasm after spasm of pure ecstasy. With each wave of orgasm, the stone slipped lower and lower, until eventually it oozed out of her body back onto the bed, dewy-wet and shining with her juices.

'Beautiful. Like watching an oyster giving up its pearl,' sighed Jake, easing himself back up the bed till he was lying beside her face to face. 'I'd better clean that one up and give it a quick polish before your husband sees it.'

'You're terrible,' giggled Julia. 'You'll do anything or anyone to make a sale, won't you, Jake Meyer?'

She seemed to have conveniently forgotten that it was she who'd dragged him into bed this morning and not the other way around.

'Not true,' said Jake as he padded barefoot into the master bathroom, pulling up the jeans he hadn't had time to take off. 'I wouldn't screw Antonia Jacobs if she promised to buy the Star of India from me.'

Julia giggled again. Ron Jacobs was another studio boss, her husband's great rival, and his wife was what was politely referred to in Beverly Hills society as 'plus-sized'. 'Don't be mean,' she scolded. 'Toni has a glandular problem; it's not her fault. She's got a heart of gold.'

'Yeah, and an arse of lead,' said Jake, turning on the gold taps at one of the his 'n' hers black onyx sinks in Julia's bathroom and gently scrubbing the stone with soap and water. It never ceased to amaze him how women like Julia could show such genuine loyalty and sisterhood towards their girlfriends, but thought nothing of screwing over their poor schmuck husbands. Of course, Al Brookstein might be doing the dirty on his wife too. A guy like that must have bimbos all over him, day and night. But he'd be hard pressed to find a better lay than the one he'd married. Jake should know.

'What time do you think your old man might get back?' he asked, slipping the cleaned stone into a dry felt pouch in his pocket, then scouring the carpet for the few smaller strays that had fallen off the bed before. 'He's not gonna flake on me, is he? 'Cause I've got a lot of people interested in these pinks.'

Julia's beautiful, miraculously surgery-free face instantly hardened. She didn't give a damn who else Jake slept with, but she'd never forgive him if he let another woman touch those diamonds. She was, in so many ways, a woman after his own heart.

'He'll be here,' she said frostily. 'I told him three o'clock, to give us time to ... you know.'

'Negotiate?' suggested Jake, stuffing the rest of the diamonds into his briefcase and pulling his black T-shirt on over his head.

'Exactly,' said Julia.

Just then a door could be heard slamming downstairs and a loud, nasal voice began echoing round the house. 'Ju-Ju? Jules? Are you there, honey?'

Julia's face drained of as much colour as her professional fake-bake tan would allow, and she looked with wild-eyed panic at Jake. 'Oh my God!' she whispered. 'It's him; it's Al. He's twenty minutes early, the stupid jerk. He's *never* early!'

Jake shook his head, looking remarkably unperturbed. 'Some people are so thoughtless.'

'This is not a joke,' hissed Julia, her voice half-whisper, half-sob. 'What the hell are we going to *do*?'

Grabbing her yellow Fred Segal sundress from the floor Jake threw it at her, then pulled her roughly up off the bed and on to her feet. 'Get into the bathroom and get dressed,' he said. 'Lock the door. And take this with you.' Reaching into his jeans pocket, he pulled out the enormous rock that moments ago had been throbbing between her legs and thrust it into her bewildered hand. 'Go! I'll deal with things here.'

Straightening the bed in lightning-quick time, he opened his briefcase and hurriedly emptied the remaining pinks back onto the black satin bedspread. He barely had time to slip on his handmade Italian loafers and straighten his blonde mop of hair before Al Brookstein stormed in, looking far from happy.

'What the fuck are *you* doing here?' he snarled at Jake. 'Where's my wife?'

'She's in the bathroom, looking at a fuck-off pink diamond I brought back from Siberia,' said Jake breezily. 'What do you think of these?' He gestured to the jewels sprinkled across the bed.

Ignoring him, Al marched over to the bathroom but found the door locked. 'Julia?' he called. 'You in there?'

'Oh hi, Al. I didn't hear you come in.' Appearing in the doorway in her cute yellow sundress and flip flops, her long honey mane tied back in a ponytail and her skin still slightly flushed from sex, she looked both utterly desirable and a picture of innocence. Al, a short, beetle-browed man in a crumpled suit who looked every one of his fifty-two years, softened slightly.

'Jake was showing me some diamonds,' Julia smiled. 'Aren't they beautiful?'

'Hmmm,' said Al, fingering the pink stone she handed him and calculating how much Meyer might try to charge him for it. The thing was almost the size of a fucking golf

7

ball – never a good sign in his book. 'He couldn't show you downstairs?'

Julia looked worryingly blank for a moment, but Jake came to her rescue.

'I wanted her to see the colour against a black background,' he said casually, 'so we came up here. Nice bedding by the way, Alan. Very P. Diddy. Come and have a look.'

Torn between annoyance at Jake, who he was sure was mocking him, and desperation to steer his young wife towards the smaller, more affordable diamonds, Al grumpily walked back over to the bed. He was a wealthy man, but Julia's diamond obsession would have tested the bank account of the Aga Khan. Like many of Hollywood's rich and powerful men, Al Brookstein had developed a distrust of Jake Meyer that bordered on loathing. Not only did the bastard look like Daniel Craig, with the sort of washboard abs that few fifty-something husbands could aspire to, but he was always sniffing around Julia and her friends, dangling bling in front of them like a fucking drug dealer. The mere sight of his distinctive blue and silver Maserati in the driveway just now had already brought on Al's chest pains.

'Pretty,' he said grudgingly, picking up a mid-sized stone. 'How much?'

'*Al*,' Julia chided him. 'I'm sorry, Jake. My husband has no soul.' She was about to come out of the bathroom, but thought better of it when an unmistakably fishy whiff of sex drifted up from her body, retreating instead for a surreptitious wash while Al was still distracted.

'Not at all,' said Jake brightly. 'I'm always happy to cut to the chase and talk business. Perhaps you and I should go downstairs, Mr B? Get down to the nitty gritty, as it were.'

'I'm not necessarily buying anything from you today, Meyer,' said Al, in the hopeless tone of a man who knows he is already defeated. 'Let's get that straight right off the bat.'

'I want the big one!' yelled Julia from the bathroom.

Jake smiled. Sometimes his job really was too easy.

An hour later, pulling out of the Brooksteins' wrought iron gates onto North Canon Drive, Jake gave a little whoop of triumph. He'd just sold a three-carat hunk of GGG for six hundred and fifty thousand dollars, to a man famed throughout the entertainment business for being one of the toughest negotiators in Hollywood. Flicking the switch to let the top down on his beloved customised convertible, he luxuriated in the sunshine that seemed to pour out of the LA sky like an inexhaustible stream of liquid butter, even in December. He often missed London, his mates, the pub, the know-it-all taxi drivers, the women with breasts that jiggled when they moved, and faces that moved when they talked. But he had to admit that Los Angeles could be a pretty spectacular place to live too, especially on days like today.

Heading down the canyon into Beverly Hills proper, speeding past the seemingly endless rows of naff Persian mansions with their manicured lawns and vast, vulgar statues of lions in gold or marble guarding their gates, he couldn't resist putting in a brief, gloating call to Danny. He imagined his brother freezing his arse off on a Manhattan street somewhere, soaked to the bone in icy drizzle, and began to feel even more pleased with himself as he punched out the familiar number.

'Dan?' The phone rang only twice before Danny picked up. 'You'll never guess what I've just done.'

'Not now Jakey,' came the terse reply. 'I'll ring you back.'

And to Jake's astonishment, Dan hung up on him.

'Well, that's just bloody charming, that is,' grumbled Jake to himself, pulling into one of the subterranean parking garages on Rodeo. He was closer to his twin brother than to anyone else on earth, and loved him unconditionally, but they had always been deeply competitive. Every Christmas, back home in London, they compared notes on their earnings for the year. For the last three years Danny had just pipped Jake to the post, but today's coup with Brookstein would turn the tables for sure. He'd been looking forward to rubbing his brother's nose in it – in the nicest possible way, of course – but now he was going to have to wait. And though Jake had many good qualities, patience had never been one of them.

Stuffing the pouch containing his remaining simulants into the glove box of the car and locking it, he headed for the elevator. Late lunch on his own at Nate 'n Al's was hardly the celebration he deserved. On the other hand, their chicken matzo ball soup put even his mother's to shame. After the marathon fucking session he'd just had with Julia, followed by the adrenaline rush of pulling a fast one on her husband, he'd worked up quite an appetite.

On the other side of the country, Danny Meyer was in the midst of a deal of his own. Unfortunately for him, his client was not a rookie like Al Brookstein, but a hard-nosed Russian jeweller known simply as 'Vlad' who'd once worked the infamous Udachnyi mine in the frozen Siberian plains of Yakutia, and who knew an overpriced stone when he saw one.

Poring over his diamond balance, a sort of miniature old-fashioned kitchen scale, in the back room of his dingy little store in Queens, Vlad placed the second of Danny's five stones in one pan and, with tweezers, began adding tiny weights to the other pan. It was mesmerising to watch this big oaf of a man, his hands as fat and clammy as bear paws, perform the delicate operation with such consummate skill. Danny stood back to let him work, concentrating on maintaining his poker face while the jeweller made his own assessment of the diamonds he'd brought him, judging each stone according to the 'four Cs' that everybody in the industry worked from – colour, cut, clarity and carat.

Danny wouldn't have been foolish enough to try to cheat an old hand like Vlad on carats. The stones were all tens and eights (one tenth or one eighth of a carat), as the Russian would soon discover for himself. But on clarity, he *had* chanced his hand, claiming all five diamonds were 'perfect', a technical term meaning that a grader would have to magnify them at least ten times to be able to identify any blemishes, when in fact only three fully met that standard. He could only pray that at the end of a long day, and in such dreadful light, Vlad might slip up and miss the small inclusions he'd omitted to mention.

Unlike Jake, however, this wasn't to be Danny's lucky day. Pulling out a standard, 10X colour-corrected loupe, Vlad lifted the stone out of the scale and examined it closely.

'What the fuck ...' he mumbled, his broad giant's brow furrowing into a frown. 'You theenk I'm fucking blind? Perfect my ass. This is an SI one. Maybe even a two. Is worth half the price you asking.'

'Bollocks,' said Danny, doing his best to look affronted. There was nothing for it now but to bluff it out, and pretend that he hadn't noticed the small inclusion, or internal scratch, himself. If Vlad believed he was being deliberately cheated – if he was sure of it – things had the potential to turn very nasty indeed. 'There's nothing wrong with that stone. Let me have a look.'

Vlad passed him the loupe, and Danny made a great show of looking very closely, as if unsure that what he was seeing was a blemish at all.

'Are you talking about the feather, top right? Come on. I can barely even make it out.'

'Barely?' The Russian looked at him witheringly. 'You said "perfect".' Carefully rewrapping each of the stones in diamond paper, he handed them back to Danny. Then, very ominously, he clapped his hands. Seconds later, two even burlier figures emerged from the shadows behind him.

'All right, mate, calm down,' said Danny, swallowing nervously, his eyes swivelling around the room scoping out the nearest means of escape. He'd been in many a sticky situation during his years in the business and knew how to handle himself in a fight, but these odds weren't good and he knew it. 'How long've we been doing business together, eh, Vlad? It was an honest mistake.'

He could see the Russian thinking about it for a moment. Clearly, everybody in the room knew what had really happened. Honest mistakes from diamond dealers were rarer than a flawless four-carat rock, and Vlad was nobody's fool. But if he was two parts thug, he was three parts opportunist. Suddenly the power dynamics of the transaction had shifted in his favour. He might as well make use of that.

'Thirty grand, all five,' he barked.

Danny started to protest. 'Are you smoking fucking dope? The other stones *are* perfect, and that feather's a VS one at most.'

'*Very small*,' Vlad laughed mirthlessly. 'You calling that inclusion *very slight*? I see Manhattan apartments smaller than that feather. You treeck me, you a-hole.'

'They're worth three times what you're offering, and you know it,' said Danny truthfully.

'Thirty thousand,' repeated Vlad. 'Or twenty-five and I break your fucking fingers.'

The heavies behind him cracked their enormous knuckles with relish. What the hell did Russian mothers feed their kids, wondered Danny. Miracle-gro?

'All right, you bastard,' he said bitterly. 'Deal. But that's the last trade we ever do, my friend.'

'You damn right it is,' wheezed Vlad, pulling out wads of filthy banknotes from a drawer in his desk. 'I see you in my store one more time, Danny Meyer, I fucking kill you.'

Danny's first stop was the nearest Bank of America.

After fifteen years in the business, he was used to carrying hundreds of thousands of dollars' worth of stones hidden about his person, in chewing gum, fountain pens, even sewn into the fly flap of his trousers, but he'd never got comfortable wandering around with cash, especially not in New York. It was almost closing time and the branch was full of commuters running end-of-the-day errands. Everyone seemed happy, glad to be out of their offices or off the bitterly cold streets. A few people ahead of him in the line were even exchanging pleasantries with one another, a rare sight indeed in this city. Just as he reached the cashier's window, the witching hour of six p.m. struck, and the girl at the counter firmly waved a 'position closed' sign in his face. It was turning out to be that kind of a day.

'Come on, darling, give a guy a break,' he pleaded, shooting his hand under the clear plastic so she couldn't fully close the shutter between them. 'It's Christmas.'

'I'm an atheist,' she shot back wryly. But something about Danny's face made her hesitate. He was handsome in a brutish, gangster sort of a way, and his broken nose and sexy British accent reminded her of one of those guys from *Lock, Stock*. He also had the most exquisite eyes she'd ever seen, the same liquid purple as grape-juice.

'So? I'm Jewish,' he smiled, sensing her weakening, and realising belatedly that she was actually very pretty in a young Demi Moore sort of a way. 'But that doesn't mean I can't spread a bit of festive cheer. Look, I'll make you a deal. If you let me deposit this wodge burning a hole in my pocket, I'll take you out for the biggest cocktail we can find; how's that?'

'Make it dinner and it's a deal,' said the girl, suddenly deciding that she'd like nothing more than to be the recipient of this divine man's festive cheer for the evening. Removing the position closed sign, she reopened her window, her eyes widening as Danny shoved the filthy bundle of hundreds tied with twine through to her side of the plastic glass wall.

'Early Christmas present,' he grinned. 'From my Aunt Fanny in Maryland.'

The girl rolled her eyes. 'Hey, don't know and don't wanna know, OK? But dinner'd better be somewhere good.'

It was four hours later before Danny finally remembered to call his brother back.

'Oh, cheers,' said Jake grumpily. 'Nice of you to remember my existence.' Danny could hear the noise of a raucous bar behind him, with a lot of over-excited female voices. 'Why d'you hang up on me before?'

'Sorry,' said Danny, turning the sound down on the TV. Having reluctantly dropped the bank girl back at her apartment earlier – Chiara; lovely, melodious name – he was now back home himself, at his loft pad on Broadway and Bleeker, drinking a hot whisky toddy in bed in front of the latest Tivo-ed episode of *EastEnders*. 'I was in the middle of something.'

'Woman?' asked Jake.

'Sadly, no. A deal. But after you called the whole thing went seriously shape-au-poire.' He told Jake about his little miscalculation with Vlad, and how he'd narrowly escaped a serious going-over from the jeweller's heavies. 'I tell you, all that back and forth we had about staying out of Africa 'cause it was too dangerous … Russia's getting just as bad. He made me sell him the whole bloody lot for thirty grand. I'm at least sixty out of pocket now.'

'Don't worry, bruv,' said Jake, unable to keep the smile of triumph out of his voice. 'I'll be happy to lend you a quid or two till you get back on your feet.'

Danny sighed good-naturedly. 'All right then, come on, you're obviously dying to tell me. What masterpiece of salesmanship have you pulled off now, you jammy little sod?'

Jake, who'd been waiting all day to share his good news with somebody, gleefully lingered over every detail of this morning's events, from Julia Brookstein's fabulously responsive, gym-toned body to the gleam of genuine satisfaction in Al Brookstein's eyes when he clinched the deal, convinced he'd just struck himself a hard bargain.

Danny's reaction, however, was less admiring than he'd hoped.

'GGG?' he said incredulously. 'Have you totally lost it? What if he has the thing independently appraised?'

'He won't,' said Jake confidently. 'He's already asked me to set it for him as a pendant. Insisted I "throw that in" in fact, as part of the deal. If he was gonna get it checked out, he'd do it now, before I set it.'

'But anyone who sees a pink that size is gonna know instantly it can't be real. Did you say three carats?'

'Yeah,' Jake laughed. 'Trust me, if this were London or New York, I'd agree with you, but things don't work like that out here. People in LA assume you can get anything you want for the right price. Striped blue bananas, snow in August, diamonds the size of a plum. This is Al King-of-Hollywood Brookstein we're talking about. Everyone'll think he paid ten million, and hey presto, he "found a way" to get a super-sized pink. The word impossible doesn't mean much in this town.'

'Oh yeah? What about the word "prison"? Have they heard of that one in Governator-ville?'

'Give me a break,' said Jake. 'We make a living selling contraband; we're not fucking Tiffany's. Brookstein doesn't want to explain to the judge how he came to pay six hundred grand cash to a dealer, with no receipt, any more than I do.'

'All right, well how about "bankrupt" then,' said Danny. 'Does that ring any bells?' His earlier festive spirit seemed to have waned. 'You can't keep doing this, Jake. It only takes one punter to catch you out flogging a fake and our reputation is shot. Everything we've worked for could be wiped out overnight. This affects both of us, you know.'

'Whatever,' grumbled Jake. 'You're just jealous 'cause I made six hundred in a day *and* had sex with one of the most beautiful women in America, while you got taken up the arse by a fat Ruski and blew three hundred bucks on dinner with a tart from the bloody bank.'

Despite himself, Danny laughed. He was furious with Jake for taking such a stupid risk – in their business partnership as in life, Danny had always been the more sensible, practical one, struggling to rein in his brother's daredevil temperament – but maybe Jake did have a bit of a point. His encounter with Vlad *had* left him feeling more than a little bitter.

'She wasn't a tart, unfortunately for me,' he said, smiling as a furious Pam St Clement, all caked blue eyeshadow and dangly plastic earrings, loomed up as Pat Butcher on the plasma screen in front of him. 'I tried to get her back here for a coffee but it was nothing doing. Great pair of knockers she had, and lovely dark hair. Funny too. Italian.'

'Oh dear, oh dear. You're not falling for her already, are you?' Jake teased him. Danny had a romantic side, a quiet hankering for stability and perhaps even some real love in his life that Jake had always found baffling and amusing in equal measure. Who needed true love in their business, when there was a steady stream of no-strings-attached hot sex on tap? 'Mum won't like that. If she's an Iti she's bound to be Catholic, which'll go down about as well as a fart in a space-suit back home.'

'God, Mum,' Danny groaned. 'Have you got her Christmas present yet?'

It was already early December. In a little over a week both brothers would be heading home to London for Hanukkah and then Christmas. Culturally the Meyers were

Jewish to the core, but they weren't big synagogue-goers, and had never seen the point in boycotting Christmas, which they looked on as a perfectly good opportunity for more eating and drinking, not to mention a great excuse for the giving and receiving of yet more diamonds. Both Jake and Danny looked forward to their winter trip home all year, as a chance to catch up with old friends in St John's Wood and to soak up the atmosphere of the grimy, cold, ridiculously expensive city of their birth. After fifteen years in America, the twins remained British to the core, and had never fully conquered their homesickness for London.

'You'd better not try to pass off any of your GGG rubbish on her.'

'On Mum?' said Jake. 'Christ, I'm not *that* stupid. She'd have my bollocks off with the electric carving knife before she'd even unwrapped it. I was thinking of using the last of those marquises we picked up in Amsterdam this summer. Make her up a nice ring.'

'If you do, let me know and I'll do the earrings,' said Danny. 'Listen bruv, I ought to go. It's past my bedtime here you know.'

'Crap,' said Jake. 'You just want me off the phone so you can get back to your *EastEnders* fix on BBC America, you sad git.'

'Oh, piss off,' grinned Danny, hanging up. That was the problem with having a twin. You could never put anything past them. Sometimes he felt like Jake knew him better than he knew himself.

# Two

Peering out into the wet darkness of the late London afternoon, Scarlett Drummond Murray looked at her watch, an antique Franck Muller her father had given her for her twenty-first, and tried to decide whether it made sense to close up for the day early.

On the one hand it was almost Christmas, and she didn't want to miss any shoppers looking for a last-minute brooch or eternity ring for the women in their lives. This being Notting Hill, one of the most expensive enclaves of the city where even a poky little dolls-house mews could set you back two million, there were plenty of local investment bankers, long on money and short on time, who'd think nothing of running into a store like Bijoux and dropping tens of thousands on jewellery for their wives or mistresses in a matter of minutes.

On the other hand, it was almost six, she wanted to get to Fresh & Wild before it closed and buy some supper and a can of dog food for Boxford, her adorably stupid springer spaniel, and the weather outside was so truly foul, it was hard to imagine anyone braving Westbourne Grove tonight on their way home from work.

'What do you think, Boxie?' she asked, flinching at the violence of the rain-cum-sleet as it pounded the empty pavement. 'Shall we make a break for freedom?'

The dog thumped his tail enthusiastically on the floor, his stock response whenever he heard his name mentioned, and returned to the serious business of mauling his mistress's discarded Ugg boot. Scarlett, who knew full well that he would have thumped his tail just as hard if she'd said 'Come on Boxford, what about a nice trip to the vivisectionist?' decided she would take this as a yes, and switched the 'open' sign in the doorway to 'closed'.

Gosh, she was tired. Pulling down the blinds, her back and shoulders ached like an old woman's. It was an effort to lift the heavy trays of jewellery, all her own designs, out from the glass display cases and into the safe at the back of the shop. She really must try to make it to yoga at the Life Centre this week, for her mental health as much as her poor muscles. Heaven knew she'd have precious little time to channel her inner calm once she got home to Scotland for Christmas.

At almost six foot, with long molasses-brown hair and a perfect, willowy figure, Scarlett Drummond Murray had originally come to London to work as a model, one of the first 'aristo girls' as they were known – Jasmine Guinness, Honor Frazer, Stella Tennant – to be snapped up by a big London agency. But despite her striking beauty: porcelain pale skin, lightly freckled across the bridge of the nose, wide-set amber eyes, cheek bones so sharply prominent you could have served sushi on them, she wasn't a natural model. Having grown up in a family that set little store by looks, especially hers (her father's pet name for her growing up was 'giraffe'), Scarlett had never developed the confidence to go with her ethereal good looks, and was clumsy when she moved. She was also hopelessly dreamy, and found it impossible to concentrate on shoots, which often involved standing in front of a camera for hours on end with nothing to do but keep turning one's head this way or that. Inevitably her mind would wander to more interesting things – the latest Oxfam report on famine in Congo, her girlfriends' love-life problems, whether or not she'd remembered to leave fresh water in Boxford's bowl before she left the flat that morning – and take her eye off the ball just at the crucial moment, to the frustration of the photographer and crew. Catwalk work was even worse.

Scarlett was forever missing cues because she was too busy backstage, trying to comfort the make-up girl whose boyfriend had just announced he was gay, or missing flights to important shows because she somehow managed to get her days muddled up.

It was a relief to her agency as much as to her when she finally decided to quit modelling and go into business for herself, as a jewellery designer. With no formal design training, never mind business experience, even her friends privately thought her latest career change offered little prospect of success. But Scarlett had proved them all wrong. With the modest nest-egg she'd saved from modelling, she put down a deposit on the tiny premises in Westbourne Grove just before the area exploded as a property 'hot-spot' and watched it treble in value in the space of eight years. During this period, as well as learning on the job and from the veritable library of self-help books she'd picked up from Waterstone's – *Small Business for Dummies*, *Make Jewellery Design Work for You*, *Be your own Book Keeper* – she diligently attended night classes at the London Business School. Armed with her newly acquired business acumen, and a natural flair for design and eye for beauty that no course in the world could have taught her, she launched Bijoux with a small party the day after her twenty-second birthday. By the end of the first year she had established suppliers and a steadily growing customer base, with a good smattering of repeat business. Eighteen months in, she was turning a consistent profit, and it wasn't long before her store became synonymous with all that was hip and vibrant about Notting Hill, a bastion of boho, young London style.

Now, at twenty-seven, Scarlett was a reluctant regular on the pages of *Tatler* and *Harpers & Queen*, and rarely did a month go by without one of her pieces being featured in *Vogue* or *In Style*. Now that they no longer had to deal with her scattiness professionally, her old colleagues from modelling days were more than happy to support Scarlett as a designer, and she often found model friends and photographers willing to work for her for knock-down rates, or even sometimes for free. Once she started her Trade Fair campaign, raising awareness about corruption in the jewellery industry and the widespread use of 'blood' diamonds – diamonds originating from war zones, usually in Africa, and smuggled onto the market illegally – the goodwill towards both her and Bijoux had snowballed still further. These days, Trade Fair was almost on a par with PETA, the anti-fur animal rights group, as the London fashion crowd's cause of choice.

Picking up a diamond and emerald brooch in the shape of an apple with a single bite taken out of it – she'd christened the piece 'Eve's Temptation' – Scarlett lovingly ran a finger over the shimmering stones. To her, each of her creations was like a child, unique and beautiful in their own way. She poured so much love and care into her work, that she still found it hard to sell a much-loved piece to a buyer who seemed unworthy of it – a spoiled housewife, or a rich man buying thoughtlessly for a girlfriend who'd be more impressed by the Bijoux box than the work of art inside it.

The polished diamond beneath her fingertip felt cold and smooth. Closing her eyes, she tried to imagine what it had felt like to the hands, almost certainly black and impoverished, who had first plucked it from the earth, ending its fifty or perhaps even a hundred million years of subterranean existence. Very different, that was for sure. It would have felt warm. Rough. To all outward appearances, worthless. The long journey each stone made before becoming part of a brooch or ring somewhere on the other side of the earth had always seemed impossibly romantic to Scarlett. She knew she represented the safe, sanitised, wealthy end of the diamond food-chain, but she still felt a close emotional connection to everyone who had helped each stone along the different legs of its journey – the miners, drivers, cutters, polishers and appraisers – before it arrived at her workshop.

Her over-developed social conscience, already an irritating thorn in the side of the diamond cartels and multinational retail chains, was part nature, part nurture. Always a sensitive and loving little girl, she grew up in a uniquely sheltered and privileged world in her family's ancestral stately home in Scotland, Drumfernly Castle. Had it not been for the many long childhood summers spent in South Africa, at her Aunt Agnes's game reserve near Franschhoek, she might never have seen a black face until the day she left St Clement's Girl's Boarding School in Inverness to make her own way in London. As it was, by the time she began modelling she had long since developed a passionate interest in African affairs and the injustices of globalisation. Never, ever would she forget her first trip to Cape Town, driving past the corrugated iron shacks of the shanty towns, where thousands of Aids-stricken people sweltered in the hundred-degree heat, whilst less than two miles away their white neighbours lounged by swimming pools, plainly visible from the shacks, congratulating themselves on how cheaply they'd bought their property, and wondering aloud where else in the world you could enjoy a full lobster supper with a decent bottle of Pinot Grigio for the equivalent of five US dollars.

Loading the last of the jewellery trays into the safe, she closed and locked it with a satisfying 'cl-clunk' and reached up to the peg by the door for Boxford's lead.

'Come on, you big lug,' she said, ruffling his tangled fur and clipping the lead onto his collar, whilst simultaneously removing her tattered left Ugg boot from his slobbery jaw and slipping it onto her foot. 'We'd better get a move on if you want to eat.'

Outside the rain was even colder than it looked. Stepping into it from the warm cocoon of the shop felt like getting out of a sauna into one of the showers at St Clement's, so freezing it made you gasp for breath. Dressed for the cold but not the wet – the sky had been as crisp and blue as a butterfly's wing when she set out for work this morning – it wasn't long before Scarlett was soaked to the bone. Her Ugg boots squelched audibly with each step, and icy water ran off the sleeves and back of her sodden suede coat like hundreds of miniature mountain streams, joining forces with the torrents running in the gutters as she crossed Portobello Road.

'You need an umbrella, love!' shouted the fish 'n' chip man from across the road. 'Wanna borrow mine?'

'Thanks,' Scarlett yelled back. There was very little traffic but the noise of the rain was deafening. 'But I think it's a bit late for that now. We're almost home anyway.'

Cheered by this exchange, she stepped up her pace, dragging poor Boxford from puddle to puddle on their way to the local organic supermarket. Even on a horrid, grey day like today, Scarlett adored Notting Hill. The friendliness, the sense of community, the quirky, boutiquey shops of Portobello competing for space and custom with super chi-chi stores like Matches and Anya Hindmarch. In the eight years since she'd moved here, she'd seen the area go from genuinely bohemian, a home to artists and artisans from all walks of life, to its current status of 'Belgravia of the North', a stomping ground for hedge fund millionaires and their tacky Russian wives, with their furs and Bentleys and round-the-clock nannies for their baby-Dior-clad offspring.

But she could never bring herself to join the new breed of Notting Hill-haters. Yes, there was a lot of new money coming in, an inevitable result of the crazy property hike. But there was still a mix of rich and poor, alternative and mainstream, arty and financial, that couldn't be found anywhere else in London. Ten-million-dollar mansions still stood cheek by jowl with council blocks, and the pound shop on Kensington Park Road did every bit as brisk a business as the Paul Smith on the corner. People *talked* to each other here, on the street, in shops and cafes. There was a palpable sense of belonging, so much so that as a single girl Scarlett never felt uneasy walking home alone late at night, as she would have done elsewhere in the city.

Fresh & Wild was closing up as she arrived, but Will the manager took pity on her bedraggled state and let her in anyway. 'As long as you're quick,' he added, holding Boxford's lead for her while she darted inside, slipping through the empty aisles, all beautifully hung with holly and mistletoe for Christmas. 'The football starts in an hour and I'm not missing kick-off for anyone.'

Five minutes later, armed with some smoked tofu, leeks, expensive organic chocolate and a quarter of a pound of lean minced beef for Boxie – a terrible extravagance, especially at these prices, but he'd been such a patient boy today she decided he deserved it – she was off again, head down against the wind, walking back towards Ladbroke Grove and the beckoning warmth and comfort of her flat.

Having ploughed almost all of her savings into the business, Scarlett's two-bedroom conversion in a dilapidated Victorian villa was at the distinctly cheap and cheerful end of the market. But with her flair for colour and innate sense of style, she'd transformed it into a haven of warmth and homeliness, her refuge from the cut and thrust of the jewellery business and from life in general. A passionate hater of minimalism, in jewellery as well as interior decor, she'd crammed the flat with colourful treasures from her travels. African masks and brightly woven textiles from Mexico and Bolivia were thrown together with a carefully selected handful of inherited antiques: an inlaid mahogany and walnut desk of her grandmother's, Victorian and over-the top ornate; a library full of ancient atlases and bound maps that she loved chiefly for their dusty, leathery smell; and in the so-called 'master bedroom', her pride and joy, a Jacobean four-poster hung with vintage lace and linen curtains, so big that she couldn't fit so much as a bedside table next to it and had to climb out of the foot of the bed every morning.

As soon as she'd squeezed through the door, dumping her shopping bags unceremoniously on the hall floor, she ran to fetch two towels from the bathroom, one for Boxford and another for herself. It was a further five minutes before either one of them was dry enough to progress through to the sitting room, Scarlett having shed her boots, coat, sweater, socks and sodden jeans and wearing nothing but a red vest-top, matching bra and pair of M&S white cotton knickers. Happily, the flat was already toasty-warm. Having grown up in a draughty castle in Scotland, central heating was one of the few ecologically unsound luxuries in which Scarlett indulged to the full, and she didn't hesitate to turn on the gas fire full blast so that Boxford could settle down comfortably in front of it on his favourite, tatty armchair.

'Bloody bills. Honestly, don't they know it's Christmas?' she grumbled, going back into the hall and scooping up a huge pile of brown envelopes along with a smattering of white ones – Christmas cards, probably – and carrying them into the kitchen along with the groceries. Flicking the radio on to Classic FM for the carols and lighting a Diptyque Myrrh candle, the ultimate smell of Christmas, she set about warming Boxford's mince and chopping leeks for herself, intermittently opening post as she went.

Making the cardinal sin of opening the white envelopes first, she was punished when the first one turned out not to be a Christmas card, but a letter from her mother, Caroline.

*Looking forward to seeing you, darling,* it began, unconvincingly. *I'm writing to remind you to pick up my food order from Harrods before you drive up, and all the decorations from Peter Jones. You can help me with those when you get here. Pa's been complaining that the parlour looks awfully drab.*

Scarlett felt the first stirrings of annoyance prickle across her skin. 'Help you, my arse,' she mumbled crossly. 'I'll be doing the whole darned thing, just like every other year.' And why on earth couldn't her mother get the Harrods hamper delivered like everybody else? Last year the stench of the Stilton sweating on the back seat for fourteen hours had made the drive almost unbearable, and she kept having to reach into the back to prise Boxford away from the apple and clove spiced sausages. Not to mention the fact that a trip into Harrods tomorrow on the busiest weekend of the year, followed by a second detour to her brother Cameron's house in Chelsea, would mean they wouldn't be able to set off until close to lunchtime, slap bang in the middle of the worst of the holiday exodus traffic. Next year she was *definitely* taking a plane home for the holidays, carbon footprint or no carbon footprint. She'd rather plant a rainforest with her bare hands than go through that nightmare drive one more time.

*Also darling, I know Cameron will want to share the driving,* Caroline went on, *but I do think it's important you let him rest as much as possible. He's been terribly busy at the office lately and he desperately needs a break.*

And I don't? thought Scarlett furiously. Cameron, her older brother, sole heir to Drumfernly and the rest of the Drummond Murray family fortune, had always been the apple of their mother's eye. Now an investment banker, clawing his way up the ladder at Goldman Sachs and already earning a second small fortune, he'd become even more insufferably self-important recently, glued to his Blackberry as though the world would stop if it lost contact with him for even a minute. Scarlett wouldn't have minded so much if he, or any of her family, had taken her own career a bit more seriously. But none of them had given her the slightest praise or encouragement for her achievement with Bijoux, or for the huge strides she'd made in her Trade Fair campaign. The only thing Caroline Drummond Murray was interested in for her daughter was a successful marriage, which in her book meant marriage to the eldest son of one of a select group of Scottish families, no matter how dull or uninspiring he might be. And on this front Scarlett was determined to remain an abject failure.

Too pissed off to read any more, she ripped open another white envelope and pulled out a glossy, stiff-backed card with a picture of the Rockefeller Center ice rink and Christmas tree on the front. Inside, to her joy and relief, was a letter from Nancy, her oldest and closest girlfriend, crammed with gossip and plans for Scarlett's New Year shopping trip to New York. Nancy was based in LA, trying to make it as a scriptwriter, but her family were dyed-in-the-wool New Yorkers and she always spent the holidays there. The thought of her five-day mini-break with Nancy was the only thing keeping Scarlett even faintly sane as another Christmas at Drumfernly loomed.

'Oh, shit! Bugger, bugger, bugger!'

Leaping to her feet she turned off the gas and pulled Boxford's charred mince in its smoking pan off the hob. Climbing up on to the table, still in her knickers and vest and with her long damp hair stuck to her back like seaweed, she hurriedly disabled the smoke alarm before it could go off and annoy the neighbours. 'Sorry, Boxie darling,' she said, opening the tiny barred window a crack to let out the fumes and salvaging what was left of the good meat with a wooden spoon as the dog padded through into the kitchen, tail wagging. 'I'm afraid it's half rations. I got a bit distracted.'

Deciding that the rest of the post could wait, she gave him his meal, padded out with a bit of Pedigree Chum mixer, and set about preparing her own food. When focused, Scarlett was actually a decent cook, and had been an ardent fan of fresh organic ingredients long before it became fashionable. Not usually a big drinker, the prospect of tomorrow's drive and all the wrapping and packing she still had to do tonight was so depressing that she ended up opening a bottle of Jacob's Creek and finishing almost all of it while she ate, flicking idly through the latest copy of *Forever*, the diamond industry's quarterly trade magazine.

'Oh, look, Boxie, look!' she slurred excitedly, stumbling upon a feature about her Trade Fair fundraiser last month at the Dorchester. 'They're actually writing nice things about us for once. Can you believe it?'

The event, an auction hosted by two of Scarlett's more successful model girlfriends, had been attended by the usual do-gooder crowd of charity junkies – bored, wealthy wives mostly, who liked to soothe their consciences after a hard day exercising their husband's credit cards at Boodles by 'giving something back' the only way they knew how: getting their hair and Botox done, slipping on a couture dress and dropping five hundred pounds a head on a ticket for a glamorous charity dinner at one of London's top hotels.

'You must stop it,' Scarlett told herself firmly, skimming through the gushing review and accompanying pictures of Jemima Khan looking as horse-faced and inbred as ever. 'Don't be so judgemental.' As much as she might disapprove of her patrons' lifestyles, she needed both their money and their high-profile support if her campaign was to have any chance of success. Thanks to the hostility of the cartels, Trade Fair got precious little good PR. She should be grateful for this article, however creepily sycophantic it might be, and for the socialite supporters who made it possible. Scribbling down the name of the journalist on the back of an envelope, she made a mental note to call and thank him in the morning.

Skipping past a piece on the two-million-pound revamp of Cartier's flagship on Bond Street, her attention was caught by a picture of the Meyer twins, Jake and Danny, arm in arm and grinning at some trendy new jeweller's in New York.

*Flying the flag for British bespoke expertise in the diamond trade*, read the accompanying blurb, *Solomon Stones' founders*

*Jacob and Daniel Meyer enjoy some Stateside hospitality at the new Max Peterson store on Park Avenue.*

'Wankers!' Scarlett heard herself yelling at the page. She'd definitely overdone it on the old Pinot. 'Flying the flag for grasping, unprincipled womanisers more like it.'

She'd met the Meyers only once, last year at an industry function in Amsterdam, but already knew them well by reputation and had disliked both of them on sight. Arrogant, vain and immensely impressed by their own perceived 'charm', she'd watched them oil their way around the great and the good at the party like a pair of Cockney jellied eels. With their cosmetically white smiles, year-round tans and loud, wide-boy suits, they radiated insincerity and self-interest like a pair of politicians running for office. Well known for their shady business practices and, far more unforgivably in Scarlett's eyes, for their continued willingness to buy stones from tainted sources like Congo and Angola, they were nevertheless welcomed by high society in London and America, fêted as much for their good looks and reputed prowess in bed as for their beautiful, cut-price diamonds.

Jake, the cockier of the two, had been foolish enough to make a half-hearted pass at her in Amsterdam, so she'd had an opportunity to examine the fabled 'Meyer magic' at close quarters. Personally, she couldn't see what all the fuss was about. Fine, so he was regular-featured, but then so was Ted Bundy, and he wore enough Gucci Envy to fell an elephant at fifty yards. Was she really the only woman in London immune to his charms? The only woman who cared about the appalling conditions in Africa that Jake and his ilk were helping to perpetuate?

At least spending the holiday immured at Drumfernly with her parents would mean she was in no danger of running into the Jake-and-Danny show. When the Meyers came back to London at Christmas, the It-girls, models and wives that made up the core local diamond-buying market

– not to mention Bijoux's own customer base – seemed to degenerate into an embarrassing flurry of excitement, like giddy schoolgirls. Always listed in *Tatler*'s top five 'Most Eligible Bachelor' rankings, despite the fact that neither of them had lived in London for aeons, both Jake and Danny were considered big society draws. It made Scarlett's blood boil.

Still, this was no time to be wasting mental energy on Jake stupid Meyer. She still had everything to do before tomorrow, and a mountain of wrapping paper, Sellotape and ribbon waiting in a reproachful pile on her bed. She'd better get stuck in before the wine really got the better of her, and she forgot which present was for whom.

# Three

'So I told him,' said Cameron, drawing breath for the first time in at least a minute, 'I said, "Listen Muhammad," I said, "I don't care how rich you are, or how your grandfather's grandfather used to do business. We are Goldman Sachs. We are *the* premier investment banking organisation *on this planet*. And we do our deals, our way. Now are you in or are you out?" And of course, the poor little guy's balloon was well and truly popped after that,' he laughed. 'It's always the same with the bloody A-rabs. All they need is a firm hand, and next thing you know they're eating out of it.'

'Hmm,' said Scarlett, who'd tuned out of her brother's self-aggrandising monologue well over two junctions back on their torturously slow slog up the M1. 'Well, never mind. It sounds like you did the best you could.'

'What do you mean?' snapped Cameron. 'I just told you, I nailed that little dweeb. Sheikh bloody Muhammad might be a big noise in Kuwait, but he's a pretty small fish in the sort of waters Goldman swim in, I can tell you.'

'But didn't you say earlier that his net worth was somewhere north of ten billion?' said Scarlett, casting around for any scrap of information from his tedious, long-winded speech that she could remember.

Cameron gave an unimpressed shrug of his thirty-year-old, associate shoulders. 'So?'

'Well, nothing. It's just I'm sure I saw in the paper the other day that Goldman's market cap is around thirty billion. So doesn't that mean that this chap, this one "little" man, could buy up a third of your entire company if he wanted to?'

'I'm afraid it's not that simple,' Cameron snorted, adding patronisingly, 'I wouldn't give up the day job if I were you, Scar. You wouldn't make much of an i-banker.'

He didn't appreciate being caught out on the facts by his dippy little sister. Since when did Scarlett know what a market cap was, anyway?

Scarlett, in fact, couldn't have been less interested in her brother's latest professional 'triumph' if he'd been recounting it to her in Urdu. On previous journeys with Cameron, she'd passed the time by playing an adapted mental version of 'pub cricket' whereby she scored a run every time he said the words 'Goldman Sachs', a four for any regurgitated American business-school phrases like 'think outside the box' or 'step up to the plate', and a six for real clangers such as 'I'm gonna blue-sky this with my boss'. But after last Christmas, when she'd racked up a century before they'd even got past Luton airport, she decided the game was no longer enough of a challenge.

Besides, her head was throbbing so badly, it was all she could do to concentrate on the road, never mind listen to the constant stream of drivel emanating from the passenger seat. Having collapsed into bed at three o'clock that morning with bits of Sellotape still stuck to her hair, she'd been woken up at six with a pounding hangover to the sound of workmen drilling up the road outside her window. From there the morning had gone from bad to worse, starting with cleaning up a big pile of dog-shit in the kitchen (poor Boxford's beef hadn't agreed with him) and progressing to the hell-on-earth that is Harrods' Food Hall on the Saturday before Christmas. After an hour and a half of queuing, smiling politely while tourists pushed in front of her, trod on her foot, and engaged in piercingly loud conversations in their own various languages within millimetres of her battered eardrums, she finally emerged onto Walton Street weighed down with overpriced cheese, meats and chocolate like a packhorse, only to find that her car had been ticketed and was in the process of being clamped – with poor Boxford howling in the back!

Much screaming and a fifty-pound bribe later, she was on her way again, but on arrival at Cameron's gorgeous townhouse by the river in Chelsea, she found him still asleep and not yet packed, curled up in bed at noon in his Conran silk pyjamas like the Sultan of bloody Brunei.

She'd been furious at the time, of course. But now, five hours into their (at least) ten hour journey, she rather thought she preferred him asleep.

Desperate to take advantage of the lull in conversation, she switched on the radio. Her head hurt too much for music, so she plumped for Radio 4, hoping that the sooth-ing tones of Jenni Murray on *Woman's Hour* might calm her battered spirits. They listened in silence to a repeat of last Sunday's *Thought for the Day* – some sweet rabbi from Leeds talking about the importance of tolerance at Christmas, and the close bond between Judaism and Christianity – and through a series of light-hearted, festive news items about drunk and disorderly carol singers and a parrot who could apparently recite ''Twas the night before Christmas'. But the mood in the over-stuffed grey Volvo changed dramatically when a report came on about the American mine-owner Brogan O'Donnell, and the mysterious lung and throat cancers affecting workers in his Russian diamond mines.

'It's hard to describe the bleakness of Yakutia,' the Scottish reporter was saying, his feet crunching audibly across the Siberian ice. 'This remote region of Russia produces over ninety-eight per cent of all the country's diamonds – that's twenty per cent of the world supply of gemstones. Everything here – the entire landscape – is white-grey, and the cold is absolutely … paralysing.' You could hear the biting wind whistle in the background and the poor man struggling to get his breath. 'A lot of people are making fortunes here, many of them foreigners, like the American billionaire Brogan O'Donnell, chairman of

O'Donnell Mining Corp. But for the miners, working in these utterly appalling conditions day after day … it's a very different story. When you're struck down with a serious illness in Yakutia, there's precious little help on offer.'

For the next several minutes, a series of O'Donnell workers, most of whom had asked to be allowed to remain anonymous, told their stories via an interpreter. In flat, dispassionate voices, they recounted their symptoms – all hauntingly similar – the shortness of breath, coughing spells, chest pains so acute they found themselves suddenly unable to stand, never mind work. They described a world in which lung cancer was merely a final insult, set against a lifetime of subsistence-level pay – miners in the former Soviet Union were some of the worst paid in an industry notorious for exploiting its workers, far worse off in real terms than their South African counterparts – abysmal mine safety records, a total lack of healthcare, education, even basic sanitation facilities in their living quarters. It was heartbreaking.

'How can they be so bloody stoic about it?' said Scarlett furiously, swerving into the fast lane in her fury and only narrowly missing an HGV, whose driver beeped loudly and shook his fist as she passed.

'They're used to it,' said Cameron blithely. 'I daresay it's a lot better than it used to be under the commies, and what's their alternative? Planting turnips in the permafrost?'

'Their *alternative* is to have greedy bloody employers like O'Donnell forced to comply with basic pay and safety regulations,' spluttered Scarlett, 'as they would have to in any other industry. It's a bloody disgrace! People wouldn't buy those diamonds if they knew what was going on.'

'Oh, come on,' Cameron laughed. He looked smugger than ever in his bespoke tweed jacket, an incipient double chin quivering beneath his silk Turnbull & Asser cravat. 'Even you can't be so naive as to believe that.'

'Those mines are causing cancer,' said Scarlett, ignoring

him. 'It's O'Donnell Mining Corp's fault those men are dying.'

'That's pure supposition,' said Cameron firmly. 'I'll bet you they all smoke, every last one of them.'

But Scarlett shushed him and turned up the volume. Amazingly, Brogan O'Donnell himself was giving an interview. Famed for his hostility towards the media he almost *never* spoke to the press. But suddenly the car was filled with his voice, a surprisingly gentle, measured baritone and not at all the strident, belligerent American drawl Scarlett had expected.

'I'm not saying life in those mines isn't tough,' he was telling the BBC reporter calmly. 'Life in former soviet Russia is tough for most people, and Yakutia is a place of incredible physical and environmental extremes. What I am saying is that O'Donnell Mining Corp provides far better working conditions than existed there previously. And that we are continuing to improve those conditions as best we can, introducing social programmes, and yes, education and health provision are both areas we need to focus on. But you're talking about a region with almost no existing infrastructure. It isn't simply a case of throwing money at the problem.'

'Bullshit!' Scarlett exploded, so loudly that poor Boxford woke with a start from a very pleasant dream he was having about chasing pheasants and started barking plaintively, unsure where he was or what on earth was going on. 'Don't make it sound complicated, you arsehole. Pay those poor men enough to feed their families!'

But even she had to admit Brogan sounded worryingly plausible, the fair-minded capitalist doing his best for his workers under extraordinary and challenging conditions.

'The diamond business is good for Russia, and for this part of the country it's a genuine lifeline. There is no evidence whatsoever to link isolated lung cancer cases to our mines. It's not as if we're digging for asbestos.'

'Exactly,' nodded Cameron.

'Most of the campaigners trying to shut us down have never even been to Yakutia,' continued Brogan. 'They have no idea what a vacuum would be left if businesses like mine pulled out, or were priced out of the market here by the unworkable labour laws and health insurance premiums they're proposing.'

'The guy sounds like a smart cookie,' said Cameron, knowing how much it would annoy his sister. 'It's easier to get all holier-than-thou about it, but the fact is these Ruskies need him.'

'Yes, they do,' Scarlett shot back, livid. 'And Brogan O'Donnell exploits that need. Criminally, in my opinion. Those poor men are dying like flies, and listen to him. He doesn't give a damn.'

'Yes, well, that makes two of us,' yawned Cameron. Turning up the heating on Scarlett's horrible Scandinavian car, he tipped his seat back and soon fell into a contented, dreamless sleep.

Rising from the surrounding pine forest and sea mist like a vast, grey ship breaching a wave, Drumfernly was widely considered to be one of the most beautiful estates in north-east Scotland. Ten miles inland south of Inverness, the castle was a turreted granite masterpiece. Once used as a hiding place for Bonnie Prince Charlie, it had been in Drummond Murray hands since it was built in 1520, and a watertight entailment ensured that it would remain so for many generations to come. If Cameron had no sons, the estate would pass to his nearest male relative, however distant such a person proved to be. Once identified, they would have to agree to revert to the surname Drummond Murray, and to have their children do the same. They would also be obliged to spend a minimum of six months of the year 'in residence' at Drumfernly. If they baulked at either of these conditions, the inheritance would pass to the next male in line, and so on and so on until a willing 'taker' was found.

So far, no one had baulked, and it wasn't hard to see why. With its long, winding drive lined with fir trees, interspersed with crumbling bridges spanning the crystal-clear waters of its salmon stream, its Rapunzel towers and three-foot-thick medieval wooden doors, Drumfernly was like the fairytale castle from a Grimm Brothers' story. Every time she came home, Scarlett was struck again by its beauty, and for a moment would wonder how on earth she could have so dreaded coming back here.

But only for a moment.

'Darlings!' Caroline Drummond Murray, dressed in a nightie, dressing gown, parka and Wellington boots, crunched her way across the gravel to greet her children. It was nearly midnight, but the moon was full and bright and the stars out in full, so she had no need of the torch wedged like a baton in her coat pocket. 'At last!'

Ignoring Scarlett, she opened the passenger door and helped Cameron, who moments ago had been slumped back against the headrest, snoring loudly, out into the chill night air. 'Poor thing, you must be shattered,' she said solicitously.

'I am actually,' he yawned, kissing her on both cheeks and allowing her to lead him into the warmth of the house. 'I don't suppose there's any chance of some late supper, is there?'

'Er, excuse me?' Having opened the back door for Boxford, who was now running around the lawn ecstatically, peeing like a garden sprinkler, Scarlett was busy heaving presents and suitcases out of the boot. 'Some help would be nice.'

'Don't be silly, darling,' said Caroline brusquely. 'Cameron's exhausted. Bring in what you need for tonight and I'll send Duncan out to help with the rest first thing in the morning.'

Too tired to argue, Scarlett did as she was told, and after a brief but delicious kitchen supper of kedgeree – good old Mrs Cullen had excelled herself again – collapsed on to her childhood bed. Her bedroom was just as it had always been, as unchanging in reality as in her memory: a small turreted octagon at the top of the east wing of the castle, with thick stone walls that felt cold to the touch even in hot summer, and a high wooden bed piled even higher with linen sheets and ancient, rough woollen blankets against the winter chill. A few dog-eared photographs of former family pets, or long-since sold ponies, remained stubbornly Blu-tacked around the mullioned window, next to the smattering of Pony Club rosettes that had once been Scarlett's greatest source of pride.

*What a long time ago that was,* thought Scarlett. Before she knew it, she was deeply asleep.

By the time she woke the next morning, bright winter sun was burning its way through the cracks in the shutters. Getting woozily to her feet, still wrapped in the scratchy woollen blanket – Christ, it was cold in here – she hopped gingerly across the floor and opened them fully, flooding the room with sunshine so dazzling it made her sneeze. Pulling on her discarded clothes from last night – faded blue jeans, Ugg boots and a Gap wool sweater with a giant snowflake on the front – she headed straight downstairs for breakfast.

'Hello poppet.' Her father, Hugo, absorbed in the *Sunday Telegraph* sport section and a plate of congealing fried egg, kissed her absently on the cheek as she sat down. Short, fat and bald, with a kindly, ruddy-cheeked face and a permanently bewildered expression, Hugo Drummond Murray looked absolutely nothing like his beautiful daughter – although he was responsible for both Scarlett and Cameron's unique hazel eyes. Dressed permanently in an old pair of corduroy trousers and a hunting jacket so threadbare that it was now more darn than tweed, he looked to Scarlett like a cross between Tweedledum and Friar Tuck, with perhaps a hint of Prince Charles thrown in for good measure. How he had ever come to marry a pushy socialite like her mother was a mystery not just to her but to most of Scotland.

'Hello Pa,' she smiled. 'Any bacon still on the go?'

'Not sure,' said Hugo vaguely. He was immersed in a double-page spread on fly fishing in Slovenia. 'I think your brother may have finished it earlier. There are plenty of eggs though. Shall I ring for Mrs Cullen?'

'No, don't be silly,' said Scarlett. 'I think I can manage to scramble myself a few eggs.'

After a satisfying breakfast of egg on toast, washed down with two pint-sized mugs of hot, fresh coffee, she was starting to feel a bit more human. But the peace wasn't destined to last long.

'Ah, Scarlett dear, you're up at last.' Caroline, looking immaculate and whip-thin as ever in a navy-blue Country Casuals twin-set to match her eyes, swept regally into the kitchen. Once a beautiful woman, she was now what would most easily be described as 'handsome'. Blessed with the same high cheekbones and clear complexion she had passed on to her daughter, she would have looked younger than her fifty-two years if it weren't for her permanently erect posture and penchant for formal, tailored clothes, even when relaxing at home. Noticing Scarlett's dirty jeans and unwashed hair, she wrinkled her perfect little snub nose disapprovingly. 'Really, darling, you might have changed. You look like something the cat's dragged in. Have you even washed?'

'No,' said Scarlett patiently. 'The water was arctic in my room, as usual, and there were no towels. As for changing, all my stuff's still in the car. Cameron was too "shattered" to help me unpack last night, remember?'

'Do stop frowning like that, darling, it's terribly aging,' said Caroline. She loved her daughter, contrary to what

Scarlett might believe, but had never understood her, even as a toddler, which had inevitably made for a distant, combative relationship. Cameron was more like her: uncomplicatedly ambitious, and a natural social snob. She favoured him because he made it so easy for her to do so, while Scarlett ... well, Scarlett had always been the cuckoo in the nest at Drumfernly. Her childhood compassion for injured birds or animals had morphed, during her teenage years, into a worldview that seemed positively communist to Caroline: not wanting to marry appropriately, if at all, fraternising constantly with blacks and mine-workers and God knew who else, running off to London, dressing like an impoverished hippie.

'Duncan's bringing your cases in now,' she said brightly. 'You can help me look at these place settings for tonight's dinner, then pop up and wash your hair before we go into Buckie. All right?'

'Buckie?' Scarlett groaned. 'What for? I don't want to go into Buckie, Mummy. I want to stay here and relax.'

'I dare say you do.' Caroline looked suitably disapproving. 'But you can't leave me and Cameron to do *all* the work. It's the pre-Christmas raffle at the church this afternoon. I've put you down to do the teas.'

Scarlett sighed. It was terribly strange, coming from London where she ran her own successful business and was respected as a leader and decision-maker, to Drumfernly where everybody treated her as though she were still a wilful six-year-old.

'What's Cameron going to be doing?' she asked suspiciously, unable to keep the resentment entirely out of her voice, 'apart from drinking Reverend Timothy's sherry?'

'Your brother will be mingling,' said Caroline stiffly. 'As the future laird, that's what's expected of him. It might look easy to you, but it's a very heavy responsibility on his shoulders,' she added crossly. 'Sometimes I think you forget that.'

'Are you going, Pa?' Scarlett turned to her father, once her mother had disappeared in search of the place cards. Evidently dinner tonight was going to be another social hoopla, not the quiet night in with shepherds' pie and telly that Scarlett desperately longed for.

'Going? To Buckie?' Still glued to his newspaper, Hugo gave a little shudder. 'Good God no. Not my cup of tea at all.'

'Cup of tea, Mrs McIntyre?'

Scarlett smiled sweetly at the crotchety old woman who'd made her life such a misery as her primary-school teacher. She was older and leatherier than Scarlett remembered her, but beyond that wasn't much changed. Then again, nothing in Buckie ever changed much.

The pre-Christmas raffle was being held in the same, draughty old church hall that had housed every village event since before Scarlett was born, and that still smelled of the pungent combination of disinfectant and incense that she remembered so well from her childhood. Standing here, pouring tea for Mrs McIntyre and all the other old biddies, her life in London felt like a dream. It was hard to believe that this time two days ago, she'd been sipping a soy latte behind the counter at Bijoux, negotiating the sale of a thirty-thousand-pound diamond bracelet.

'Is it free?'

The old woman's whiny, nails-on-blackboard voice brought her back to earth with a jolt.

'I'm sorry?'

'The tea, Scarlett, the *tea*.' She pronounced it 'tay'. 'Are you selling, or giving it away?'

'Oh, sorry, yes, it's free,' blushed Scarlett, feeling like a naughty ten-year-old again. 'But if you'd like to make a donation, there's a box at the end of the counter there.'

Taking a steaming cup and a hefty handful of custard cream biscuits, Mrs McIntyre shuffled off, shamelessly ignoring the donation box. Mean old cow, thought Scarlett.

Just then Caroline wandered over, arm in arm with a paunchy middle-aged man Scarlett vaguely thought she recognised.

'Darling, you remember Hamish Sainsbury? You used to ride together on the beach at Elgin all those years ago.'

Hamish Sainsbury! Good God! They'd never been great friends, but she did remember him and his brother leading the pack on those long, dreary riding-school hacks. He could only be three or four years older than her, but he'd aged dreadfully. With his pasty, puffy face and red, watery eyes, he looked to be in his mid forties at least, and couldn't have taken a shred of exercise in the last decade. She supposed that was what staying in Banffshire did for you, and thanked her lucky stars once again that she'd escaped.

'Well, you weren't exaggerating, Caroline,' said Hamish, staring with gummy admiration at Scarlett's tight green cashmere polo neck where it clung to her breasts. His voice was even more ludicrously plummy than she remembered it. 'She's even more beautiful than I remembered. I'd never have thought it possible.' To Scarlett's horror, he picked up her hand and planted a wet-lipped kiss on the inside of her wrist.

'Hello, Hamish,' she said as politely as she could, snatching back her hand and wiping off the revolting snail's trail of saliva on the back of her jeans. Cliff Richard's 'Mistletoe and Wine' began blaring out over the ancient speaker system, and she said a little prayer that Reverend Tim might call the raffle soon so they could all go home. 'Can I get you some tea and biscuits?'

'Not for me thanks,' he said, patting his spreading tummy fondly. 'Got to watch the old figure.'

'Oh Hamish, what nonsense. You've got a fine, trim figure,' lied Caroline.

'Well, I don't know about that,' he mumbled, turning

back to Scarlett. 'But in any case, your mother's been kind enough to invite me over for dinner at Drumfernly this evening. I wouldn't want to ruin my appetite.'

Scarlett's heart sank. Her mother inviting single local landowners over for dinner could only mean one thing: she was match-making again. Just when she'd thought her first day home couldn't possibly get any worse.

Her only consolation at dinner was that, for once, Cameron had also had a local 'prospect' foisted on him, a deathly shy pudding of a girl called Fiona, whose father just happened to own the finest grouse moor in Scotland.

'Your m-m-mother tells me you're a banker,' Scarlett overheard the girl stammering timidly at the other end of the table. The Great Hall at Drumfernly was a huge, high-ceilinged room with stone walls and floors that tended to amplify people's voices, the worst possible place for a stammerer. 'Is that terribly d-d-difficult?'

'No,' said Cameron rudely, turning away. Unlike Scarlett, he was all for finding a rich, titled wife whose wealth and position could complement his own. But he didn't do fat girls, and that was that.

Seeing Fiona blush red as a beetroot, Scarlett longed to go over and rescue her. But she was too far away to make conversation without shouting over all the other guests, and besides, Hamish clearly had no intention of letting her out of his clutches. Wedged like an unhappy sardine between him and her totally deaf uncle William, she was trapped both physically and conversationally.

'I always say it's closer to ballet than to sport,' wittered Hamish, now fifteen minutes in to his specialist topic of salmon fishing, a subject that held about as much interest for Scarlett as fossilised dinosaur turds. 'And of course, even the tying of the flies is an art, a dying art. If you've ever seen a dozen bead head nymphs being properly tied, and I mean *properly* tied, it's a thing of beauty, I can tell you.'

Unable to bear it a moment longer, Scarlett bravely tried to change the subject.

'Jewellery design, the personal, hand-crafted sort of work that I do, is a dying art too,' she said. 'So much of what people buy nowadays is mass produced, even at the top end of the market, the Tiffanys and Aspreys and what have you. There's either cheap handmade jewellery in silver and glass, or factory-finished diamond and gemstone pieces. Very little in between.'

'Scarlett's got a little shop,' Caroline interjected patronisingly from Hamish's right. 'It's become quite a hobby for you, hasn't it darling?' She'd hate for a catch like Hamish to write her daughter off as a committed career girl, unsuitable for marriage.

'How splendid!' he replied, surreptitiously pressing his kilted thigh against Scarlett's woollen tights – hardly the greatest fashion statement, but her parents' steadfast refusal to pay for heating in the castle's public rooms left her little choice. 'So important to have interests, I always say, especially living up here. Girls do need something beyond the children and the home, especially once the hunting season's over.'

Scarlett almost choked on her beef fillet.

'Bijoux is not a hobby, Mother, as you well know,' she said firmly. 'It's a business, and a thriving business at that. And happily,' she turned to Hamish, 'I don't live up here. I live in London, where we "girls" have all sorts of interests outside children and the home, and where I'm delighted to report there is no hunting season.'

'Ha, ha, jolly good!' Hamish laughed loudly, as if she'd made some great joke. 'Well London's marvellous for a time too, before one marries. I sometimes regret not spending a year or so there myself, seeing the world a bit and all that. But these estates don't run themselves you know.'

'Indeed not,' murmured Scarlett's father from the head of the table, apparently forgetting that he himself relied wholly on a team of professional estate managers to run Drumfernly and couldn't name the various crops in his fields to save his life.

Scarlett sighed. She should know better by now than to try to get into a debate with the likes of Hamish, men who considered a year in London to be 'seeing the world'. What on earth would he make of Africa? she wondered. His life, like her parents', was so sheltered and parochial, she couldn't possibly expect him to understand hers.

But Hamish, it seemed, was made of sterner stuff than she gave him credit for. Undeterred by her complete lack of interest so far, he decided to make another ill-fated sally into the conversational fray.

'You've heard about our Hogmanay celebrations over at Kinlochry this year?' he said brightly to the table at large. 'The reels'll be spectacular. I do hope you'll all be there.'

'Of course we'll be there,' said Caroline, returning his enthusiastic smile with a beamer of her own. Really, it wouldn't kill Scarlett to show a little more interest. 'The whole county's in a spin about it.'

'In that case, I wonder if I might make so bold,' Hamish turned back to Scarlett, 'as to reserve the first dance of the Dashing White Sergeant for you, Miss Drummond Murray?'

'Oh, that's very kind,' said Scarlett, crossing her legs as the only means of removing them from his insistently pressing thigh, 'but I'm afraid I won't be in Scotland for New Year. I'm going to New York with a girlfriend.'

'You never mentioned New York to me,' said Cameron, sounding put out. 'We spent twenty minutes talking about our New Year plans on the drive up yesterday, and you never said a thing.'

'*You* spent twenty minutes talking about *your* plans,' said Scarlett pointedly. 'I never got a word in edgeways.'

'Well, I must say, I think you might have told *me*,' said Caroline, who for politeness's sake was trying not to show

how livid she was. 'Naturally I assumed you'd be here, with the family.'

'But Mummy, we only ever spoke in terms of Christmas,' said Scarlett plaintively.

'Well, who is this girlfriend?' asked Caroline. 'You're going to tell me it's that dreadful American child from St Clement's, aren't you?'

For unexplained reasons, Caroline had always disapproved of Nancy. Scarlett could only imagine it was because she was the only American girl at the school. The fact that her ancestors had come over on the Mayflower or that her parents owned half of Park Avenue meant little in Scotland, where the right tartan and regiment were everything.

'Nancy isn't dreadful, she's lovely,' she said wearily. 'She's been hugely helpful to me in trying to spread Trade Fair's message in the States.'

'Trade Fair is my sister's other little hobby,' Cameron explained scathingly to Hamish. 'Or rather, her hobby horse. It's all about saving the Sambos in the diamond mines from the evil British white-slavers. Isn't that right, Scarlett?'

'Look, I'm sorry Mummy, I really thought you knew about New York,' said Scarlett, ignoring him. 'But I've been looking forward to it for ages, and I can't let Nancy down.'

'Hmm,' sniffed Caroline, 'of course not. It's only your poor *family* you feel able to let down.'

'Trade Fair,' said Hamish, who'd clearly been spending the last two minutes trying to think of something devastatingly witty and amusing to say to impress Scarlett. 'What a terribly appropriate name, for one as *fair* as you to have chosen for your campaign. Do you get it?' he smiled, evidently pleased with himself. '*Fair?*'

Even Caroline forgot Hamish's estates and seven-figure yearly income at that point, and glared at him witheringly.

*

Later that night, in bed, Scarlett remembered the Trade Fair comment and started to giggle. Poor old Hamish. It wasn't his fault his family were so inbred he'd been left with the IQ of a cow-pat. Still, she was sure there were plenty of well-to-do Scottish girls who'd be delighted to marry him anyway – sweet, fat Fiona had looked positively keen when the men switched seats at pudding. He'd be much better off with her.

Pulling the mountain of blankets up to her chin as their sheer weight finally began to generate some warmth, she let her thoughts drift to Nancy and New York. She imagined the sales at Bergdorf Goodman and Barney's, and started to fantasise about stocking up on cut-price Marc Jacobs, and the late dinners they'd have together at the 21 Lounge. But then her mind turned involuntarily to Yakutia, and the terrible stories she'd heard on the radio yesterday about the conditions in the O'Donnell mines, and she felt a sharp stab of guilt. How could she be so shallow, thinking about shoes and sweaters and cocktails, when she knew what those poor men were going through? How could she waste so much mental energy on pointless arguments with her family, when she knew first hand about so much genuine suffering in this world? And particularly in *her* world, the diamond business.

Ignoring her mother's house-rules, she pulled back the covers to allow a whining, shivering Boxford into bed beside her. Cocooned in their combined body-heat, she fell into a fitful sleep, peppered with dreams of salmon fishing, Madison Avenue, and the tyrannical, smiling face of Brogan James O'Donnell.

# *Four*

Brogan O'Donnell put his head back and smiled contentedly as the girl beneath his desk began unzipping his flies.

His office was on the thirty-third, penthouse, floor of
an all-glass block on Wall Street, with breathtaking views
across the water to Ellis Island, the Statue of Liberty and
beyond. Today the city had been transformed into a magical snowscape, an urban Narnia sparkling beneath a clear,
lapis-blue January sky. Gazing out of his floor-to-ceiling
window, Brogan felt like the emperor of a great kingdom,
surveying his lands. Life didn't get a whole lot better than
this.

'Slower,' he murmured, reaching down and entwining
his fingers in the girl's hair so he could pull her head back
and forward in the rhythm that he wanted. She was one
of Premiere New York's more recent signings, a Ukranian
redhead with legs like a camel, and a quirky, striking face
most notable for its full, wide mouth, an oral replica of
the Lincoln Tunnel. Since founding the model agency as a
sideline business eight years ago, Brogan had consistently
used it as a private brothel, taking girls for himself when
he wanted to and occasionally offering them to friends and
business associates who had earned his particular favour.
There was always the odd girl who refused his advances.
Most model bosses would have fired them, but Brogan had
learned long ago that it paid to keep one's friends close and
enemies closer, and never doled out retribution. There
were plenty of new girls willing to oblige him, many of
them from backgrounds of desperate poverty, like Dascha.
From the skilful, enthusiastic way she was working her

tongue up and down his cock now, cupping his balls in her hands as she licked and sucked, it was clear she was no novice at pleasuring her bosses, or any man who might be able to offer her some advancement.

'Oh, God that's good,' he moaned, slowing her pace still further to try to prolong his enjoyment. Aware that he was dangerously close to coming, he tried to turn his mind to other things, like tonight's big party at the new Tiffany Store on Madison Avenue. All the great and the good of the diamond fraternity would be there – dealers, cutters, designers, independent mine owners like him, and of course the cartels. Privately, Brogan found these sorts of events rather a bore. He was always getting collared by some diamond-crazed crone or other hoping to cut a private deal, or by journalists asking tiresome questions about conditions in his mines. But he had to go tonight. One of the top De Beers executives was in town, and however successful one became in the diamond business, one could never afford to snub De Beers. Not even the great Brogan O'Donnell was above a little schmoozing.

Still, he hoped the store's PR people would keep the worst of the journalists at bay. Recently, the whole 'blood diamond' controversy seemed to have exploded into the national consciousness to a worrying degree. First there was that godawful film, with Leo DiCaprio running around Sierra Leone with some kaffir, repenting of his sins as a smuggler. Then came a series of tiresome 'celebrity' campaigns, railing against De Beers and their chief rival Cuypers for knowingly allowing stones from war-torn countries onto the mass market.

The whole thing irritated him intensely. What did these people expect? There would never be an Africa without war, never. As far as Brogan was concerned – and he considered himself well informed on the subject, having operated on the continent for more than a decade – most African blacks were little more than savages, corrupt to the core and utterly undeserving of the sympathy lavished on them by bleeding-heart Hollywood democrats. So what if they spent their diamond money on guns? Let them fuck up their own lives if they wanted to. Nobody was forcing them to do it, least of all the buyers paying vitally needed hard currency for their stones.

About two years ago things had gotten so bad that he'd decided to pull O'Donnell out of Africa altogether and focus on his Russian mines. But now these fucking parasite journalists were starting to ask questions about his safety record and workers' rights in Siberia too! It was ridiculous. He'd even had to go on record with the BBC, defending the company's practices in their Yakutian mines. A few months ago, no one outside the industry had ever heard of Yakutia, but now suddenly every liberal eco-worrier and their dog wanted to sponsor a miner there.

'Everything OK, Mr O'Donnell? You want I'm doing something different?' The girl looked up from between his legs, her head cocked to one side like a curious dog. She seemed bewildered by his softening erection, and could tell that something was wrong.

Brogan looked down at her, and immediately felt himself hardening again. Her pink lipstick was smudged around her glorious, over-wide lips and her chin glistened with saliva and the sweat of her efforts. He didn't think he'd ever seen anything more wantonly desirable.

'Get up here,' he said, smiling. 'I want to fuck you.'

Pushing back his chair so she could climb out of her cramped hiding place, he helped her to her feet, then turned her around and bent her over the desk. Yanking down her True Religion jeans – she was so skinny, he didn't even need to undo them but could pull them right off – and cheap Victoria's Secret panties, he drove himself into her, releasing all his pent-up anger and aggression with every thrust.

Dascha oohed and ahed obediently, but it couldn't have

been much of a pleasure ride for her; it was over so quickly. Once he'd come, he lay slumped over her for a moment, his heavyset, bulldog body pressing down on her fragile frame like a paperweight on a flower. Then he withdrew, wiping himself with a tissue from the box on the desk and pulling up his pants while she did the same.

'If you want some more, I can wait?' she said helpfully, reaching into her purse for face wipes and make-up, re-applying her lipstick as if nothing of any importance had just happened. 'I don't have any jobs this afternoon.'

Brogan smiled. 'No, no, that was fine,' he said. 'But I appreciate you coming by. I can tell you're going to be a great asset to Premiere.'

Once she'd gone, his mind turned quickly back to tonight's party. Apart from the De Beers and Cuypers guys, there were a number of other people he wanted to see. Nothing gave Brogan quite the same thrill as crushing a business rival, and there was one particular individual, one of his American competitors in Russia, whose company he'd recently had the pleasure of annihilating, who was rumoured to be coming tonight. Having grown up dirt poor himself, a fighter who'd worked hard and played dirty for every cent he'd ever made, Brogan never let go of the ruthlessness that had made him such a rich man. The diamond business was notoriously clubby. Having no family name, no connections and, crucially, being a gentile, had put him at a hell of a disadvantage in his early years as a trader and smuggler, before he hit the big time buying up cheap, poorly man-aged mines in Congo and Zaire. By the time he moved into South Africa, and later Russia, he was already a wealthy man, and doors that were once locked to him had begun, slowly, grudgingly, to open. But he'd got to where he was without asking anything of anybody. If people wanted to try and paint him as the Big Bad Capitalist Wolf now, that was their problem. In his own mind, he was the living embodiment of the American dream, and he dismissed all criticism of himself and his company as straightforward envy.

'Sir?' The voice of his secretary, the coolly efficient Rose, drifted over the intercom on his desk.

He hit speaker. 'Yes. What is it?'

'It's Mrs O'Donnell on line one. Are you available to take the call?'

Brogan thought about it for a second. 'No. Tell her I'm in a meeting, will you, and I'll call her back in about ten minutes? I need some time to get my head together. She's in rather a fragile state at the moment.'

'Will do,' said Rose, and the line went dead.

Walking over to the window, looking out at the snow sparkling like a billion tiny diamonds in the dazzling winter sun, he thought about his wife, Diana. He knew, or thought he knew, what this call would be about: another early miscarriage. They were on their fourth cycle of IVF – his sperm apparently preferred attacking one another to racing towards the egg, plus Diana had some sort of cysts that made the whole thing difficult her end – and the specialist had already told them on Monday that it wasn't looking good. Brogan himself couldn't have cared less about children. He'd never much liked other people's, and he already had a business empire to leave to posterity. But he knew Diana felt utterly bereft without them, and he wanted to make things right for her.

Despite his workaholism, serial infidelities and complete lack of remorse, in his own way Brogan did love his wife. Diana was precious to him, like a rare bird that he daren't release or even stroke for fear of damaging it in some way, but which he cherished from a distance. Born into a well-off, stable family from Connecticut, she was everything that he wasn't: educated, gentle, secure in herself in a quiet, unassuming sort of way. Making love to her wasn't exciting in the way that screwing young models was exciting. It was more like sticking your scalded hand into cool water

– a sort of blissful relief. Congenitally incapable of showing affection in any normal, expected ways, he tried to express his love by showering her with diamonds, real estate and other expensive, though not necessarily romantic gifts. When she failed to react with the hoped-for enthusiasm, he withdrew further, deepening the already vast divide between them. Having a child, he knew, would be the one sure way to bridge that divide, a gift for which she would remain slavishly and everlastingly grateful. But infertility was the one problem in his life that money alone couldn't solve. He'd already paid top dollar for the best IVF specialists in the world, but so far nothing seemed to be working, leaving Diana increasingly desperate and Brogan feeling furious and impotent in more ways than one.

He did feel sorry for his wife. But he also hoped she wasn't going to use this latest setback, if she was bleeding again, as an excuse to cry off tonight's party at Tiffany. Wives were expected at these events. He needed her there, looking stylish and making intelligent, ladylike conversation with Mrs De Beers and Mrs Cuypers.

If the IVF had fucked up, they could always try again.

Meanwhile, across town in Greenwich Village, Nancy and Scarlett were up in one of the guest bedrooms of Nancy's parents' palatial brownstone, trying on outfits for tonight.

'It's ridiculous,' said Scarlett, standing in front of the full-length mirror in her bra and knickers, 'I go to so many of these things nowadays, but I'm still never sure how to pitch it. Should I go for sober businesswoman?' She held up a severe black Calvin Klein suit with a killer pencil skirt.

'Very Angelina-at-the-UN,' said Nancy.

'Or wild, artistic genius?' Pulling her newest acquisition, a tiered, multicoloured Marchesa gypsy skirt, out of its bag, Scarlett held it to her waist and twirled around and around.

'I'd go for the skirt,' said Nancy, looking at her friend's

flawless model figure with good-natured envy. 'Everyone in New York lives in black; you'll stand out more in colour. Besides, I can't very well wear my red flamenco number if you turn up dressed all CNN.'

Nancy Lorriman and Scarlett Drummond Murray had been firm friends since the age of thirteen, when Nancy had arrived at St Clement's School for Girls in Inverness, shivering like a polar explorer in her lightweight, American clothes and wondering if she'd landed on the set of a *Munsters* remake, and Scarlett had taken her under her wing. Physically, they were as different as different could be, with blonde, curvy Nancy standing almost a foot shorter than Scarlett, who as a teenager was as tall, pale and skinny as an unripe stick of asparagus. But they immediately recognised one another as kindred spirits – bright, independent minded, romantic and, in Nancy's case particularly, harbouring a strong rebellious streak.

Nancy's father had sent her to St Clement's on a whim, having seen the school advertised in the back of a magazine, and developed a notion that Scotland was a land of beauty and mystery in which his daughter couldn't fail to blossom. The fact that the school itself looked like Cinderella's castle had been an added bonus, and besides, he was running out of options in New York, where Nancy had already been expelled from two schools, and was hardly being welcomed with open arms by others.

A sweet kid, but highly intelligent and consequently easily bored, Nancy also suffered from being the only child of very wealthy, older parents, who spoiled her with material things but left her too much in the care of nannies, and were far too over-protective. Yearning for freedom and adventure of the sort she read about constantly in books, Nancy spent much of her early life giving her nannies the slip, and running off on her own into the Manhattan streets that became her private playground.

To say that St Clement's came as a shock, with its rigid

rules and routine, revolting food and sub-zero dormitories, would be a serious understatement. She contemplated running away, but Scarlett soon convinced her that there was really nowhere to go – Inverness had little to offer in terms of urban excitements. They would simply have to rely on each other's company and make their own excitement, tormenting their poor teachers with a litany of pranks and amusing their classmates with tales of their latest misbehaviour.

Somehow both girls made it through their Highers without being expelled, and both achieved creditable grades. After Scarlett went to London to model, Nancy raced delightedly back to the States to study journalism at NYU, and the two girls lost touch for a while. But when they reconnected a few years ago, it was as if nothing had changed. Scarlett might now be a hot-shot designer and Nancy an up-and-coming Hollywood screenwriter, but at heart they were still the same two mischievous misfits they'd been at school.

'What do you think?'

Nancy had poured herself into a pillar-box-red dress with a ruffled train that clung to her curves like shrink-wrap. All she needed was the beauty spot and little-girl voice and she'd be the spitting image of Marilyn Monroe.

'I think the rest of us might as well not bother,' said Scarlett, truthfully. 'You'll out-sex every woman there by a hundred to one.'

'Good,' said Nancy, beaming. 'I'm tired of being single, and I'm tired of living in a city where most women's idea of dressing up is wearing a visible diamanté thong with their Juicy sweatpants. I mean, if you can't go to town at Tiffany's, right?'

'Right,' said Scarlett. She, too, was tired of being single. She hadn't had a date since October, and that was a disaster as the guy had turned out to be married. But between Bijoux and her Trade Fair commitments, there never seemed enough time to look for suitable men. It didn't help that most guys in the diamond business were sharper than razor blades and about as trustworthy as Jeffrey Archer in a witness box. Certainly she didn't hold out much hope of breaking her romantic duck tonight.

The original Tiffany store on 5th Avenue at 57th Street was such an iconic New York landmark, forever associated with Audrey Hepburn and the glamour of the *Breakfast at Tiffany's* days, that the decision to open a second Manhattan location featuring younger, hipper designers sent shockwaves through both the jewellery industry and the city. Plans for the new store, its interior and layout, had been more closely guarded than the Kremlin's nuclear defence procedures, so there was much excitement and anticipation surrounding today's grand unveiling.

Not until six p.m. were the brown hoardings masking the building at last removed and the red carpet rolled out onto the sidewalk. A huge swathe of Madison Avenue had already been cordoned off by this time, as police struggled to hold back the swelling crowd of press and civilian gawpers who'd come to watch the first big celebrity party of the year get underway.

They weren't disappointed. By six fifteen, a steady stream of limousines were arriving, discharging their famous occupants onto the sidewalk from where, after a quick red-carpet twirl and wave, they'd disappear into the sumptuous new building. Actors, singers, politicians and a smattering of A-list socialites swarmed into the atrium one after another, mingling with the unknown but usually infinitely wealthier scions of the diamond business, be they producers, dealers or buyers.

Scarlett, with her designer's eye, was more struck by the astonishing array of pieces on display in open, laser-alarmed cases, and by the beauty of the store itself, than by the star-studded guest list.

'Have you seen what they've done with the light in this foyer?' she gasped admiringly to Nancy. 'It's like standing in the centre of a princess-cut diamond, and working one's way out. Each of those ante-rooms is like one of the facets, do you see?'

'I'll tell you what *I* see,' said Nancy. 'I see George Clooney standing by the bar on his own. I'm gonna try and score a date.'

Once again, Scarlett marvelled at her friend's limitless confidence as she watched her sashay across the marble floor, Louboutin heels clacking and red satin bottom wiggling sexily like Jessica Rabbit. Still, why not? She looked so jaw-droppingly fabulous tonight, Gorgeous George might just have met his match.

Feeling distinctly less fabulous herself – she'd plumped for the gypsy skirt, which was divine but more girlie than sexy, a white ruffled peasant blouse and flat jewelled sandals – she lingered a little longer over the jewellery cases by herself, before finally steeling herself to go and mingle. Small talk had never been a forte, but there were influential people here who could really help her with her Trade Fair campaign. She'd kick herself in the morning if she hadn't plucked up the courage to talk to any of them.

Meanwhile, in a busy corner of the mezzanine level, Diana O'Donnell was nodding absently at the South African woman talking to her, wishing she were anywhere but here. Brogan had insisted she come tonight, practically marched her here at gunpoint, but all she could think about was the tiny fertilised egg that was right now working its way out of her body, unable to cling on to life. The doctors were forever telling her not to personalise things.

'Don't think of it as a baby, Mrs O'Donnell,' they said. 'It's really only a tiny ball of cells, nothing more.'

But to Diana it was much, much more. It was a child, her child. Each of those tiny fertilised specks contained within them the entire sum of her hopes for the future.

Losing one felt like having her heart ripped out, and it got worse every time.

'I said to Michael the day I married him,' the South African woman was saying in her piercing, Afrikaans accent, 'I said, "Michael, I don't care how many diamonds you sell, or how many millions you make. I will *not* share my bed with your *bloody* mobile phone." He's pretty good about it most of the time, but you know what the New Year's like in our business: hectic, hectic, hectic.' She laughed, looking to Diana for affirmation, and Diana dutifully laughed back.

'Is Brogan addicted to his BlackBerry as well?' asked the woman, grabbing a passing waiter and helping herself to a caviar and quail's egg blini, which she dispatched into the recesses of her ample stomach in under a second. She really was a remarkably unattractive girl, thought Diana. Like a female sumo wrestler, if female sumo wrestlers got to be sponsored by Ungaro. Then again her husband, a squat, toad of a man deep in conversation with Brogan, was no oil painting either.

'BlackBerry addiction is the least of my husband's problems,' rejoined Diana, sadly. Then, realising she might have said too much, added, 'but all successful men love their work, don't they? I think that great, overwhelming drive must be part of their appeal.'

Downstairs on the ground floor, an eight-piece jazz band struck up the first chords of 'Night and Day'. A few brave couples drifted idly onto the makeshift dance floor, but most remained glued to the various bars, raising their voices to be able to continue their conversations about how much x stone sold for at auction, or exactly what the mark-up was on some of the more outrageous Tiffany pieces.

'You're paying for the name, of course,' Danny Meyer was explaining to a busty television actress, the star of NBC's latest mobster drama, as he handed her a mojito. 'Half of these pieces are semi-precious, but the prices are gemstone all the way.'

'You think you can do me a better deal?' the girl asked flirtatiously. He was a little short, but she adored his confidence and had already decided that his North London accent was quite the sexiest thing she'd heard in years. He was definitely more interesting than the standard-issue New York suits who usually asked her out.

'Sweetheart, trust me; I can do you a *much* better deal. I'm purely a diamond man myself, but I work with some of the best private jewellers in the city, real craftsmen. Any of this lot, half price,' he said, sweeping his arm in the general direction of the glass cases surrounding them, much as a market trader might wave away a competitor's inferior stall of bananas.

'Don't believe a word he says.' Jake, vulgarly resplendent in a cream Miami Vice suit with a big seventies collar, pink shirt and silver Sean John silk tie, appeared behind his brother like a grinning ghost. 'He'll rob you blind soon as look at you, won't you Dan?'

'Annalise, this is my twin brother Jake,' said Danny, rolling his eyes melodramatically. 'And if you can trust a man in a suit that loud, you deserve to get done over.'

'Hi,' said Annalise, thinking how much she would enjoy being 'done over' by Jake or Danny, or perhaps even both of them together. 'Your brother here's been trying to talk me out of buying from Tiffany.'

'I should think so too,' said Jake, reaching across her to grab a mojito of his own. 'We're Jewish, you see. Paying retail's against our religion. Have you seen who's here tonight, Dan?'

Danny laughed. 'Everyone's here. Can you be a bit more specific?'

'Up there, boring the tits off Michael Beerens from Cuypers.' He pointed up at Brogan, at the same time puffing out his chest and brilliantly mimicking the great man's wide-legged stance and self-important, Julius-Caesaraddressing-the-troops posture. 'Silly twat. He really thinks he's Tony fucking Soprano, doesn't he?'

Annalise giggled. 'Who is he?'

'A knob-cheese,' said Jake.

'More like a big cheese,' explained Danny. 'Brogan O'Donnell. He's worth billions of dollars. Owns a bunch of diamond mines in Russia and a load of other businesses, mostly in Africa: model agencies, property development companies. Last I heard he was cleaning up in real estate in Cape Town.'

'He's a twat, though,' said Jake. 'Loves the sound of his own voice, always running round town with models on his arm, girls half his age.'

'You can talk!' said Danny. 'Talk about the pot calling the kettle black.'

'I'm not married. Or old,' said Jake defensively. 'Brogan must be fifty if he's a day. I reckon he's had a Michael Douglas eye-job since we last saw him and all. Shall we go and take a closer look?'

'In a minute,' said Danny, who wanted to be left alone to get back to the serious business of chatting up Annalise. 'Looks like he's already being accosted at the moment. Hey, hang on? Don't we know that girl?'

'The one in the gypsy skirt?' said Annalise, curiously. 'I noticed her earlier. There's something very striking about her, don't you think?'

Jake looked up and clocked Scarlett, her chiselled, beautiful face clouded as usual by a furious expression of righteous indignation, like a schoolgirl who'd just been given an unfair mark on her chemistry test. The flouncy shirt and skirt she was wearing didn't do much to accentuate her to-die-for figure – at last year's ball in Amsterdam, she'd been dressed to kill in a clinging gold Shirley Bassey number that still haunted his dreams – and yet Annalise was right. There *was* something striking about her, even amongst all tonight's perfectly coiffed and polished Park

Avenue princesses. Or perhaps *especially* amongst them. Scarlett Drummond Murray was that rare thing, a natural beauty, even if she did do herself up to look like a Scottish air hostess.

'Yeah, we know her,' he said. 'She's that jewellery designer from Notting Hill who wants to save the world, remember? Bono in a bra. We met her in Amsterdam.'

He wondered what Scarlett wanted with Brogan O'Donnell, of all people. It was clear from her stern, determined face that, whatever was on her mind, she was about to give the poor sod a piece of it.

'Come on,' he said gleefully, grabbing Annalise by the hand and pulling Danny along with her. Jake loved a good scene. 'Let's get a ringside seat before the fireworks start.'

Scarlett, in fact, had been enjoying a fruitful conversation with one of the senior Tiffany staffers, and was starting to feel she might actually be getting somewhere persuading him to sign up to Trade Fair, when something about Diana O'Donnell caught her eye.

It wasn't just her fragile beauty. She'd have expected a man like Brogan to have acquired a beautiful, much younger wife, although perhaps not one with quite so much self-evident class. In a demure, knee-length cashmere wrap dress and pearls, with her flawless skin and caramel-blonde hair swept up into a loose chignon, Diana looked the epitome of good breeding, a racehorse out of place amongst so many cheap, leggy standardbreds. But it wasn't even that that drew Scarlett's gaze. Rather it was the huge, unspoken sadness that seemed to radiate out of her like light from an SOS flare. From time to time Diana would smile at the big, blowsy woman talking to her, feigning attention, but the smile was even sadder than the blank, faraway expression she wore the rest of the time. Scarlett, who was sensitive to these things, was overpowered by an urge to go over and hug her; so much so that she made her excuses to the nice man from Tiffany and was already three-quarters of the way up the stairs when she found herself within earshot of Brogan's own conversation.

'It's wearing, more than anything,' he was saying, 'having these ignorant do-gooders stirring up discontent amongst one's workforce. Those miners welcomed me like the fucking Messiah when I first moved into Yakutia. To have an American employer who clothed and fed them after what they were used to? Jesus, they thought my mines were fucking Disneyworld. These journalists and save-the-whalers have no concept of how dire things were in Siberian diamond mining ten, twenty, thirty years ago. But now *I'm* the one being crucified in the press because a few of them have got lung problems? They've all smoked since they were twelve!'

'It's the same story in Africa, as you know,' Michael Beerens, Cuypers' head man in the US, replied despond-ently. 'We're proud of our record of improving workers' rights, and of our efforts in aid provision for the countries we work in. We spend millions of dollars, year-on-year, on health and education programmes for our mining com-munities. But do the press ever want to focus on that? Of course they don't. There'll always be ill-informed liberals who choose to see the diamond industry as exploitative, as white against black.'

'Sure,' said Brogan bitterly. 'Because the blacks only had however many thousand years to make something of their own natural resources, right? But of course they were far too busy killing each other and running around the bush with spears to think about that, weren't they? Developing their oh-so-admirable tribal cultures, the ones where the kids get raped and the sick get cast out of their piss-pot vil-lages to die. That's what these bloody campaigners are so keen to protect at all costs.'

'Steady on now, old man,' said Beerens good-naturedly. 'I'm not saying I don't sympathise. But there are subjects where it's impolitic to speak too freely, especially at an event like this. You know that.'

'Damned right I do,' said Brogan. 'Political correctness was what drove me out of Africa. But it's like a disease in this industry now; it follows you wherever you go. I could open a mine in Maryland, Virginia and still get some yapping bitch from Trade Fair whingeing that I was responsible for every lung cancer case in the state.'

Rooted to the spot on the stairs, Scarlett had momentarily forgotten her compassion for Diana. With each overheard word the red mist in her brain grew thicker until she thought she might be about to spontaneously combust with rage. She couldn't care less if Brogan O'Donnell thought of her as a 'yapping bitch'. In fact she was greatly encouraged that he'd heard of Trade Fair at all, especially as they had next to no presence in America. But as for implying she and her fellow reformers were ignorant of the reality of life in the diamond mines, never mind his appallingly racist views about Africa – views that Michael bloody Beerens and his cronies obviously shared, whatever they might say publicly – well, it was nothing short of outrageous.

Barging into their little huddle without bothering to introduce herself, she began lashing out at Brogan, her anger fuelled by the raw adrenaline of confrontation.

'Tell me, Mr O'Donnell, when the Americans liberated Auschwitz, would it have been acceptable if they'd simply transferred all the inmates to nicer, cleaner prisons and offered them a decent meal? Should the Jews have been grateful to be kept under lock and key by you, simply because you treated them better than the Nazis?'

'Oh dear.' Brogan raised a bored eyebrow at Michael. 'We seem to have attracted the attention of the evening's token lunatic. Be a good girl and go and rant at someone else, would you? My friend and I are talking.'

Pointedly turning his back on Scarlett, he tried to resume his conversation, but she wasn't about to be brushed aside that easily. Noticing that Beerens seemed distinctly more perturbed by her intrusion than Brogan – Cuypers, like De Beers, avoided controversy as assiduously as Brogan O'Donnell seemed to court it – she aimed her second scud in his direction.

'I'm surprised a legitimate businessman such as you, Mr Beerens, would be comfortable to be seen endorsing Mr O'Donnell's loudly proclaimed, racist views. Is that how you view Zulu culture?' Pulling out the Dictaphone that she always carried with her from her sparkly Indian evening bag, she made a great show of pressing the record button. 'As a bunch of savages, "running around the bush with spears"?'

'Of course not,' he spluttered, looking over Brogan's shoulder for his wife with the panicked expression of an ambushed landing-party leader from the Starship Enterprise, begging Scotty to beam him up. 'I don't know what you thought you heard, but you've taken Mr O'Donnell's remarks entirely out of context. Ah, Marigold, there you are my dear. We must go.' Grabbing the hand of the enormous woman in a lurid pink and green tent dress who'd been monopolising poor Diana for the last ten minutes, he scuttled off in the direction of the staircase from where Scarlett had just come.

'Congratulations,' said Brogan calmly, looking at Scarlett with undisguised contempt. 'You've managed to ruin his evening. What a marvellous sense of achievement that must be for you.'

His voice was somehow even more surprising in person than it had been on the radio. Deep, rumbling, almost reassuring, it seemed entirely at odds with his belligerent, larger-than-life physical presence. He was more attractive than she'd imagined him too, albeit in a short, bull-doggish sort of way. He wore his thick, dark hair cut very short, not quite military-style but not far off, and even in an expensive, bespoke suit and tie managed to look more like a nightclub bouncer than a billionaire mine owner. It wouldn't have surprised her to learn he had murdered someone with those outsized, bear-like hands, and she certainly couldn't imagine him using them to tenderly caress his porcelain doll of a wife.

'Brogan? Is everything all right?' Freed from Mrs Beerens' clutches, Diana dutifully made her way back to her husband's side. He was clearly furious with the pretty, oddly dressed English girl, although something about her made Diana want to smile at her anyway.

'Not really,' he barked, his coolness beginning to slip. 'This *person*,' he looked at Scarlett as if she barely merited the description, 'took it upon herself to lecture me on … Christ, what was it again? Something about Auschwitz … when I was in the middle of an important discussion with Cuypers.'

'I'm sorry, Mrs O'Donnell, I didn't mean to upset your evening.' Scarlett turned to Diana. 'But I'm afraid your husband was saying some unforgivable things about Africa. I'm also afraid that his devil-may-care attitude to his Siberian mine workers' lung cancer is a disgrace. But perhaps he thinks a Siberian miner's life is worth intrinsically less than an American's.'

'It is,' said Brogan bluntly. He was starting to grow mightily tired of this irritating young woman. 'Tell me, what is your interest in my diamond mines, exactly? Are you in the business yourself? Some sort of cancer researcher looking for funding? Or have you just overdosed on the latest Amnesty International report?'

'My name is Scarlett Drummond Murray,' said Scarlett, drawing herself up to her full five-foot-eleven so she stood taller than Brogan even in her flip flops. 'I run a jewellery design business and store in London, and I founded the Trade Fair campaign that you and your friend Mr Beerens were making such ill-informed comments about just now.'

'Ah. Of course.' Rather disconcertingly, Brogan smiled,

as if this explained everything. 'Well, as pleasant as it's been to meet you, if you don't mind, Scarlett, I shan't sacrifice what's left of my evening pointing out to you the glaring weaknesses in your so called "argument" for closing down half the world's diamond mines. My wife is tired.' He wrapped a protective, conjugal arm around Diana, but succeeded in looking more mafia-minder than devoted husband. 'I have neither the time nor the inclination to waste my breath on silly little rich girls who insist on meddling in matters they clearly don't begin to understand.'

Infuriatingly, Scarlett found herself temporarily lost for words as he swept arrogantly past her back down into the atrium. She thought she caught an apologetic look from Diana, who did indeed look tired close up, as she hurried after him, but she couldn't be sure. By the time she'd thought of a comeback, Brogan was well out of earshot and surrounded by an impenetrable mob of sycophantic hangers-on on the floor below. Moments later, Diana's floor-length mink was produced from the cloakroom and the pair of them had disappeared into the snow.

Suddenly aware that a number of people were giving her odd looks, Scarlett turned round in search of Nancy, who hadn't been seen since setting off after Gorgeous George. But her nightmare seemed set to continue as she found herself running slap bang into a grinning Jake Meyer.

'You?' she said crossly. 'That's all I bloody need. What are you doing here?'

'Now, now,' said Jake, kissing her on both cheeks. 'That's not a very warm welcome for one of your fellow countrymen, now is it?'

He looked more tanned than ever in that ridiculous white suit, and his teeth were so white they practically glowed whenever he opened his mouth – something he seemed to do an awful lot, exercising that famous Meyer gift of the gab.

'We actually came up here to congratulate you, didn't

we, Danny? About time someone brought that pompous prick O'Donnell down to size.'

Danny gave a brief nod before turning his attentions back to Annalise.

'I'm not sure I did cut him down to size,' said Scarlett ruefully, 'although I'm surprised you care one way or the other. You'd buy diamonds from the devil himself if the price was right. You and O'Donnell are two peas in a pod.'

'We are not,' said Jake hotly. 'I'm nothing like that creep. Come and dance with me and I'll prove it to you.'

'I don't think so,' stammered Scarlett as he grabbed her hand and began yanking her in the direction of the dance floor. Didn't he remember Amsterdam? Apparently not. Either that, or one dose of rejection wasn't enough for him. Refusing to take no for an answer, he bundled her down the stairs despite her indignant yells.

'I mean it, Mr Meyer, let go of me,' she insisted. But the noise of the party was now so loud, with hundreds of voices echoing off the angled glass walls, her protests were drowned out before they'd begun.

'Stop moaning,' said Jake, leading her into a waltz with such expert skill that she found herself compelled to follow. 'One dance won't kill you. Besides, it's the only way we can hear each other talk in here without shattering an eardrum.'

'And what makes you think I want to talk to you?' said Scarlett petulantly. She was amazed at the speed and sureness with which he whisked her around the floor. Somehow she'd never have put him down as a dancer.

'The fact that you haven't stormed off yet,' said Jake matter-of-factly. 'Look, I can understand what you have against Brogan. My uncle Solly died of lung cancer, so I know what those poor Russians are going through. O'Donnell's a nasty piece of work, totally heartless, and everybody in the business knows it. But what's your beef against me and my brother? I mean, come on. You barely even know us.'

'I know you smuggle stones out of war zones,' said Scarlett, indignation and the pace of the dance making her face flush.

'No you don't,' said Jake. 'You've heard rumours, that's all, and you choose to swallow them.'

Scarlett gave him a withering look. 'Come on. You don't seriously expect me to believe you go to Angola twice a year on holiday?'

'Beautiful country,' teased Jake, pulling her body closer as the tempo of the music slowed into a sultry rallentando, 'and the fishing's amazing. You should go some time.'

'This is ridiculous,' said Scarlett crossly, pulling away. 'I don't know why I'm even talking to you. You clearly haven't a shred of remorse for the human suffering you turn a blind eye to every time you trade one of those diamonds.'

'That's not true,' said Jake, looking hurt. 'None of us like what's going on out there. But Brogan's right about one thing. Robbing countries like Angola and Zaire of their diamond income isn't going to help those poor people.'

'It will in the long term,' insisted Scarlett.

'*The long term*?' Jake looked at her pityingly. She really didn't have a clue. 'What use is that to them? Those countries need our dollars now, today. They don't have the luxury of a long term and nor does my business. Danny and I didn't make the rules, Scarlett. We're just playing the game like everyone else.'

'Please. Don't give me that self-justifying crap,' said Scarlett loudly. Unfortunately, just at that moment the music stopped, and the entire dance floor was treated to the spectacle of her haranguing Jake Meyer like a school ma'am. Blushing an even deeper red – she really was adorable when she blushed, Jake decided – she lowered her voice to a whisper. 'Plenty of dealers choose to operate ethically. At Bijoux I wouldn't dream of using anything I suspected of being illegally or immorally sourced.'

'*I wouldn't dream of using anything immorally sourced.*' Jake mimicked her prim outrage perfectly. 'Give me a break, Pollyanna.'

'I wouldn't!' said Scarlett vehemently.

'Well, maybe you don't have to,' said Jake. He wasn't sure why he felt the need to defend himself and his motives to this uppity, judgemental posh bird, but somehow he just did. 'Not all of us were born in a castle and given a whopping great trust fund for our twenty-first, you know. It doesn't take much effort to be a champagne socialist.'

'A champagne ... how dare you!' Scarlett spluttered. 'You know nothing about me.'

'Danny and I worked like dogs building up Solomon Stones,' said Jake.

'As did I, building up Bijoux,' retorted Scarlett.

'And I reckon we've made a pretty damn good job of it,' he went on, ignoring her. 'So save your lectures for the people who really deserve them, like O'Donnell. I never gave anyone lung cancer. Leave me out of it.'

The music started up again, which Scarlett took as her belated cue to leave. This time Jake didn't try to stop her as she strode angrily off the dance floor in search of Nancy. Finding her drunkenly giggling by the front doors, surrounded by a drooling gaggle of some of Manhattan's most eligible men, she dragged her off to one side.

'Hey, what gives?' said Nancy, aggrieved. 'I was just getting into the groove back there.'

'I'm leaving,' said Scarlett bluntly. One look at her face, all narrowed eyes and flared nostrils, told Nancy that her friend was in the most almighty huff.

'What, now? Why? You were dancing with that divine bit of rough in the white suit a few minutes ago. What went wrong?'

'Your eyesight, that's what went wrong,' said Scarlett

tetchily. 'Jake Meyer is anything but divine. I was only dancing with him because he forced me, and because I thought, foolishly, that I might be able to talk some sense into him.'

Nancy sighed. She adored Scarlett, but she did wish that her friend would occasionally take off her save-the-world hat and simply relax and have fun.

'Look, if you really want to go, I'll give you the keys,' she said, delving into her gold clutch bag. 'But I think you should stay. I've got more hot guys back there than I know what to do with.' She gestured to the eager posse of admirers behind her. 'It's like shooting fish in a barrel.'

'Thanks, but I'll pass,' said Scarlett. After two frustrating conversations, first with Brogan O'Donnell and then with Jake, she was ready to punch someone, and certainly not in the mood to make small talk with Nancy's cast-offs. 'You be careful, OK? Don't do anything I wouldn't do.'

'I won't,' said Nancy, privately thinking that that didn't leave her with too many options, other than getting into unnecessary political arguments with every guy who wanted to sleep with her. 'See you at home.'

Meanwhile Jake, who had also lost his appetite for the party, managed to track down Danny.

'Where's Annalise?' he asked, finding his brother alone and morose at the ground-floor bar.

'Gone,' said Danny. 'Some bloody Adonis with a hedge fund called Chip or Chuck or something damn stupid like that turned up. Next thing you know she was climbing into the back of his Vanquish.'

'Her loss,' said Jake supportively. 'Imagine her having to shout out "Chip! Chip!" when she comes. He'd better have an awfully big todger to compensate for a name like that.'

Danny gave a half-hearted smile. 'What about you? What happened to Scarlett?'

'Disappeared up her own arse,' said Jake, irritated. 'She's a gorgeous bird, but honestly, she doesn't half bend your ear about all this ethical trading wank. I almost felt sorry for Brogan by the end of it.'

'Blimey, I don't,' said Danny. 'Did you see how drop-dead gorgeous his wife was? By far the best-looking woman here.'

Jake noticed the dreamy expression on his brother's face and took him firmly by the shoulders.

'No,' he said, looking him right in the eye. 'Do you hear me, Danny? N-O spells no. Mrs O'Donnell is very definitely off limits.'

'I know *that*,' said Danny, shrugging him off. 'I'm not stupid. I'm just saying . . . she's got something.'

'That's right,' said Jake. 'It's called a billion dollars in the bank, and an old man with half the Russian mafia at his beck and call. Promise me you'll steer clear.'

Danny looked puzzled. It was unlike Jake to take a throwaway remark so seriously. 'Relax,' he said. 'I promise.'

# Five

Six months after the Tiffany party, London was enjoying a rare summer heatwave that seemed to have infected the city's inhabitants with a quite uncharacteristic joie de vivre. People on the streets began smiling and waving at one another in the mornings, commiserating that they were forced to spend such a gorgeous day stuck in an office, and bemoaning the general lack of air conditioning. Stifling, stuffy Tube trains emptied as commuters opted to walk or cycle to work, thronging to the parks and banks of the Thames like salmon swimming upriver to spawn. There was plenty of 'spawning' going on too. Everywhere you looked lovers seemed to be strolling hand in hand, the women with their legs and cleavages at last on show, the men looking happy but at the same time awkward and British in their shorts and flip flops, as if the soaring temperatures had forced them all to pretend to be Italians, without providing the requisite tanned skin and laid-back manner needed to pull the look off.

Nature had also risen to the occasion. Even in the heart of the city, window boxes and tiny, postage-stamp front gardens exploded into riotous colour, with poppies, freesias, roses, clematis and buddleia bushes all jostling for position and their share of the apparently endless sunlight. Cafes and pubs battled with stuck-in-the-mud local councils to be allowed to put tables and chairs on the pavements, and illicit smokers hung out of every window, enjoying the summer smells of freshly mown grass and Starbucks' iced Frappucino.

At Bijoux Scarlett had thrown open all the windows

and doors, and done her best to allow the spirit of summer inside with the help of huge porcelain water pitchers filled to the brim with daisies, dandelions and other pretty weeds she'd gleaned from Holland Park earlier. She'd never seen the need for the vastly expensive, imported flower arrangements that so many smart shops went in for in their window displays, when there was a plentiful supply of free, home-grown flora out there for the taking. For Boxford's sake as much as her own, she'd also invested in two expensive Conran ceiling fans, which left her permanently windblown and dusted with pollen, but which did at least keep the worst of the punishing temperatures out.

'It really is very beautiful.'

The young woman holding the platinum and amethyst pendant in her hands looked down at it longingly. 'I particularly like what you've done with the diamond setting, so subtle. I'd hate it if it were all ...'

'Sparkly?' offered Scarlett.

'Yes. You know, overdone,' agreed the woman. 'Still, fifteen thousand pounds. It's not cheap, is it?'

'No,' Scarlett admitted, admiring her own handiwork over the customer's shoulder. 'No, it's not. I think it looks exquisite on you, but I quite see that it's not something one can just splash out and buy without a second thought.'

It was funny: when it came to her Trade Fair campaign she was quite capable of being pushy, yet with her own designs she'd never mastered the art of the hard sell. The thought that she might be pushing someone into buying a piece they didn't really want, or worse, couldn't afford, seemed straightforwardly wrong to Scarlett, no matter how many times wiser heads described it as 'business sense'.

'I'll take it off the display for a few days if you like,' she said kindly, 'while you think it over. I'm afraid I can't really hold it any longer than that.'

Inside a not-so-small voice was shrieking *What the hell are you doing? Your business is going under; you can't hold it at all!* But the woman looked so relieved and hopeful, Scarlett hadn't the heart to play hardball. Besides, in the past she'd won many a loyal customer through being reasonable and patient. Perhaps this was simply a delayed sale?

God, she hoped so.

It was astonishing how a thriving business like Bijoux could have been brought so low in such a short space of time. This time last year she was going great guns, with a healthy waiting list of bespoke orders shoring up the retail business and suppliers queuing up to work with her. Now it was as if everything Scarlett touched turned to dust in her hands, as if somebody had put a hex on her. And she had a pretty shrewd idea who that somebody might be.

After their very public run-in in New York, it became painfully apparent that Brogan O'Donnell had the knives out for Scarlett. In the four years since she'd started Trade Fair, she'd made a number of powerful enemies. It was safe to say that none of the big jewellery chains or diamond mining groups much liked her, and there were plenty of corrupt government officials from Mozambique to Moscow who wished fervently that she and her meddlesome crew of cronies would take up some other crusade. But not until she crossed swords with Brogan had she realised quite how damaging a truly personal vendetta could be, to her campaign as well as her livelihood. It seemed there was no aspect of her life that his malevolent influence couldn't touch.

At first, the intimidation was gradual, so much so that at times she questioned whether Brogan was masterminding it at all, or whether she was simply being paranoid. Trade Fair was the first thing to suffer, as one by one she found her speaking engagements being cancelled for vague, unspecified reasons. Those venues that did bother to come up with an excuse were far from convincing. The concert hall in Geneva claimed to have double-booked itself for Scarlett's two-night run, an unheard-of error for the efficient Swiss to make. Still, at least they'd had the decency to warn her in advance, unlike the Corn Exchange in Cambridge, who called only hours before she was due to go on-stage with her slide show to announce that they'd been overrun by rats (*rats!*) and forced to shut up shop for the night.

If it had happened once, it might have been bad luck; twice, a freak of coincidence. But in the six months since she'd met Brogan, she'd mysteriously lost all but two of her public-speaking gigs. Quite apart from the lost money and time, it was a serious blow to the campaign's momentum, as so much of Trade Fair's success was built on word of mouth, as Scarlett travelled from city to city.

And it wasn't just Trade Fair that was suffering. By February, her problems had started to spread to Bijoux too. All of a sudden suppliers she'd worked with for years began refusing to do business with her.

'But Johnny, this is madness,' she'd remonstrated with her longest-standing diamond dealer when he pulled the plug on her by phone. 'If it's a price issue, surely we can talk about it?'

'It's not the price, Scarlett,' he said awkwardly.

'Well what, then? Something personal? Whatever it is, you can be honest with me. We've known each other long enough.'

'It's nothing personal, truly.' She could hear the tension in his voice on the other end of the line, and was left with the strong impression that he was enjoying the conversation even less than she was. 'It's purely business. I just ... I can't sell to you any more. We're oversubscribed, and I just can't do it. I'm sorry.'

Johnny Fitzhammond was a brilliant diamond man, always had been, but there was no way he was 'oversubscribed'. An ex-crack addict, he'd been almost destitute when Scarlett started working with him. She knew for a fact that none of her major competitors in London trusted him enough to forgive him his past.

No, it was patently clear that Brogan had got to him. Just as over the next few months he'd get to her other suppliers, the magazines who sold her advertising space, even some of her clients. If it hadn't been for her online business, she might have gone under altogether, and she still wasn't out of the woods yet. Thank God she'd bought the store outright rather than leased it. At least that meant Brogan couldn't knobble the landlord and hike her rents up.

Boxford, his shaggy coat blown into a bizarre, spiky up-do by the ceiling fan directly above him, gave his mistress a reproachful look as the young woman customer left the shop empty handed.

'Oh, don't you start,' said Scarlett, crossly. 'She'll come back, all right?'

Sitting down cross-legged on the floor, her legs unusually bronzed from the sun and as long as two slender saplings in the pair of frayed denim shorts and pink espadrilles she was wearing, Scarlett pulled the spaniel into her lap.

'Sorry, old boy,' she said, ruffling his knotted, dangly ears. 'I shouldn't take it out on you.'

It had been a tough few weeks.

It all started with the anonymous, threatening letters. Scarlett dismissed the first one as the work of some crank. But when two more arrived, each more luridly menacing than the last, she called the police. No one at Ladbroke Grove station seemed particularly interested. The problem, apparently, was that none of the letters contained an explicit death threat.

'Come back to us if something 'appens,' the bored duty sergeant told Scarlett dismissively.

'Like what? Waking up with a carving knife between my shoulder blades?'

'It's probably just kids tryin' to wind you up, miss. Try not to worry.'

Scarlett tried not to worry. The next morning she woke

to find her car tyres had been slashed and a laminated note super-glued to her windscreen:

*NEXT TIME IT MIGHT BE YOUR NECK*

This, surely, the police would have to take seriously.

'I do sympathise, miss,' the WPC who came round to the flat said apologetically. 'It's terribly upsetting when something like this happens. But chances are we're still dealing with local kids up to no good.'

'*Kids*?' said Scarlett, exasperated. 'Kids use spray paint. They don't have laminating machines. Most of the ones round here can't even spell "neck". I know who's behind this and he's no kid, believe me.'

'Hmm, so you said,' said the policewoman, in the sort of conciliatory tone she might use to pacify a violent lunatic. 'The American billionaire diamond chappie.' She made Brogan sound like Scarlett's imaginary friend. 'You see, the problem is that without any actual *evidence* of him being involved, Miss Drummond, there's not a lot we can do. These sorts of empty threats towards someone like your-self, in the public eye, they're a lot more common than you'd imagine. You'd be amazed.'

I'm amazed at your incompetence, thought Scarlett furi-ously. What the hell did she pay her taxes for? But once she calmed down, she could see that perhaps the policewoman had a point. The Brogan theory did sound a bit far fetched when one actually said it out loud.

As a last resort she'd turned to Cameron, who'd trained as a lawyer before he joined Goldman, to see if there might be something she could do to protect herself legally.

'Like what?' he laughed, over lunch at the Wolseley. 'Sue him for your Autoglass bill on the windscreen? Don't be silly, Scar. You haven't a shred of evidence that O'Donnell was involved in any way, and frankly I find the idea quite preposterous. You and your little gaggle of *Tatler* groupies are far too small fry for a man like him to be bothered with.'

'He didn't seem to think I was such small fry when I met him in New York,' Scarlett shot back defensively. 'He was busy telling the head of Cuypers how much damage Trade Fair has done to his business before I interrupted him.'

'Yes, well, perhaps you shouldn't have interrupted him,' said Cameron piously. 'What do you expect if you go around baiting big businessmen and generally making a nuisance of yourself?'

'Hold on.' Scarlett shook her head. 'A moment ago you said you thought I was being preposterous. Now you think he *is* involved, but it was *my* fault for provoking him? You think I'm responsible for getting my own tyres slashed?'

'I think whoever was responsible did you a favour. That car's a bloody eyesore. Tell you what,' Cameron snorted with laughter, 'it was probably Jeremy Clarkson! Saving the streets of West London from wanton vehicular ugliness!'

'What about a restraining order?' asked Scarlett, who didn't find the situation remotely funny.

'On O'Donnell? No chance. They'd throw you out of court.' Wiping his wet lips with his napkin, Cameron looked his sister in the eye. 'If you honestly think this is Brogan O'Donnell's doing, and you're worried about it, the solution lies in your own hands. Give up this nonsense campaign of yours, write him an apology for whatever foolishness you got up to in New York, and let bygones be bygones.'

'Bygones?' Scarlett pushed back her chair in defiance. 'Over my dead body.'

'Yes, well. Let's hope not,' said Cameron.

Jake Meyer fixed the waiter with a frosty stare.

'There must be some mistake,' he said. 'There's nothing wrong with that card. Run it through again.'

He was sitting outside at Il Sole on Sunset, soaking up the Californian sunshine and gossipy lunchtime atmosphere in the enchanting company of Greta Saltzman, the sultry

German-born wife of the producer Michael Saltzman, and one of his most generous clients, when his Amex was returned to him a second time.

'Sir, I don't mean to be rude,' said the waiter, looking equally frosty. 'But we've run this card twice now. Perhaps you'd like to take care of the check another way?'

Cracking his knuckles, Jake got to his feet.

'Or perhaps you'd like to do as I ask, sweetheart, and run it through your machine. Again.'

It wasn't a question. The waiter hesitated for a moment, but taking in Jake's biceps bulging through his Abercrombie T-shirt and the murderous violet-blue eyes narrowed beneath his blonde bed-head of hair, he decided to plump for caution. Sighing heavily, he scurried back into the restaurant.

'It's really not a big deal, you know,' said Greta, who'd also clocked Jake's Power Ranger arms and was hoping to put them to better use than waiter-bashing once she got him home. 'I'm happy to pay.'

'No way,' said Jake. 'Thanks, but I'll give them my bleeding watch if it comes to that. I'm not taking your husband's money.'

Greta roared with laughter. 'You won't take his money, but you'll take his wife? And what about all the thousands you've taken off him for diamonds over the years?'

'That's different,' said Jake. 'That's business.'

'And me?' Greta looked at him archly, her slanting, playful eyes dancing with desire and expectation. 'What am I?'

'You, my dear, are purely pleasure,' growled Jake, returning the look. He did love a flirtatious woman. What was the point of being sexy if you were too uptight and prissy to do anything about it, like the saintly Scarlett Drummond Murray? 'All's fair in lust and war. But that doesn't mean I can fleece your old man for lunch. Trust me, if you were a bloke you'd understand the difference.'

It was awkward being embarrassed like this in front of

Greta and the other wealthy diners, pretending not to be watching the unfolding drama from their neighbouring tables. In LA, and in Jake's business particularly, appearances were everything. It was acceptable to be in debt, but totally unacceptable to drive a shitty car, for example, or to have one's platinum Amex turned down in public. As long as you appeared successful, no one much cared whether you actually were.

But Jake himself cared deeply, and the business side of his life had been distinctly rocky lately. Things were not yet that bad – he was pretty sure today's Amex problem was a technical hitch, rather than a total absence of credit – but it was fair to say that the triumphant high on which he'd ended last year, screwing over the Brooksteins, seemed light years away now.

After a fraught Christmas in London, he'd promised Danny he'd put the kibosh on using simulants, and he'd stuck to his word. With the exception of the Brookstein deal, they'd never made up a huge part of his income anyway. But there was no doubt that a return to purely legitimate diamond trading involved a lot more work and effort than he'd been used to of late, and in particular a lot more travel. This was the perennial diamond dealer's dilemma: you needed to travel, often on long, risky trips to far-flung corners of the world in order to source the best ice at the best price. But if you abandoned your patch for too long, you ran the risk of some rival moving on to your turf and nabbing your clients before you got back.

With the Oscars in February, no dealer in their right mind could afford to leave LA before March. In past years, that's what most of Jake's competitors had done, disappearing as soon as the awards were over. Low on stock himself after the Oscar season frenzy, Jake would typically use simulants like cubic zirconia, YAG or GGG to tide him through the spring months, cleaning up while his competition was out of town. Then he'd run his own, shorter trip to Africa in June, before the summer rush, and when the LA market was already overwhelmed with dealers trying to offload their newly acquired product. It was a strategy that had served him well for years, and made him the most profitable 'independent' in town.

This year however, unable to sell synthetic stones, he'd been forced to join the March exodus. By the time he got back into town in late May, having been delayed a week by a deeply unpleasant stint in a Kazakhstani jail, some chancer called Tyler Brett was all over his clients like a fucking rash. What was particularly galling was that Tyler was in fact an ex-daytime-soap star, considered something of a heart-throb amongst Hollywood women of a certain age. The guy might not know a decent diamond from a packet of peas, but he sure as fuck knew how to sell himself, and he'd stolen a march on Jake big-time.

'Sorry about that, sir.' The waiter, all smiles now, had returned to their table. 'I don't know what the problem was, but it seems we were third time lucky.'

'Great,' said Jake coldly, signing the check. The guy could smile and make nice all he liked. If he thought he was getting a decent tip now, after showing him up in front of Greta like that, he could whistle for it.

'So.' Greta slipped on her oversized Oliver Peoples sunglasses. They were all the rage in LA this season, which Jake thought a shame, given that they hid pretty girls' faces and made them look like giant bugs. 'Your place or mine?'

'Yours, definitely,' said Jake. He'd long ago made a policy decision never to bring women home unless he was really serious about them – which was never. The last thing he needed was some married bunny-boiler knowing where he lived. 'You are sure Michael's away?'

'Positive,' she smiled, allowing him and the rest of Sunset Boulevard a glimpse of her sky-high legs in a crotch-skimming white sundress. 'We shouldn't leave together though. I'll go first and wait for you at the bottom of Stone Canyon.'

Watching the Mexicans on valet duty drool surreptitiously as she curled herself into her pink Lamborghini, Jake began to perk up. So what if Tyler 'nine-inch' Brett was having a good few months? His novelty value would soon wear off, and the diamond-hungry wives at the Brentwood tennis club would be beating down Jake's door once again. In the meantime, he'd just enjoyed a damn good lunch and was about to get the best head in Hollywood from Greta Saltzman. Things could be worse.

'Meyer!'

Al Brookstein's booming, furious voice shook the air like an earthquake as he spotted Jake from across the street.

'I want a word with you, you son of a bitch! You sold me a lump of frikkin' glass!'

In a split second, Jake weighed up his options. He could stay and try to reason with the irate Al. Technically he could deny the accusation – GGG wasn't glass; it was garnet, and for six hundred grand he could hardly have expected the real deal – but one look at Brookstein's red, straining face told him his chances of success were slimmer than Nicole Ritchie on a diet. Halfway across Sunset now, weaving his portly form through the angrily beeping traffic, the veins on his temples stuck out so far that Jake could see them from here.

If he waited for the valet to bring his car, they might as well serve him as fresh chopped liver on tonight's menu; Al was clearly going to skin him alive in about twenty seconds. No, the only thing for it was to make a dive for his keys and run for the car himself.

Leaping across tables like James Bond, spilling drinks and plates of mung bean salad as he went, he reached into the valet booth for his car keys on their distinctive white and blue Tottenham Hotspurs fob, and bolted past the trash cans into the parking lot. By some miracle, no one had boxed him in. He could jump into the driving seat and go.

His fingers were trembling so much, it took a second or two to start the ignition and auto-lock the doors. As soon as he slipped the Maserati's silver gear stick into drive and began to pull forward, Al rounded the corner of the alley, shaking his fist like a cartoon baddie.

'I'll kill you!' he roared. 'I'll fucking rip your fucking balls off, you British prick!' The next thing Jake knew, he'd lowered his bald head and began running straight at the car, charging it like some sort of crazed bull.

Slowly, Jake edged the Maserati forward – there was nowhere else to go, and he didn't want to kill the guy. But Brookstein kept on running, finally flinging himself on the bonnet, where he landed with an almighty, chassis-buckling thud.

'Get out of that car!' he yelled, battering the windscreen with his fists. It would have been comic had Jake not been convinced that with a few more blows he might actually break the thing and climb inside, broken glass and all. He hadn't felt this frightened since the time his parents took him and Danny to Whipsnade Zoo for their tenth birthday, and they'd broken down in a field of monkeys, who proceeded to jump all over the car, stripping it of everything portable from windscreen wipers to hubcaps, baring their teeth and shrieking uncontrollably all the while.

On that occasion, he'd memorably wet his pants. This time, he decided to take the more dignified option of fighting back. Speeding up into the alley, he swung the car sharp right onto Sunset. Al clung on manfully for a couple of seconds, but soon fell to the ground, curling up and rolling to the safety of the sidewalk like a hedgehog. Jake's last image of him in the rear-view mirror showed him bruised but still screaming, waving a wrenched-off wiper like a dagger at Jake's tail lights.

'Fuck!' he shouted, letting off steam himself as adrenaline

gave way to the nausea of relief. 'Holy fucking FUCK! How did he know?'

He'd known the Brooksteins long enough to realise that neither of them would ever think unprompted of 'verifying' one of his stones. Someone must have put the idea into Al's head. He wouldn't mind betting that that someone was an iron-jawed *Melrose Place* has-been called Tyler.

'I'll kill him,' he muttered to himself, surveying the dent and scratches Al had left on the front of his beloved car as he sped through Holmby Hills and on towards Stone Canyon. 'If that little fucker's been badmouthing me, I swear to God, I'll kill him.'

How ironic it would be if, after years of scamming, the whole simulants thing came back to bite him just when he'd sworn off it for good. He could already imagine the 'I-told-you-so's from Danny. Although recently his brother had been so distracted, no doubt mooning over yet another unsuitable woman, he probably wouldn't register what an almighty fuck-up this was.

But then again, he might. Perhaps it was best if he didn't tell Danny just yet? He'd come to some sort of arrangement with Brookstein, who'd have to calm down eventually. Either that or die of a coronary, either of which would suit Jake's purposes admirably. Hopefully with a bit of sweet talking, he could get Julia to help plead his case, although God knew how he was going to afford to pay her old man back, even in part. The first priority was to get his car fixed. Left as it was, it would serve as a visible daily reminder to the LA gossips of a story that was probably already flying round town like Chinese Whispers: the great Al Brookstein going psycho on Jake the Rake at Il Sole, after Jake sold him a fake diamond.

Christ. Whichever way he looked at it, this was going to hurt Solomon Stones.

'Omigod! What happened?' Greta, who moments ago had been starting to get pissed at Jake for keeping her waiting, now stared at his battered car and sweating, anxious face with genuine concern as he pulled into Stone Canyon Drive. 'Did you get in an accident? Are you OK?'

'No, and not really,' said Jake. 'I'll tell you about it later.' Getting out of the car to greet her, he realised he was still shaking. 'Listen, G, I never thought I'd hear myself say this. But I'm kind of not in the mood for sex right now. D'you mind if we take a rain check?'

Greta kissed him on the cheek.

'Not at all,' she smiled. 'I don't know when Michael will next be out of town, but I'm sure it won't be long. I'd much rather have your full attention.'

'Thanks,' said Jake, staggering dazedly back to the Maserati. 'I'll call you.'

'I won't hold my breath,' said Greta, without rancour. She liked Jake, but she had a wealth of other lovers to choose from. 'Take care of yourself, OK?'

Jake gave her an uncharacteristically nervous smile.

'I'll try my best.'

# Six

Scarlett unscrewed the top of her purified water bottle for the second time in as many minutes and took a deep, thirsty gulp. Why had nobody warned her that the Siberian summer was so *hot*? Strolling along Ulitsa Lenina in Yakutsk, Yakutia's capital city, past the endless jewellery boutiques showcasing the region's diamonds in a dazzling array of colours and settings, she felt the energy seeping out of her like moisture from a withered vine. Ugly sweat patches had formed under the sleeves of her Gap T-shirt, and even in linen trousers and sandals she felt uncomfortably overdressed for the ninety-plus-degree heat.

She'd arrived here last night, courtesy of an Aeroflot flight from Moscow that she wouldn't forget in a hurry. Wedged between a snoring, farting Georgian businessman and a middle-aged Muscovite woman who brought new meaning to the term 'white-knuckle flyer' (her screams must surely have been audible from the cockpit, if not the ground, every time they ran into turbulence), she'd collapsed into bed at the Sails Hotel on the main town square without taking much stock of her surroundings. Only this morning, at breakfast (a surprisingly cosmopolitan spread of pastries, fruit and cold meats and a vast improvement on the food she'd been offered on her last trip to Russia) did she realise that her room was 'armoured'. Tinted windows of bulletproof glass complemented a decor of concrete with subtle accents of reinforced steel, which did rather make her wonder what the majority of her fellow guests did for a living. But as she was here on Trade Fair business – and as the only other hotel in town was the extortionately priced

Polar Star, where a cocktail would set her back roughly as many roubles as her entire suite at Sails, she had little option but to make the best of it.

Catching sight of a bench up ahead, nestled beneath a tired-looking plane tree, she made a beeline for it, sinking down gratefully onto its wooden slats and luxuriating in that rarest of Yakutian commodities, shade. This entire sterile, barren city was at once so rich and so poor, so crammed with jewels and money and light, and yet so unutterably blank and depressing. While the rest of Siberia crumbled uselessly around it, a living museum of its own, past great-ness, Yakutsk was all about the future, about the Sakha Republic's vast diamond wealth, and what that money could build. But if this was the best they could come up with – bulletproof hotels and breezeblock jewellery stores? Well, it just went to show that money wasn't everything.

Tonight – in six hours precisely, in fact – Scarlett would address a packed hall of diamond miners, some of the poorest men in the whole of Sakha, many of whom would have travelled hundreds of miles to hear her speak. It was a daunting thought. Using an interpreter was always diffi-cult. She'd done it on numerous occasions in Africa, during Trade Fair's early days, but somehow the atmosphere was easier amongst the smiling, Swahili rabble than it was here, in this stark, alien country, in front of such dour, hard-bitten working men. Nor were her nerves eased by the certain knowledge that in a matter of days, perhaps even hours, Brogan O'Donnell would hear about her little foray into his backyard, stirring up trouble.

She looked at her watch and thought briefly of her father, as she did every time she saw its battered, familiar strap and rose gold face. She pictured him asleep in his comfy chair in the study, with the three o'clock at Kempton still crackling out from his ancient Roberts radio. It was rare for Scarlett to get homesick for Drumfernly, but Yakutsk was the sort of place that could make one homesick for anywhere.

Heavens, twelve o'clock already. She'd better scoot back to the hotel and shower before Gregori from the union turned up.

'Relax. This is Yakutia,' Gregori grinned. 'Everybody else in that hall will have had at least four vodkas before they sit down. Have another.'

She'd expected the miners' union rep to be a typical Russian – monosyllabic, with a paunch spilling over polyester trousers and all the charm of a traffic warden with a migraine. Instead, Scarlett found herself passing a remarkably pleasant afternoon at the hotel bar with a good-looking guy about her own age, who seemed intent on delivering her to the podium drunk.

'I can't, honestly,' she giggled. She'd only had two gin and tonics, but the seventies-themed bar was already starting to look blurry, a psychedelic mish-mash of orange and brown. Russian barmen were notoriously easy on the mixers. 'It's all right for them; they don't have to give a speech. Besides, they're used to it. Isn't the average Siberian miner's diet eighty per cent alcohol?'

'At least,' Gregori smiled, ignoring her protests and ordering a third cocktail for both of them. 'Now, where were we? Oh yes, you wanted the cancer statistics. It's all a bit ad-hoc I'm afraid. But these are the best numbers I have.' He reached into his briefcase and handed her a sheaf of cheap-looking printer paper, covered in spreadsheets with a few handwritten addendums in the margins.

'Can you summarise?' Scarlett asked hopefully. Numbers tended to swirl before her eyes at the best of times. After two stiff drinks, he might as well have handed her the Enigma code.

'Sure.' He took a gulp of his cosmopolitan. 'This column here shows the number of confirmed cases in the last three years.'

'These are all O'Donnell employees?'

'Yes,' he nodded. 'Page two shows you comparable numbers for Alrosa miners.'

'The government diamond interest?' asked Scarlett, scanning the figures where Gregori pointed.

'Correct. I know it looks a lot, but that's about the average level of lung cancer occurrence for adult males in this part of the Russian Federation. Everybody smokes.'

'I know, I know,' said Scarlett, sighing. 'It'd make my work an awful lot easier if they didn't.'

'But the O'Donnell workers are at well over twice that level,' said Gregori, directing her back to page one. 'Statistically, everything points to the fact that there must be some particulate matter in those pits that's fucking with those guys – excuse my language. Brogan O'Donnell knows it. He just doesn't want to address it, and why should he when labour here is so cheap and plentiful?'

Scarlett shook her head. Poor Gregori. He was educated, but he could identify with the diamond miners and their struggles in a way that she never could. These dying men were his friends, his uncles, his brothers. No wonder he looked so angry.

'What they need is organisation,' he went on. 'Someone to help them harness the power of their numbers and their situation.'

'That's why I'm here,' said Scarlett. 'This is exactly the sort of work Trade Fair needs to be doing. We've had quite a bit of success in South Africa, helping the unions ...'

'I know,' said Gregori, 'and that's great. But Russia is completely different.'

'In what way?'

He frowned, searching for the right words. 'It's hard to explain. Russians, Yakuts, they're a very proud people. They won't thank you for your charity, the way that a South African might.'

Scarlett looked at him quizzically.

'You'll find it a lot harder to whip up international

sympathy for white Russian miners than you will for black Africans,' Gregori blurted. 'I'm sorry if that sounds racist but it's true. I love these men; they're my people. But they aren't cute and cuddly. There is nothing ... adorable about them.'

'Nothing *adorable*?' Scarlett laughed.

'I'm putting this badly,' said Gregori. 'Just don't expect miracles tonight, OK? They need help, but they don't know they need it. Especially not from a woman. A *foreign* woman,' he added, meaningfully.

'Come on,' said Scarlett. 'I'm sure they can't be that bad.'

Now it was Gregori's turn to laugh. 'Don't you believe it. Why do you think I've been buying you drinks all afternoon? Trust me, Scarlett, you're going to need them.'

He wasn't wrong.

The sight of some three hundred, semi-inebriated Yakuts crammed into an auditorium in the former Soviet Party headquarters was enough to make her contemplate bolting.

'Oh God,' she whispered to Gregori, who stood beside her on stage as the last of the men took their seats. 'My knees are shaking. I shouldn't have come.'

'Nonsense,' said Gregori. 'You'll be fine.'

Her audience seemed to divide into two distinct camps: the glarers and the leerers. On balance, she thought she slightly preferred the latter, who at least took the trouble to muster the occasional smile. But they were hardly the world's most welcoming bunch, and it took all of Gregori's cajoling to get them quiet enough to allow her to begin speaking at all.

'Thank you all for coming,' she began falteringly. 'I know some of you have travelled a long way to be here, and I really appreciate it.'

A few men in the front row began talking amongst

themselves. Scarlett looked helplessly to her translator, a fat, bored-looking woman who relayed her words without an iota of enthusiasm first in Russian and then in the local Yakut. By the time she'd finished, the front-row conversation was already spreading backwards and becoming quite animated, with miners laughing and passing cigarettes amongst one another like naughty schoolboys.

Suddenly Gregori bellowed something in Russian. A couple of hecklers yelled back, after which a full-scale slanging match erupted for almost a minute. When it was over, Gregori turned back to Scarlett, as calmly as if he'd just been adjusting her mic.

'You can continue now,' he said brightly. 'Everybody is very interested in what you have to say.'

For the next twenty minutes, Scarlett ploughed through her speech, stopping every thirty seconds or so for the suicidal translator to do her thing. With the exception of the night she lost her virginity to a ham-fisted schoolboy called Roland with a nervous sweating problem, it was without doubt the longest twenty minutes of her life.

'O'Donnell Mining Corp is systematically killing you.'

Silence.

'The power to fight Brogan O'Donnell lies within your own hands.'

More silence.

'Yakutia's diamonds are *your* wealth, *your* resources, *your* livelihood. They should be paying for the best healthcare, the best hospitals, the best schools in the federation. You don't *have* to see that money disappear into American pockets, into Brogan O'Donnell's pockets, while you suffer in silence.'

Not a murmur.

In the end, hoarse with the effort of making herself heard and winded with deflation at the lack of reaction, she sat down to the faintest ripple of forced applause. No one, it seemed, had any questions, and within sixty seconds the hall had emptied almost completely.

'What a fiasco.' Dropping her head into her hands, she groaned loudly. 'You know, it's ironic. I came out here to make a difference, to prove to myself that I wasn't going to let Brogan intimidate me, that I was going to bring the fight right to his bloody doorstep. But these people don't want a fight.' She shook her head in exasperation. 'All they want is a free bar.'

'You're wrong.' The Scottish accent caught Scarlett's attention immediately. 'Isn't she, Gregori? Why d'you think they travelled so far to be here? They want help. And they'll have listened to what you said tonight, even if they don't show it. They're not used to being lectured by pretty wee girls, that's all, and they don't know Trade Fair from a horse's arse. Let's just say you're not the messiah they've been expecting.'

'That's just what I've been telling her,' said Gregori, clapping the small, ginger-haired man on the back. 'Scarlett, this is Andy Gordon. He's the BBC correspondent out here, God help him. Andy, meet Scarlett Drummond Murray.'

'A pleasure.'

'You're the one who did the report for Radio Four at Christmas,' said Scarlett, impressed. 'That was a terrific piece, by the way. It's what first got me interested in Yakutia, in fact. Up until this year Trade Fair's been almost exclusively in Africa.'

'Well, we're happy to have you, believe me,' beamed Andy. 'These poor bastards need all the help they can get. I don't suppose you fancy a drink, do you?'

'Another one?' groaned Scarlett.

'Please,' mocked Gregori and Andy in unison. 'We've hardly started.'

The three of them soon found themselves ensconced in a

comfortable corner booth at one of the lesser-known hotel bars in downtown Yakutsk.

'It's as ugly and soulless as every other waterhole in this godforsaken town,' said Andy cheerfully, 'but they know me here, which means we won't get ripped off, and they actually serve some decent Scotch if either of you get bored with vodka.'

The Yakut clientele eyed them warily as they sat down; unsurprisingly, thought Scarlett, given what an odd trio they made: Gregori, all brooding Dr Zhivago handsomeness, led the way, followed by the pint-sized figure of Andy, grinning like a ginger garden gnome, and Scarlett bringing up the rear, a willowy, freckled Alice in Wonderland and quite clearly the only non-prostitute female in the room.

'I feel like such an idiot.' Scarlett began beating herself up again the moment her Glenfiddich arrived, noticing with alarm that the barman seemed to have left them the entire bottle. 'I should have done more research, understood a little of the culture before flying out here half cocked, thinking I could actually make a difference. I was just so determined to bring the fight to Brogan, to get involved ... but he was right. I *am* naive.'

'There are worse crimes than naivety, you know,' said Andy kindly. 'Anyone can sit on their arse and pontificate about the world's injustices. But not many people get on the fucking plane, write a speech, pull off an event like tonight with all the organisation that entails. No wonder Trade Fair's got O'Donnell rattled.'

'Thanks,' said Scarlett. 'But I'm not sure I did pull it off. Those men thought I was a joke. They don't believe I can help them.'

'You can't,' said Gregori. 'No one can unless they're prepared to help themselves. But tonight was a step forward. They came to hear you speak, they listened, they stayed to the end.'

'You mustn't take it personally,' agreed Andy. 'Rapturous

applause was never on the cards. These blokes don't do emotion, OK? I've watched some of them listen to their doctors telling them they've got inoperable lung cancer, and it barely elicits a shrug.'

For the next forty-five minutes he filled Scarlett in on everything he'd learned researching the O'Donnell miners for his BBC report, and for the in-depth feature he was currently writing for the *Sunday Times*.

'The cancer cases are compelling,' he told her, 'but you'll never pin that on OMC in a court of law, not in a million years.'

'So what are you saying?' Scarlett's frown deepened. 'We should just give up?'

'Not at all. The diamond industry is acutely sensitive to bad press, as you know – Brogan O'Donnell more so than most. I'm doing my bit to get this story out there. But Trade Fair can help. Enough media pressure and Brogan will have to act. At the very least I'd like to see him paying for medical care.'

'Meanwhile, we unions have to get our own act together,' said Gregori. 'We have to insist on better mine safety, better pay, better conditions. And we will. It's a slow road, but we're getting there.'

'Well, you can count me in,' said Scarlett, her cheeks flushed with alcohol and renewed passion. 'Brogan O'Donnell's nothing but a schoolyard bully. He's already tried to intimidate me into keeping my mouth shut, but he doesn't scare me a bit.'

'He should,' said Andy, deadly serious all of a sudden. 'This is Russia. Inconvenient people "disappear" here every day. The hoods call themselves mafia, but that's a polite term. The truth is they're nothing more than hired assassins, farming out their services to the highest bidder, no questions asked. And your friend Brogan's one of the highest bidders in Siberia.'

Scarlett fell silent. When Cameron had tried to warn her

off provoking Brogan, she'd dismissed him out of hand. But here was someone who truly cared about these diamond miners, who was risking his own life and reputation to help bring them justice – and even *he* was urging caution. She thought about the bulletproof glass in her hotel room window, and for the first time felt a cold prickle of fear beneath her skin.

'I'm not telling you to drop it, and I really hope you don't,' said Andy, sensing her change in mood. 'I'm just saying you can do as much good, if not more, from London or New York than you can out here.'

'But even at home you should take basic precautions,' chimed in Gregori. 'Check your phones. Make a habit of looking underneath your car before you start it in the mornings.'

'Oh, come *on*,' laughed Scarlett. But neither of the men cracked a smile.

'Sorry to be the harbinger of doom, sweetheart,' said Andy, refilling her glass. 'But if they can lock up Khordorkovsky and throw away the key, they can certainly get you.'

# Seven

Aidan Leach jerked his wiry hips to Justin Timberlake's 'Rock Your Body' with about as much sense of rhythm as a deaf, elderly nun.

By far the oldest, ugliest and un-coolest individual of either sex on the dance floor, Brogan O'Donnell's chief attorney and self-proclaimed 'friend' was nonetheless surrounded by female admirers in various stages of undress. Bungalow 8 was usually renowned for its strict, Studio 54-style door policy. It wasn't enough simply to be rich here. You must also be suitably beautiful, famous or otherwise captivating to be admitted as one of New York's genuine in-crowd. And yet somehow, Aidan Leach, a man with all the charm of a festering bed sore, had become a semi-permanent fixture.

Brogan's influence helped. As did Leach's bank balance, persistence, and the fact that he owned a twenty per cent share in Premiere, and so was guaranteed to turn up with some of the most beautiful girls in Manhattan on his arm. Even so, you'd have thought management would have drawn the line somewhere. With his dandruff-splattered shoulders and cheap shiny suits – he could easily have afforded the best tailoring money could buy, but was notoriously penny pinching, one of the character traits that Brogan admired in a lawyer – he looked more like a New Jersey accountant than a top attorney. Instantly recognisable for his height (he was six foot five), tiny, deep-set, bird-like eyes and prominent Adam's apple, his ugliness was not even mitigated by being generic. Nor did he possess the sort of wit, charm or dynamism that can sometimes make an unattractive but successful man desirable in the eyes of women. No, Aidan Leach had one thing and one thing only that the girls fawning over him wanted – access to Brogan O'Donnell. Happily for him, many of them were prepared to do just about anything to get it.

'Come over here, baby,' he crooned, summoning a nubile young Latina into his inner circle. 'Hurry up, 'cause you're taking too *long*,' he added, grimacing in a cringe-worthy attempt at JT Karaoke. The girl made her way over, smiling as she nudged disgruntled rivals out of the way, and began gyrating her gold lamé-clad butt in Aidan's direction.

'What's your name?' he bellowed in her ear, trying to make himself heard over the din as his bony hands slid all over her breasts, like a horny BFG.

'Carrrrrla,' she purred, rolling her 'r's in a sultry, Salma Hayek fashion.

'Aidan,' he shouted back, pulling her against his body so she could feel his meagre erection pressing into her back. 'You wanna take a break, Carla? Go get a drink?'

'Sure,' she beamed, aware of the envious, dagger looks of the other models as she slipped her arm around his waist. 'Lead the way Meester Leach.'

'Ah, so you know who I am?' Aidan smiled smugly.

'Of course,' said Carla, quite prepared to massage his ego as well as his dick if it would catapult her to the front of the line on the best jobs. 'You're an important man in this city. Everybody know who you are.'

The bar was packed, but as soon as Aidan arrived a stool materialised out of the ether. Immediately taking it for himself rather than offering it to the girl, he sat down, spreading his gangly legs like a crab opening its pincers, and ordered two martinis.

Positioning herself between his legs with her back to the bar, Carla ran a long, red-taloned finger up the inside of his polyester-covered thigh.

'So,' she drawled. 'Now that you have me here … what d'you want to talk about?'

Aidan was about to make some quip about talking being the last thing on his mind, when his inside jacket pocket began vibrating. 'Sorry,' he said, whipping out his cell phone with a flourish, like a cowboy brandishing a gun. Seeing the name 'Brogan' flash across the screen, he turned it around to show the girl, who looked duly impressed, before lifting it to his ear.

'Hey boss,' he yelled. 'Whassup?'

'*Whassup?*' Even on the crackly long-distance line, Brogan sounded scathing. 'Jesus, Aidan, enough with the jive talk, all right? You are not black.'

Stung, but grateful that no one else could hear him being so summarily put down, Aidan smiled and nodded, trying to act like nothing had happened. Tragically, his hero-worship of Brogan was not an act. It always hurt him when the boss exposed their 'friendship' for the master/servant relationship it really was.

'How's Moscow? Have you had time to do any scouting while you were out there? Find us some new girls?' he asked, trying to get back in Brogan's good books. Premiere had professional, employed model scouts in all the major capitals, including Moscow, but both Aidan and Brogan liked to indulge themselves with a little freelance dabbling when they travelled. It was one of the few 'interests' they genuinely had in common.

'One or two,' said Brogan, without enthusiasm, thinking of the dead-eyed Georgian twins he'd amused himself with last night. 'Nothing to write home about.'

'Well, worry not,' oiled Aidan. 'I've got us a great Latina here. If she's any good in the sack I'll pass her on to you when you get back. My treat.'

'I don't need you to find me pussy,' snapped Brogan. There were times when he was happy to play along with his attorney's drooling schoolboy enjoyment of the freebies on offer at Premiere, but tonight wasn't one of them. This trip had been a washout. He was pissed off with Russia, with the unions, with the shitty excuse for a hotel his PA had booked him into, and with being away from home generally. Diana was starting yet another IVF cycle this week – her fifth – and he didn't like leaving her.

'It's insanely hot over here,' he grumbled. 'I've been in Yakutia the past two days, trying to sweet-talk the unions into dropping their demand for health insurance. Why can't these people get it through their thick, Slavic skulls that I am not about to admit liability for those wheezing, work-shy sons of bitches? I mean, do they have any idea how much lung cancer treatment costs?'

Aidan shook his head and mumbled something conciliatory.

'You'd have thought they'd be happy to be employed,' Brogan ranted on. 'It's not as if they have so many other, more attractive options.'

'Well, quite. So why sweet-talk them?' said Aidan. 'Tell them pay and conditions are what they are, no health coverage, and they can take it or leave it.'

'Hmm,' growled Brogan, who'd certainly thought about it. 'Maybe I should. But the men are scared. Some upstart from the union, Gregor something-or-other, has been whipping them into a frenzy. When's that Harvard report gonna be finished?'

As soon as the first cancer cases emerged, Aidan had taken the precaution of commissioning an official scientific investigation to disprove any link between air quality in OMC mines and the workers' respiratory problems. With a multi-million-dollar research grant at stake, there was never much doubt about what the eminent scientists' findings would be. But Brogan wanted his answers today, in black and white, for shareholders, the press and anyone else who asked.

'All this bad feeling isn't good for business,' he

complained. 'An unhappy worker is an unproductive worker, and I've got a lot at stake out here.'

'I know,' said Aidan. 'I'm on it.'

'Really?' Brogan's tone sounded ominous. 'The way you were supposed to be "on" Trade Fair and that meddlesome Drummond Murray woman?'

Carla's hand had been creeping ever further up Aidan's thigh while he was on the phone, and was now coiled unashamedly around the modest bulge in his pants. As enjoyable as this was, it was making it hard for him to concentrate. Holding up five fingers to indicate he'd be back shortly, he slipped outside to take the rest of the call in the relative quiet of the street.

'Scarlett Drummond Murray?' he asked, playing for time, as if there could possibly be another. 'She's no threat to us. Trade Fair hasn't been active for months.'

'Wrong again,' seethed Brogan. 'The stupid bitch was here, in Yakutsk, less than a week ago.'

Aidan swallowed nervously. 'In Yakutsk? That's not possible. Are you sure?'

'Am I sure?' Brogan roared. 'Yes, Aidan, I'm sure. Three hundred of my miners turned up to hear her speak! The whole fucking province is talking about it.'

'All right, all right. Calm down,' said Aidan firmly, struggling to conquer his nerves. This was a major fuck-up on his part – how the hell had Scarlett arranged this without his knowledge? – but he'd learned long ago that it never paid to apologise to Brogan, or admit a mistake. There were no prizes for honesty with the boss.

'So she gave one stupid speech. So what? We're squeezing her tighter and tighter in London, financially, professionally, personally. Soon she'll have to drop the ball with this ridiculous campaign of hers.'

'I'm not interested in *soon*,' spat Brogan. Pacing his suite at the Ararat Park Hyatt in his purple silk pyjamas, he picked up a brass paperweight from the desk and hurled it across the room in frustration, shattering the bedside lamp. Fucking ugly thing anyway. Three thousand bucks a night and his suite looked like it had been furnished from a goddamn K-Mart catalogue. 'I want that girl out of my hair *now*. Yesterday.'

He'd always prided himself on his cool, even-tempered public image. When he lost his temper, or lashed out at enemies or business rivals, he preferred to do it in private. At the Tiffany party, he'd been no more than mildly reproving of Scarlett when she'd shown him up in front of Michael Beerens and his wife, spewing her socialist nonsense like Trotsky with Tourette's. But he never forgot a slight. Nor did he ever knowingly leave a declared enemy unpunished, or allow threats to his business or personal life to go unchecked.

The morning after that party, he'd phoned Aidan from the car before he even got to his office, and set the wheels of retribution in motion. That was over six months ago. Scarlett should have been dead in the water long before now.

Brogan had never liked Aidan, but he was an excellent attorney. Crucially, he understood the concept of 'plausible deniability' – the importance of keeping Brogan's hands clean – and could usually be relied upon to do whatever was asked of him quietly, efficiently, and without sharing unnecessary and potentially damaging details of his working methods with his boss. It was unlike him to leave a task unfinished, as it seemed he had done with Scarlett and her Trade Fair campaign. But one mistake was one mistake too many.

'I don't care how you do it,' he said bluntly. 'But I want Trade Fair to disappear. I want *her* to disappear. Do we understand each other?'

'Of course.' Aidan did his best to sound confident. 'Loud and clear.'

After Brogan hung up, he took a deep breath and tried

to clear his head. Outside the club, a growing gaggle of wannabes had assembled, some of the girls dressed in little more than their underwear, but for once Aidan's mind wasn't in his pants. His career was on the line here, his entire relationship with Brogan at risk. He needed to think.

He'd been too complacent about Scarlett; that was the problem. He'd considered her and her charity such small fry that he'd delegated the task of scaring her off to his London underlings. Clearly, that had been a mistake. It never occurred to him that such a slip of a girl might be as stubborn and determined as Brogan when it came to getting her own way.

Well, if she wanted a fight, she'd got one. As far as Aidan was concerned, anyone that made him look bad with the boss deserved everything that was coming to them.

Slipping the phone into his pocket, he headed gloomily back into the club.

'Everything OK?' Carla's pupils dilated wildly as she handed him his drink. She'd obviously taken advantage of his absence to shovel buckets of Colombia's finest up her perfectly straight nose.

'Not really,' said Aidan, sitting down heavily on the barstool. 'But it will be. It will be.'

Clicking his fingers imperiously for another drink, he repositioned her hand over his cock.

'Now, where were we?'

The next morning, across town in Park Avenue, Diana O'Donnell gazed mindlessly out of the window of her penthouse apartment. It was a glorious day. The sun blazing down on Central Park was bright and dry, a welcome change from the cloying, humid summer weather that for weeks had had New Yorkers sweating in their cars and offices like melting ice lollies, deserting the city at the weekends in search of cooler breezes on the coast. Trees bright with blossom provided welcome shade for the shorts-and-vest-clad multitude that had thronged to Manhattan's only real green space to enjoy the heatwave, content to venture outside now that the sauna-like mugginess had passed.

Briefly, Diana contemplated joining them. Perhaps it would do her good to get some fresh air? But on balance, she thought not. It was strange to feel, on the one hand, so desperately, achingly lonely, and on the other so frightened of normal human contact. As a teenager, she'd thrived on the buzz of New York City, the daily banter with the hot-dog sellers and street vendors, the sense of community, of a unique, shared energy that made this greatest of cities feel so constantly, throbbingly alive.

Of course, New York was still alive. It was she who had died, suffocated in the gilded cage of her marriage and the private hell of her battle to conceive a child, a battle that lately seemed to have sucked all the joy and excitement and beauty out of the world. It had got to the point where she no longer trusted herself to be around other people without bursting embarrassingly into tears.

'Come on, Diana, get a grip,' she said out loud, walking over to the fawn suede B&B Italia couch and flicking on CNN. Perhaps some footage of the real tragedies unfolding in Iraq and Darfur and Somalia might help jolt her out of this ridiculous, relentless depression.

When she'd first met Brogan, over fifteen years ago now, they'd both been such totally different people. She was a twenty-year-old art student from an old-money family, revelling in the freedom of living alone in the big city for the first time in her short, sheltered life. Never wildly ambitious, as least not in the traditional sense, she was passionate about her art, and soon became an accepted part of the rich, bohemian set that hung around the cafes of the East Village, talking about Dali and disarmament, daringly eschewing their republican parents' politics. Very pretty in a neat, American, un-exotic sort of way – had she been born a generation later she'd have been snapped up as a model for Abercrombie & Fitch or Tommy Hilfiger – she was never short of boyfriends, but tended to go for the long-haired, idealistic types who liked to rant against Reagan and encouraged her to go Dutch on dinner.

Then she met Brogan, and stepped into a whole new world.

At thirty-eight, almost two decades her senior, he'd blazed into Diana's life like a comet of worldly self-assurance, as experienced and confident as she was innocent and naive. Already a multi-millionaire and big noise in the diamond fraternity, as well as a renowned Manhattan playboy, he had the sort of charisma and presence normally associated with movie stars or certain rare types of politician. He was also, in Diana's eyes at least, extremely good looking, with his thick dark hair and broad, powerful shoulders, the antithesis of all the weedy, earnest guys she'd dated in the past. Later, she would describe their first meeting, at a party at the Plaza, as the archetypal bolt of lightning. Until Brogan smiled at her, she'd never have guessed she could be so powerfully attracted to a rich, middle-aged, unreconstructed republican. But there it was. She was smitten.

For his part, Brogan's attraction to Diana was more thoughtful and considered, at least at first. He was pushing forty, and ought to acquire a wife. Whomever he chose must be beautiful, naturally, young but not silly, reasonably educated, socially connected and ideally independently wealthy. Diana Frampton ticked every box. She was also, he rapidly discovered, kind hearted, quick witted and funny. It wasn't long before his feelings for her deepened, to the point where he felt quietly confident that they must now qualify as this much-talked-about 'love', an emotion that thus far in life had eluded him completely, but which he had gotten along perfectly well without.

They married in a quiet, low-key ceremony on Nantucket, where Diana's people had a summer home.

Brogan loathed the island on sight – cutesy clapboard houses and khaki-wearing trust fund kids called Chipper were complete anathema to the boy who'd grown up semi-feral, roaming the streets of Brooklyn. But it didn't matter much. After the honeymoon (St Barts) he brought her back to the city, and set about controlling every aspect of their married life as closely and ruthlessly as he always had his businesses.

With no close family, or even real close friends of his own – his parents had broken up when he was eight, and he'd rarely seen either of them since his teens – Brogan lacked what the shrinks he despised would have referred to as a 'blueprint' for marriage. He loved Diana, in the same way that he loved his vintage wine collection or his wardrobe full of exquisitely tailored Savile Row suits. Like them, he treated her with care and respect, protected her fiercely from anyone who threatened to take her from him, and considered his husbandly duties done. She had beautiful homes all over the world, free rein with his credit card, and access to the best designers, beauticians and hair people in the world. What more could a woman want?

It never occurred to him to be faithful. He considered it contrary to the male nature, an unnecessary and unnatural restriction of his freedoms. But he did all he could to insulate Diana from his mistresses, compartmentalising his business, social and married lives as thoroughly as a CIA double agent. To this day, Brogan believed that if only he were able to give her the child she craved, his wife's life would be happy, fulfilled and complete. The idea that Diana might want more than simply material and maternal comforts – that she might want intimacy and trust with the man who shared her life and her bed – was one that he'd never grasped, despite her repeated attempts to explain it to him.

An image of a weeping refugee child calling hopelessly for his mother filled the screen. Aware of the tears starting to prick her own eyes, Diana changed channels. *Everybody Loves Raymond* was on, one of her favourite shows, and she soon found herself smiling, lost in the bickering, domestic banter between Ray and Deborah. She was so engrossed, it took a few moments to register that the intercom buzzer from the lobby was going off.

'Who is it, Rico?' she asked the doorman, getting up to answer it but still keeping half an eye on the TV. 'If it's a delivery, you can sign; I'll tell Mr O'Donnell I okayed it.'

'Ees no delivery, Mrs O'Donnell. Ees a friend of your 'usband. 'E says he has something very valuable, for your 'usband, and he must speak to you in person. Very important business.'

Diana frowned. In all her years with Brogan, he had never once invited a business associate to the apartment, never mind authorised them to discuss anything 'very important' with her.

'What's his name?' she asked.

There was a long silence on the other end of the line, followed by some muffled talking. Eventually Rico's voice came back on.

'Meester Vincent Van and Go,' he said seriously.

Diana giggled. Who was this clown? 'Do you mean Van Gogh? Is that what he said his name was?'

'Yes, yes,' the doorman seemed pleased. 'He say you know hees work very well. Mr Vincent.'

'All right,' said Diana, well and truly intrigued by now. 'You can send Mr Vincent up.'

A minute later, she heard the elevator whooshing to a halt and its occupant emerge onto the landing. Before he had a chance to knock, she'd opened the door.

'Mr Van Gogh, I presume?'

Danny Meyer grinned, his whole face seeming to open up and burst with life, like a freshly cut grapefruit. 'At your service. May I come in?'

Diana hesitated.

'It's a bit late for that now, don'cha think?' said Danny. 'If you thought I was a murderer you shouldn't 'ave buzzed me up. Besides, look at me. I've got nowhere to hide my axe.'

He spread his arms and legs, like someone waiting to be frisked by airport security. In a tightly cut cream linen suit, open-necked shirt and sandals, he looked more like a dapper war correspondent than a crazed killer. Diana relaxed.

'Hold on,' she said, cocking her head to one side and examining him more closely. 'Don't I know you from somewhere? I'm sure I recognise your face.'

'Danny Meyer,' he said, shaking her hand. 'We've never met – unless you count our eyes meeting across a crowded Tiffany store in the depths of winter.'

'Ah yes, of course, Tiffany's,' she said, nodding. 'You were there with your brother, right?'

'Never mind my brother,' said Danny hastily. 'Just remember, I was the handsome one. Look, can I come in? I've got something I'd like to show you.'

Following her into the apartment – fucking hell it was palatial; the couch alone was bigger than his place – he admired her pert bottom in simply cut Gap jeans, and the way her clean hair hung loose to her smooth, brown shoulders. He'd half-expected her to be Chanel-ed up to the eyeballs, but was glad to see she preferred the casual look at home.

'Is this something to do with my husband?' she asked, leaving him standing in the drawing room while she wandered into the kitchen. 'Would you like some coffee, by the way?'

'No, and no thanks,' Danny called back. 'But I'll have tea if you've got some. Only if it's made with boiling water, though, in a pot. And only if it's actually tea and not some soy orange leaf bollocks. Otherwise I'm fine.'

Diana re-emerged, smiling, and sat on the couch, gesturing for him to do the same. 'Maria will do her best. You don't ask for much, do you?'

It was so long since she'd been alone in the company of another man, or even another person, that she was surprised by how easy and enjoyable she found it to talk to him. There was something warm and reassuring about Danny that put her immediately at ease, despite the oddness of the circumstances.

'So come on,' she said brightly. 'What's all this about? Ridiculous pseudonyms, claiming you have business with my husband.'

'I wanted to see you,' Danny blurted out. 'I wasn't sure I'd get access, so I made up a bit of a blag. Everyone told me Brogan guards this place like Fort Knox.'

Diana smiled wryly. 'He doesn't need to. You'd be surprised how few people call on us. But you still haven't said what it was you wanted to see me about.'

Aware he was blushing, and wishing for the thousandth time he shared Jake's cool insouciance when it came to beautiful women, Danny fumbled in his inside jacket pocket and pulled out a small, but infinitely delicate baguette diamond ring.

'I'm in the diamond business,' he said.

'Like Brogan ...' mumbled Diana idly, turning the band over between her fingers.

'Well, sort of. I'm much smaller fry,' said Danny truthfully. 'Mostly I deal in cut stones, but every now and then a finished piece comes my way that I try to find a home for. Ever since I got my hands on this one ...' he swallowed nervously, 'I've been thinking of you. I can't explain it really. I just thought it was perfect. For you.'

Diana held the ring up to the light. The setting was antique, she guessed nineteen thirties, and very simple: a white gold rope twist with the baguette glistening above it like a fifty-seven-faceted snowflake. No doubt about it, it was a work of art, and very much to her own, understated taste. It was also the exact opposite of anything Brogan would buy for her.

Turning back to Danny, she looked at him quizzically.

'You came here to sell diamond jewellery? To *me*?'

'I know,' he blushed again, 'I've lost my marbles, haven't I? You've probably got a million bucks' worth of ice in your dresser drawer already.'

'Several million,' said Diana matter of factly.

'Of course you have,' mumbled Danny. What the fuck had possessed him to come here on such a ridiculous errand? Just because his dreams had been haunted by images of Diana's sad, radiant face ever since the night of the Tiffany party; because he hadn't been able to make love to other girls without fantasies of her naked body creeping into his consciousness; that was no reason to show up at the woman's home like a stalker with a ring so cheap her husband might use it to tip a waiter. She must think him a right deranged prick. 'Look, sorry, it was stupid of me,' he said, reaching for the ring. 'Another piece of bling is the last thing you need.'

'No, no,' said Diana vehemently, snatching it back. 'I love it. I want it, I really do. How much?'

'Er ...' Nonplussed, Danny struggled to think of a figure. He'd love to have made a grand romantic gesture and given it to her outright, but he couldn't afford to, not this month. He was already carrying Jake as it was this year. 'Ten?'

'Ten thousand?' Diana laughed. 'Don't be silly; it's worth far more than that and you know it. Believe me,' she gestured to the master paintings and priceless artefacts strewn round the apartment like so much Z-Gallery trash, 'I'm the last person you should be underselling to. I'll give you fifteen for it, and even that's a bargain.'

Danny smiled. 'I see you know your diamonds, Mrs O'Donnell.'

Diana shrugged. 'After fifteen years of marriage to Brogan, I ought to.'

'I'll tell you what.' Taking the ring from her, Danny

slipped it back into its royal-blue velvet box. 'I'll let you have it for fifteen grand, on one condition.'

'A condition?' Diana laughed. 'Two minutes ago you wanted to sell it for ten!'

'Have dinner with me tonight,' said Danny.

'Excuse me?'

'Dinner. That's the condition. Have dinner with me tonight. I'll bring the ring, and we can close the deal over a civilised bottle of Guigal.'

All at once the laugh died on Diana's lips and the playful sparkle left her eyes, replaced with the same dull, aching stare he remembered so vividly from the Tiffany party.

'I can't,' she said quietly.

'Why not?'

His voice was gentle and encouraging, but still it took her an age to answer.

'Brogan,' she said eventually. 'He wouldn't like it.'

'So don't tell him,' said Danny. He made it sound so simple, so unthreatening. 'Anyway, he's travelling, isn't he?'

'Yeees,' said Diana tentatively, not thinking to wonder how Danny knew this piece of information. 'But—'

'Great,' said Danny. 'We'll go somewhere quiet, a little local bistro I know where the food's good and no one'll bother us.' Seeing the anxiety etched on her face, he took a leap of faith and rested one hand lightly on her denim-clad knee. 'Sweetheart, it's only dinner. I'm not gonna jump on you, I promise. Much as I might like to.'

Diana hesitated. He was right, of course. How had she, an intelligent, rational woman in her mid-thirties, reached a point where she was too frightened even to leave the apartment for a simple dinner, just because Brogan was away? She'd become scared of her own shadow these days.

'All right,' she said, letting out a deep, long-held breath. 'Fine, I'll do it. I'll have dinner with you.'

Only after Danny had left the apartment did the folly

of what she had agreed to really hit home. She, Diana O'Donnell, was going on a dinner date with another man, an attractive, flirtatious man. She must be out of her mind! Brogan routinely had her followed when she went out alone. Even if he didn't do that this time, what if he called home and no one answered? She'd have to come up with a cover story for where she was – she never went out alone – but her mind had gone a complete, panicked blank.

'Don't overreact,' she told herself sternly. 'You're meeting a dealer, with a view to buying a ring. It's no different to walking into a jewellery store.'

Danny's blue eyes, kind face and sonorous, deep English accent had nothing to do with it. Nothing at all.

Later that evening, Danny sat alone at a corner table at Jean Paul's, a minuscule cafe-cum-bistro round the corner from his apartment, wiping his sweating palms on the table-cloth and wishing he didn't feel so sick with nerves.

What if she bottled it? It wouldn't be the end of the world, he told himself. God knew he'd been stood up by enough women in the past. But somehow tonight's date with Diana – if it was a date; was it a date? – had assumed massive, terrifying significance. He didn't know what it was about her – that combination of beauty, vulnerability and a repressed spirit yearning for release – that was so hard to describe, or even capture in his memory. But she'd got to him in a way that no woman had since … well, since ever, really.

He was well aware how ridiculous all this was. He barely knew the woman, she was married, and way out of his league on almost any scale you cared to measure: wealth, breeding, beauty and probably brains too. For this reason, he'd said nothing about today's activities to Jake, or indeed to anyone. If he crashed and burned with Diana, he wanted to do it in private.

'You still wait, or you wanna order now?' The surly,

pinch-faced waitress stood sullenly at his elbow awaiting a response. Danny had been coming to JP's for years, addicted to the outstanding food and the cosy candlelit atmosphere. But the service was without doubt the worst in all Manhattan.

'I'll wait,' he said firmly, watching the waitress grimace as though he'd just squirted lemon juice in her eye. 'She's not very late yet. Give us a few more minutes.'

The harridan shuffled off, muttering something half audible about 'obviously a no-show' and 'waste of a table'. Danny wasn't a religious man, but he closed his eyes and said a little prayer that she was wrong.

'Sorry I'm late.'

When he opened his eyes again, the first thing he saw was Diana, radiant in a floaty cream lace sundress and sandals, dancing her way through the maze of tables like an angel.

'I know it sounds insane, but I wanted to make sure I wasn't being followed, so I took a bit of a circuitous route.'

Danny's eyes glowed with relief.

'I'm just glad you're here,' he said, beaming. 'Please, sit down. I'll get us a bottle.'

The waitress, who'd been buzzing around his table like a fly on a turd for the last twenty minutes, now seemed intent on ignoring him. But he wasn't bothered by the delay. As far as he was concerned, the longer this evening lasted, the better.

'Perhaps we should get the business part out of the way first,' said Diana, reaching into her white Mulberry handbag and pulling out a crisp JP Tyler check. 'Fifteen thousand. It's from my private account, so Brogan needn't know.'

Danny relieved her of it, handing over the ring box with a frown. 'Are you always so nervous about your husband's reactions?'

Diana began playing awkwardly with her napkin.

'You're buying a ring, not a shipment of uncut heroin. Would he really care?'

She laughed bitterly. 'Yes, he'd care. He's a generous man, but *he* likes to be the one to buy my jewellery.'

'Controlling, then?' asked Danny. It was a dangerously personal question to put to a woman he'd just met. But something about Diana gave him the feeling that she was burning to open up to somebody. 'You mentioned being followed.'

'I suppose he is controlling.' She was staring at the napkin again, as if it were a map that could somehow lead her out of her troubles. 'He doesn't see it that way, though. To him, it's a way of showing love. He thinks it's his job to protect me. Like a child, or an endangered species or something.'

'He sounds like a right nut-job,' said Danny robustly.

Diana laughed. 'Oh, I don't know. Maybe I'm the "nut job", as you put it, for sticking with him.'

'Yeah.' Danny looked at her seriously. 'Maybe you are.'

As the evening wore on, and the wine started to flow, conversation came more easily. They chatted happily about everything from art to politics to the diamond business. Danny was surprised to learn how little she knew about the nitty gritty of Brogan's vast mining empire.

'I know he had political problems in Africa years ago, and that's why he pulled out,' she said, lassoing a stray linguine onto her fork. 'Moving to Russia was supposed to put a stop to all of that, but he's come in for a lot of flak recently for conditions in his mines.'

'D'you think that's unfair?' asked Danny, genuinely curious. Diana looked surprised by the question.

'I don't know,' she said. 'I've never been there. From what I understand, the workers have more rights with O'Donnell Mining Corp than they had before, working for the Russian government.'

Danny smiled. 'Isn't that a bit like saying that AIDS is better than cancer? I mean, a shit life is a shit life, isn't it?'

'That's what my husband's opponents say,' said Diana. 'He's become quite obsessed with these Trade Fair people. He thinks they're against free enterprise. He particularly loathes the English girl, the one who accosted him at the Tiffany party. She's a friend of yours, isn't she?'

'Scarlett? Not really,' said Danny. 'My brother wants to get into her knickers. Then again, that applies to half the women in London, so I wouldn't say they were exactly close.'

'Do *you* support her campaign?'

Danny thought about it for a minute. 'No,' he said. 'Not really. I hate to agree with your bloody awful husband, but I think she's naive. The diamond industry is grossly unfair, granted, but then show me a business that isn't. Not that I approve of the conditions in Yakutia, especially in your old man's mines.'

They finished their entrées, and silence fell for a moment as the hostess with the leastest cleared away the plates. Although the restaurant was full, the low buzz of muffled conversation acted as an effective sound barrier, and their corner table felt safely intimate. Covered with a simple red cotton tablecloth and lit by a single candle, it was also dark enough to hide in, the low light and cramped physical space – Danny's knee was necessarily brushing Diana's under the table – lending it an unavoidably romantic air.

Whether it was this, or the wine, or a more general sense of panic that the meal was drawing to a close, Danny found himself reaching across the table for her hand and blurting out the question he'd been dying to ask all night.

'Why *do* you stay with him? I mean, it's obvious you're unhappy. And it's not like you have any children together or anything.'

To his horror, at the mention of the word 'children' Diana burst into tears.

'Oh, darling, no, please don't cry,' he said, passing her a clean handkerchief from his jacket pocket. 'I'm sorry, that was crass of me. Your marriage is none of my business.'

'It's OK,' she sniffed. 'It's not the marriage; it's the children, or rather the lack of them. Oh God, Danny!' Piece by piece, the entire, long story of her IVF rollercoaster, the years of desperate hope and ultimate crushing despair came tumbling out.

When she'd finished and at last cried herself out, he inched his chair around to her side of the table so he could put his arm around her.

'Sorry,' she mumbled, embarrassed. 'I don't know why I'm telling you all this.'

'I do,' said Danny gently. 'Because you can't tell Brogan.'

She looked up at him through eyes red and bleary with tears. He was so solid and sure and gentle, and he understood her so well. The urge to climb into his lap, curl up into a ball and shelter in his arms for ever was almost overwhelming.

'Come back to my place,' he said, seizing the moment. 'For coffee,' he added hurriedly, not wanting to scare her off. 'We can talk some more. It's only round the corner.'

Diana looked at his face, searching for some clue, some reassurance that she was making the right decision. Then, to her own surprise as much as Danny's, she heard herself saying 'OK. Let's go.'

Danny's apartment was less than reassuring. She'd never seen quite such a stereotypical bachelor pad in her life.

Although a loft, with the high ceilings and big windows beloved of urban single males and advertising directors shooting commercials for expensive coffee makers, the flat was small, with one all-purpose living space leading off into a single master bedroom and bath. There wasn't a print or colour or vase of flowers in sight, but the money saved on interior design had clearly been spent on gadgetry – a huge plasma TV dominated the living room, which also boasted state-of-the-art Bose speakers, an automatic retractable glass skylight and a pair of matching Lazyboy reclining chairs in chrome and black leather.

Walking into the kitchen area, she noticed that the gas hob still had its plastic showroom wrapping on. The two fridges contained nothing but alcohol and coffee, and the food cupboard revealed only two tins of Dean & DeLuca's martini olives and a super-sized jar of Marmite.

'Not much of a cook?' she asked, as Danny forgot the coffee and uncorked a decent bottle of Sangiovese instead, grabbing two crystal glasses from the dishwasher.

'It's a crime to cook in New York,' he said cheerfully. 'Best restaurants in the world. Come, sit.'

As he flicked on the stereo (Joan Armatrading was already loaded – his seduction music?) lit candles, and filled her glass with the richly aromatic, purple wine, Diana couldn't help but wonder how many other hundreds of women he must have tried it on with up in his spider's lair. She could practically feel the sticky, silken thread of his web on her bare arms, and shivered.

'I know what it must look like,' he said, reading her thoughts exactly. 'But I said I wouldn't jump on you, and I meant it. Not unless you want me to, that is.'

It was a joke, but the next thing he knew Diana was kneeling over him on the sofa, kissing him on the lips with totally unexpected passion.

'What was that for?' he asked breathlessly when she pulled away.

'I don't know,' she said, honestly. 'I've never been unfaithful to Brogan before. Never.'

She'd sat back down, and although Danny was desperate to touch her again, he sensed it would be more politic to wait.

'So what's changed? If you don't mind my asking.'

She shook her head, either unwilling or unable to answer the question.

'Is he faithful to you?'

Another head shake.

'So why ... ?'

'Because,' she said, almost angrily. 'Because I'm married to him, Danny. Because he wasn't always the way he is now. I mean, he was always driven. But these last few years, since he became super wealthy, since the model agency and all of that bullshit, he's changed. I don't know what it is about diamonds, but they bring out the very worst in people. Haven't you found that?'

'Yes,' Danny admitted. 'Yes, I have. But they can only bring out what's already inside. Your husband isn't a good man.'

'Oh, I see. And you are, I suppose?' Diana raised an eyebrow teasingly.

'Perhaps not,' he said seriously. 'But I wouldn't treat a dog the way that Brogan treats you, darling. And that's God's honest truth.'

He kissed her then, slipping his warm hands under the soft lace of her dress and finding them suddenly full of her small, pert, bra-less breasts.

'Christ, you're sexy,' he whispered. 'Your old man must be out of his mind to mess you around.'

Diana closed her eyes, and for the first time in years let go of her emotions. She knew it was 'wrong' to betray one's husband. And yet every inch of her flesh seemed to cry out in rightness. Despite Brogan's best efforts at concealment, she was no fool, and she knew that he cheated on her regularly with girls from his agency. In the beginning it had hurt her deeply. Now it was more like a dull, aching grief, an outward symptom of a much deeper cancer that had long ago eaten away the heart of her marriage. Did she stay with him out of love and loyalty, as she told herself? Or out of fear? Tonight, talking to Danny, she'd started to wonder for the first time if perhaps it was the latter.

As for sexual desire, it was so long since she'd felt what

she was feeling now – that delicious, physical tugging, like an erotic rip tide, sucking her into the vortex of pleasure and need – she was amazed she was still capable of it. Sex with Brogan had become a military operation, planned around ovulation charts and hormone injections. Perhaps, subconsciously, the IVF had distracted her, prevented her from having to face everything else that was wrong between them. Either way, there was something about Danny's touch, the touch of a kind, desiring stranger, that unlocked every trapped sexual nerve in her body. She had never wanted someone more.

Tentatively, she put a hand on his thigh. It felt like a slab of concrete wrapped in suit pants.

'I feel so nervous, it's crazy,' she whispered, as his hands began exploring her bare back, easing the dress down over her slender shoulders. 'Like a teenager.'

'Speaking of teenagers,' said Danny, fumbling with his fly, 'I'm afraid I might not be able to hold out much longer. You're far too exciting for your own good, Mrs O'Donnell.'

Wriggling out of his clothes with the speed and skill of an Olympic swimmer, he pulled her down onto the floor, laying her gently on the fluffy sheepskin rug between the couch and the fireplace. Marvelling at her body in the flickering candlelight – she was tiny, and as softly rounded and pale as a Renaissance marble statue – he began slowly peeling off her panties, revealing a sleek blonde bush already damp with desire.

'Oh fuck,' he mumbled, under his breath. 'Fuck, fuck, fuck.' And with one swift movement he guided himself inside her. She was so slick and ready, it felt like diving into warm paraffin oil. He came in a matter of seconds.

'Oh my God, I'm so sorry,' he murmured into her hair afterwards. 'That never happens to me. I can't believe that just … oh God, have I blown it? Angel, why are you crying?'

'It's not you,' she sobbed, swallowing air in great gulps like an inconsolable child. 'Or rather, it is you. You were lovely. That was lovely. It's been an awfully long time, that's all. Since I've felt ...'

'Happy?' offered Danny. 'Desirable? Because Christ knows you are. You're a fucking goddess. Brogan doesn't know what he's got.'

'I was going to say "safe",' said Diana, leaning in to his thick mass of blonde chest hair and breathing deeply. 'And he *does* know what he's got,' she added. 'I know it'd be easier to believe otherwise, but he loves me. He just doesn't know *how* to love me.'

Danny sat up miserably and put his head in his hands. 'Judging by tonight's performance, neither do I. Can I blame the wine?'

'You don't have to blame anything,' said Diana, kissing him on the cheek. 'It was perfect. Wrong, but perfect.'

'Don't say that,' said Danny, his face falling. 'Don't say it was wrong.'

Reaching for her dress, she slipped it on over her head, then sat on the couch to pull her panties back on.

'Where are you going? Can't you stay the night?'

She smiled and shook her head. 'If I don't come home tonight, Brogan'll smell a rat for sure.'

'But he's in Moscow,' pleaded Danny. 'How's he gonna know?'

'I've told you,' said Diana. 'He watches me.'

'Well, how should I reach you? When can I see you again?' asked Danny. He could hear he was sounding desperate, but didn't know how to stop himself. He felt ridiculous, sprawled naked on the floor while she stood over him, fully dressed and checking her purse in case she'd forgotten anything.

'I don't know,' she said, sadly.

'But how ... ?'

'Danny,' she interrupted him, 'please. I don't have any

answers for you. Not tonight. But I'll think of you, I promise.' Reaching into her purse she pulled out the ring box. Clicking it open, she slipped the sparkling band onto her finger. 'Every time I look at this.'

And before he could think of anything else to say, she'd gone, closing the apartment door behind her.

# Eight

Gazing out of the taxi window as the driver sped through the Scottish countryside, Scarlett thought again how beautiful the Banffshire landscape was in autumn. Thanks to the swathes of evergreen forests, their pines and fir trees crammed together like battalions of Nordic sentries, it wasn't an entirely russet view. Some might say that the intermingling of dark green leaves with the amber of the deciduous woods made the Scottish autumn less dramatic, less striking than the uniform golden blanket of somewhere like Vermont, or even the New Forest. But to Scarlett, the contrasting colours heightened the season's charms. Throw in the pale-grey granite architecture, and vast, low sky with its deadened light, like a ceiling of frosted glass, and the overall effect was one of such romantic wilderness it was impossible not to be seduced, even without the sentimental attachments of childhood.

'There she is, look,' said the taxi driver, as the tips of Drumfernly's turrets inched into view above the tree tops. 'Is it guid to be home, miss?'

'It is,' said Scarlett wistfully. 'Actually, it really is.'

Tomorrow was Hugo's birthday, his seventieth, and a huge ball with reels and bagpipers had been organised for tonight. Scarlett, who hadn't been home since Christmas, had had predictably mixed feelings about the trip. She was looking forward to seeing her father, and to giving him the gift she'd been making for him for the past four months– a beautiful pair of enamel and platinum cufflinks in the colours of the Drummond Murray tartan. She was also grateful for the chance to get away from London, and all the pressures at work that seemed to have been piling ever higher on to her shoulders with each month that passed.

Despite the awful incident with her car, the disappearing suppliers and customers, and the threatening letters and phone calls she was still receiving regularly (she'd given up reporting them to the police, who plainly didn't give a monkey's, but kept a careful log of everything herself), she was working flat out on Trade Fair at the moment. Determined not to give in to Brogan's crass bullying tactics, she'd just gone public with a new and very successful ad campaign, featuring naked black girls apparently being 'lanced' by diamond tipped spears. One image in particular, of a black woman holding up her baby whilst being shot at with a giant, James Bond-esque revolver firing diamond bullets, caused a furore in all the art and lifestyle magazines, and had even been picked up abroad. It hadn't hurt that the shot was taken by a world-famous fashion photographer, an old friend of Scarlett's; nor that Cuypers had made the error of making a public complaint to the Advertising Standards Agency, claiming that the black background, illuminated only by diamonds, was designed to encourage people to link the Trade Fair pictures with their product. (Which of course it was, although Scarlett was thrilled to have the chance to deny any such connection publicly, thus generating yet more attention for her campaign.)

But it wasn't all good news. Thanks to Brogan's efforts, Bijoux was still suffering. She'd also been forced to become more security conscious, installing expensive intruder alarms both at the shop and at home, and hiring a semi-permanent 'doggie-guard' for Boxford whenever she was away. Mrs Minton from downstairs adored the spaniel and spoiled him rotten, but Scarlett still felt anxious leaving him for more than a few hours. She'd wrestled with her conscience over her decision to fly up to Scotland, rather than drive, as it meant a whole three-day weekend without him. But in the end she decided it was simply too much of a slog for such a short trip. She needed a real break and, as long as she avoided any major run-ins with Mummy and Cameron, this was her first chance all year to have one.

'Actually,' she said, as the driver swung the grey Rover into the bumpy driveway, 'can you leave me here? I'll walk the rest of the way.'

'Are ye sure?' he asked, pulling over. 'It's still a guid mile up to the castle, you know.'

'I know,' Scarlett smiled. 'I grew up here, remember?'

'Aye, course you did,' the driver blushed. 'Silly o' me. But are you sure you want me to leave you?' He looked awfully doubtful, as if she'd asked him to set her down in the middle of Mogadishu.

'Quite sure, honestly,' said Scarlett. 'I'll enjoy the walk, and my bag's not heavy. How much do I owe you?'

'Darling, good heavens, where did you spring from? And what on *earth* have you been doing? Your face is as flushed as a tomato.'

Caroline Drummond Murray greeted her daughter with her usual, tactful grace. Draped over a cream brocade chaise longue in the drawing room, her face and neck covered with Pond's cold cream like a newly-iced cake and with an open copy of the *Telegraph* spread over her knees, she had clearly been enjoying an afternoon siesta when Scarlett walked in.

'It was such a glorious day, I thought I'd walk up the drive,' said Scarlett brightly, determined not to be drawn into an argument in minute one. 'There are so many rabbits running around, it's like *Watership Down* out there.'

'I know,' drawled Caroline, turning back to the *Telegraph*. 'I must remember to tell Duncan to shoot some more of them. He's getting terribly lazy in his old age.'

'Oh no, Mummy, come on, leave the poor things be,' said Scarlett, horrified. 'What harm do they do?'

'Rabbits?' said Caroline. 'Is that a serious question?

They're pests, darling, you know that. Let's try and save our bleeding heart liberalism for the Africans, shall we, and leave the rabbits out of it?'

'Where's Daddy?' asked Scarlett, keeping her temper with an effort. She might be a bleeding heart, but at least she had a heart to bleed. Sometimes her mother's callousness was beyond the pale. 'I want to give him his present.'

'Well you can't,' said Caroline, flicking over to the sports pages. 'No family presents till tomorrow; that's the actual day. It was Daddy's request,' she added, catching Scarlett's thunderous look.

'Where is he?'

'Fishing, I think, with Cameron. I'm not sure where they went exactly.'

'Cameron's here already?' Scarlett raised an eyebrow. 'Leaving the office on a weekday? That's not like him. I'm amazed Goldman Sachs could possibly spare him,' she added, a touch bitterly.

'They can't,' said Caroline, frostily. 'He's heading back to London first thing tomorrow, for a *weekend* meeting, if you can believe that.'

Scarlett thought of the countless weekends she'd spent working or travelling for Trade Fair, but said nothing.

'He's devoted to Daddy and Drumfernly, but he pushes himself too hard. It was quite an effort for him to get here, never mind being dragged off to that ghastly, cold river the moment he arrives. Your father can be terribly thoughtless at times.'

It hadn't occurred to Caroline that she hadn't even got up to greet Scarlett, never mind offered her a cup of tea after her long journey. Losing herself in the racing results, she didn't even notice when Scarlett mooched off to her room to unpack, until the door clunked shut behind her.

Upstairs, Scarlett was looking at the photograph on her dressing table. The only shot she'd kept and framed from her modelling days, typically for Scarlett it was a group picture – showing her clapping with a gaggle of other girls at the end of the Lacroix catwalk show – but she still stood out a mile, her amber eyes glowing like coal embers amidst the sea of blonde, blue-eyed beauties, her legs going on for miles beneath the tiniest of black satin mini-dresses.

Gosh, it all seemed like a terribly long time ago now, she thought with a sigh, kicking off her trainers and flopping down on the bed. On the chair in the corner, Caroline had already laid out the rust-coloured taffeta dress she expected her to wear for the party tonight, the same hideous puffball monstrosity she'd worn to every Drumfernly cocktail party and hunt ball since she turned eighteen. Aware that her mother was envious of her youth and good looks – Scarlett's brief success as a model had been very hard for Caroline — she rarely protested at being forced to dress as one of the ugly sisters at home. After all, it wasn't as if anyone of any interest was going to be there tonight. She was here for her father, who she very much doubted would notice if she turned up naked and sprayed in silver paint, much less in her familiar get-up as an eighties prom queen-slash-conker.

By seven o'clock, the 'carriages' had started arriving in force – ancient Land Rovers mostly, or Volvos splattered so liberally with mud they could have doubled as army camouflage vehicles – and a battalion of tweed and taffeta-clad matrons, their pearls glinting in the moonlight, crunched their way across the gravel and into the ballroom. Once inside, they sheered off from their kilted, red-faced husbands like so many teenagers at a school dance, congregating in same-sex groups, the better to gossip about the latest scandal at the Women's Institute or the whispers about the new gay vicar at Aberfeldy.

'Caroline, darling, you look divine,' one of the husbands gushed admiringly as she greeted him at the door. 'What a goddess! The old boy couldn't ask for a better birthday present.'

'Oh, Jock, you're too killing,' Caroline simpered, happily. 'I've had this dress for years. Do go on in.'

In fact, the clinging, grey, floor-length number from Ann Taylor had been shipped up to Scotland at great expense two weeks ago, since when a legion of local seamstresses had altered it almost daily until it fitted Caroline's lithe body like a second skin. With her dark hair piled up on top of her head in a more intricate version of her usual, severe bun, and all the Drummond Murray family diamonds at her throat, ears and wrists, she looked positively regal. Thanks to the cold cream, her skin also glowed like moonlight. Tonight, for once, Scarlett would have a tough time upstaging her, she thought happily.

Meanwhile Hugo, the birthday boy, looked faintly ridiculous standing beside her. Short, round and happy in his tattered kilt, and already three sheets to the wind on malt, he looked like Snow White's drunken pet dwarf.

By the time Scarlett came downstairs, the party was already in full swing, with all the usual suspects getting stuck in to the booze and swaying mindlessly to the same Scottish dances played at every Banffshire party since time immemorial.

'About time.' Cameron, immensely pleased with himself in white ruffled shirt, kilt and knee socks, his sporran perched obscenely over his groin like a Highland merkin, grabbed her by the arm. 'Where've you been all afternoon? Poor Mummy's been run off her feet.'

'I fell asleep,' said Scarlett, hitching a rust taffeta puff-sleeve back up on to her shoulder. She'd lost a lot of weight, thanks to the stress of the last few months, and the dress was constantly threatening to fall off her tiny frame. 'I've had a hell of a week. Besides, Mummy's spent the entire afternoon on the sofa. It's Mrs Cullen who's done everything, as usual. Anyway, you can't talk. You've been fishing all day with Dad.'

'We were discussing estate business,' said Cameron pompously. 'He's not getting any younger, you know. He needs more help up here.'

'I agree. So help him,' said Scarlett, seeing where this was going.

'Me? Don't be ridiculous,' Cameron snapped. 'I can't just up sticks and leave the office whenever I feel like it. This is a very crucial stage in my career. I could be less than twenty-four months away from partnership. *You* should make the effort.'

'In case you hadn't noticed,' said Scarlett, smiling woodenly at her Godparents as they passed, 'I have a business of my own to run.'

'Oh, come on,' said Cameron patronisingly. 'Your little jewellery shop is hardly in the same league as my banking career. You're going to give it up eventually anyway, when you marry.'

'Says who?' said Scarlett indignantly. 'Anyway, why the hell should I be the one to lose out? Drumfernly's your inheritance, remember, not mine.'

Cameron frowned.

'The estate affects the whole family,' he said sanctimoniously, 'although that's just the sort of selfish attitude we've all come to expect from you.'

'*Selfish?*' Scarlett looked suitably flabbergasted.

'Yes, selfish,' said Cameron. 'What else do you call those appalling advertisements with the naked blacks? Poor Mummy nearly died of shame. Can you imagine how that went down in Buckie?'

Scarlett was on the point of replying that she didn't give a fuckie about Buckie, and that Trade Fair's adverts were already making a real difference in the industry, when she found herself being literally wrenched out of her brother's grip and pulled on to the dance floor.

'Remember me?'

Hamish Sainsbury, her would-be suitor from Christmas, had obviously been taking assertiveness lessons. Either that, or he'd read in *Farmers' Weekly* that single ladies all swoon over a forceful man. Freshly returned from a tour of the vineyards in Southern Portugal, his face was as red as boiled lobster. His paunch, if anything, had grown in the ten months since Scarlett had last seen him, and now sat like a basketball, balanced atop the rim of his straining cummerbund. For once he'd opted for a traditional black evening suit instead of a kilt, a small mercy for which Scarlett thanked the heavens as he threw her around the floor like Fred MacStaire.

'Goodness, Hamish, you're a jolly energetic dancer,' she panted. She was pleased to get away from Cameron, but talk about out of the frying pan.

'Been having lessons, actually,' he said proudly, jerking her backwards in an ill-advised attempt at the mambo – ill advised as the band were playing 'Green Grow the Rushes O', which didn't exactly lend itself to flights of Latin passion. 'Getting rather good. Though obviously it helps when one has such an inspiring partner.'

Scarlett smiled through gritted teeth. She was in danger of getting serious whiplash.

'D'you mind awfully if we get a drink?' she said, at last managing to interrupt him between twirls. 'I'm gasping for a gin and tonic.'

'Of course, of course,' said Hamish, looking pleased at the chance to get her into a quiet corner. 'Come on. I'll beat a path through the heaving masses.'

Five minutes later, enjoying the first cool sips of her drink in the relative peace and quiet of the Great Hall, Scarlett felt flooded with relief. In fact, the respite turned out to be temporary. Hamish, though well meaning, could bore for Scotland. After fifteen minutes of listening to him droning on about the merits of traditional Portuguese wine-making techniques, she was starting to wish she'd opted for a quick death on the dance floor. By the time the gong sounded for dinner and the rest of the guests surged towards the tables like a plague of tartan locusts, she'd reached the point where it was a genuine struggle to keep her eyes from closing.

'Dash it,' said Hamish, consulting the whiteboard next to their table, 'how infuriating. We aren't seated together. You're here and I'm ...' he scanned the lists, 'all the way over on table twenty-nine. With Emma bloody Cavendish, if you can believe it. *Such* a tedious woman. Hey, I know. What do you say we swap the place cards about a bit? I can shufty this chap over there.' He picked up the name card next to Scarlett's. 'Magnus Hartz,' he frowned. 'Never heard of 'im. And then I can sit next to you.'

'Too late I'm afraid.'

Scarlett spun around. Behind her a tall, dark and quite jaw-droppingly handsome American man in a lounge suit and without a tie, was addressing himself to Hamish.

'I'm sure Miss Cavendish is quite lovely. But I've been looking forward to making Miss Drummond Murray's acquaintance all evening. Magnus.' He extended a smooth, manicured hand towards Scarlett, who took it, mute with embarrassment. Then, gesturing at the chair in front of Hamish, he said: 'If you'll excuse me,' and sat down without waiting for a response.

Hamish, whose assertiveness course had not yet got as far as teaching him how to see off taller, handsomer male rivals, mumbled something about returning straight after coffee and sloped miserably off to his fate.

'So.' Magnus, who was even better-looking close up – all jutting jaw bone and smouldering brown eyes – began buttering a bread roll. 'You're the famous Scarlett Drummond Murray. You're considered quite the scarlet woman around here, you know, for those diamond adverts of yours. My grandmother actually described you to me as "racy". I knew I had to meet you after that.'

'Oh,' said Scarlett, still utterly tongue-tied. Not only was he the most desirable man ever to have crossed the threshold at Drumfernly – possibly to have crossed any threshold, anywhere – but of course, she'd had to meet him whilst dressed as a copper meringue. 'Who's your grandmother?'

'A lady called Jane Verney-Cave.' Magnus dispatched the roll in two easy bites. 'She's a friend of your mother's, I believe.'

No. Not possible. This broad-shouldered American Adonis couldn't possibly be the grandson of a wizened old crone like Mrs VC.

'But ... you're American,' stammered Scarlett lamely. Honestly, she was going to start dribbling in a minute. What was it about attractive men that made her regress into something approximating an advanced case of Alzheimer's? Happily, Magnus seemed not to notice.

'My mom, her daughter, met my dad in college,' he said, pouring them both a glass of red from the bottle in the middle of the table. 'I grew up in Seattle, lived there all my life in fact, but Mom always brought us home to Scotland in the vacations.'

'Really?' said Scarlett. 'In that case, I can't believe we've never met before.'

'Weird, isn't it?' said Magnus, gazing unashamedly into her hazel eyes, then down over the smooth white skin of her collarbone to the creamy swell at the tops of her breasts. That gross dress didn't do her any favours, but nothing could detract from her incredible cheekbones, or the sexy curl of her soft, wide lips. 'I guess we should start making up for lost time.'

Never had a Drumfernly dinner party flown by so quickly. Scarlett barely touched her loin of venison, and only managed a couple of spoonfuls of Mrs Cullen's ambrosial chocolate mousse because she needed something to do with her hands. Magnus turned out to be not just gorgeous but funny too, regaling her with stories of his dour Scottish grandmother trying to negotiate a mob of skateboarding kids in downtown Seattle on her one and only visit stateside, and how as a kid he used to stuff fistfuls of haggis into his pockets when she wasn't looking so he wouldn't have to eat the 'rancid stuff'. He was a lawyer, apparently, a career that, along with accountancy, usually had Scarlett's eyes glazing over with boredom. But Magnus could make a bus timetable sound gripping. He was also gratifyingly interested in her career, and the harassment problems she'd been having at Bijoux.

'I take it you reported all this already?' he said.

Scarlett nodded. 'The police looked at me as if I were mad.'

'So maybe you take matters into your own hands? Try and get ahold of some evidence yourself. Show 'em something concrete that they'll *have* to take seriously.'

'Like what?' she asked. 'They've already seen the letters.'

Magnus shrugged. 'How about installing CCTV cameras at your store?'

'Already have them.'

'Or at home, then? Put a voice recorder on your phone.'

Scarlett thought about it. 'I could do, I suppose. It all seems a bit Secret Squirrel though, doesn't it? Besides, Brogan does everything anonymously, through his goons. He's hardly likely to ring up and say "Hi, it's me, drop your campaign or else."'

'Was that supposed to be an American accent?' Magnus laughed. 'That's terrible!'

Scarlett laughed too. For the first time in months, work problems seemed blissfully far away. Sitting here, flirting with Magnus, they didn't even feel particularly important.

The two of them spent the rest of the evening hiding from Hamish, who was being helped in his mission to woo Scarlett by Caroline, who kept trying to 'steer' Magnus towards other, supposedly eligible single girls.

'You must meet Clementine,' she said, tugging him away from her daughter with a force belied by her tiny frame. 'She still needs a partner for the Dashing White Sergeant, don't you, Clemmie?'

Magnus dutifully performed two dances with the girl, who was nice enough but had an ass the size of Washington, not to mention two left feet, before slipping back to rescue Scarlett from the clutches of the apparently unstoppable Hamish.

'Jeez,' he said, once he'd finally prised her free. 'Is your mom always that pushy?'

'Oh yes,' said Scarlett ruefully. 'And controlling. She as good as forced me to wear this awful thing tonight.' She looked down at her dress in shame.

'Why didn't you tell her to take a hike?' said Magnus. 'I mean, no offence or anything, but you're not twelve.'

He was quite right of course. It was ridiculous the way she let Caroline walk all over her.

'I know,' she sighed. 'I suppose the truth is I can't face having it out with her. I know you Yanks believe in getting everything out in the open, but we Brits are far too repressed for that. If we see something unpleasant, we tend to bury it. Life's easier that way.'

'If you say so,' he said, reaching out and touching the fabric of her dress just where her waist narrowed below the bodice, rubbing it between his fingers so that the cheap taffeta crinkled like a crisp wrapper. It was intended as a jokey gesture, but Scarlett jumped as an unmistakable spark of raw attraction flew between them.

'Is there somewhere ... quieter ... we could go?' Magnus whispered hoarsely.

Scarlett nodded frantically. She wanted him so badly, the dress was in danger of melting from the heat of her body.

'We shouldn't leave together, though. I'll slip off to the loo and meet you at the foot of the kitchen stairs in five minutes.'

It was ten minutes before he finally rejoined her, panting as if he'd just got back from a battle zone.

'OK, so your mother actually has a problem,' he said, looking over his shoulder as if she might be on his tail as he spoke. 'She was shoving me at this one girl, Fiona? I swear to God, the woman was practically unzipping my flies!'

Scarlett giggled. 'Come on,' she whispered. 'Follow me.'

Taking him by the hand she led him through the maze of corridors and narrow, winding stone staircases that made up the rabbit warren of Drumfernly's upper storeys. After much twisting and turning, Scarlett led him into a neat, virtually empty bedroom.

'This your room?' he asked, admiring the view of rolling moonlit parkland from the single window while Scarlett bolted the door.

'No,' she said. 'Someone might come looking for me there. This is one of the old servants' rooms. We hardly ever use this part of the house. Hence the dust.' Coming up behind him, she dragged one finger along the stone window ledge, leaving a trail in the thick grey layer of grime like miniature ski-tracks through dirty snow. Turning around, from one mesmerising view to another, Magnus pulled her in to his arms.

'You're like Rapunzel in her tower,' he said, pulling out the tortoiseshell hair clip at the base of her neck and allowing her glossy river of hair to ripple down her back.

'What does that make you?' sighed Scarlett, closing her eyes in delight as she felt his cold hand on the zipper at her back, releasing her from the confines of the hated dress. 'Prince Charming?'

'I'm afraid not,' he whispered, planting a kiss on the hollow beneath her collarbone as the dress slithered to the floor. 'I'm flying back to America tomorrow. Believe me, I wish I weren't, but ... I have to be honest with you. I can't promise happy ever after.'

'That's OK,' said Scarlett, equally seriously. 'I'll take happy now.'

Being more of a cotton M&S knickers girl than a Victoria's Secret siren, she never normally wore matching underwear, but tonight by some miracle (hooray!) she'd actually put on one of her sexier combos: a pale-pink lace strapless bra with matching, barely-there panties and hold-up stockings. Magnus, however, was too intent on removing them all to pay much attention to the detailing. Her body beneath the frumpy dress was a revelation – a little on the skinny side, perhaps, but curved in all the right places. Her breasts, as round and soft as twin peaches, were the same milky white as Häagen Dazs vanilla ice-cream, the freckles across their tops like loosely sprinkled chocolate powder. As for her lower body, quite apart from its sheer length – she was almost as tall as he was, and most of that was leg – she was as toned and taut as a long-distance runner. There wasn't a hint of cellulite on her cute, boyish butt, and the paradise of skin between the tops of her stockings and lace trim of her underwear was as firm and unsullied as a baby's.

Scarlett's enthusiasm seemed to more than match his own. Tearing off his shirt, oblivious to the popping buttons, she began running her hands all over his torso, revelling in the size and strength of him, her fingers probing his chest hair and tracing the lines of his pectoral muscles like a blind sculptor trying to memorise form and texture.

'I might be a little out of practice,' she mumbled between kisses, as he pushed her back on to the bed. 'It's been a long time since my last relationship.'

Magnus grinned, scooting down the bed and peeling off her stockings with his teeth. 'It's OK,' he said. 'It's not like confession. You don't have to tell me when your last time was.'

Scarlett giggled.

'And besides, this is not a relationship. So just lie back and enjoy yourself.'

Which is exactly what she did. He was an astonishingly skilful lover, by turns slow and teasing, strong and hungry. At one point, while he was going down on her, she found herself wondering whether he was one of those people who could tie cherry stalks with their tongues, an image that made her laugh so hard she almost couldn't come. Most men would have taken offence at being laughed at at such a delicate moment, but Magnus was incredibly relaxed and confident enough to take her lack of inhibition as a compliment.

Afterwards, she insisted on returning the favour, taking his hard, ramrod-straight dick into her mouth despite his protests that he'd really rather just make love to her.

'Honestly,' she said, her treacle-dark hair spilling over his tensed stomach as she licked slowly around the tip of his cock, 'I want to.'

Feeling him in her mouth, literally tasting his desire for her, was the biggest turn-on of all. Deep down she'd never lost the insecurity about her looks that she'd had growing up. She wasn't the sort of knowing, sophisticated, sexy girl who could lure a man in with a provocative look or a flash of her short skirt and she couldn't remember the last time she'd been with a man who wanted her as much as Magnus plainly did. Certainly she'd *never* been with one even half as good looking, or as fantabulous in bed, as he was.

In the end, they made love into the small hours, collapsing at last only when neither of them had an ounce of physical energy left in their body. They were far enough away from the Great Hall not to be able to hear noise from the party, and only the occasional distant grumble of one of the last departing car engines broke the still calm as they lay side by side, staring contentedly up at the ceiling.

'Isn't it funny how free you can be with one night stands?' said Magnus. 'Almost as if not knowing the other person makes it easier to be yourself.'

'I wouldn't know,' said Scarlett truthfully. 'You're my first.'

'Oh, God, sorry,' he frowned, propping himself up on one elbow. 'I hope ... I mean, I didn't mean to offend you. Tonight meant something to me, it really did. It's just—'

'Relax,' said Scarlett, smiling and laying a finger gently across his lips. 'I'm not offended. You live in Seattle; I live in London. You're a lawyer; I'm an artist. We both work all the hours God sends. It would never work.'

They relapsed into silence.

'I'm happy I met you tonight,' said Marcus at last, just as Scarlett was drifting helplessly off into sleep. 'You're an incredible woman.'

'Thanks,' she said drowsily. 'So are you. An incredible man, I mean. Not woman. Definitely an incredible ... man.'

The last thing she remembered was Magnus's smile as he leaned over and kissed her on the forehead. When she woke in the morning, he was gone.

Caroline, needless to say, was livid about Scarlett's disappearing act.

'I don't believe it!' she exploded, when Scarlett shuffled dreamily into breakfast the following morning in an ancient dressing gown of Hugo's she'd found stuffed in the back of the spare-bedroom cupboard, and started helping herself to tea from the pot. 'Where the hell have you been all night? Cameron almost sent out a search party.'

'Really? How sweet of him to have almost cared,' said Scarlett, taking her cup of tea to the opposite end of the table where her father sat, and wishing him a happy birthday. 'But as you can see I'm fine. How was the rest of the party?'

'Terrible,' said Caroline, melodramatically. 'Poor Hamish Sainsbury didn't know what to do with himself after you ran out on him.'

'Really?' said Hugo absently. 'He seemed to be making rather a good fist of it with Lettie Gillingham when I shuffled off to bed. Glued to one another like a couple of barnacles, they were.'

Scarlett grinned at her father, who grinned back. Hugo Drummond Murray had never quite shared his wife's passion for marrying their only daughter off to the nearest chinless laird with a heartbeat.

'First you make a fool of yourself, and us, with those obscene advertisements of yours,' said Caroline furiously. 'Then you embarrass Daddy and me in front of all our friends by running off in the middle of your own father's seventieth.'

'It wasn't the middle,' protested Scarlett. 'Plenty of people left before we did ... I mean, before I did,' she corrected herself hastily. But her mother wasn't buying it.

'And to cap it all, after all the trouble I went to, inviting decent, single, eligible men for you to mingle with, you spent the entire evening with that ghastly American, who mysteriously vanished at exactly the same time you did. People aren't stupid you know, Scarlett.'

'Some people are,' said Scarlett with a meaningful look, taking a piece of buttered toast from her father's plate and biting into it, spraying crumbs everywhere. 'There's nothing ghastly about Magnus, believe me.'

Closing her eyes for a moment, she smiled, reliving the touch of his hand on her body and the brush of his stubble against her cheek.

'Oh, for pity's sake. He's married you know,' spat Caroline.

If she was looking for a reaction from Scarlett, she wasn't disappointed. All the colour drained from her face.

'No. He can't be. Daddy? D'you know anything about this?'

Hugo frowned at his wife. He loved Caroline, but he

wished she didn't always have to put the cat amongst the pigeons.

'I *believe*,' he said slowly, 'that he's separated. That's what Jane said, anyway. Separated, about to be divorced.'

'In other words, he is still married,' reiterated Caroline, before stalking off, slamming the kitchen door behind her in twinsetted fury.

'She'll get over it,' said Hugo, once she'd gone. 'Nice chap, was he, this Marcus fella?'

'Very. I mean, I thought he was,' Scarlett corrected herself. Her mother might have been stirring the pot – separated and married weren't quite the same thing – but it was rather suspect of him not to have mentioned his wife, ex, or whatever she was, at all.

Hugo shuffled his paper awkwardly. 'Might he be, you know … a prospect?'

'I'm afraid not, Daddy,' said Scarlett kindly. She knew it worried her father that she was still unmarried. Being single at twenty-eight seemed positively spinster-like to his generation and class. It bothered her to think of Hugo, old and lonely at Drumfernly, fretting about her future, egged on in his fears by her meddlesome mother. 'Apart from anything else, he's already on his way back to America. And I have my work here.'

'Ah, thinking of work,' said Hugo, relieved to have a chance to change the subject – the ground felt shaky beneath his feet whenever he found himself drawn into topics other than fishing, shooting or hunting – 'a Mrs Minton called for you at the crack of dawn this morning.' He handed her a slip of paper with a London number on it. Scarlett felt her heart leap into her mouth.

'What did she say? Is Boxie all right?' she asked, panicked. If anything had happened to that dog, she'd never forgive herself.

'Dunno. Your mother took the call,' said Hugo. 'But I think she said it was something to do with your shop.

Wanted you to ring her back urgently, apparently.'

'If it was urgent, why didn't somebody bloody well wake me?' barked Scarlett, her nerves making her snappy as she grabbed the cordless kitchen phone and started dialling.

'None of us knew where you were,' said Hugo reasonably. 'I'm sure it'll be all right, darling. Probably just a customer grumbling about an order or something.'

But looking at her ashen face a few minutes later as she put the phone down, it was clear that things were very far from all right.

'What is it, poppet?' he asked gently, laying a gnarled, weather-worn hand on her shoulder. 'Can I help?'

'It's Bijoux,' said Scarlett. 'There was a break-in last night. They took everything, then threw in a couple of petrol bombs on their way out. It's gone, Daddy. The shop's completely gone.'

It was three days before the police forensic teams had finished combing the site for evidence, and another four before the insurers were satisfied and the painstaking clean-up operation could begin.

Standing in the burnt-out shell of the shop floor in the late afternoon with a nervous Boxford sniffing around at her heels, Scarlett struggled not to cry. Only a thin line of orange tape and a couple of bollards separated what had once been her beloved store front from the street outside, and the streams of gawpers peering into the wreckage. She knew people meant well, but it still felt wrong and intrusive, like having strangers turn up to your mother's funeral and demand front-row seats with the family. These people would never know how much the place had meant to her, how many of her hopes and dreams had been contained within these charred and ravaged four walls. Since it had happened, she'd tried to be strong and practical – she had to be, especially dealing with the police – but inside all she wanted to do was curl up into a ball and sob.

The flight back from Scotland had taken an age. In a complete daze, wrenched from the unexpected joy of her night with Magnus, who apparently wasn't quite what he seemed after all, then plunged into the full-on horror of what was unfolding in London, it was all she could do to put one foot in front of the other, never mind deal with the arsey staff at British Midland when she got to the airport.

'I'm afraid that flight's completely full,' the girl at check-in had informed her chirpily, relishing the word 'completely' to an almost sadistic degree. 'To be honest, I'm not even sure if we can get you on the three o'clock, not at this late stage.'

'Please, this is an emergency,' babbled Scarlett. 'Perhaps someone would be prepared to give up their seat, if I paid them?'

'Oh, good gracious no,' said the girl. 'We couldn't possibly ask any of our customers to do that.'

'Surely there's something you can do?' said Scarlett desperately.

Matters hadn't been helped when Caroline, who adored a good drama and had insisted on coming to the airport with Scarlett and Hugo, piped up: 'Oh, come on, darling, it's hardly an emergency, now is it? The thieves are already long gone, and it's not as if you aren't fully insured. Why don't we go and have a nice lunch somewhere on Princes Street and do some shopping and you can hop on a plane tonight?'

The ensuing slanging match had been so loud and protracted that in the end the check-in girl 'discovered' that they did in fact have one remaining seat and, having fleeced Scarlett for a full-fare ticket in upper class, let her on the plane. But any relief Scarlett felt was to be short lived.

Nothing in Mrs Minton's tearful phone call had prepared her for the carnage that met her eyes when she walked into what had once been Bijoux. At first there was nothing to see but soot-blackened walls and grey dust an inch thick coating every available surface. It was as if a tiny, localised volcano had erupted right where the counter used to be, spewing destruction in every conceivable direction. But as the forensic team showed her, beneath the petrol-bomb damage, what had taken place was not the smash-and-grab job it appeared but a slickly executed, professional raid.

'None of the glass was smashed by hand,' said the young inspector from the serious robbery squad that first evening, trying to maintain his professional detachment – it wasn't often he got to deal with women as beautiful as Scarlett. 'These panes shattered from the heat of the fire, and the debris from the collapsing ceiling. When they took the jewellery, each lock was meticulously picked. They knew what they were doing. Your safe was decoded on site – they didn't take it with them – and your Banham's alarm system was professionally disabled. Great pains were gone to not to leave any bio traces behind.'

'Bio traces?' Scarlett looked confused.

'Fingerprints, hair, body fluids,' said the inspector, trying not to notice the way her breasts swelled with emotion beneath her grey cashmere sweater. 'Of course, that was what the petrol bombs were for, to destroy anything they might have left. But from what we can tell so far, it was an unnecessary precaution. Even the relatively undamaged areas are clean as a whistle.'

An unnecessary precaution? thought Scarlett with a shiver. It was only thanks to the quick response of the London Fire Brigade that no one had been killed.

'Your CCTV was knocked out, we believe as much as an hour before the fire began. They knew what they were looking for there as well,' the inspector went on.

'So what are you saying?' asked Scarlett. 'That it wasn't local kids breaking in on the off-chance?'

'Definitely not,' said the inspector. 'That much we know. Unfortunately, that's about all we know at the moment,

Miss Drummond Murray. Which is where we're hoping you'll be able to help us.'

There was never the slightest doubt in Scarlett's mind that Brogan O'Donnell was behind this. To her, it was the clear culmination of a pattern of threats and escalating, minor attacks, the decisive blow against her business that his anonymous henchmen had been promising for months if she didn't dismantle Trade Fair. But the problem of proving it was evident, even to her. When given a pencil and paper by the police and asked to write out a list of her potential enemies, she was horrified to find that it ran to two pages. Her anti-corruption work made her unpopular with a lot of people, not just Brogan. From the cartels to the independent mine-owners and dealers, everyone with a vested interest in keeping the diamond supply lines open and the labour costs down had a motive for making her suffer. Add to that her business rivals, disgruntled ex-boyfriends and the usual line-up of local nutters, and the playing field was wide open.

Nancy, bless her heart, had offered to fly out to London and help deal with everything.

'I can at least walk Boxie and do the grocery shopping while you get back on your feet,' she protested, when Scarlett refused the offer.

'Thanks, but there's actually not that much to do,' said Scarlett sadly. 'The insurance claims are all filed, and the investigation itself is out of my hands. The police have as good as admitted to me that they're never going to find who did it, but they're going through the motions, and I've told them all I can.'

The remaining big things on her to-do list were the refurb of the building, to be paid for out of the insurance money, after which she supposed she would sell it, and the daunting task of starting from scratch, working on some new designs and rebuilding her lost stock. The pieces themselves were insured, thank God, but nothing could insure against the loss of clients, angry that their promised rings and brooches were gone and unwilling to wait the months it would take Scarlett to produce new ones. Worse still, the fire had destroyed all of her sketches, so ideas as well as finished work had been lost. If the aim of the attack had been to sound the death knell for her business, Scarlett had a sinking feeling it might have been successful.

'Ah, good, I'm glad you're on time.' Cameron, looking smugly immaculate in a new Paul Smith suit, glanced impatiently at his Rolex, frowning as he picked his way across the sooty debris towards his sister. 'Gotta get back to the office by six. Big deal today. China.'

Among the myriad annoying habits he'd picked up since working for an American bank was this penchant for speaking in staccato, one-word sentences. The implication presumably being that he was far too busy and important a person to be bothered with such trifling matters as conjunctions, or even verbs.

'Thanks for coming,' said Scarlett, listlessly. Emotionally, the last thing she needed in a crisis was to have her tiresome, know-it-all brother around. But Cameron did know about financing, and the sort of costs involved in a total business rebuild. It had been a week since the break-in, and she still hadn't begun to look at the figures. She could use his professional advice. 'What do you think?'

'About what? The building itself?' he sniffed, shaking some offending dust off the toe of his perfectly polished brogue. 'Write off. To be honest, it's so tiny I'm amazed you ever managed to work from here. Far too small for most retail operations, even when you get it shipshape.'

Scarlett bridled. It had been such a stunning shop in its day, an oasis of calm and beauty. But she didn't say anything.

'My advice is to do the cheapest, most basic refit possible and whack it on the market,' said Cameron. 'Won't be worth much though,' he added tactlessly.

'I had it valued last year,' said Scarlett, feeling tearful and defensive despite herself. 'Winkworth said I might get seven fifty for it.'

Cameron laughed. 'For this mouse hole? I don't think so, Scar.'

Inevitably, the conversation deteriorated. Utterly unable to comprehend his sister's emotional attachment to the business she had begun from scratch six years ago, Cameron fired out one gloomy pronouncement after another, like so many poison arrows. He also felt strongly that if the attack was intended as a warning from the diamond cartels, she should listen to it.

'You must start acting responsibly, Scarlett,' he said sanctimoniously. 'Whoever did this obviously means business. You should drop this silly Trade Fair nonsense and keep your head down, before someone gets seriously hurt.'

'People are already getting seriously hurt,' Scarlett shot back indignantly. 'All across Africa they're dying in unnecessary wars, shot with bullets paid for by the likes of Brogan O'Donnell.'

'I'm not talking about the bloody Africans,' snapped Cameron. 'I'm talking about you. Or Mummy and Daddy. Who knows who these heavies may target next?'

Scarlett, who hadn't considered that she might be putting her family in danger, paused momentarily, running a frazzled hand through her hair. Outside the sun was setting, the daylight dying like a wood-starved fire. Was that what would happen to Trade Fair in the end? Would it peter out with a whimper, after all her hard work?

'But you can't give in to bullies,' she said eventually, trying to convince herself as much as her brother. 'Don't you see? That's what O'Donnell's counting on. That I'll cave under the pressure.'

'Oh for God's sake, Scar, get a grip on reality. I very much doubt if Brogan O'Donnell even remembers your name, let alone took the time out of his business day to supervise this little enterprise.' He ran a hand down the peeling paintwork, pulling off a strip of wall like dead skin. 'It'll be some local dealer you've pissed off, some hood with a few thugs on his payroll. I mean, let's face it: you're not exactly Bono, the new face of world peace, are you? None of the big boys even know who you are.'

At this point Boxford, sensing his mistress's blood pressure rising, took matters into his own paws and made a pre-emptive strike against Cameron's trouser leg, clamping the fabric between his powerful jaws and tugging until he produced a satisfying ripping sound.

'For fuck's sake!' Cameron howled, shaking his leg uselessly as the spaniel bit down even harder, thumping his tail on the ground in delight. 'Can't you even control your fucking dog? This suit cost me a small fortune.'

'Boxie, get down!' yelled Scarlett, whose head had started to thump rhythmically and whose temples were now starting to ache. 'Boxford! Drop!'

Giving her a puzzled look, as if the word 'drop' meant nothing to him, Boxford continued worrying the remains of Cameron's right trouser leg until something on the street caught his attention. The next moment he'd bounded over the orange tape and up to a tanned, blonde man in jeans and a blue striped shirt. Squatting down on his haunches, the man petted the dog fondly. Scarlett instinctively smiled, until he looked up and she saw to her horror that it was none other than Jake Meyer, looking as twinkly eyed and pleased with himself as only Jake Meyer could.

'Hello, Scarlett,' he drawled, his deep, resonant North London accent cutting through the twilight air like a rumble of thunder. 'Lovely dog. What's 'is name?'

'Boxford,' said Scarlett automatically, forgetting to ask him what on earth he was doing here.

'And there's nothing remotely lovely about him,' added Cameron, staring down at his ruined suit in horror, his flabby jowls shaking with rage. 'I've a good mind to charge you for this,' he seethed at Scarlett. 'There's nothing wrong with that animal that a lethal injection wouldn't fix.'

'He was sticking up for me,' said Scarlett, wresting Boxford away from Jake with some difficulty and pulling him close. 'He could tell you were being vile.'

'You asked for my advice and I gave it to you,' said Cameron bluntly. 'Your business is finished, and this campaign of yours is downright dangerous. If you carry on with it after this, you're even more stupid than that mindless animal of yours. See if you can talk some sense into her,' he added to Jake, as he hobbled furiously back to his Porsche.

Jake stood up and stepped gingerly over the orange tape. Showing a disappointing lack of loyalty, Boxford broke away from Scarlett again and began curling himself affectionately between his legs.

'Friend of yours?' he asked, nodding towards Cameron's disappearing car as it sped away in the direction of the City.

'My brother,' sighed Scarlett. 'He's a banker. I thought he might be able to give me some practical advice, but all he came here for was to rub my nose in it. I assume you've come to do the same,' she added bitterly, leaning back against the cleanest part of the wall in the hope it might stop her head from exploding.

'Why would you assume that?' said Jake amiably. Physically, he was the polar opposite of Magnus: shorter, broader and blonder, a bull terrier to Magnus's elegant, long-legged whippet. But he had the same smiling, easy confidence. If she didn't disapprove of him so thoroughly, she would probably have found it rather attractive.

'Because you also think Trade Fair is stupid,' she said wearily, 'and that I've brought all this on myself. Right?'

'I never said it was stupid, just misguided,' said Jake, idly scratching the top of Boxford's head.

'Why aren't you in LA, anyway?' asked Scarlett suspiciously. 'Don't tell me you've tired of fleecing the bimbos of Sunset Boulevard and decided to move back home.'

'Me? Tired? Never!' Jake grinned. 'I'm here on business for a few days, that's all. I heard you'd been done over, so I thought I'd stop by and—'

'Gloat?' said Scarlett.

'I was going to say, see if there was anything I could do to help,' said Jake patiently. 'What are you doing for supper?'

'Supper? Oh, I er ...' Caught off guard, Scarlett wracked her brain for a suitable excuse, but arguing with Cameron seemed to have used up the last ounces of her mental energy. 'I'm, er ... I was just going to grab a sandwich, actually. There's so much still to do here.'

'Like what?' said Jake. 'This is a job for the builders, not you and a can of paint-stripper. Besides, it's getting late.'

He was right, of course. In fact her dinner plans had revolved around opening a bottle of Merlot on the couch at home with Boxford and feeling sorry for herself, but she wasn't about to admit that to Jake. A small, insane part of her wanted to call Magnus – to discover that he didn't have a soon-to-be-ex-wife after all, and was itching to ride to her rescue on his white charger – but she resisted the urge. This was no time to be wallowing in romantic fantasies. Besides which, on a more practical note, she realised she didn't have his number.

'You won't function properly if you don't eat a decent meal,' said Jake. Picking up Boxford's lead from the counter, he clipped it onto his collar, grabbing Scarlett's tatty brown briefcase with his free hand. 'Your dog agrees with me, don't you boy?'

'Traitor,' Scarlett hissed at Boxford, who'd definitely taken a shine to Jake and seemed thrilled that an evening walk was in the offing. But her resolve was waning. A decent meal and some company, even Jake Meyer's company, suddenly seemed preferable to yet another night at home, drowning her sorrows. 'I have to be home by ten,' she said sulkily.

'Eleven, latest,' said Jake. 'I promise.'

'And I need to go to my flat first, to drop Boxie and change.'

Jake looked her up and down. In a pair of tattered jeans and a dark-blue polo neck, with her dark hair pulled back into a tangled bun and only a smudge of day-old black eyeliner on her otherwise un-made-up face, she looked tired but somehow still adorably ravishable. After all the perfectly groomed, blonde mannequins in LA, scruffy brunette chic made a welcome change.

'You're fine as you are,' he insisted. 'I know this little place in St John's Wood; it's very casual. And the dog'll go down a storm.'

The 'little place in St John's Wood' turned out to be a sprawling, six-thousand-square-foot mock-Tudor villa, set back off a leafy, suburban road.

'What are you doing?' asked Scarlett, as Jake pulled the black Range Rover, his London car, into the forecourt. 'Where's the restaurant?'

'This is the restaurant,' he said, laughing. 'Welcome to Casa Meyer. Don't look so panicked. My parents don't bite, and Mum makes the meanest roast chicken dinner this side of the Edgware Road.'

Scarlett was about to protest that she couldn't possibly impose on his mother, and had she known he was asking her to a family dinner she'd never have come, when the passenger door opened and she found herself enveloped in the sensory explosion that was Minty Meyer.

'Lord above, there's nothing of her! There's nothing of you!' she screeched, wrapping two podgy arms around Scarlett's ribcage and squeezing. The scent of Chanel Number Five was overwhelming, and her floral silk shirt so loud that if night weren't falling Scarlett would have been tempted to put on sunglasses against the glare. 'Jake, put the dog in the garden with Bella and get him some tripe and water; you know where it is,' said Minty, grabbing Scarlett's hand without drawing breath. 'Come in, come in, come in! Look, she's shivering with cold, the poor girl, and no wonder, not an ounce of fat on those bones. Doesn't your mother feed you?'

'Scarlett doesn't live at home, Mum,' said Jake, opening a side gate for a thoroughly overexcited Boxford. 'Bella' turned out to be an eager little bulldog bitch with a spring in her step that he clearly felt boded well for their relationship. 'She's a jewellery designer—'

'I don't care if she's the Queen of Sheba; she needs a good meal,' said Minty firmly. 'I wouldn't let you or Danny out of the house looking like skeletons, now would I?'

Not much danger of that, thought Scarlett, looking at Jake's enormous trucker's shoulders straining the cotton of his shirt as he strolled up the front steps.

'Now stop interrupting me please, Jacob, and go and tell your father to open the wine. And put the lounge fire on!' she yelled after him, as he disappeared into the house, abandoning Scarlett to her clutches.

In fact, once she'd got used to the volume and the constant prodding and poking – Mrs Meyer was clearly not a big believer in the idea of personal space, and continued to grab, squeeze and otherwise molest her throughout the course of the evening – Scarlett found herself warming to Jake's mother. She might be loud and vulgar, but she was also kind and loving, and welcoming in a way that Scarlett's own mother would never have been to a surprise dinner guest.

Ushered into a reception room almost the same size as Drumfernly's Great Hall, but smothered in enough soft furnishings to fit out a Vegas hotel – thick velour curtains in a truly hideous cat-sick pink hung from the windows, tied back with enormous black and white silk bows, and every sofa was piled high with silk cushions in a dizzying array of colours and fabrics – Scarlett found herself being forced into a chair and plied with enough canapés to feed a small African nation. By the time Jake finally reappeared, having fed and watered Boxford and fixed himself a large gin and tonic, she was already starting to feel like a French goose on a foie gras farm.

'Is she always like this? With the food, I mean,' she whispered, when Minty disappeared into the kitchen in search of yet more caviar blinis. 'I've just been force fed more than I normally eat in a week.'

'This is nothing,' he laughed. 'Wait till we sit down to dinner.'

He wasn't kidding. The dining room, an even more opulent space than the 'lounge' (complete with baronial marble fireplace, full-sized crystal chandelier and, at the far end of the room, Minty's astonishingly tiny wedding dress suspended from the ceiling in a glass case, like a sleeping Snow White) was dominated by a twenty-foot onyx table, on which was spread a feast that reminded Scarlett of childhood history-book pictures of Roman banquets. There were four people eating: Jake, herself, Minty and Rudy. For this intimate, 'casual' family gathering, Minty had laid on a roast chicken *each*, along with overflowing bowls of floury roast potatoes, parsnips, salads, butter-drenched sweetcorn, and a gravy boat roughly the size of a child's head filled to the brim with delicious-smelling, piping hot gravy. Having thought she couldn't manage another bite, Scarlett suddenly felt her stomach give an audible rumble and her mouth start to salivate.

'This looks incredible, Mrs Meyer,' she said honestly, as Minty heaped a Ben Nevis of roast potato onto her plate. 'I'm so sorry for imposing myself like this on your family meal. Jake never mentioned—'

'Nonsense, nonsense, we always have last-minute guests on Friday nights. Besides, I enjoy cooking, especially when my Jakey's home.' She gazed at her son with unashamed admiration, and Scarlett saw in an instant where all the Meyer brothers' cocksure confidence had come from. Her poor husband, ploughing quietly through his own mountainous meal at the head of the table, barely got a look in. 'Have you and Jakey been friends for long?'

'Well, we're not exactly ...' began Scarlett awkwardly, unsure how she might finish the sentence without either lying or being unforgivably rude.

'We've known each other a couple of years,' said Jake, coming to her rescue. 'Scarlett's a designer and a campaigner for mine workers' rights. She thinks Dan and I are responsible for all the wars in Africa,' he added, mischievously.

'Don't be silly, Jacob, why on earth would she think that?' said Minty, impaling a caramelised carrot on her fork and dunking it in horseradish sauce. Turning to Scarlett, she added proudly, 'My boys' diamonds are the best on the market. Take a look at this.'

For one awful moment Scarlett thought she might have been about to remove the rainbow blouse, as her pudgy, diamond-encrusted fingers delved beneath the fabric, deep into the fjord of her cleavage. Instead, mercifully, she retrieved a platinum chain, on the end of which hung a pendant of such breathtaking vulgarity it was hard to put into words. A sunburst of yellow and pink diamonds, it looked like something 50 Cent might give to his girlfriend, or Indiana Jones might use to unlock the secrets of the holy grail.

'I'll bet you've never seen anything quite like *that*,' she boasted, beaming from ear to ear.

'No, no I haven't,' said Scarlett truthfully. 'Never.'

'I designed that myself, with the most stunning stones the boys bought me for my sixtieth. Just imagine how many Africans they must have helped with that piece alone.'

'I'm afraid it doesn't work quite like that,' began Scarlett tentatively, but Minty waved away her objections, steamrollering her way through the conversation with the same unstoppable good humour she used to silence Jake and his father, waxing lyrical about how her sixtieth birthday had been the best she'd ever had, and how it was all thanks to her darling, thoughtful boys.

'You look tired, my dear,' she said, changing the subject at last after a full five-minute monologue. 'Is everything all right?'

'Scarlett's had a bit of a shock recently,' said Jake, explaining about the break-in and arson attack at Bijoux. 'Because of her charity work ...'

'With the Africans?' asked Minty.

'Yeah, because of all that, she's upset some of the big mine owners. So now they're trying to get back at her.'

Scarlett looked surprised. Cameron and the police had been so dismissive of her suspicions of Brogan, she hadn't expected Jake to take them seriously either.

'You really think it could have been O'Donnell?' she asked him hopefully.

'After what you told me in the car about the threats you've been getting, I'd say it was odds on. Not that you'll ever pin it on him. That bastard's more slippery than a used condom.'

'Jake, language.' It was the first time Scarlett had heard his father speak – after forty years of marriage to Minty, he must be sorely out of practice – and even then he didn't look up from his roast chicken.

'Yes, Jacob, really,' his mother agreed. 'I'm sure Scarlett doesn't want to hear that sort of talk, not after all she's been through. I hope you were insured, my dear.'

'Oh, yes, yes, thank goodness,' said Scarlett. 'It really wasn't that bad. I can rebuild the business.' She felt unaccountably embarrassed discussing what had happened. Even her skin had started tingling with a very British urge to play down the situation, and she was pretty sure she was blushing.

'Jake's had some business trouble of his own out in America,' said Minty. 'More apple sauce?'

'Er, no, thanks, I'm fine,' said Scarlett, intrigued. 'What sort of trouble?'

'It's nothing,' said Jake, shooting his mother a for-God's-sake-put-a-sock-in-it look. 'A couple of down months, that's all. Solomon Stones are doing fine.'

'Yes dear, but Daniel's numbers were more than twice yours in September, weren't they?' said Minty. 'That's not normal.' Having missed the first dirty look he'd given her, she caught this second one, but misinterpreted it as brotherly jealousy. 'My boys are very competitive with each other,' she whispered conspiratorially to Scarlett. 'Jake especially is used to being the best. He doesn't like to be beaten by Danny, do you, sweetheart?'

Now it was Jake's turn to blush. Scarlett, who couldn't remember ever having seen him wrong-footed, couldn't help but smile. It was tough to keep up one's suave, Casanova image with a mother like Minty. It occurred to her how surprising it was that he'd invited her to his family home, and allowed her to see his carefully constructed public persona being debunked so remorselessly. For a passing moment, he went up in her estimation.

By the time dinner was finally over, and Scarlett had gorged herself still further on apple pie and fresh whipped cream, she'd started to have sympathy for those poor fat people on Jerry Springer who had to be winched out of their houses by a crane. It was late, but when Jake suggested a moonlit stroll to 'walk things off', she jumped at the chance, desperate for some cool night air and an opportunity to see if her limbs still functioned.

'If I die of a clogged artery in the night, I'm blaming you,' she said, following him out onto the street as they set out up the hill towards St John's Wood proper.

'Mum was right; you needed a good meal,' said Jake,

taking off his coat and draping it over her shoulders. 'You'll sleep like a rock tonight.'

'I feel like a rock,' grumbled Scarlett. 'I feel like Ayers bloody rock.' But in fact the inner, warming sensation of a full stomach, and the gentle caress of the evening breeze on her cheeks was making her deeply content in a way that she hadn't been since making love to Magnus. Christ, she really must stop thinking about Magnus.

'So what *is* your plan?' asked Jake, slowing his pace to give her time to catch up. 'Are you going to reopen the shop?'

Scarlett's face fell. 'I honestly don't know. I don't think I can afford to, not immediately. Plus I have so many commitments with the campaign—'

'Ah, of course. The campaign.' Jake rolled his eyes.

'I'm not giving it up, you know,' said Scarlett hotly. 'Not on your nelly.'

'Has anyone ever told you you sound like a Head Girl when you get angry? From one of those posh schools?' said Jake. '"Not on your nelly",' he mimicked her cut-glass accent brilliantly. 'Give me a break.'

Scarlett took the teasing in good part. 'Your parents are lovely,' she said after a while.

'Thanks.' He gave her a broad, genuine smile. 'Mum can be a bit full on.'

'Oh, but I adore that; she's so bubbly and warm. And she obviously dotes on you,' added Scarlett, knowingly.

Jake shrugged. 'She's a Jewish mother; what can I say? She really liked you, by the way. She normally gives a major cold front to women she suspects of being interested in me or Danny. Especially shiksas.'

Scarlett stopped in her tracks. 'I am not *interested* in you!' she said, horrified. 'My God. The arrogance!'

'Keep your hair on,' said Jake, walking on ahead. 'I never said you were. I said Mum might have assumed you were, that's all.'

'Why would she assume that?' spluttered Scarlett. 'On what possible basis—'

'She thinks all women are after me,' said Jake matter of factly. 'In fairness to her, most of them are.'

Not sure whether he was joking or not, Scarlett said nothing. He was almost at the top of the hill now and hadn't looked back, leaving her little option but to run panting after him.

'Hold on,' she gasped when she reached the top. 'I need to catch my breath.' Sinking down on to a bench, she sat slumped forwards, waiting for her lungs to recover. Jake, who seemed irritatingly amused by her exhaustion, came and sat beside her.

'I actually came by your shop today to make you a proposition,' he said.

Slowly, Scarlett sat up, fixing him with a deeply suspicious look.

'Oh, so *now* we get to it,' she said. 'Somehow I thought tonight's cosiness must be too good to be true.'

Jake frowned. 'Do you ever get down from that high horse of yours?'

The jab hit home and for a moment Scarlett was silent.

'All right then,' she said eventually. 'Prove me wrong. What's your proposition?'

'You think O'Donnell's out to get you,' said Jake. Scarlett nodded. 'I agree. If we're both right, this won't be the last time he tries to pull something. He obviously has ... people ... in London he can use. People who don't much care who they hurt.'

'You're depressing me,' said Scarlett. Under the lamplight her pale skin looked golden, bathed in an eerie, electric glow. 'The proposition?'

'You want to rebuild your business, but you're worried about money.'

She nodded again.

'You *don't* want to wind down your Trade Fair campaign.'

'Absolutely not. If anything, this shows how much we're rattling the big players like Brogan.'

'I agree,' said Jake. Catching her astonished look, he added, 'Look, it's not rocket science. I'm not saying I support what you're doing. I think it's all a load of old wank, if you want the truth. But if you didn't matter to these guys, they'd leave you alone.'

Silence fell again. Jake was staring straight ahead, looking out over the treetops of Regent's Park. Studying his profile, the strong jaw, perfectly straight nose and slightly jutting chin, Scarlett was grudgingly forced to admit that he was quite revoltingly handsome, even if all he cared about was making a fast buck.

'So what's your proposition?' she asked again. 'If you don't want me to drop Trade Fair?'

Jake turned and looked at her. 'Come out to LA.'

'I'm sorry?' said Scarlett.

'London's too dangerous and too expensive,' he said. 'Your insurance money won't go far here. In LA it'd buy you a fantastic space in a prime area.'

'Yes, but my business is here,' said Scarlett, stating the obvious. 'My suppliers, my clients, all my contacts.'

'I'll supply you in LA,' said Jake.

'You?' Scarlett looked suitably gobsmacked.

'Yes, me,' said Jake, visibly put out. 'Fair prices, no funny business. You need a supplier, and I could do with a steady retail outlet to supplement my private sales.'

'Come on,' said Scarlett, her old scepticism returning. 'I only buy clean stones, stones that I can verify. You and Danny still source from Angola, for God's sake!'

'Everything I sell you will be clean as a nun's arse,' said Jake. 'That's a promise. I'll also feed you clients, for a cut obviously.'

'Obviously,' said Scarlett.

'Hey, don't knock it. I've got a little black book of contacts on the West coast going back fifteen years.'

'Yes, I can just imagine the contents of your little black book.' Scarlett looked disapproving. 'I really don't think this would work, Jake.'

'That's because you're being narrow-minded and letting your feelings for me cloud your judgement,' he shot back, undeterred. 'If you're rattling Brogan now, just imagine how much more impact Trade Fair could have in the States. You're talking about the biggest diamond-buying market in the world. Think about it.'

Scarlett thought about it. The idea did have a certain appeal.

'You could still do private commissions for your London clients. All I'm talking about is setting up a physical presence in LA, a new store. You want a fresh start, right?'

'Well, yes,' she admitted. 'But I never envisaged leaving London. What if Brogan thinks I'm running away? That he's driven me out of town?'

'Who cares what he thinks?' said Jake. 'You can prove him wrong soon enough when you get out there, and Trade Fair's on the cover of *Vanity* fucking *Fair*. Come on, Scarlett. Think big!'

'I don't know. I'm not sure I'm really an LA sort of a person,' she said lamely. 'Isn't it rather shallow?'

'It's a fucking paddling pool!' laughed Jake. 'But they'll love you. Honestly. You have no idea how much a posh British accent, never mind a castle and a title, means to them over there. Class is the one thing these people *can't* buy, and you've got it in spades. I'm telling you, I know this market. We'll rake it in.'

If anyone had told her yesterday that by midnight tonight she'd be seriously contemplating upping sticks and moving to Los Angeles, of all places – and not just moving there, but moving there to go into business with *Jake Meyer*! – she'd have looked at them as if they'd lost their mind. But maybe now she was losing hers. Because whichever way she turned it, it *did* seem like a good idea, or at least like a possibility. If Trade Fair cracked the States – if she cracked the States – there'd be no stopping her.

'I know it's a big decision,' said Jake, who was a good enough salesman to know when to stop pushing. 'All I'm asking is that you think about it. All right?'

He mustn't sound desperate. He'd come up with the idea himself only a few days ago, after he heard what had happened at Bijoux, but already he'd come to see partnership with Scarlett as the answer to his prayers. He hadn't wanted his mum to scare her off at dinner, but the truth was his business was suffering more than he cared to admit and had been for some time. Scarlett might be irritating, and her bear-baiting campaign would no doubt bring him a whole new set of problems to contend with. But a joint venture in LA – a new store, fronted by this beautiful, aristocratic, talented girl – would go down a storm, he just knew it. Finally he'd have the bazooka he needed to blow Tyler Brett out of the water.

'All right,' said Scarlett, trying to conceal her own excitement, and not sound like a drowning woman who'd just been thrown an unexpected lifeline. 'I'll think about it.'

# Nine

Diana O'Donnell turned up the volume on the stereo and kicked off her shoes.

Ella Fitzgerald's 'Have Yourself a Merry Little Christmas' boomed out of Brogan's new, state-of-the-art Japanese speaker system as she twirled happily around the chalet, wiggling her bare toes in the luxurious softness of the carpet. All around her, white oblong place cards, bearing names carefully crafted in festive red and green calligraphy, lay scattered on the floor like so much stiff confetti. Two Filipina maids were busy polishing the antique dining table and setting out the best silver candelabra. And behind Diana, in the bespoke Nordic pine kitchen, another two were preparing this evening's appetisers – miniature Swiss cheese soufflés with a light, white truffle sauce – and privately wondering what on earth had got into their usually restrained, and often downright miserable mistress.

As usual, the O'Donnells were spending Christmas in Colorado, at Brogan's sprawling chalet-cum-mansion in Telluride. He had bought the property six years ago, since when he had spent fewer than sixty days here – five days every Christmas, plus one long skiing weekend in March each year – but a skeleton staff were kept on payroll all year round, in case he loaned the house to friends or business associates, or slipped up here for a snatched night away with one of his mistresses. Diana, who wasn't a skier and often passed on the March trip, was an even shadowier presence in the chalet than her husband, appearing each Christmas like one of Dickens's ghosts before flitting back to New York. The staff at Telluride, as at all her houses, had grown used to seeing her sad and listless, fulfilling her wifely hostess duties with the forced enthusiasm of a newly drafted recruit setting off for war.

But this year she was different. Smiling, chatty, animated. Dancing to cheesy Christmas songs. Spending hours perched on top of a ladder, decorating the thirty-foot tree that dominated the open-plan entrance hall in a riot of gaudy, clashing colours, a radical departure from the subdued silver and white themed trees of previous years.

'I'll have what she's having,' whispered one cook to the other, watching Diana pirouetting around the living room like a five-year-old.

'That'll be sex,' her friend whispered back. 'Either that woman has a new lover, or I'm the next Julia Roberts.'

'I do hope so,' said the first cook, slicing truffle shavings onto a silver tray. 'God knows she deserves a bit of fun, poor woman. His majesty gets enough.'

Sex, in fact, was the one thing Diana was missing. Danny had left for England two weeks ago, bringing their thrice-weekly lovemaking sessions to an agonisingly abrupt end, and wouldn't be back till January. And Brogan, who usually demanded his conjugal rights at least every other night, had become mysteriously tired this vacation and barely touched her all week. He blamed a troublesome cough he'd developed recently that he seemed unable to shake, but Diana suspected his lower libido had more to do with Natalia, Premiere's latest star model and one of their guests for tonight's Christmas Eve dinner. Apparently in Telluride by coincidence, with friends, the girl seemed to be spending an awful lot of time in 'meetings' with Brogan. This time last year, Diana reflected, a mistress's presence at such a special, family time of year would have wounded her deeply. Now, she was almost grateful for the distraction – anything to keep Brogan off her back, literally and metaphorically, and throw him off the scent of her blossoming affair with Danny.

She wasn't sure when her feelings for Danny had shifted from desire and affection to genuine love. Maybe it was the day after her birthday in November when he'd taken her dancing at a tiny, throbbing little salsa place in the Bronx that reminded her of her happy, carefree student days, and on the subway home had given her a present – a first edition of *Wind in the Willows,* her favourite book as a child. The night before, Brogan had taken her to the Four Seasons, dropped two thousand dollars on dinner and champagne, and presented her with an eight-hundred-thousand-dollar diamond choker. And she'd felt nothing but sadness. The sadness of knowing that the communication gap between the two of them was too wide now to ever be bridged, with or without Danny.

When Brogan asked her later where she'd got the book, she told him a girlfriend had given it to her.

'Damn stupid present,' he growled dismissively. 'What the fuck do you need with a children's book? Lisa knows we don't have kids.'

Of course, everyone knew the O'Donnells didn't have kids. Sometimes Diana felt like the most famous childless woman in Manhattan. Somewhere along the line, her failure to conceive a child with Brogan had become what defined her as a person. But slowly, thanks to Danny's love, the layers of disappointment and grief were being peeled away. The fun, free-spirited girl who had once existed was clawing her way up out of the grave and back into the land of the living.

Of course, there were still plenty of problems to be faced. Her time with Danny was still snatched and furtive, and they often had to cancel rendezvous at the last minute if Brogan's travel or dinner plans changed. Danny's impatience with these restrictions was growing. The night before he left for England they'd had a titanic row about her marriage, and why she didn't 'just end it'.

'You talk about it as if it were like selling a car!' she yelled back at him. 'Ten years of marriage isn't something you "just end". We have a life together. There was so much love there once.'

'And what about the love here, now?' said Danny, exasperated. 'Doesn't that count for anything? What about the way he treats you, spying on you, caging you up like some fucking trapped animal? How can he love you if he doesn't trust you?'

'Well he's right not to trust me, isn't he?' said Diana, fighting back tears. Danny had never understood her guilt over their affair, but it ran deep. The way he saw it, if she knew Brogan had been fucking every twenty-one-year-old with a pulse for years, why the hell should she care about his feelings? He didn't want to consider the possibility that, despite all the pain he'd put her through, the love bond between husband and wife might still be intact.

Thankfully, they'd made things up before he left, and all his phone calls from London had been so full of love and longing that Diana felt reassured they were back on track. Contrary to his fears, she didn't 'get off' on the illicit, secret nature of the relationship at all. She had the same fantasies he did about marriage and children and happy ever after – about starting again. But for her, a new start would demand a painful ending to something that, for better or worse, she had striven to save and nurture for most of her adult life.

Despite these tensions, falling in love with Danny had given her a new lease of life. When they spoke this morning – she'd slipped out early to Main Street on the pretence of doing some last-minute Christmas shopping, and taken his call in a quiet corner of Gucci – he'd promised to engineer some sort of romantic getaway when Brogan flew to Antwerp in February, and it was the prospect of this that had her twirling around the chalet now like a love-struck teenager.

'Mrs Diana?' One of the maids broke her reverie. 'You

want to do those placements now? Or should we go ahead and make up the table first?'

Bending down, Diana scooped up a handful of cards and began plonking them at random around the table. She wasn't even reading the names.

'There you go,' she said, beaming. 'I always say it's better not to overthink these things. Don't you agree, Joyce?'

'If you say so, ma'am,' giggled the maid. No doubt about it, whoever the mystery man was, her mistress had got it bad.

Meanwhile, in London, Christmas Eve at the Meyer household was already well under way.

Minty, who'd rather saw off her fingers with a rusty penknife than see either of her sons marry a non-Jewish girl, was nevertheless enthusiastic about Christmas and all its rituals, especially those that involved eating, drinking and generally making merry. It was the one time of year when both her boys came home, and that alone was excuse enough for celebration and for the giant fake Christmas tree ('I can't be doing with all those dropped needles! At my age?') that towered over the space that Minty liked to call the 'foyer' like a vast, silver rocket.

'Danny, bring us another beer, would you?' Jake, sprawled out on the settee in sweatpants and a Tottenham hoodie, called into the kitchen for his brother. 'How long are you gonna be on that bloody phone for? Chelsea almost scored just now.'

'All right, all right, I'm coming,' Danny called back. 'We already know the score, you know.'

'That's not the point!' yelled Jake.

Reaching into the cavernous fridge for two bottles of Stella, Danny tried to put his game face on. He'd been trying to ring Diana back for the last hour – he just needed to hear her voice again – but her cell had been resolutely switched off, leaving him feeling ludicrously bereft and rejected. He must get a grip. If he kept moping around the house like a wet weekend, Jake was bound to sense something was up. And once his twin brother got the bit between his teeth, he never let go.

Wandering into the lounge, he joined Jake on the couch and tried to focus on the football. The Chelsea/Spurs match was months old, but it was a Meyer family tradition to spend Christmas Eve watching all the best of the season's matches, lovingly recorded by Minty, back to back. Even Rudy, who'd never followed the premiere league, dutifully sat in his corner armchair, eating himself into a peanut coma and sporadically shouting out 'Come on, you muppet!' when he felt it was required of him.

'Any word from Scarlett?' asked Danny, unable to concentrate.

Jake shook his head. 'She's in Scotland, up at Castle Creepy,' he said, stuffing a handful of pretzels into his mouth. 'I don't wanna bother her over the holidays.'

Scarlett had agreed to the LA plan, much to both brothers' delight, and was now just waiting on the completion of her sale of Bijoux. Contrary to Cameron's assertions, she'd got an excellent price for the place, and she and Jake had spent much of the last two weeks on email, excitedly trawling the internet for possible sites for the new LA store.

Although surprised by their partnership – bringing Scarlett on board had been entirely Jake's idea – Danny was fully behind it. He didn't want to make things worse for Jake by banging on about it, but he couldn't help but be concerned at the degree to which the ridiculous Tyler Brett had encroached on the LA side of Solomon Stones' business. A joint venture with someone as high-profile and, crucially, as legit as Scarlett (after Jake's dalliance with simulants last year, they needed to be whiter than white) might finally turn their flagging fortunes around.

'Things are moving fast, though,' said Jake. 'Did you see

that interview she did in *Marie Claire*? Great pre-publicity for us.'

Danny looked at his brother archly.

'You mean the one where she's wearing that little gold number with all the cleavage? Yeah. I saw it,' he grinned.

'Can't say I noticed what she was wearing,' mumbled Jake, unconvincingly.

It was perfectly plain to Danny that his brother fancied the pants off Scarlett. The bickering, the repeated, unnecessary dropping of her name into conversations, the constant comments about her being 'too thin', or 'too tall' or 'too up herself' for his taste were all classic giveaways. In fact, this was the only part of the LA plan that bothered him. Jake had a bad tendency to become obsessed with women until he slept with them, then lose interest overnight. Fine if the woman was a social friend or even an occasional customer, but not at all fine with one's business partner. Happily, so far at least, his interest in Scarlett appeared to be entirely one-sided. For the first time Danny could ever remember, Jake seemed to have set his cap at a girl who was utterly immune to his charms.

'Oi, come on, ref! What was that about?' Jake sprang to his feet, as excited about some presumed off-side infringement as if he'd been watching the match live at Old Trafford. 'Did you see that?'

'Shocking,' said his dad, waking up with a start. 'The man needs a white stick.'

'Anyone up for the pub?' asked Danny. It was no good; he couldn't stop thinking about Diana. He had to get out of the house.

'What, now?' said Jake. 'There's still fifteen minutes of extra time.'

'All right, well, I'll see you there then, yeah?' said Danny. And grabbing his coat, he shot out of the front door before anyone could question him further.

Outside, a light dusting of snow had fallen, enough to

turn the city streets from dark grey to light, without quite achieving true whiteness. It was bitterly cold, but the wind that had whipped through North London earlier in the day had died down, and Danny enjoyed watching his breath hang in the air in front of him as he walked, like the smoky puffs of a small dragon.

New York would be groaning with snow by now, he thought idly, and Telluride must be beautiful. Say what you like about the Yanks, but they knew how to pull the stops out at Christmas – fairy lights everywhere, piped carols in the malls, eggnog lattes. He pictured Diana standing in the snow, as pale and tiny as a winter sprite, and felt a wave of longing bowl him over, flipping his stomach like a pancake. How the fuck was he going to make it through the next two weeks without her? And how the fuck was he going to live the rest of his life if she didn't leave that son-of-a-bitch husband of hers and marry him?

He wanted so badly to confide in Jake. In the past, they'd talked to each other about everything, especially women. But he knew he couldn't, not this time. Apart from the fact that he'd made Diana a solemn vow not to breathe a word of their affair to a soul – a vow that was in his interests as much as hers – he also knew that Jake would go absolutely spare if he knew. They were already taking a calculated risk with Brogan by going into business with Scarlett. But banging the guy's wife was a whole different order of magnitude. Not even Danny could see the big man forgiving and forgetting that one. And if he chose to, Brogan could make life very difficult indeed for Solomon Stones.

When Brogan got back to the chalet around six, after a day's skiing with Natalia and her imaginary friends, he seemed to be entirely his normal self. The maids fixed him his usual bourbon and soda, and he spent a typical fifteen minutes downstairs on the couch, skimming through the business papers and unwinding before heading up to his room to change.

'Is Mrs O'Donnell home?' he asked casually, downing the remnants of his drink as he climbed the wooden stairs.

'Yes, sir, of course,' said the maid. 'She's in the bedroom. I think she might be sleeping.'

Diana, in fact, had just woken up from a doze and was on her way into the shower. The water was already running, its hot jets pounding the slate floor of the wet room, and thin wisps of steam were winding their way into the bedroom, mingling with the lavender and sage scents of her favourite Bougies candles.

The hiss of the shower was so loud that at first she didn't hear Brogan come in. Turning around, she was startled to find him standing immediately behind her.

'Darling. You scared me,' she said, instinctively wrapping the towel more tightly around her.

'Did I?' Yanking the towel away with unnecessary force, he grabbed her naked body and pulled her to him. His hand on the small of her back was cold from clasping the bourbon glass. But his eyes were even colder.

'Is something wrong?' asked Diana.

Brogan didn't respond. Instead, pushing her back on to the bed, he pressed his whole body weight on top of her and began fumbling with his fly.

'Honey, stop,' Diana laughed nervously. 'Come on. We have ten people coming for dinner in less than an hour. I need to get ready, and so do you.'

He looked at her. For the rest of her life, Diana would never forget that look. Like a wounded animal fighting for its life, she saw hatred, fear and rage swimming in his eyes. The next thing she knew, he was inside her, grinding painfully against her, fucking her with a roughness and violence she'd never known in him before.

'Brogan, stop!' she cried out, panic starting to seep into her. 'What is this? You're hurting me.'

She was so dry, he felt enormous inside her, like a rolling pin grating against sandpaper. But he ignored her cries, thrusting faster and harder, biting painfully into her shoulder as his frenzy mounted. Finally climaxing, with a noise like a sob, he withdrew, zipped up his pants and walked wordlessly into the bathroom, leaving her shaking and whimpering on the bed while he splashed cold water onto his face.

By the time he came back out, she'd slipped on the dress she was wearing earlier – still in shock, her nakedness was making her feel even more vulnerable – and stood by the dresser, staring into space.

'I don't understand,' she whispered, cowering away from him. 'Why ... ?'

But she didn't get any further. Lunging across the room, he swung his fist at her face with such force and sudden-ness that she didn't have a second even to raise her arms in defence. The next thing she knew she was flying across the room, her back slamming into the far wall like something out of a bad action movie.

'How could you do it? *How!*' Brogan roared. 'Did you really think I wouldn't find out?'

Hauling her up off the floor like a rag doll, he hit her again, a slap across the mouth this time but still hard enough to draw blood.

Numbed with adrenaline and shock, Diana felt no pain, but merely stared at him, mute and incredulous.

'I thought you were better than that. Better than all the other cheap, money-grabbing whores.' Another punch to the ribs sent her sliding to the floor again. One of her eyes had closed up, but with the other she looked up and saw tears streaming down his cheeks. 'But you're not. You're just the same. You're just the fucking same!'

Some time passed. She wasn't sure if it was seconds or minutes. Brogan had gone back to the bed and sat down, his head in his hands. He was shaking, she thought crying, but it was hard to tell. Her senses were playing tricks on her. Her vision was blurry and even sound seemed muffled. She was aware of blood pouring from her lip and pooling into her lap, soaking the white dress. And yet a part of her felt oddly calm, relieved, almost, that the dreaded moment of discovery and confrontation had at last arrived.

'Danny Meyer.' Brogan was speaking again, apparently to himself. 'Danny fucking Meyer, of all people! Some two-bit dealer, some nobody.' He shook his head. 'What can he possibly give you that I don't?'

'Time,' said Diana, gently. 'Affection.'

'I give you affection!' shouted Brogan, turning to look at her. Diana reached up and touched her bloodied face, but said nothing. 'I shower you with gifts, with jewels, with clothes. I buy you beautiful homes, fill them with whatever you want. I get you the best fucking doctors ... is that what it is?' he asked desperately, as though the thought had just occurred to him. 'Are you mad at me for not giving you a child?'

'No!' said Diana. 'Of course not. I'm not even mad at you. I'm unhappy, Brogan, that's all. I'm lonely.'

'So what? So you go creeping off to have sex with that slimeball? That *fuck*! You're lonely, so it's all OK?' His rage was building again. Diana scrambled back away from him into the corner, but he made no move in her direction. Instead he picked up one of the scented candles, a sauce-pan-sized glass circle, and threw it onto the floor, sending glass and hot wax flying in every direction.

'Is it OK when *you* sleep with girls from your agency? When you bring them to our homes?' Diana challenged him bravely. 'What about Natalia?'

'That's different,' said Brogan.

'Why?'

'Because I'm a man, that's why. It's different for men. We need variety. Besides, Natalia means nothing to me. I've always respected you.'

Diana let the ridiculousness of this statement hang in the air between them. It was Brogan who spoke again.

'Do you love this guy?'

It was bizarre. She was the one lying bruised and bloodied on the floor. And yet in that moment it was Brogan who seemed the more vulnerable.

'I do,' whispered Diana. 'Yes, I do.'

Letting out a great bellow of grief and fury, Brogan flew at her again, lifting her by the shoulders and shaking her so violently that Diana could feel her brain rattling back and forth in her skull. Scared she might pass out, she at last found the strength to start fighting back. Flailing out wildly with her legs, she landed a couple of useless kicks against his stomach before hitting him more by accident than design in the balls.

'You bitch!' hissed Brogan, releasing his grip as he clutched his groin. Aware that this might be her one and only chance to escape, Diana ran, flinging open the bedroom door and throwing herself blindly down the stairs.

'Mrs Diana?' The maid came out of the kitchen and gasped in shock when she saw Diana's swollen face. 'Oh my God!' she shrieked. 'What happen?'

'Mr O'Donnell,' panted Diana, pulling on the nearest pair of snow boots and a quilted jacket just as Brogan staggered onto the landing. 'Please ... try and stop him.' And she bolted out of the front door like a hunted fox, running for her life.

The next twenty minutes were a blur. At first she was sure she could hear Brogan behind her, and all she wanted to do was put as much distance between them as possible, weaving in and out of side streets and pitch black alleyways until pretty soon she had no idea which way was up. Not until she was convinced she'd lost him did she start to feel the cold. The snow boots and jacket were woefully inadequate protection against the minus-ten-degree temperature, and her bare legs and hands had long since gone completely numb. Only yesterday she'd been reading about some drunken revellers who'd died of exposure earlier in the season after failing to find their way back to their piste-side condo. She had to get indoors, and quickly.

At the end of the street she saw a late-night convenience store, a place where the local kids who were too young to get into the bars used to hang out after hours. She'd never been inside – she and Brogan weren't really convenience-store people – but had passed it hundreds of times, and always thought it looked cosy and inviting, with its nineteen-fifties advertisements and its old-fashioned milkshake counter. Quickening her pace, but too cold to run, she limped towards the light it threw out over the street.

'Can I help you?' asked the spotty teenage kid behind the counter, on autopilot, without looking up from his Nintendo DS Lite.

'Phone,' whispered Diana. Her teeth were chattering so much, she could barely get the word out. 'I need a ph-ph … I need to make a call.'

'Holy crap!' said the kid, at last looking at her properly. 'You want me to call the cops? You want some, er, some hot tea? Carl!' He yelled out back to his colleague. 'Get me some blankets from the closet and some hot water. We got a situation here.'

Diana's skin, by this point, had turned a mottled shade of blue, a combination of bruising and cold. Her left eye was swollen like a plum and fully closed. The gash on her lip had stopped bleeding, but a lump the size of a Babybel cheese was forming there, and enough blood had already spilled down her dress and jacket to make it look as though she'd been stabbed.

'Please,' she stammered. 'I just need a phone.'

Luckily for her, the two boys insisted on wrapping her in thick layers of coats and blankets, sitting her under the store heater and thrusting a mug of hot, heavily sweetened tea into her frozen hands before they would agree to let her use the portable phone.

'I can call the cops for you, if you want?' the pimply boy offered sweetly. 'Or the hospital?'

'That's OK,' smiled Diana. She was warming up now, and tried not to think about the throbbing pain in her fingers and face as the blood supply slowly returned. 'I can do it. I need to call a friend of mine f-f ... first.'

The barman at the Red Lion on Old Broad Street had rung the bell for last orders twenty minutes ago, but nobody seemed to be paying a blind bit of attention.

'Don't you people have homes to go to?' he shouted good naturedly through the drunken din. 'It's Christmas Eve. Go to bed.'

'Shut up and have a drink, Charlie,' Jake shouted back.

'What about a lock-in?' proposed another wag.

Like most of tonight's crowd, the Meyers were regulars at their local pub, an ugly mock-Tudor, turreted affair sitting incongruously between two even uglier sixties council blocks behind the Tube station. But the ambience in the Red Lion was great: real old-school North London camaraderie, and Charlie Whitford was the most accommodating landlord for miles around, regularly serving after hours and always quick with a joke or a juicy piece of local gossip.

Jake sat between Minty and Danny at a corner table, watching the multicoloured fairy lights round the bar flash on and off and wondering whether any of them would be sober enough to walk home unaided. It was touch and go. Rudy had already lapsed into a deep, drunken sleep by the fire, and Minty had reached the stage of regaling the group at the next table with dirty jokes, cackling at her own daring like a ruddy-faced fishwife. Danny was stuck in to his sixth or seventh Harvey's Bristol Cream, and showed no signs of slowing down. After four beers Jake was none too steady on his feet himself.

Still, he must have been in a better state than the rest of them, as he was the only one to notice Danny's phone vibrating its way across the table, buzzing and jumping like a scalded insect. Unthinking, he picked up.

''Ello?'

'Darling it's me, it's Diana.' The American woman's voice on the end of the line sounded weak and quavering. 'Please don't panic. But Brogan knows. He just came home and—'

'Brogan?' Jake struggled to make sense of things through his alcohol-induced fog. 'Who is this?'

'Danny?' Diana's voice was barely audible now. 'Is that you?'

Only at this point did Danny pick up on what was happening. He tried to snatch the phone from Jake, but Jake whipped it behind his back.

'Don't play silly buggers,' said Danny crossly. 'Who is it?'

'Some bird called Diana. She said something about Bro ... oh my God.' The pieces fell slowly into place. 'It's Diana O'Donnell, isn't it? Tell me you're not seeing her.'

But Danny was in no mood to explain. Throwing himself bodily across the table, sending beer glasses and ashtrays flying, he wrestled the phone out of his brother's hands.

'Diana?' he asked breathlessly. 'What's up? Are you OK?'

'Oh Danny!' Hearing his voice, she at last let go of all the fear and tension and burst into uncontrollable sobs. It was almost a full minute before he could get any sense out of her. 'Brogan knows about us.'

'How?' Cupping the phone to his ear, Danny waved frantically for the raucous drinkers around him to pipe down. 'Try to speak up, darling. I can't hear myself think in here.'

'I don't know,' sobbed Diana. 'I've been as careful as I could, but he has people everywhere.'

'*Darling*?' said Jake in horror, but Danny ignored him.

'Well, what happened? What did he say?'

'He didn't *say* much,' said Diana bitterly. 'He came home, had sex with me ...'

Danny visibly winced.

'... and then he ... he ...' She was crying again now, unable to go on.

'It's OK,' said Danny soothingly, trying to control his own rising panic. 'Did he hurt you?'

Diana was silent.

'Angel, you must tell me. Did he hurt you?'

'A little bit,' she whispered. 'I'm OK. I don't know. My face is beaten up pretty bad.'

Danny gripped his glass so hard it shattered. Minty reached for his bloodied hand but he shooed her away.

'I managed to get out of the chalet,' said Diana. 'I'm in a convenience store right now. Some boys are ... taking care of me.'

'OK,' said Danny, sensing she was about to lose it again. She was clearly still very disoriented. 'Put the boys on the line. Let me talk to them for a second.'

He walked outside, his left hand still dripping with blood. Sobered by shock and the crisp night air, he managed to talk calmly to the boy from the store, instructing him to get Diana straight to the hospital and to have his friend call the cops on the way. By the time he'd spoken to Diana again, reassured her, and promised to have air tickets to London waiting for her at Denver airport on Christmas morning, everyone else had left the pub and staggered home. Only Jake, leaning ominously against the locked front door, was waiting for him, his face half hidden in shadow.

'So,' said Danny wearily, slipping his phone back into his jacket pocket. 'Now you know.'

'Yeah,' snarled Jake. 'Now I know.'

The next thing Danny knew, he was flat on his back on the icy pavement, fending off a volley of punches.

'Diana O'Donnell?' Jake roared, between blows. 'You stupid fucker! You've ruined us! How could you bang Diana O'Donnell? Brogan'll have our balls in a fucking pickle jar!'

'I'm not "banging" her,' said Danny, shielding his face with his forearms. 'I love her, all right? I'm in love with her and I'm gonna marry her, and I'm sorry about everything else and lying to you and all that, but I—'

'Marry her?' The punches stopped.

Danny, not sure whether the respite was permanent or not, lowered his arms an inch.

'Yeah,' he said, a slow smile spreading across his face. 'Yeah, I think so. If she'll have me.'

'And what about Brogan?' said Jake, getting to his feet. This affair, and Brogan's discovery of it, was just about the worst news he could imagine. But he'd never heard Danny talk about marriage before. Things were obviously serious. 'Has she left him?'

Danny's face darkened. 'He roughed her up tonight. I've just sent her to the hospital. I think he might have raped her,' he added bleakly. Then, to Jake's amazement, he started to cry.

'Hey, come on, bruv.' Jake put his arm around him. 'It's all right. It'll all work out all right in the end, you'll see.'

But at that particular moment, neither of them was sure they believed him.

# *Ten*

Nancy Lorriman drew wolf-whistles from the construction guys as she crossed the parking lot at LAX and headed for the terminal.

An unseasonably cold January had forced the normally scantily clad LA girls into jeans and sweaters, but thankfully it was a look that suited Nancy. With her blonde bob and cute, curvy, Marilynesque figure, she looked sexier in a pair of fitted Sevens and a tight, lemon-yellow sweater than most women did in hot pants and heels. Her trademark fire-engine-red lipstick and flirtatious smile didn't hurt either. She was clearly a woman who revelled in male attention, and was used to getting it.

Today she had more reasons than usual to be happy. She'd just had her first script optioned, a difficult political thriller that she'd been writing on and off for over two years. And she was on her way to pick up Scarlett, her best friend in the world, who'd miraculously decided to open a new jewellery store in LA in an effort to spread the gospel of exploitation-free diamonds to the American public.

No one had been more shocked than Nancy when Scarlett announced that not only was she moving to LA, but she was also going into business with Jake Meyer. Like most girls-about-town in LA, Nancy knew Jake as a reprobate playboy, a womaniser with a ready smile and an even readier condom. At the moment Scarlett seemed obsessed with some Seattle lawyer she'd had a fling with last fall. But Jake's sly charm was legendary, and Nancy was far from convinced that her friend would remain immune to it indefinitely, especially with the two of them working side by side.

Still, those were all worries for the future. Right now she had all the fun of showing Scarlett around town to look forward to, not to mention the treat of having her as a housemate while she looked for a place of her own to rent.

She walked into the arrivals lounge to find Scarlett already there, perched patiently on her luggage reading a thick book called *Sierra Leone, The Truth Behind The Conflict*.

'Plane landed early,' she smiled, jumping up to hug her friend. 'Thanks for coming to get me.'

'Why didn't you call my cell?' said Nancy, taking charge of Scarlett's single suitcase. 'I could've gotten here earlier if I'd known. Is this all you brought? Where's Boxford?'

'They're keeping him at the airport overnight. There's a vet's surgery here; can you believe that?'

Nancy looked concerned.

'Oh, don't worry. He's still a little groggy from the tranquillisers, that's all. I'm coming to get him first thing in the morning.'

'So this case?' Nancy looked at it doubtingly. 'This is it?'

'I only packed summer clothes,' said Scarlett, shivering in her cut-off jeans shorts and vest as they stepped outside into the cold wind. 'I thought it was supposed to be permanent sunshine here.'

'Ah, yes. Another of LA's many myths, I'm afraid,' smiled Nancy. 'You'll get used to it. I'll take you to the Grove tomorrow for some winter gear. We might invest in some fake tan too,' she added, wrinkling her nose at Scarlett's pasty white legs, 'for when the sun does come out.'

Nancy's car, a beat-up vintage Thunderbird in the same lemon yellow as her sweater, was her pride and joy, and Scarlett dutifully admired its gorgeousness as they pulled out of the airport onto the palm-lined boulevards. Taking in the tall, swaying trees, eight-lane roads and scruffy, low-built store fronts, she felt small and very far from home.

'Don't worry,' said Nancy, swinging on to Lincoln once she saw the queue of static red tail lights on the 405. 'This side of town is pretty crappy. But there's a lot of beauty here. Wait till you see my house.'

Her place was indeed enchanting. Nestled high in the Hollywood Hills above Laurel Canyon, it was a rustic, white wooden cottage-cum-cabin, surrounded by fruit trees and magnolias. Wind chimes hung from bushes in the garden, ringing a welcome to Scarlett as she walked up the path. They were only a few minutes above Sunset Boulevard, but it felt like being deep in the countryside. Boxie was going to love it.

'It's idyllic,' gasped Scarlett. 'No wonder so many writers and artists come to live here. I feel like I could design just about anything in this secret garden.'

'It does feel like a secret garden, doesn't it?' said Nancy proudly. 'Come and take a look inside.'

A wraparound porch led to wooden doors – Scarlett noticed Nancy had left them unlocked – which opened on to a light-filled sitting room. A comfy, white, shabby-chic sofa faced the big window. To the left was a simple farmhouse table and chairs, on which sat a vase full of home-grown flowers, dog roses, hawthorn berries and various sprigs of sprouting green. To the right was a wall smothered from floor to ceiling in bookcases, groaning with old, leatherbound first editions of the classics – gifts, no doubt, from Nancy's wealthy family. Set off the living room was a small, bright kitchen, with faded red cupboards and a stove that looked like something out of a Doris Day movie. A small window looked out over the garden, and on its ledge Nancy had planted various potted herbs, which sent a smell of rosemary, basil and thyme wafting into the air, competing with the sweet, heady scent of the flowers.

'Wow.' Scarlett beamed. For some reason she'd pictured

LA as all concrete and glass. But Nancy's cottage was like something out of Snow White. 'I may never move out.'

'Oh, please don't!' said Nancy, grabbing her hand and leading her through to the bedrooms and bathroom, each room as small and white and perfect as the next. Scarlett's room had a painted pine bed, made up with the most exquisite antique linens, a chest of drawers, and a tiny dressing table in the corner.

'I'm afraid there's no hanging space, just a hook on the door,' said Nancy apologetically, 'but I've cleared some space in my closet for you to hang a few dresses.'

'It's perfect,' sighed Scarlett, sitting down on the edge of the bed. 'Really. Thank you so much for letting me stay.'

'Are you kidding?' said Nancy. 'I've been going totally stir crazy up here on my own. We are going to have *such* a ball.'

Once Scarlett had showered, changed and taken a cat nap, she re-emerged into the living room to find the porch doors open and a delicious smell of rosemary chicken floating out into the night air.

'Are you hungry?' asked Nancy, setting two chipped china plates down on the table along with knives and forks and a pottery jug of homemade lemonade.

'I am now,' said Scarlett. Wearing the one sweater she'd brought with her, a threadbare grey cast-off of her father's that reminded her of him and of home, and a pair of bright-green sweatpants, with her shower-wet hair pulled back off her face in an Alice band, she looked unchanged from the gauche, gangly schoolgirl Nancy had first met all those years ago. 'So come on,' she said eagerly, helping herself to the wasabi nuts from a bowl in the middle of the table. 'Fill me in. What's been going on since I saw you?'

'Precious little compared to your life,' said Nancy, plonking a hefty pot of chicken stew between them before ladling a scoop on to Scarlett's plate. 'No robberies, no fires. I'm starting to think I lead a pretty dull existence, actually.'

But as they ate, she told Scarlett about her writing and the joy of at last selling her screenplay: 'It's only an option, and the money's barely enough to buy me a new set of crockery, but it's a start, you know?' before moving on to the typically tangled web of her love life.

'What about you?' she asked, having finished filling Scarlett in on her dizzying array of recent lovers. 'Any news from Seattle's answer to McDreamy?'

Scarlett gave a coy smile. 'We're emailing,' she said. 'We said we wouldn't, but I decided over Christmas that I ought to at least let him know I was moving here. I had to get his address from his grandmother. I felt about fifteen.'

'And? So? What's happening?' said Nancy impatiently.

'Nothing,' Scarlett shrugged. 'He's in Seattle. We might see each other at some point I guess, but ...'

'But what?'

'Oh, I don't know,' sighed Scarlett. 'I suppose I'm sort of waiting for him to make the first move. I don't want to look too keen and ruin it all. Besides, I've got a lot on my plate here for the next few months. I don't have time for a relationship.'

'Well, the second part of that sentence is complete bullshit,' said Nancy robustly. 'That's like saying you don't have time to eat or go to the bathroom. But the first part, I couldn't agree with you more. Play a little hard to get. Works every time.'

Scarlett laughed. 'How would you know, Lorriman? You've never had to play hard to get in your life.'

After a difficult year, and a typically fraught Christmas at Drumfernly, she'd been quietly dreading the move to LA. Jake had gone unnaturally quiet on her over the holidays, which she hoped wasn't a sign of cold feet on his part. Even if it wasn't, she was miserably aware that they'd have a mountain to climb once she got here, building a brand new business from scratch, not to mention generating momentum for her campaign. Many was the night she'd woken up in a cold sweat, convinced she was making a terrible mistake, with Jake, the move and everything. But sitting here now with Nancy, in this picture-postcard house, laughing about men and toasting the future, she finally began to relax.

Tomorrow was a new day. And really, how bad could it be?

'Jesus Christ.' The real-estate agent honked her horn loudly as yet another smug Prius driver pulled into the car pool lane in front of them. 'Where do these people get off? Dumbest law *ever*, letting 'em use the car pool as single drivers, just because they splashed out on some eco bullshit car. Now we all have to sit in goddamn traffic.'

Beside her in the passenger seat, Scarlett turned up the faltering AC to full. It was noon, and yesterday's chilly weather seemed to have evaporated overnight as a sweltering sun pounded remorselessly down on the windscreen. She'd woken up at five with jet lag, schlepped back to LAX in a taxi to collect Boxford and rushed back to Nancy's for a lightning shower before the agent had arrived to collect her at nine a.m. Since then they'd spent the entire morning driving around the city looking at possible sites for the new store, and Scarlett's high spirits of the night before had long since melted away. Apart from the heat, choking traffic fumes, and irritating presence of Carla, the agent – a hairsprayed harridan of indeterminate age with nails like talons and a voice so grating it could shave parmesan – the property they'd seen so far was all of a shockingly poor standard.

'Spaces like this on Rodeo or Canon go for up to two or three thousand a *day*,' insisted Carla, showing Scarlett round a dirty, breezeblock square on a nondescript street in West Hollywood. 'You gotta have some imagination, honey. This place could be byuuudiful with a little bit of TLC.'

Scarlett thought of the boarded-up windows and 'closing down sale' signs in the windows of the neighbouring stores, and decided that no amount of TLC could turn this dump into a successful, high-end jewellery boutique.

'Do you have anything smaller, but in a better area?' she asked hopefully.

'Like where?' Carla looked nonplussed.

'Well that's the whole point, I don't know,' said Scarlett. 'I was hoping you might be able to show me some of the options. Perhaps if we drove by some of the better-known jewellers? Neil Lane, maybe, or some of the up and coming designers? Jenna Halliday has a store in Los Feliz, I believe. Is that far from here?'

It turned out that everywhere was far from here. Carla tried rat run after rat run, but traffic choked every available street and it seemed to take an age to drive a few short miles. In the end they'd headed back to the freeway and Beverly Hills, with Scarlett feeling exhausted and utterly disoriented, staring out of the window and thinking longingly of her dear little shop on Westbourne Grove.

Carla's cell phone rang, and an irritating cacophony of Latin beats filled the stifling car.

'Carla Berenger.'

'Hey Carla.' Jake's low, distinctive voice rumbled over the speakerphone like thunder. 'It's Jake Meyer. Is Scarlett still with you?'

'She sure is,' said Carla, smiling for the first time all morning and automatically checking her hair in the driver's mirror. Even on the other end of a phone line, women wanted to look their best for Jake. 'You're on speaker, honey.'

'How's it going?' he asked cheerfully. He certainly sounded full of the joys of spring this morning. 'Seen anything promising?'

'Not yet,' said Scarlett grimly. She didn't want to let rip about how ghastly everything had been till she was out of

Carla's earshot. She was also mildly pissed off with Jake for not calling yesterday to welcome her to LA, or at least to check she'd got there safely, and was not in the mood for chit-chat.

'Where are you now?'

'Almost at Beverly Hills,' said Carla, when Scarlett didn't answer. 'The traffic's been a nightmare; we're a little behind on our schedule.'

'Great,' said Jake. 'Would you drop Scarlett off at the News Cafe on Robertson? I'll take her to lunch, and then I've got somewhere I'd like to show her.'

Carla's lips puckered into a tight anus of disappointment that she was not to be included in their lunch and afternoon plans. Having sat through an excruciating morning with this stuck-up, whingeing British stick insect, the least she deserved was a little face time with Gorgeous Jake.

'Remember, we signed an exclusive,' she said petulantly. 'Who found you this new site?'

'Friend of a friend,' said Jake, not losing any of his chipperness. 'Don't worry Carla, you'll get your commission, whatever we take. A deal is a deal.'

'I'm really not hungry,' said Scarlett, who would happily have traded places with Carla and lunched alone. 'Why don't we go straight to the—'

But Jake wasn't about to be put off. 'See you there,' he said briskly, and hung up.

The News Cafe was a bustling, scene-y restaurant, popular with the wealthy shoppers of Robertson Boulevard, and when Scarlett walked in there was a queue.

'Hello, stranger.' A beaming Jake kissed her on both cheeks, earning her dagger looks of envy from the bimbos waiting for tables, who'd been enjoying his attention until Scarlett arrived. In bright yellow Bermuda shorts and a white Ralph Lauren shirt with yellow piping, he looked like a catalogue model for the new season's cruise wear, and she noticed that he failed to remove his Oliver Peoples wraparound sunglasses when he kissed her. 'Expecting snow, were we?'

He laughed teasingly at Scarlett's corduroy trousers, Ugg boots and fleece combination, the latter borrowed from Nancy's wardrobe and several sizes too small for her, its sleeves stopping midway between her elbows and wrists.

'It was cold when I arrived,' said Scarlett, feeling stupid, her cheeks flushing from heat and embarrassment. 'It must be fifteen degrees warmer today.'

'Well take your fleece off, then,' said Jake, ignoring the glares from the other waiting customers as the smitten hostess showed him straight to a table.

'I'm fine,' snapped Scarlett, pulling it more tightly around her. Underneath she was wearing only the skimpiest of vests, and she was paranoid she might have sweated right through it so he'd be able to see her nipples. 'Let's just order, OK?'

'All right, Little Miss Sunshine. What's eating you?' said Jake, at last removing his shades and fixing her with his intense, violet-blue eyes.

'Nothing,' grumbled Scarlett. 'It was a frustrating morning, that's all.'

Jake, whose own morning had been anything but frustrating (he'd spent most of it in bed with the new Grey's Anatomy actress, with whose anatomy he was now intimately familiar) watched her as she studied the menu. Still pale from yesterday's flight, and with deep shadows under her eyes from her jet lag, she wasn't looking her best. As for that ridiculous, child's sweater she was wearing, it made her look as though she'd climbed into the dryer herself and shrunk her entire torso. But the cute smattering of freckles across her nose, the huge eyes like pools of liquid amber and the endless legs that, even hidden beneath those awful gardening trousers and folded under the table, managed to attract admiring glances from men around the room, all set her apart from the other women here. If there was such a thing as an X-factor – something that caught the attention, without discernible effort – then Scarlett had it in bucketloads.

'Well cheer up,' he said, signalling to a passing waitress, who shot over to their table like a big-breasted meteor. 'I'm taking you somewhere this afternoon that's bound to put a smile on your face.'

'The airport?' said Scarlett wryly. 'Do I have time to go home and pack?'

Jake grinned. 'Now, now, less of the sarcasm. Not even you can be ready to throw in the towel after one morning.'

He ordered a smoked turkey salad for himself and a mixed sashimi plate for Scarlett ('trust me, you'll love it'), and spent the five minutes while they waited for it to arrive filling her in on the latest with Danny and Diana. He'd given her a head's up about the affair over Christmas, but it was hardly necessary. By New Year's Eve, the break-up of the O'Donnell marriage was *the* hot story amongst the diamond fraternity from London to Cape Town, with Danny alternately painted as a knight in shining armour, albeit with a kamikaze streak, or a malicious home-wrecker, depending on whom you talked to. Rather to Jake's surprise, Scarlett hadn't appeared to be nearly as concerned about developments as he'd expected. Whether she was underestimating Brogan's talent for revenge, or whether she felt that as she was already on his hit list, it didn't much matter if Danny and Jake were too, he couldn't tell. Either way, he was grateful that it hadn't crossed her mind to pull out of their partnership. He needed her now more than ever.

'D and D are coming into town this afternoon as it happens,' he said, pouring her an ice-cold glass of Pellegrino. 'The press are camped outside Danny's apartment in New York day and night. He wanted a bit of a breather.'

'Won't they just camp outside your house now?' asked

Scarlett, tentatively trying a mouthful of sashimi. He was right; it was delicious.

'I've got the highest hedges in Hollywood,' said Jake proudly. 'Had 'em grown specially to keep all the angry husbands out. Oh, lighten up,' he added, clocking her frown of disapproval. 'I'm only kidding. If you don't have plans tonight, you should join the three of us for dinner. We've got a table at Mastro's. There'll be more diamonds in that restaurant than in the whole of Kimberley, trust me. You can hang out with your future customers.'

Scarlett's only plan had been a hot bath and bed – Nancy had a date tonight and wouldn't be back till late – but despite her exhaustion she was hugely curious to see Danny and Diana together in the flesh.

'All right,' she said, finally allowing herself to smile. 'That'd be nice. Thanks.'

Her smile broadened when they left the restaurant in Jake's Maserati, and began flying through the alleys of downtown Beverly Hills like a blue and silver bullet.

'Where'd you learn to drive?' she asked, impressed. 'Brands Hatch?'

'Nah. Running away from the cops,' said Jake. 'That was a joke too, by the way.'

A few minutes later they pulled up outside a tall, slim store on Canon. Leaving the car right outside, Jake hopped onto the sidewalk, opening the passenger door for Scarlett.

'Here we are,' he said, smiling. 'What do you think?'

Scarlett stepped inside. The space had most recently been used as a clothes store, a designer sample place if the few plus-sized Armani pantsuits and odd pairs of last season's Prada boots were anything to go by. It was narrow, not more than fifteen feet across at the front, but it stretched back for what looked like miles, opening out at the rear through French doors onto a charming paved patio, complete with a moss-covered stone fountain and tubs full of early-blooming spring flowers. Right now the walls were painted a drab grey, and the floor inside was covered with a hideous, sticky-brown linoleum. But with some pots of white paint and a little of Scarlett's natural flair, it could be something really special. It was also on one of the prime retail streets in Beverly Hills, sandwiched between Louis Vuitton and a day spa that looked like the world's most expensive spaceship.

'I think either you won the lottery, or you're pulling my leg,' she said. 'We can't possibly afford this. Can we?'

Jake shrugged. 'It'll be a stretch,' he said. 'But I reckon they've seriously undervalued the rent. Take a look at this.'

Whipping his BlackBerry out of the pocket of his Bermuda shorts, he opened a spreadsheet attachment and took Scarlett through a simple set of figures. 'I think we can do it, if neither of us eats anything but baked beans on toast for the rest of the year.'

'Why on earth is it so cheap?' asked Scarlett, trying to keep a lid on her excitement.

'Dunno,' said Jake. 'Not much frontage? Plus the last two businesses here folded within a year.'

'They must have been pretty badly run then,' said Scarlett, looking around again, imagining the possibilities. 'I never dreamed we could get anything so prime. Where did you find it?'

Jake tapped his nose knowingly. 'Little bird. So what do you reckon? Should we make the guy an offer?'

'Are you crazy?' said Scarlett. 'Of course we should. Get him on the phone right now!'

Jake laughed. He loved the way that Scarlett only seemed to have two gears – stop, or full speed ahead.

'Half an hour ago you wanted to go back 'ome,' he said.

'Yes, well, that was half an hour ago,' she beamed. 'I'm

serious. Call him! Oh, and I hope you didn't mean it about giving that horrendous woman Carla a commission. She was completely useless, and we can't afford it.'

Jake gave her a look of renewed respect.

'You know, for a tub-thumping hippie, you're not as naive as you look.'

'Thanks,' said Scarlett drily. 'I'll take that as a compliment, shall I?'

When she told Nancy about dinner with the twins and Diana, her friend's anti-Jake radar shot up.

'He's up to something. He has an agenda,' she announced cryptically, whilst rubbing scented body lotion into her inner thighs. 'Tell him you changed your mind.'

'But I haven't changed my mind,' said Scarlett, holding up two dresses against herself, one red and one white. She was determined, for once, not to look like something the cat sicked up when Jake saw her, if only for the sake of her pride. 'I'm really curious to see those two together. I'm hoping Diana might be able to shed some light on her evil ex-husband and what he did to Bijoux. After all, if it weren't for him, I wouldn't be here.'

'In that case I might write and thank him,' said Nancy, unselfconsciously spritzing her newly trimmed bush with Penhaligon's Victorian Posy. 'Boxie, drop!' She pulled a pair of bright-red satin panties out of Boxford's jaws and put them on, admiring the fit in the mirror. 'God, I hope Jason has a big dick,' she muttered to herself. 'He looks like he does, but so many of these ball players are a big disappointment when it comes to the shorts department.'

'Nancy!' Scarlett giggled. 'You're terrible. I thought this was a first date.'

'It is,' said Nancy, grinning wickedly before returning abruptly to their original conversation about Diana. 'Remember, Brogan isn't her ex-husband yet. She's only been with Danny Meyer five minutes. She could still go back to him, so be careful what you say tonight. Loose lips, and all that.'

'I don't think she's going back to him,' said Scarlett, opting for the red dress. The white one would have to wait till she got a tan. 'According to Jake, he beat her up pretty badly when he found out about her and Danny. No woman would go back to that.'

'You'd be surprised,' said Nancy. 'Wow,' she added, turning around and seeing Scarlett in the dress. A floor-length halterneck, it fitted her beautifully and showed off a good amount of creamy-white cleavage, as well as a tempting expanse of bare back. 'Very sexy. That'll get Meyer's attention for sure.'

'I'm not trying to get his attention,' insisted Scarlett crossly. 'For the last time, Nance, he's my business partner, and that's all he'll ever be. I felt like making a tiny bit of an effort, that's all. Is it too much?'

'Of course not,' said Nancy, stepping into her own dress for the evening, a crotch-skimming little black number that looked fit to split the moment she sat down. 'You look lovely, as always. Just watch your back with that guy, OK? He's bad news; you heard it here first.'

'Actually, I've heard it everywhere,' said Scarlett under her breath. But Jake had come up trumps today – it looked like they were going to get that store space. And if she couldn't enjoy a simple social dinner with the man, it didn't say much for their future as business partners.

'Don't worry,' she said. 'He absolutely, categorically won't try anything. But if he does ...' she did her best Charlie's Angel karate chop, complete with 'hi-yah' noises, 'I'll be ready for him.'

It was a beautiful LA evening. The palm trees lining Rodeo and Canon Drives swayed gently in the breeze beneath a riotous sunset of pinks, oranges, purples and blues that no jewel on earth could hope to imitate. All across town, automatic sprinklers began springing to life, watering the immaculately trimmed lawns and clipped box hedges that had spent the day bathed in sunshine, as pampered and spoiled as the people who owned them.

No wonder everything's such a vivid, emerald green, thought Scarlett. This city must be plant heaven.

Unfortunately, it definitely wasn't traffic heaven. Having wasted a good twenty minutes getting siphoned the wrong way around the Beverly Hills one-way system, and used some very unladylike language abusing the makers of her Thomas Guide City Map, Scarlett finally arrived at Mastro's half an hour late.

'Sorry,' she said earnestly, weaving her way through the dimly lit tables and past the piano player towards Jake and Danny's table. Jake had changed into a suit and tie, much to Scarlett's relief, as Danny and Diana were both casually dressed in chinos and T-shirts, and only a handful of women in the restaurant appeared to have dressed up for the evening. 'I got a bit lost.'

'Not to worry,' said Danny, smiling broadly and offering her his hand. 'We only just got here ourselves. What can I get you?'

'A vodka and tonic please,' said Scarlett.

'Got any ID, miss?' the penguin-suited waiter gave her the once over.

'I'm sorry?'

'Do you have any proof that you're over twenty-one?'

Scarlett flushed with pleasure. 'I'm afraid not. But how marvellous that you think I might not be.'

'I'm afraid we can't serve you alcohol without a valid ID,' said the waiter pompously. Scarlett insisted she was fine with water, but Jake kicked up a stink, and eventually a vodka and tonic, long, cool and chock full of ice and lemon was brought to the table.

'So, how are you liking La La so far?' asked Danny. Scarlett noticed the way his left hand lay possessively over

Diana's right on top of the table when he spoke. She'd only glimpsed him once before, in New York a year ago, also the only night that she'd seen Diana. Danny looked the same, a rougher-round-the-edges version of Jake, though somehow more approachable than his brother. But Diana was different. Scarlett remembered her from the Tiffany party as projecting an air of such sadness and vulnerability. Tonight, however, she looked positively radiant, glowing with love for Danny, whom she glanced at and touched constantly, her face beaming with happiness despite the still-healing bruises around her eye and the gash on her lower lip, that she hadn't bothered to try and disguise with make-up. She wore the ring that Danny had given her the first night they met. Other than that she wore no jewellery, Scarlett noticed, although a white band of skin clearly marked the spot covered, until recently, by her wedding ring.

'I'm not sure,' said Scarlett. 'It's too early to say, I suppose. The house I'm staying in is divine, and it looks like Jake has found me a wonderful space for the new store. If we get it,' she added, cautiously.

'We'll get it,' said Jake. No one would know the effort of will it took for him to keep his eyes away from Scarlett's bosoms, edibly gift-wrapped as they were in that unforgivably sexy dress. 'I'm telling you, it's a done deal.'

'And what about you guys?' asked Scarlett. 'How have you been coping with ... everything?'

No one spoke for a moment, and she worried she might have pried too far and somehow put her foot in it.

'We're fine,' said Diana, squeezing Danny's hand tighter.

The truth was, it had been a hellish few weeks. To say that Brogan had taken her departure badly would be a major understatement. After the attack in Telluride, he'd oscillated wildly between violent threats and bouts of pleading that left Diana winded with guilt. So far, Danny seemed to be taking a sanguine view of his 'if I can't have her, no one can' ranting. But Diana knew her husband too well to dismiss his reactions as so much hot air. She hadn't had a full night's sleep in weeks.

'We're very grateful to Jake for giving us a bolthole here,' she said, forcing a smile. 'Living at Danny's apartment has been like being in a cage at the zoo. We've been desperate to leave New York, but neither of us had the money to spend on hotels.' Catching Scarlett's look of surprise, she explained, 'Brogan's cut me off from all my credit cards and closed our joint account. My parents have sent me some cash to tide me over, very kindly. But I'm too old to run back to Daddy for an allowance, so I want to make that money last.'

'Can Brogan do that?' asked Scarlett, frowning. 'You were married for years. Surely some of that money is yours by right?'

She didn't know why, but she liked Diana. Even in her current, happier state, she inspired strong feelings of protectiveness in Scarlett, a desire to stand up for the sisterhood. Scarlett hoped they might become friends.

'We've got a good divorce attorney working on it,' said Danny. 'But these things take time. It doesn't help that Brogan's the one divorcing Diana. For adultery, if you can believe the cheek of that, the randy sod.'

'You knew my husband, didn't you?' Diana looked across at Scarlett. 'I remember him talking about you.'

'I didn't know him,' said Scarlett. 'I knew of some of the things he allowed to go on at his diamond mines, that's all, and I spoke out against them.'

'That's right,' said Diana, putting the pieces together. 'The cancer cases. Trade Fair; that's you, isn't it?'

Scarlett nodded proudly. Jake looked across at Danny and rolled his eyes.

'What?' said Scarlett crossly, catching the look.

'How's your charity going?' asked Diana.

'Slowly.'

Scarlett took another sip of her drink. She remembered Gregori and Andy from her trip to Yakutsk last summer, and their predictions about how hard it would be to get people interested in the Siberian miners' plight. Unfortunately, they couldn't have been more right, she thought guiltily, reflecting that she'd achieved precisely nothing on that front in the last six months.

'Part of my reason for coming out to LA was to try and breathe new life into it, and get the word out in the States.'

'The word out about what? Brogan's mines?' Diana frowned. 'You know, I admire what you're doing. But you can't be sure about those lung cancer cases. I mean, I'm not saying he has no responsibility. But it's a much more common illness in Russia than it is here. Those men might have had problems anyway.'

'Yakutia's not our only focus,' said Scarlett, anxious to avoid a row. 'In fact, up until last year, Trade Fair was almost exclusively in Africa. But the injustices in the diamond business are endemic, worldwide. It doesn't help that most Americans are more likely to give to animal charities than human ones,' she added bitterly. 'D'you know how much money PETA raises annually, in California alone?'

'All right, all right, no hobby horses at the dinner table,' said Jake. His growing attraction for Scarlett hadn't stopped him getting irritated by the way she insisted on chewing people's ears off about her charity bollocks *all the time*. Diana and Danny had come here for a break, not a lecture on bloody Africa. He'd hoped being away from London might have prompted her to lighten up, but no such luck, and he was starting to regret having held out the carrot of increased US exposure for Trade Fair if she moved here. She seemed far more interested in that than in their new business.

'It's hardly a hobby horse,' bristled Scarlett. 'Perhaps if

you read some of the literature I gave you, you'd have a bit more respect for what I'm trying to do. Or at least some understanding. Have you read that book on Sierra Leone yet?'

'Fine.' Jake frowned, loosening his tie. 'If I promise to read the book, do you promise to get off my case about this? You can't expect the entire world to agree with you, you know, just by nagging them into submission.'

Scarlett blushed. Was that how he saw her? As a nag?

'All right,' she said, more quietly. 'If you read the book, and you still think after that that the way you and Danny do business is OK, I'll "lay off", as you put it. For now.'

'So,' Diana, ever the peacemaker, tactfully changed the subject. 'I hear you're opening a new store here. Will you stock a range of designers, or will it be all your own stuff? I love that brooch, by the way.' She pointed to the diamond and garnet starburst pinned to the halter tie of Scarlett's dress.

'Thanks.' Scarlett fingered the brooch lovingly. 'I made this years ago, when I was just starting out. Unfortunately all my London stock was lost in the robbery and the fire destroyed most of my sketches.'

'That's the other reason Scarlett moved out here,' said Danny grimly. 'Your old man burned her London store to the ground.'

'I'm hoping the new store will be all my own work,' said Scarlett. 'But I'll have to work my butt off to produce a new line in time for our opening.'

'No!' Diana shook her head, looking quizzically from Scarlett to Danny and back again. 'Brogan wouldn't set fire ... no, no, he wouldn't. He wouldn't do a thing like that. Why?'

'Because Scarlett's campaign was making him lose face, not to mention money,' said Danny harshly. 'Why d'you think?'

Diana had been under so much pressure these last few weeks, what with leaving her marriage and all the press intrusion, not to mention trying to recover from her physical and emotional injuries, that he hadn't wanted to bother her with the details of Scarlett's situation, or her proposed joint venture with Solomon Stones. His hope was that once Diana knew, she'd begin to lose some of the guilt that she still harboured for leaving Brogan. That she might even start to hate him, once she saw that it wasn't only her life that he'd made a misery. But instead, her first instinct was to defend him. It made Danny want to scream.

'Are you sure it was Brogan?' she asked Scarlett directly. 'It really doesn't seem like him.'

Sensing her pain, Scarlett chose her words carefully. 'I can't prove it, no. But I believe he was behind what happened. We both do.' She looked to Jake for support, but he seemed to have developed a burning interest in the menu. 'Anyway, it's all in the past now. Hopefully moving out here will be a whole new start.'

Mercifully the waiter reappeared at this point and took their orders. Soon all four of them were tucking in to juicy New York steaks and fries, washed down with far too much alcohol, and all awkward talk of Brogan and the past was forgotten.

'So,' said Danny, smacking his lips as a quivering mountain of lemon meringue pie was dolloped down in front of him. 'Any ideas on a name yet? For the shop?'

Scarlett shrugged. 'I hadn't thought,' she said. 'I guess I could just call it Bijoux. Or Bijoux LA?'

'Nah. Boring,' said Jake, without looking up from his pudding, a slice of pecan pie roughly the same size as a traffic cone.

'Well what do you suggest?' said Scarlett, annoyed. Why did he always think he knew better?

'Actually,' he said with an arrogant smile, 'I've got the perfect name. Something that sums up LA, and the fantasy of what we're selling, but that's punchy enough to work as a global brand.'

'Oh really?' Scarlett looked at him sarcastically. 'Well, please, do tell. Share your wealth of zero retail experience with the group, Mr Meyer.'

'Now now,' laughed Danny. 'You two sound like an old married couple already, d'you know that?'

Jake paused for effect. Then, looking Scarlett right in the eyes, he said: 'Flawless.'

She opened her mouth to criticise, then closed it again. Jake sat back in his chair and folded his arms with the smug satisfaction of someone who knows they've just won an argument hands down.

'I like it,' said Diana.

'I love it,' said Danny. 'Scarlett?'

Damn and blast the man! Why did he have to get it right first time?

'It's not bad,' she said grudgingly.

'*Not bad*?' Jake gave her his best 'come off it, ref' look.

'I'll think about it,' said Scarlett. '*If* you read those books I gave you.'

'Deal!' said Jake, raising his glass. 'To Flawless!' he toasted. 'And all who sail in her.'

'Flawless!' said the other three in unison.

# *Eleven*

Thanks to Jake's natural talent for self-promotion, Flawless's opening party rapidly became the most talked-about social event in Beverly Hills since the Oscars.

By the time the big night finally arrived, in late March, neither he nor Scarlett had any handle on the guest list. At the last count, they reckoned that between them they'd officially asked around two hundred people, mostly contacts and clients of Jake's, with a smattering of Scarlett's London friends and charity bigwigs thrown in for good measure. Jake estimated at least double that number would show up when it came to it, drawn by the rumoured celebrity attendance and the promise of unlimited free champagne. His biggest worry was how they were going to cram so many bodies into the tiny, twelve-foot-wide store without risking a sardines-like crush. Whereas Scarlett remained stuck in a flat-spin panic, convinced that no one would show up at all.

'Are you sure you and I shouldn't be there earlier?' she'd asked Jake for the hundredth time that morning, glued nervously to her cell phone whilst stuck at the beauty parlour. 'I can do my own hair and get to the store for, say, three.'

Jake, sprawled out on a sun lounger on the roof of the Peninsula, sipping a post-breakfast Bloody Mary and topping up his tan in preparation for the turquoise silk shirt he planned to wear this evening, sighed heavily.

'The party's at seven,' he said patiently. 'No one's gonna show till half past at the earliest, and we'll both rock up at six. That's plenty of time. The last thing we need is you stuck there waiting for four hours, whipping yourself into a frenzy about no-shows.'

'But what if someone important does show up early?' pressed Scarlett.

'Perry's there all day,' said Jake. 'He knows what to do.'

Perry was the new store manager, a flamingly gay ex-dancer whom Jake had poached from Cartier, another brilliant coup. Scarlett could pay him only half what he'd been on before, but the management at Cartier had treated him like dog-shit, and his encyclopaedic knowledge of gemstones and natural people skills had been woefully under-used. At Flawless, he'd almost be his own boss, with overall responsibility for the day-to-day running of the store – a necessity while Scarlett focused on the creative side of the business. Then there was the added bonus of working in such close proximity to Jake, who wasn't above flirting with men if it helped him get what he wanted, and who had shamefully led Perry on from the beginning, hinting at a closet bisexuality that kept his admirer's hope alive.

'Besides, the whole grooming thing is important,' he added, knowing how much Scarlett loathed salons and wasting time being 'done', as she put it. 'This is not the night to show up with do-it-yourself hair, trust me. You're on show as much as the jewellery.'

Unsurprisingly, this failed to reassure Scarlett, who spent the next four hours, against her better judgement, being plucked and painted by a fat, tattooed girl called Misty whom Jake had assured her was the very best beautician in the city, but who looked to Scarlett like she'd be more at home on an oil rig or driving a truck than explaining the benefits of threading over waxing in a Japanese-themed 'retreat' on Beverly.

'You're sure it's not over the top?' she asked hesitantly, as still more heated rollers were wheeled out by Misty's mute girl assistant. Not since her modelling days had she willingly subjected herself to this sort of torture, and she was suddenly reminded of why she'd quit. 'I've always gone for more of a natural look. And Flawless is all about gem stones as natural art ...'

'The hair's great,' said Misty firmly. 'Don't touch it. I'll wrap the whole thing in plastic before we spray you. Then it's dress, shoes and you're good to go.'

'Spray me?'

The bronzing booth was the ultimate indignity. Standing stark naked in a weird sort of silver pod, her hair in curlers and an old fashioned shower cap, she felt like Norah Batty beamed up to the Battlestar Galactica. Misty, more of a butch, lesbian mechanic than ever in protective goggles and holding what looked like a blow torch, walked around her quite unselfconsciously, spraying her with instant tanning mist in some of the most embarrassingly intimate places.

However, even Scarlett had to admit that the end result was impressive.

'My God,' she gasped, looking down at her breasts ensconced in the emerald-green, Monique Lhuillier evening dress. 'I've gone up three bra sizes.'

Misty grinned. 'It's all about the shading. But hey, you know that. You're an artist, right?'

She was home by four, and had intended to spend an hour sketching a design for a new Tahitian black pearl choker that had come to her under the blow dryer. But by five thirty the suspense of waiting, combined with Boxford's persistent, resentful howling – he knew that the evening dress meant he was about to be abandoned – got too much for her, and she drove over to the store, parking her rented Prius out back and walking in through the garden. She'd added a couple of uniquely English touches – hollyhocks and roses had replaced the original Zen-plantings of orchid and bamboo, and the grey paved patio had been switched to gravel paths, hemmed in by formal, foot-high box hedges – but otherwise it was unchanged, as glorious and light-filled a sun trap as the day she'd first seen it in January with Jake.

'My, my! Don't we look a princess?' Perry exclaimed, clapping his hands gleefully as Scarlett walked in. It was Jake who'd tempted him into the job, but he'd soon come to adore Scarlett almost as much. A true aesthete, he was attracted to beauty in all its forms, and no one could deny that the willowy, ethereal Miss Drummond Murray was beautiful. She was also highly talented. After seven long years at Cartier, where designers never took a risk, Perry was overjoyed at being given the chance to watch her creative flow in such glorious, untrammelled action. Like Jake, he had no doubts tonight's opening would be a roaring success.

'One look at you and those celebrity actresses are gonna turn a-*round*,' he gushed, circling his boss as if he were appraising a sculpture. 'No one likes to be out-shone in *People* magazine.'

'*People* magazine? Are they coming?' asked Scarlett, half excited and half terrified at the prospect. 'Jake never said anything—'

'Try and breathe, honey,' said Perry soothingly. 'Our boy knows how to work the press. You just focus on being the creative genius and looking divine.'

Caterers were wandering in and out, adding the finishing touches to the bar – as well as champagne there would be various diamond-themed cocktails on offer (a 'Star of India' consisted of two parts vodka, two parts rum and a dash of cranberry soda), with only a few, light, carb-free nibbles on offer to help mop up all the alcohol. Jake was of the firm belief that a drunk customer was a happy customer. Scarlett could only pray that by tomorrow morning her gorgeous new store wouldn't have been redecorated with indelible red cocktail stains, or worse. Inside, she'd totally revamped the place, eschewing her normal love of colour and depth and focusing instead on a clean, white space reflective of their new name and new ethos. Not only were her designs and the diamonds they used flawless, the store seemed to say, but they offered customers the chance to buy beauty with a clean conscience. With Scarlett's politically correct, eco-friendly jewellery – or, as Perry liked to put it, 'Cartier with a Heart-ier' – the new Flawless offered something unique amongst LA's high-end boutiques. Tonight would be the first and most crucial test of whether that would pay off.

'Please tell me they'll come.' Scarlett turned desperately to Perry for reassurance as she fiddled unnecessarily with an arrangement of white lilies.

'Oh, sweetie. Of course they'll come,' he smiled, hugging her. He smelt of lavender and soap, like a baby, although his arms were astonishingly strong and manly, a hangover from all those years of dancing. It was the most comforting hug Scarlett had had in years. 'Trust your uncle Perry. You'll be beating them off with a stick.'

He was right. By seven o'clock, when doors officially opened, there was already an expectant line of partygoers milling around outside. Within half an hour, their numbers had swelled to well over a hundred, and Scarlett's nerves had shifted focus to the same problem that had been occupying Jake for most of last week – where the hell were they going to put them all? The arrival of Salma Hayek and her new fiancé, shortly followed by the Simpson sisters, prompted the sort of paparazzi scrimmage that Scarlett had only ever seen before on *E! True Hollywood Story*, and by the time her own friends from London put in an appearance the shop was so heaving with bodies that she could do little more than nod towards them helplessly from the far side of the room.

'Not bad, eh?' Jake, who'd rolled up late ('I knew you'd get there early. No point both of us being here') looking relaxed and happy after his day at the Peninsula, battled his way through the hordes to her side. His turquoise shirt clashed wantonly with his violet eyes and brought out both his tan and the blondeness of his artfully dishevelled hair.

Wearing a woman's charm bracelet Scarlett had designed on his wrist – he was so blatantly macho, he could get away with it – and a pair of signature Flawless diamond cufflinks, he could have been a pop star, or an unusually handsome gangster. Hundreds of pairs of female eyes bore into his back like lasers, but he seemed characteristically untroubled by the heat, flashing his I-told-you-so grin at Scarlett as he kissed her on both cheeks. 'And you thought you'd be sitting here all alone like Norma No Mates.'

'There's certainly a lot of interest,' admitted Scarlett. 'Has anyone bought anything yet?'

'Yeah,' he nodded. 'Salma ordered two pairs of earrings, and Anna May, one of my regulars, is springing for the daisy-chain necklace as we speak.'

He nodded in the direction of the open cabinets, where Perry was cupping a delicate yellow tourmaline, platinum and diamond chain between his manicured fingers while a man and a woman looked on.

'That's the most expensive piece in the store,' gulped Scarlett.

'I know,' said Jake. 'Those are my stones, remember?'

Back home in Notting Hill, she'd have expected to hold on to a necklace that valuable for months or even years, using it as a display or catalogue piece until she happened upon some freakishly big spender. But this couple looked like they were preparing to drop a million dollars on a passing whim.

'Hold on,' she said, looking at the woman more closely. 'Isn't that the girl I saw getting out of your car the other morning? The one you were snogging the face off?'

Jake looked at her blankly. 'Which morning? I do wish you'd be a bit more specific, angel.'

'My God, you're shameless,' said Scarlett disapprovingly. 'But then again, so's she. Isn't she nervous to bring her husband here? I mean, what if someone says something to him?'

Jake laughed out loud. 'This is Hollywood, not Kansas bloody City. Everyone has affairs here. Two of her old man's ex-mistresses are over there.' He turned and pointed to a pair of identikit brunettes, admiring the rings on display behind them. 'And that's his present squeeze, Leila Collins, with *her* husband, Don. Another loyal client of mine,' he added, enjoying Scarlett's evident discomfiture.

'Well I'm sorry, but I think it's awful,' she said seriously. 'Isn't anyone happily married in this town?'

'They're all happily married,' said Jake. 'Anna May's one of the happiest married women I know. And I know a few.'

After three months of working together, thrust into one another's company almost daily, Scarlett was still no better at figuring out when he meant something, and when he was teasing her – winding her up, as he put it. Suspecting a tease with Anna May, she managed a smile, which Jake returned with a mega-watter of his own.

'That's better,' he said. 'You know you're much prettier when you stop disapproving of everything for five minutes and give peace a chance. Here.' He thrust a lethal-looking cocktail into her hand. 'Have a drink.'

'Thanks, but no, I shouldn't.' She pushed it back at him. 'Tonight's work, remember?'

'Drink it,' said Jake, and for some reason she found herself complying. 'There's nothing worse than an uptight hostess.'

Watching him drift off into the sea of, to him at least, familiar faces, she began to wonder how many of the women here he must have slept with over the years. Half? Three quarters? Somehow she found the image of him jumping naked on to so many faceless bodies like an obsessive rodeo rider, deeply unsettling. So far she'd spent most of her time in LA holed up at Nancy's cottage, working on her designs, or running around town with Perry, sourcing interesting interiors for Flawless. She hadn't really been exposed to the other side of life here – to Jake's LA, with its bed-hopping, its conspicuous consumption, its all-round trashiness glinting like a fake diamond beneath the ever-shining sun. This was the side she'd dreaded back in London, when she thought about making the move. Was it really possible to live in Sodom and Gomorrah, amidst so much that she disapproved of – and not just to live here, but to sell diamonds to the richest of the rich – and not become tainted herself, infected with the same morality-eating virus that seemed to have struck down everybody else?

Nancy had managed it. And most of Nancy's friends, struggling screenwriters making ends meet as waitresses or part-time tarot readers in Topanga, convinced that their stay in LA was temporary, even after decades stuck here, trying to get a break.

Is that what would happen to her? Would she get sucked in to the black hole of LA life, telling herself year after year that she'd move back to London soon, right after the next sale/store opening/ad campaign? The thought made her shiver.

'You cold, sweetie?' Nancy, a breath of fresh air amongst all these overdone women in hot pants and jewelled flip flops slipped an arm around Scarlett's waist. With Scarlett in heels and her in flats, the height difference between them was even more comical. 'Hey, I could be your ven-triloquist's dummy!' she laughed, self-deprecatingly, gazing up at her friend. 'Then you could say whatever you wanted to Jake and his harem and blame it all on me. It's going well though, isn't it? Perry's selling up a storm to Barbie and her husband.'

'So I hear,' said Scarlett, laughing herself. The wicked green cocktail was at last starting to work its magic, and she did feel more relaxed.

'Shame there aren't any decent, single men knocking around,' said Nancy, scanning the sea of couples as best she could from her low vantage point. 'Whoa, scratch that. Jake Gyllenhaal lookalike, two o'clock.'

'Where?' said Scarlett idly.

'Over there!' whispered Nancy. 'Oh my God. Oh my God oh my God oh my God. He's coming over!'

Scarlett felt her heart leap, twirl around, then plunge back into the pit of her stomach in a complicated corkscrew motion, as if it were trying to take gold in the Olympic high dive. There, making his way towards her in a simple dark suit, a smile as wide as the Mississippi plastered across his face, was Magnus.

'Hello, stranger,' he beamed, taking her in his arms and kissing her directly on the mouth, before she had a chance to protest. 'Did you miss me?'

'Not in the least,' lied Scarlett, crossly. Really, married people had no business being such good kissers. 'What on earth are you doing here?'

'I came to see you, of course.' Magnus looked hurt. 'I know it's been months. But I haven't been able to stop thinking about you.'

'Oh, don't give me that pout,' seethed Scarlett. 'You lied to me.'

'What ... when?' he frowned.

'What do you mean, when? We've only ever seen each other once. At Drumfernly, of course, when we had our "one-night stand", as you so charmingly put it at the time. The night you conveniently forgot to mention that you were *married*.'

'Oh. That.'

'Yes,' said Scarlett caustically. 'That.'

'Look, I know what it must look like,' said Magnus. 'But honestly, Carole and I have been living apart for over two years now—'

'Save it,' said Scarlett, wishing she didn't still want him so much, even after all this time.

'Hello, handsome.' Nancy, with her usual impeccable

timing, inserted herself between Scarlett and Magnus, unconsciously thrusting her ample chest in Magnus's general direction. 'I'm Nancy, Scarlett's best friend. But I'd like to make it absolutely clear that I'd betray her without a second thought if you felt like sleeping with me. And you are?'

Magnus roared with laughter, and offered her his hand.

'Magnus,' he said, still not taking his eyes from Scarlett's. 'Is this the part where you tell me that you've already heard a lot about me?'

'Oh, I have,' said Nancy, grinning. 'None of it repeatable in public, unfortunately. It's terribly impolite not to tell a girl you're married before you seduce her, you know.'

'Jesus, I am *not* married, OK?'

'So you're divorced?' shot back Scarlett.

'Well, no. Not yet. Not officially ...' stammered Magnus.

'Don't worry about her,' said Nancy, seeing his face fall as Scarlett swept off into the crowd to mingle, shooting him a scathing look as she went. 'She's punishing you, that's all. Which you fully deserve. She'll get over it.'

'I hope she gets over it some time this evening,' said Magnus ruefully. 'I was kinda relying on staying at her place. So much for surprising her on her big night.'

Across the room, Jake was deep in conversation with the producer of NBC's latest hit legal drama when he caught sight of Scarlett storming off from the good-looking giant in the dark-grey suit.

'I'm sorry, what were you saying?' he asked. The producer stopped in his monologue, realising that Jake hadn't taken in a word.

Suit guy was whispering with Nancy now, thick as thieves. He obviously knew Scarlett well, and from his confident stance and body language, you could see instantly that he fancied himself. Jake found himself fighting an urge to wipe the smile off his face by strangling him with his blue and white Harvard tie.

'Never mind,' said the producer crossly, stalking off. Six

months ago he was struggling to pay the mortgage on his ex-wife's four-bedroom in the valley, but now he had a hit show on his hands he expected the world to stop when he spoke. He wasn't about to hang around for some two-bit diamond dealer to notice him.

Meanwhile Magnus had moved away from Nancy and was scanning the room for Scarlett, when he was surprised by a forceful tap on the shoulder.

'Hi,' said Jake coldly. 'I'm Jake Meyer, Scarlett's business partner. And you are?'

'Magnus Hartz.' Magnus smiled, revealing a mouthful of expensive dentistry to rival Jake's own. 'Scarlett and I are old friends.'

'Really?' said Jake. 'Because I couldn't help but notice she seemed less than thrilled to see you. May I see your invitation?'

'All right, look, I don't want any trouble,' said Magnus, his smile fading in the face of Jake's naked hostility. 'I came here to surprise Scarlett.'

'Yeah, well, you've done that now. So if you don't have an invitation, I'm afraid I'm going to have to ask you to leave.'

'This is ridiculous!' said Magnus. 'Half of these people don't have invites. It's a store opening, not a wedding reception, for heaven's sake.'

'Out!' Jake pointed imperiously to the door.

'Listen, you little shit,' said Magnus, finally losing his temper. 'I'm not going anywhere till I've spoken to Scarlett. Scarlett!' He shouted over the heads of the other guests, determined to get her attention.

In the middle of a discussion with a client about the latest Amnesty report on Russian diamond mines, Scarlett was in no hurry to respond. OK, so Magnus was divine beyond words, and probably only very faintly married, but if he thought he was going to swan in and sweep her off her feet ...

'Erm, it looks like your friend is in some trouble,' said the client, gently. 'You might want to get over there.'

Turning round, Scarlett clapped her hand over her mouth in horror. For there was Jake, his face beet red with exertion, physically dragging Magnus to the door while a gaggle of amused spectators looked on.

'Let go of me! Let go, you fucking thug.' Although a good six inches shorter than he was, Jake was as strong as a pit bull and just as determined. Unused to physical fights – he didn't think he'd punched anyone since school – Magnus was no match for him, and could do little more than yell as he was ignominiously ejected from the store, thrown on to the street like a sack of garbage.

'Stop it! *Stop!*' Scarlett arrived just in time to see Magnus sprawl out on to the sidewalk amid a barrage of camera flashes. 'What are you *doing*?' she turned on Jake. 'Have you lost your mind?'

'He refused to go quietly,' said Jake, dusting off his suit and re-straightening his tie like a gangster in a movie. 'I asked him nicely, didn't I, Perry?'

He looked to the store manager for support, but the poor man was too overwhelmed with delight, seeing his crush get so unexpectedly physical, he could barely get a word out.

'He left me no choice.'

'I could have you arrested for assault,' seethed Magnus. On his feet now, he dabbed at his cut cheek with a Brooks Brothers linen handkerchief.

'Up yours,' said Jake firmly. 'You were trespassing.'

'Of course he wasn't *trespassing*, you Neanderthal,' said Nancy, who'd emerged from the store and now stood by Scarlett's side.

'Stay out of this,' snapped Jake. 'Nobody asked you.'

'He's a friend of Scarlett's,' she shot back, undeterred. 'Tell him, Scar.'

'That's right,' said Scarlett. Seeing Magnus's bleeding

face, the nurse in her took over and she began to tend to him, examining the wound with her fingertips. 'He flew in from Seattle to surprise me.'

Seizing the moment, Magnus pressed her fingers to his mouth and kissed them.

It was no good. Married or not, liar or not, she'd missed him like hell.

'I'm sorry about Jake. Are you all right?' she asked gently.

'Fine,' he whispered. 'Listen, Scarlett, about my divorce . . .'

'Shhh,' she said, stroking his cheek. 'You can tell me later. Let me deal with this first, OK?'

Jake looked, as his mother would have said, as if he'd lost a shilling and found sixpence. If his hope had been to get rid of Magnus and score some macho points with Scarlett, the strategy had backfired terribly. He should have known she'd automatically be attracted to the bird with the broken wing.

'You're a disgrace,' she scolded him.

'*I'm* a disgrace? Great,' said Jake. 'So that's all the thanks I get for trying to protect you, is it?'

'Protect me?' Scarlett frowned. 'Protect me from what exactly?'

'Undesirables,' said Jake, glowering at Magnus.

'I'd hardly call him *that*,' muttered Nancy, not quite under her breath.

'Like Mr Seattle here. What exactly is it you do in Seattle, Marcus?'

'It's Magnus,' said Magnus coolly. 'And I'm an attorney.'

Jake gave a derisory laugh. 'What a surprise.'

'What's that supposed to mean?' snapped Magnus.

'Nothing.' Jake gave an innocent shrug. 'It means it doesn't surprise me, that's all. You look like a lawyer.'

And you look like a pimp, thought Magnus, eyeing Jake's

flamboyant shirt and perma-tan with ill-concealed distaste. But he bit his tongue. The last thing he wanted was to get back to fisticuffs and make himself look like a dick in front of Scarlett.

'Next time you find yourself on the wrong side of the law, call me,' he smiled, handing Jake his card. 'My specialty is human rights cases. But I'd be glad to make an exception. Any friend of Scarlett's is a friend of mine,' he added, sardonically.

Jake, furious at the implication that he was both a lawbreaker (true, but not the point) and the sort of person who might, in a month of Sundays, require the help of a loser like Magnus, searched in vain for a suitably withering comeback. But one too many cocktails seemed to have played havoc with his linguistic skills, and nothing came to him.

'I think I'm going to go,' said Scarlett, whose hand seemed to have found its way into Magnus's quite of its own accord. 'I'm pretty sure I've spoken to everyone here at least once, and people are starting to leave already.' She nodded towards the steady trickle of revellers making their way out of the door. 'Magnus and I need to talk.'

'You are joking?' said Jake. 'What if someone else decides to buy? What d'you want me to tell them?'

'I thought you said Perry could handle that side of things?' said Scarlett.

'Not on his own,' said Jake indignantly. Had he said that? Why the fuck had he said that? 'You're the designer. You're the one I dragged all these punters out to see. You can't do a runner from your own fucking launch party.'

Seeing her hesitate, Magnus saw another chance to play the good guy.

'It's OK,' he said. 'I can wait. We've got all night after all,' he added, shooting Jake a meaningful, triumphant glance. It was obvious the guy fancied her – why else would he be playing the jealous lover to such a ludicrous degree? Serve him right to have to imagine them in bed together, the violent little so-and-so.

'OK,' said Scarlett, hugging him gratefully. 'I won't be long, I promise.'

'Catch you later,' said Magnus to Jake, slipping his arm casually around the small of Scarlett's back as they strolled back into the party. Jake bit down on his tongue so hard it bled.

'Pretty girl, your partner. Banged her yet?'

Jake spun around. Terrific. That was all he needed.

'Fuck off, Tyler,' he snarled.

Tyler Brett, his hated rival, stood behind him with a girl on each arm, one of whom Jake could have sworn he recognised. Was she a porn actress from one of his Vivid Video productions? In a cream jacket and jeans, with his newly dyed black hair gleaming and a cigar clamped between twenty-thousand-dollars' worth of Hollywood White porcelain veneers, Tyler looked oilier than a tinned sardine, and a lot less palatable.

'I'll take that as a "no", shall I?' he smiled smugly. 'Not into the old "bit of rough" eh? Prefers the preppy type, does she?'

Porn Girl giggled, her eyes rolling wildly. She was clearly high as a kite.

'Cheer up,' said Tyler, who was enjoying needling Jake. 'Looks like she's bailed out your business, even if you aren't getting any pussy. Smart move, hooking yourself up with a store like this. It's gotta beat sitting around watching me take off with half your clients. Right?'

He laughed, a weird, strangled, braying sound, like a donkey being tortured. For the second time in as many minutes, Jake felt his fists twitching. But this time he man-aged to restrain himself. Brett might talk a good game, but he must be feeling the heat tonight, seeing Flawless make such a resoundingly big splash on her opening night. Not even his very public set-to with Magnus could take away what they'd achieved.

'See you around, Tyler,' he said civilly, making his way back indoors. Deciding he needed a stiff drink, he made a beeline for the bar. Within minutes he was engulfed by a bevy of beautiful, eager girls. Automatically, he turned on the charm. But for once their naked adulation gave him no thrill.

He'd lost sight of Scarlett and Magnus. But the image of that bastard's hand resting on the small of her back was seared into his memory like a cattle brand. All the happiness he'd felt earlier about the launch being such a success seeped out of him now like air from a slow-punctured tyre. This should have been his moment. His and Scarlett's together, a joint triumph. But now this fucker from Seattle had shown up and ruined it.

It was a long time since Jake could remember hating someone so much.

Two hours later, snuggled up in a booth at Jerry's late-night deli, sharing a plate of fries and a bucket-sized glass of lemonade, Scarlett and Magnus had eyes only for each other.

'So,' said Magnus, sprinkling a chip with salt and feeding it lovingly to Scarlett, like a mother bird, 'let me tell you about Carole.'

'You don't have to,' said Scarlett, thinking how odd it was that even his fingers were beautiful. 'I'm sorry I lost it with you before. I just ... I couldn't understand why you never said anything when we met. I felt like such an idiot when my mother told me the next day.'

'Don't apologise,' said Magnus. 'You were quite right. I *should* have told you. That night was so magical, I suppose I just didn't want to fuck it up. There's never a right time to bring up the wife in the attic, is there? But I should have said something. It was wrong of me.'

Their waitress, a harassed-looking woman who must have been sixty if she were a day, plonked two glasses of red wine down in front of them with all the finesse of a baby elephant, then shuffled back to the kitchen without a word.

'Where do they find these people?' said Magnus.

Scarlett giggled and took a sip of her wine. 'Eeugh,' she grimaced. 'Paint stripper. So you and ... Carole?'

'Carole.'

'You're still not divorced?'

He took a deep breath. 'We're not, no. But you mustn't read anything into that. I realise it sounds strange, but the truth is we simply never got around to it. Neither one of us has been serious enough with a new partner to think about marrying again. And until that happens, there didn't seem much point in going through all the legal hoopla, dividing assets and all that.'

'Are you still friendly?' asked Scarlett. 'I mean, what happened? How long were you together? Why did it end?'

'Whoa, whoa, easy with the Spanish inquisition,' said Magnus. 'Yes, we're friendly. She still lives in our old house. I moved into an apartment on the other side of town. Why did it end?' he shrugged. 'Who knows what makes two people grow apart? I mean, there was no big fight, no infidelity or anything like that. We'd been together since college; maybe we married too young, I don't know. Anyway, the time came to think about kids and we were both hesitant. I think that's when we started to realise that maybe we weren't right for one another, long term. She's a lovely girl. But it's over, very, very over. It has been for years. I don't talk about having a wife because I don't think of her as that any more, and neither does she.'

Scarlett scanned his face, looking for traces of dishonesty, of a story only partially told. But if he was lying, he was good at it.

'I'm sorry,' he whispered, reaching across the table and

taking her hand in his. 'Maybe part of the reason I didn't tell you was because I wasn't planning on seeing you again.'

'Thanks a lot!' said Scarlett, reaching for another chip. God, they were good.

'But I couldn't get you out of my mind, not for a day, sometimes barely for an hour. I kept wondering where you were, what you were up to, picturing you in Scotland mostly, in that fucking awful dress.' Scarlett laughed. 'Then I remembered the name of your charity, so I checked out the website one day. I couldn't believe it when I read your blog, about your store burning down. After everything you told me that night about Brogan O'Donnell and all the intimidation.'

'I know,' said Scarlett with a shiver. 'They actually torched the place that evening – while we were talking, probably.'

'And then I read that you'd moved out here, that there was a lot of buzz about your new store.'

'You've been my online stalker, in other words,' she teased him.

'Kind of,' he admitted. 'In fact, who am I kidding? Yes, totally. It got to the point when I knew I had to see you, I just didn't know when or how. And then a little bird told me about the Flawless party.'

'And here you are,' she beamed. 'It's tragic, isn't it? I can't stop smiling. Nancy's always giving me these books on dating, and they all say one should play hard to get. But I'm crap at it, aren't I?'

'You're not the greatest,' he laughed. 'I thought Nancy was great, by the way. What a firecracker!'

'She's been such a good friend to me,' said Scarlett. 'If it weren't for her, I don't think I could have stuck it in LA. The business is taking off so fast, but you wouldn't believe how stressful it's been, getting to this point.'

'Oh, I think I would,' said Magnus, shaking the last dregs

of ketchup from the bottle. 'Your partner seems like an absolute nightmare. How can you stand him?'

'Jake's all right,' said Scarlett, surprised to hear herself defending him. 'I mean, he was totally out of line tonight, with you,' she added hurriedly. 'But I have to give him credit where it's due. He's worked like a dog to get Flawless off the ground. Officially, he's only supposed to be my supplier.'

'You make him sound like a drug dealer,' said Magnus, adding, 'then again, he dresses like one, so why not?'

'He does a bit,' grinned Scarlett. 'But you know, he found us the space, negotiated the rent, hired Perry, my manager, who's an absolute gem. Most of the people there tonight were Jake's clients. He's definitely gone the extra mile.'

'He fancies you,' said Magnus, matter of factly.

Scarlett laughed loudly. 'I can assure you he does not!' she said. 'Jake and I do nothing but fight. He has the moral awareness of an amoeba, if that. We disagree on just about everything: politics, business, religion.'

'That's just foreplay,' said Magnus. 'You saw how hostile he was to me.' He pronounced the word 'hostel', one of Scarlett and Jake's few, shared pet-hates. 'That was pure, caveman jealousy.'

'I don't think so. It's more likely to be because he's used to being the best-looking man in every room and getting all the attention,' said Scarlett, running a desirous hand along the stubbly ridge of Magnus's jaw.

'Do you think he's attractive?' Magnus asked, as casually as he could.

Scarlett frowned, trying to be fair.

'Well, he's definitely not ugly,' she replied at last, taking another gulp of the barely drinkable merlot. 'Oh, come on,' she teased, seeing Magnus's face cloud over. 'Don't tell me *you're* jealous of *him*?'

'Of Neanderthal Man? I don't think so,' he scoffed. 'I'm

just surprised you chose to go into business with someone so uneducated. I mean, he's kind of a jerk.'

'He can be,' admitted Scarlett. 'Put it this way: I won't be sorry when he leaves for Africa next week. I think we both need a break from each other.'

Magnus's expression brightened.

Africa, eh? Well that was one piece of good news. Best place for a monkey like Jake Meyer.

'How long's he gone?'

'Only a couple of weeks,' said Scarlett. 'It's a relationship-building trip more than anything. He'll have to go back in the autumn for longer, to take delivery of the diamonds.'

She lightly touched on Solomon Stones' past, murky record in the area of blood diamonds, and the handshake agreement she and Jake had come to that no unethical stones would ever be used at Flawless.

'I've been giving him reading on the Sierra Leone civil war and some of the other conflicts in the region,' said Scarlett earnestly.

'Are you sure he can read?' muttered Magnus.

'But he's not remotely interested. That's the sad part. He's only doing the reading on sufferance, because he promised me he would.'

'Yes, well, not everyone's as good hearted as you, my angel.' Pushing the plate aside, Magnus took her head in both his hands and kissed her, properly, for the first time that evening. Whatever doubts he'd had about rekindling their 'fling' disappeared in that moment as he felt her hungry, warm lips part for him and her cashmere-soft breasts pressing needily.

'How far is it to your place?' he whispered hoarsely, feeling his desire growing like a tidal wave as he dropped a wad of notes onto the table.

'Ten minutes' drive,' breathed Scarlett. 'Let's get out of here.'

\*

The bumpy track leading up to the cottage was so dark, they kept losing their footing, ricocheting off one another like two drunks as they stumbled up to the garden, and in through the unlocked front door. (Magnus had taken one look at Nancy's so-called 'drive' and decided to leave his hire car on the road below.)

The instant Scarlett stepped inside she was knocked flying by a thoroughly overexcited Boxford, at once ecstatic to see her and reproachful that he'd been abandoned up at the house for so long.

'Back off, buddy,' said Magnus, watching the deranged spaniel pin Scarlett to the ground and cover her face with slobbery licks. 'That's my job.'

Boxford looked up briefly and growled.

'Boxie!' said Scarlett, shocked. 'That's odd. He's normally so friendly.' Kicking off her high heels she struggled back on to her feet. 'He's supposed to protect me and Nance from unwanted intruders, but he's a bit shit at it.'

'Really? And what about wanted intruders?' Scooping her up into his arms, Magnus carried her into the living room, laying her down gently on the worn white sofa.

'He sometimes protects us from those too,' said Scarlett, her pupils dilating with longing as she lay back and Magnus climbed on top of her, bringing his solidly handsome face within an inch of hers. 'You know, we might be better off in the bedroom, so we can lock the door.'

'Sorry.' Slipping his hand around the back of her neck, he unzipped her green dress, before lowering his mouth to her bare breasts. 'I can't wait that long.'

Scarlett didn't think she could wait, either. The weight and warmth of his body on hers, the heady scent of his cologne mixed with sweat and smoke from the party, and the ecstatic, glorious feeling of his hot, wet tongue on her nipples was more than she could bear. Having convinced herself she would never sleep with him again, and probably not even see him for years, the unexpectedness of his touch made it all the more magical.

'Fuck, I want you. I want you so badly,' he moaned, pulling at the dress until she'd wriggled out of it completely, and letting his hands slip beneath the silk fabric of her panties. 'I've tried to get you out of my head, but I can't.'

'Nor me,' whispered Scarlett, surprised by her own boldness as she unzipped his trousers and wrapped her fingers around his rock-solid erection. For a split second she was struck by the incongruous thought that his dick was exactly like him: straight, predictable and solid. She wondered if that meant Jake's cock was bent, unpredictable and slippery, then realised how wildly inappropriate it was for her to be thinking about Jake's penis at a time like this – or indeed at any time – and let go of Magnus with a start.

'What's wrong?' he asked, trying not to sound irritated. Now was really not a good time for her to be having second thoughts.

'Nothing. It's nothing,' said Scarlett. 'Something just popped into my head, that's all.'

'Yeah well, something else is about to pop here,' panted Magnus, pulling off her underwear and slipping a hand beneath her bottom so she could spread her legs more easily. 'I honestly can't hold it much longer.'

Smiling, Scarlett guided him inside her, clenching tightly with her muscles as he thrust once, twice and then came, his fingers gripping her breasts so hard she could feel the red welts appearing on her skin.

'Sorry,' he mumbled, half heartedly.

'That's OK.' Whatever slight annoyance Scarlett felt at not having had a chance to come herself was more than made up for by her delight in his desire. Knowing that she could make such a measured, cautious man lose control like that was quite a power kick.

'Sorry buddy.' Magnus grinned as Boxford came back in

from the garden, teeth bared. 'You missed your chance to savage me. The deed is done.'

He stood up and stretched. Scarlett tried not to think how faintly ridiculous he looked, still in his shirt and tie but with his pants slipping down and his now limp dick swinging like a stubby rope between his thighs. Was it weird to prefer one's lover clothed to half naked?

Boxford eyed Magnus sceptically as he bolted into the bathroom, turning his shaggy head towards Scarlett, as if to say 'who is this clown?' But he limited his disapproval to a single, short bark, and didn't make a fuss when, after a quick pee, Magnus sat back down on the sofa beside her.

Wide awake, her mind and pulse racing from the excitement of the launch and the sex and seeing Magnus again, Scarlett longed to talk. After enduring Jake's bored indifference day after day, it would be a real release to be able to unload her frustrations about Trade Fair, and the fact that they were getting precisely nowhere helping Brogan's Siberian miners, to someone who shared her passion and her social conscience. She was also dying to hear more about this mysterious Carole – the wife in the attic, as he put it.

But Magnus clearly wasn't feeling chatty. The second his head hit the pillow, he was out like a light, snoring with all the unsexy abandon of a foghorn. Tonight's performance had been a far cry from his patient, selfless lovemaking in Scotland, she thought wistfully and not without a little disappointment. Still, he'd told her at the deli that he'd be staying the whole weekend. Hopefully tomorrow she could reconnect with his romantic side, and delve deeper into his past.

# Twelve

As it turned out, one tomorrow followed the next, and she never did get around to questioning Magnus further. Instead they toppled inevitably into exactly the sort of long-distance, inter-city relationship they'd once agreed could never work, but which soon felt normal for both of them. Before she knew it, Scarlett was roasting in her first LA summer, working every hour that God sent, either in the store or in her tiny workroom up at Nancy's cottage. Vado Drive was loaded with charm, but lacking in modern amenities such as air-conditioning, and the six-by-nine-foot cubby hole Scarlett used as her office brought new meaning to the word 'sweat shop'. The same holiday months that felt so endless for LA's frazzled soccer moms, struggling to keep their fractious kids amused until September; or for their stressed-out studio exec husbands, fighting to keep their jobs and their tempers throughout blockbuster season, passed in a blink at Flawless. Most nights Scarlett collapsed into bed too tired even to think about missing Magnus, toiling away at his law firm in breezy Seattle. Autumn – 'fall' as they called it here – was supposed to be quieter, and she'd hoped she'd spend more time with him then. But by the time October rolled around, she still seemed to be running around like a headless chicken. Business was booming.

'My God. Look at them all,' said Magnus. 'They're like locusts. They're actually swarming.'

He'd flown into town tonight for the first time since June to support Scarlett at a joint PR event she was hosting with Jimmy Choo at the Chateau Marmont. Surrounded by shoe-crazed women oohing and ahing over each limited-edition stiletto, he looked distinctly out of his depth.

The hotel's famous garden had been transformed into a shoe fetishists' wonderland for the evening, courtesy of a set design company run by a friend of Nancy's. Three-foot-high red spotted mushrooms had been installed between moss-covered rocks on either side of a fake stream – how on earth did they create these things? – with artfully placed Jimmy Choo shoes 'hidden' beneath them. On top of the mushrooms sat beautifully carved and hand-painted wooden elves and fairies, draped in Flawless jewellery.

'I know,' said Scarlett excitedly. In bright orange skinny jeans, with blue and white striped maillot jersey slipping sexily from one shoulder, she looked very LA this evening – as did Boxford, whom she'd brought along in a ridiculous tartan doggie coat with 'FLAWLESS' woven into the back in diamanté lettering (a present from Perry). He was merrily raising his leg against one of the mushrooms while no one was looking. 'Isn't it great?'

After the success of their opening-night party – Jake's street brawl with Magnus had helped ensure them valuable column inches in the tabloids – Flawless had rapidly become a Mecca for hip, young Hollywood. Before long Scarlett and Perry knew most of the paparazzi by their first names, and never tried to stop them loitering outside the store, hoping for a shot of Lindsay or Paris, the way most of their competitors did. As Jake rightly pointed out, paps provided free publicity for Flawless, and their 'targets' certainly didn't seem to be bothered by press intrusion, whatever they might claim in interviews. One of the snappers, John, had even invited Scarlett to his kid's fifth birthday party. She'd have gone, too, if she hadn't been working up in Hollywood that day, shooting models for her latest Trade Fair campaign, a Russian-themed extravaganza complete with fur, fake snow, and her now trademark nude models posing as corpses in diamond-encrusted coffins. It was gruesome, but it worked. As the business gained momentum, and her designs started flying off the shelves, Scarlett finally found she had more time to devote to Trade Fair. Andy and Gregori, her friends from Yakutia, were thrilled at the direction of her new campaign, the first to focus exclusively on Siberia and the appalling conditions there.

'If you can get those pictures in any of the big US magazines, O'Donnell'll have to sit up and take notice,' said Andy excitedly, when she sent him the proofs. 'This is just the shot in the arm we need, and the kick up the backside *he* needs, the heartless git.'

Fundraising was also a breeze in LA. A good fifty per cent of Flawless's customers were professional 'charity wives', and those not already snapped up by Laurie David for her anti-SUV campaign, or committed to the ubiquitous Make A Wish Foundation, were more than happy to get involved with Trade Fair.

The only remaining fly in the ointment was the difficulty of getting US press coverage, although she was confident her gorgeous new ads would change that. Brogan had set Aidan Leach the task of keeping Trade Fair out of the US media, and he took the responsibility very seriously, more determined than ever not to fuck up after his 'oversight' with Scarlett's Yakutia trip last year. The *LA Times* had already dropped an interview with Scarlett days before it was due to run, under pressure from Aidan. Even *In Style* had heavily edited its profile of Flawless and its famous customers, eradicating every mention of Trade Fair from the published text, much to Scarlett's fury. Brogan evidently had friends in high places.

Still, she reasoned, not even he could keep her out of the press indefinitely. There was a lot of goodwill towards her in LA, where to her surprise she'd been warmly and swiftly adopted as a quirky, British outsider. Only a week ago, Lindsay Lohan's manager had been in the store, hinting that Lindsay herself might be prepared to lend her name to Trade Fair, if Scarlett could let her people know a little more about it. It hadn't happened yet, but it was all exciting stuff.

At least, Scarlett thought so. Magnus, much to her disappointment, had been less interested in her charity work than she'd anticipated. After six months 'together' – although admittedly ninety per cent of their relationship had been spent apart – she'd hoped for at least a modicum of boyfriendly solidarity. But he was so caught up in his own work – most recently he'd been working on an esoteric challenge to some minuscule piece of immigration law that he hoped, when published, would secure him his partner-ship – he had no mental energy left for her interests.

Having agreed at the outset to spend a minimum of one weekend in three together, Scarlett ended up doing all the travelling. Other than his first, surprise visit in March, Magnus had only made it down to LA once before tonight. Meanwhile, Scarlett had been ratcheting up the air miles to Seattle, a city she secretly found dull as ditchwater, spending her precious weekends mingling dutifully with Magnus's boring lawyer friends, nodding and smiling her way through corporate cocktail parties and tennis club socials till her jaw ached.

All of which wasn't to say that she and Magnus never had fun together. When he wasn't 'on duty', sucking up to his senior partners, he still had the ability to reduce her to tears of laughter. They read the same books, were interested by the same NPR news stories, and thanks in part to the enforced, long separations, the sexual chemistry between them seemed to strengthen rather than weaken with time. The last three times she'd gone to see him, he'd booked them into a swish hotel, which Scarlett thought was sweetly romantic. But it hadn't escaped her notice that nine times out of ten, *she* was the one making the effort and the sacrifices to keep the love affair going. And that on some very basic level, Magnus considered his career and interests to be more important than hers.

At least the fact that he was here tonight was some sort of step forward, and Scarlett was grateful for his support. It was four full months before the Academy Awards, but the *pre*-pre-Oscar season was already underway in Los Angeles. Every fashion-related business – clothes stores, jewellers, accessories outlets, shoe designers, hairdressers, you name it – was immersed in a fierce and frenzied competition for precious Oscar-night endorsements, bombarding actors, agents, managers and their wives/friends/dogs with free products and services, in the hope that their name might be glimpsed or mentioned on that all-important red carpet.

As the new kid on the jewellery block, Scarlett was at a distinct disadvantage, made worse by the fact that Jake had decided to disappear off to Africa for the second time this year to buy new stock just when the parties and press junkets were beginning in earnest. She felt no small pride in the fact that she'd put together tonight's celebrity cocktail party all by herself. She knew the Jimmy Choo boss, Tamara Mellon, from London, and when she heard she was in town last month had put in a tentative call, wondering if perhaps they could meet for supper and she could pick Tamara's business brain for PR ideas. It was Tamara who'd suggested the joint event – Flawless, like Jimmy Choo, was a luxury brand aimed primarily at a younger, celebrity-conscious clientele – but Scarlett had leapt at the chance.

'Tamara's such a whiz at these things,' she whispered to Magnus, smiling at one of her regular customers as they strolled past. 'I'm lucky she let me hang on to her coat tails. Oh look, there's Kate Hudson. I wonder if she'll go for my bumble bee pendant? It's very her, don't you think?'

Magnus looked at her as if she'd just let out the most horrendous fart.

'Have you heard yourself lately?' he said disapprovingly.

'You sound like a valley girl. How should I know what kind of pendant Kate Hudson wants to wear? More to the point, why should I care? Why should *you* care? She's only a stupid actress.'

'Unfortunately, stupid actresses count for a lot in my business,' said Scarlett. 'Without them, we couldn't hope to compete with the established brands. And Trade Fair would sink like a stone.'

She hated his assumption that because of what she did for a living, she was somehow more shallow, and more tolerant of the vile *US Weekly* celebrity culture than he was. Publicity was an evil, but a very necessary one. Surely he could see that, and accept it without judging her?

'I have to circulate,' she said, kissing him on the cheek. 'Are you OK here? Or d'you want to come with me?'

'Into that coven of witches?' said Magnus, surveying the army of rich girls in hipster jeans and Fred Segal T-shirts as they drooled over the merchandise, giving little squeals of delight at the kitschness of the set. 'No thanks, honey. I'll be over at the bar if you need me.'

What I need, thought Scarlett, glad-handing her way through the guests, is some bloody support. If only Jake were here, he'd be charming his way around the garden like Eden's snake, flirting for England and hard-selling her designs the way that only Jake could. She pictured him, sipping an ice-cold gin and tonic on a veranda somewhere in Africa, gazing out over a savannah sunset – was it sunset there? She could never get the hang of this time difference thing – and felt a pang of jealousy. How she wished *she* could take a month off to visit her beloved Franschhoek and tour the continent, while Jake got to stay here, schmoozing LA chicks and doing what he did best.

Over the past few months, she'd developed a grudging respect for Jake's people skills. But he still annoyed the hell out of her. He was always goading her about Magnus, and how lame she was to be doing all the running.

'He'll be Fed-Exing down his shirts next, so you can iron them for him,' he quipped, the day Magnus called to ask if she could call US Air and book his flights. 'Tell him to do his own bleeding travel arrangements. You've got a business to run.'

'Thanks for the advice,' Scarlett replied caustically, irritated because she knew he was right, 'but seeing as your longest relationship to date has been, what? Four weeks?'

'Three,' said Jake proudly.

'I think I'll follow my own judgement on this one.'

'Yeah, good idea,' said Jake. 'Maybe you can talk things over with him this weekend. When you fly to Seattle, *again*. What delights has lover-boy got in store for you this time? The Seattle-Over-Sixties-Please-God-Make-Me-A-Partner-Bingo-Championships? Bet you can hardly wait.'

'Yeah, well, it beats your weekend,' she shot back. 'Another gross, mindless shag-a-thon with some poor, unsuspecting bastard's wife.'

'Actually, the girls I sleep with are all married to *rich*, unsuspecting bastards,' smiled Jake. But though Scarlett didn't know it, he didn't enjoy the banter. Though he made light of it, he genuinely hated watching her trail around after that stuffed shirt lawyer like a loyal puppy. Ironically, it was Magnus's nominal support for her charity work that fuelled Jake's own, continued resistance to Trade Fair. It'd be a cold day in hell before anyone could accuse him of having something in common with that pompous, prematurely middle-aged knob.

But it wasn't just Jake's needling that annoyed Scarlett. Although he'd kept out of trouble with Flawless, as promised, he continued to employ unforgivably shady business practices when selling to private clients, flogging compromised or included stones for three or four times their market value where he thought he could get away with it. Scarlett was horrified. But Jake, thrilled to finally be regaining ground against the odious Brett Tyler, saw no reason to abandon tactics he'd employed successfully for years, and clearly viewed her objections as both naive and unreasonable.

'I'm your diamond dealer, not your pet,' he snapped at her the night before he flew to Cape Town, when she'd ill-advisedly embarked on another morality lecture. 'I don't tell you how to run your business, sweetheart. I'd appreciate it if you stopped telling me how to run mine.'

'But Jake, it's fraudulent!' Scarlett insisted, exasperated by his apparent total lack of conscience. 'Can't you see that what you're doing is wrong?'

'No,' he said firmly. 'I can't. I'm happy. The customer's happy. So why on earth shouldn't you be happy? You might have been too busy saving Siberia's diamond miners to notice, but Brogan O'Donnell's got my brother by the balls in New York.'

'What's that got to do with anything?' said Scarlett.

'When Tyler had me over a barrel last year, Danny kept Solomon Stones afloat,' said Jake. 'Now it's my turn to return the favour. So just butt out, all right?'

Knowing that the Danny situation was a sore point – after ten months, Brogan and Diana's divorce was no nearer completion, thanks to Brogan's stalling tactics, leaving Danny bled dry with lawyer's fees – Scarlett had backed off, for now. But her dislike of Jake's business practices hung in the air between them like a constant bad smell, as did Jake and Magnus's mutual loathing.

'Come and talk to Kate.'

Tamara, looking as radiantly glamorous as ever in a tiny aqua mini-skirt and a pair of her own aqua and chocolate-brown heels, cornered Scarlett just as she was heading to the Ladies.

'She's in love with that pendant of yours. I've told her I'm buying it if she doesn't, and I'll wear it to the Oscars myself.'

'You're an angel,' said Scarlett sincerely. 'I can't tell you how much I appreciate all this.'

'Oh bollocks,' smiled Tamara, with a dismissive wave of her hand. 'Far more fun to do these things together.'

Glancing back over her shoulder at Magnus, sulking at the bar and checking his watch ostentatiously, Scarlett couldn't have agreed more.

Sitting in the stifling waiting room of the Freetown orphanage, swatting flies away from his face with a two-year-old copy of *Time* magazine, Jake wondered if the director, Dr Katenge, was really in his office, as the receptionist had told him, or off snorting coke somewhere with his buddies like three quarters of the so-called 'charity workers' in Sierra Leone.

The country was so corrupt it made the mafia look like the Salvation Army. You never knew whom to trust. This was his seventh or eighth visit here – he couldn't remember exactly. In the past, he'd always come with Danny, and the pair of them had been whisked straight from the plane to the dealer's house, normally a fuck-off, fortified white palace up on a hill somewhere. There they'd be offered some good diamonds at a reasonable price, with no questions asked or explanations given as to their origin, supplied with a comfortable bed, a selection of willing local girls and a dizzying array of hard drugs, and left to their own devices for a night or two. After which, without having set foot out of the compound, they'd drive back to the airstrip and the rather less bountiful pleasures of 'civilisation'.

This trip was very different.

Unbeknownst to Scarlett, about a month ago he'd read one of the books she'd given him. Written by a boy soldier from Sierra Leone, it painted a horrifically vivid picture of the country's civil war through the eyes of a child. Though he'd die rather than admit it to Scarlett, the book had affected Jake deeply. He realised with a sharp pang of remorse that the last time he'd been here, living it up with Danny at some warlord's pad, this kid had been less than a hundred miles away, terrified and alone in the jungle, watching his mum and dad being sliced to pieces by some machete-wielding madman. He also realised that there was every chance that this same madman, or at least his bosses, controlled the very diamond mines from which he was buying ice to sell to the spoiled housewives of Beverly Hills.

Scarlett had been ramming this shit down his throat for so long now, he'd learned to switch it off completely, dismissing her impassioned lectures as so much irritating white noise. But this lad's stark, honestly written book had jolted him out of his stupor. Jake was no saint, he knew that – not like Magnus the holier-than-thou civil rights lawyer. He was quite happy ripping off clients with more money than sense, or doing the dirty with their wives and girlfriends when he thought he could get away with it. But the atrocities that had gone on here and were still going on, in countless other diamond-producing parts of Africa? That shit was of a whole different order. Suddenly the well-worn arguments he'd trotted out to Scarlett about the blacks bringing it on themselves, or the damage that boycotting conflict diamonds would do to African economies, sounded laughably hollow.

What the fuck was this Katenge wanker playing at?

'Mr Meyer?' A pretty, very dark-skinned woman in a shift dress and sandals emerged from the director's office and held out her hand. 'Sorry to keep you waiting. I'm Doctor Katenge.'

'Hi. You're ... ? Wow.' He stumbled to his feet. 'Thank you for seeing me.'

She laughed at his confusion. 'You were expecting a man? Or someone older?'

'Both, actually,' he admitted. 'They say it's a sign of ageing when you start to think that doctors and policemen look young. I must be knocking on a bit.'

Dr Katenge smiled. 'Nonsense. You're in the prime of your life, Mr Meyer. I've had fifteen-year-olds turn up on my doorstep looking older than you do.'

Knowing a little about what they might have been through, Jake wasn't surprised. He'd heard about the St Catherine's orphanage through a friend in New York, another transplanted North London Jew who was heavily involved in fundraising for a charity called Hope for Children. At first the friend had thought Jake was joking.

'This is a wind-up, right? You and Danny wanna start giving something back to Africa? Give me a break!'

'Not Danny,' said Jake, mildly offended that the idea he might choose to do something selfless provoked such instant disbelief and hilarity amongst his friends. 'He's got enough on his plate right now. Just me.'

'Blimey, you are serious,' said the friend. 'What do you want to know?'

Jake wasn't sure. Part of him felt a prat. He'd read one book, and now he wanted to wade in like the Lone Ranger and start changing things? After telling Scarlett *she* was naive?

'I'd like to find a small charity, something that isn't already funded by one of the big, Save Africa foundations, that works with kids from the diamond-mining areas.'

'I can give you a thousand,' said the friend ruefully. 'They all need cash. Want to narrow it down any more?'

'A group that isn't run by a muppet,' said Jake. 'Or some greedy bastard with his hand in the till.'

'Ah, well, that's a little tougher,' admitted the friend. 'It's pretty much every man for himself out there. I mean, some of the NGOs do good work, but they all take bribes. It's part of the culture.'

'Sod the culture,' said Jake. 'I'm buggered if I'm gonna line the pockets of those fuckers. I want to deal with someone I can trust.'

'All right,' said the friend. 'Give me a few days. I'll dig up some names and get back to you.'

When he heard about St Catherine's, a small, church-run orphanage on the outskirts of Freetown that took in teenage girls who'd been raped by the rebels, and their unwanted, ostracised babies, Jake thought it sounded like a good place to start. Following Dr Katenge through the gaudily painted corridors, peering into rooms stuffed with tatty, broken toys and noisily happy toddlers, he was confirmed in this impression.

'How many children do you have here?'

'Right now, twenty-eight,' said the doctor, scooping a lost little girl into her arms without breaking stride and depositing her in another overcrowded nursery room two doors down. 'We have had as many as forty. That's not including the mothers, of course, most of whom are children themselves.'

Turning down a second, smaller corridor, she led him into a classroom with two rows of old-fashioned desks and a teacher, a white man in his twenties, standing at a blackboard at the front. Each desk was occupied by a smiling black girl – some of them were heartbreakingly young, not more than eleven, Jake guessed – all of whom swivelled round to stare at this unexpected, not to mention handsome visitor.

'Carry on, Mr Harris,' said Dr Katenge. 'We're not staying.'

'What are they learning?' asked Jake, wiping the sweat off his forehead as they continued the tour. It was stiflingly hot.

'Not much.' Dr Katenge sighed. 'Their teacher is a volunteer, on loan to us from Unicef, but he only comes for two hours, twice a week. Very few of the girls can read or write; only half speak English. He's trying to give them basic instruction in childcare and health and safety – how to sterilise a bottle, what to do if their baby has a fever, contraceptive advice. One or two will learn other skills, to help give them a chance of a job once they leave us. We have a computer, so they can practise typing.'

'Only one?' said Jake, trying not to look as shocked as he felt. Passing the kitchen and dormitories, he saw that the girls were sleeping on rush mats on the floor and living off maize meal and chicken scraps. He couldn't understand why they all looked so happy.

'We're lucky to have that,' said Dr Katenge. 'To be honest with you, Mr Meyer, it's not a priority. Most of these girls are from rural communities – villages where the RUF arrived one day, maiming and killing and raping – which are now slowly rebuilding.'

Jake wondered guiltily whether his specific diamonds had contributed to this death and destruction, but said nothing.

'Unfortunately, in Moslem culture there is no place for these children born of rape, or their mothers,' said Dr Katenge. 'They're considered an embarrassment, a shameful reminder of a past that everybody in Sierra Leone wants to forget.'

They were back in her office now, a simple whitewashed room with a desk, four filing cabinets and a big hamper of children's books and teddies stuffed in the corner. Dr Katenge gestured for Jake to sit in the lone, fraying armchair, while she brought her own chair around from the other side of the desk.

'Our main role is community liaison,' she told him. 'We train counsellors to go back to these villages. We talk to the grandmothers; they're often the key. If we can get the grandmother to hold a child, just once, that's often all it takes to forge a bond and break down some of the prejudices keeping these poor girls from their homes.'

Jake looked at her earnestly, uncomfortably conscious of his fifteen-thousand-dollar Rolex burning into his wrist like a brand.

'How can I help?' he asked humbly. 'What do you need?'

Dr Katenge smiled broadly, her straight, white teeth lighting up her pretty, open face. 'Everything.'

Jake had never fancied black girls – even in the old days, he'd never taken advantage of the hookers on offer up at the dealer's mansion – but he thought he could make an exception for Dr Katenge.

'Lots of the international diamond companies are giving money to Sierra Leone now, but it's all for show. They want it to go towards something visible, something they can wave in front of their shareholders, like shiny new school buildings or libraries. They're not interested in small, community projects like ours.'

For the first time, Jake detected a trace of bitterness in her gentle, patient voice.

'These girls don't need a library, or even an education,' she murmured, shaking her head at the stupidity of the world. 'They need their families back.'

'So, what can *I* do?' asked Jake. 'I don't have millions to give,' he added hastily, thinking of Danny's disintegrating business and mounting divorce-attorney fees, 'but I would like to help.'

'Air-conditioning for the centre would cost about five thousand dollars,' she cut to the chase. 'Counsellors' wages run to around the same, per year.'

'That's all?' Jake looked amazed.

'That's all,' she smiled. 'We receive contraceptives free, but we could use more of everything else: antibiotics for the babies, paracetamol, whatever you can get. We need beds, sheets, toys, clothes for the kids. I could go on.'

'That's OK,' said Jake, looking at his watch. He'd sell it as soon as he got back to the States. 'I'll get you the air-conditioning tomorrow. And I'll wire you a year's wages for two more counsellors before the end of the month.'

Dr Katenge looked at him quizzically, as if seeing him properly for the first time.

'Thank you,' she said, shaking his hand. 'You're a good man, Mr Meyer.'

'Trust me, Dr Katenge,' Jake laughed. 'I'm not.'

She walked him out to the street, past a waiting room full of tired women, all hoping for a meal from the St Catherine's drop-in centre.

'You know, the most important thing you can do for us,' she told Jake, as he climbed into his rented four-by-four, 'is to spread the word in America. The American women who wear diamond rings from Sierra Leone on their fingers? They don't know what's happening here. If they knew, they'd help us. They'd help my girls.'

Jake thought about Julia Brookstein and her diamond-obsessed cronies and wasn't so sure.

'Listen, there's something I haven't told you,' he said, his mouth dry with embarrassment. 'I'm a diamond dealer myself. I've bought stones from here, in the past, from some pretty terrible people. So, if you don't want my money—'

She stopped him, laying a hand on his arm.

'The past is the past,' she said gently. 'We're very grateful for your money, Mr Meyer, believe me. Drive safely.'


Back in his room at the Cape Sierra, a complex of beach villas with the dubious reputation as the best hotel in Sierra Leone, Jake peeled off his sweaty clothes and showered before settling down on the bed to check his messages.

There were only four: two from Danny, wanting to know when Jake would be back with the diamonds and how much over the odds he'd had to pay to follow Scarlett's strict new ethical guidelines, one from his mother, Minty, reminding him to take his malaria tablets, and one from the girl he'd been screwing on and off in LA, demanding to know what the hell he thought he was playing at, disappearing on her like that without so much as a phone call.

'I know it's difficult, like, with Richard,' she said, her whiney, vacuous voice slicing into the dry, air-conditioned atmosphere like a razor. 'But I thought you and I had something special. Guess I was wrong.'

'Guess you were,' said Jake aloud, switching off his phone, but not before deleting her number from his address book. Silly cow. This always happened when he slept with a woman more than twice. They got clingy. He really must stick to his own rules next time.

Opening the minibar, he pulled out a warm Budweiser – nothing in the fridge was cold. The electricity must have gone off again while he was at the orphanage – and drank it, trying to think about the things he'd seen today and block out his disappointment that Scarlett hadn't bothered to ring.

It was her Jimmy Choo thing at the Chateau tonight. She'd done well, putting that together at such short notice. He ought to ring, say congratulations, see how things had gone. But he couldn't bring himself to do it, knowing that Magnus would be there, hovering in the background like an overgrown weed, no doubt slagging him off to Scarlett like he always did.

Recently his innate dislike of Magnus had blossomed into something more sinister, or at least more all-consuming. He couldn't put his finger on it, but he simply didn't trust the guy. The self-satisfaction would have been bad enough on its own. But the way he had Scarlett running around after him like a puppy, the way he controlled every aspect of their relationship from the geography to the timing ... it all smelt faintly fishy to Jake. An expert in infidelity himself, he knew the signs of a fellow cheater: the secrecy, the un-predictable flashes of romance, the righteous indignation when challenged. If Magnus were being faithful to Scarlett, he'd eat his hat. Of course, proving his suspicions was quite another matter.

Closing his eyes, he lay back against the pillow. Stupid bloody Magnus. Within minutes he was asleep, beer bottle still in hand, dreaming about the classroom at St

Catherine's, machete-wielding rebels, and Scarlett, running naked through the garden of the Chateau Marmont.

# Thirteen

Brogan O'Donnell surveyed the eleven nervous, sycophantic faces around the boardroom table with a feeling of immense wellbeing.

He had friends – successful, shrewd businessmen – who'd seen their authority over their own companies eroded over the years at the hands of a difficult, headstrong board, and determined never to make the same mistake himself. Unlike other CEOs, he wasn't necessarily looking for the brightest and best at O'Donnell Mining Corp. Why shell out millions of dollars in options and incentives trying to poach some whiz-kid with a Harvard MBA out of Goldman Sachs or Tyler Stanley, just to have them turn around and try to knife you in the back the second you gave them a chance? Headhunters were always going on about hiring guys who were entrepreneurial and hungry. But Brogan knew how easily a board of eleven hungry guys could turn him into lunch. There was only room for one entrepreneur at O'Donnell, and he was it. Give him a bunch of solid, reliable yes-men any day.

Not that any of them had much to complain about. It was November now, which meant year-end bonuses were around the corner, and everyone at the table knew that they'd enjoyed a stellar year. The Yakutia mines were now more profitable than ever, far outstripping the volatile African holdings of most of O'Donnell's major rivals, and the international diamond markets were as buoyant as Pamela Anderson's breasts in the Dead Sea.

Without consulting any of them, Brogan had committed five per cent of the year's profits – a big chunk of change – to high-profile charity causes in both Africa and Siberia. But if anyone had nursed private doubts over the move, they felt a whole lot better now. In a matter of months, they'd seen the firm's image shift from that of heartless Yankee plunderer, to concerned, responsible global player. And it was all thanks to a few well-placed magazine features, and one hugely sympathetic Fox News interview, depicting Brogan as the new caring face of capitalism.

Not only had the shift gone down well with share-holders, but it had bolstered Brogan's image in the divorce courts too. With Diana unwilling to use pictures of her beaten face as evidence – 'I'm sorry,' she told Danny, 'but it's below the belt. He'd never done anything like that before, and that isn't why I left him' – there was nothing to stop Brogan's excellent divorce attorney from painting his client as the wronged, innocent party. Anyone attending the hearings would have thought him the most devoted husband on earth, showering his young wife with every conceivable material comfort, undergoing humiliating and painful fertility treatment to provide her with the child she so craved, only to have it thrown back in his face when she ran off into the sunset with a handsome business rival.

That was the part Danny liked most – hearing himself described as Brogan's 'rival', when he could barely afford laces for his shoes. It was right up there with Brogan's claim that he'd never been 'physically or emotionally' unfaithful to Diana. But again, without proof (Diana had no pictures or written evidence of his many affairs, and the girls in-volved had all been paid handsomely for their silence) there wasn't a lot they could do to stop the PR rollercoaster from rebranding the former monster as a latter-day saint.

In fact, of all the things that had gone right this year – O'Donnell's results, Premiere being named newcomer of the year for their newly opened Cape Town office, the amazing sex he was having with his latest twenty-three-year-old Slovakian girlfriend – it was crushing Diana and

Danny in court, and financially, that had given him the most pleasure.

After Diana left him he'd spent a week locked away in Telluride, refusing to speak to anyone, not even Aidan Leach. Winded with shock and grief, terrified by how keenly he felt her loss, for the first time in his adult life he wasn't sure what to do. Diana had had years to say goodbye to the marriage, watching it unravel like a snagged sweater from her lonely prison on Park Avenue with each endless passing day. But their problems, and her unhappiness, came as a bolt from the blue to Brogan. Every day, he waited for her to return, like a bewildered toddler lost in a supermarket aisle. When she didn't, he felt the closest he'd ever come to panic, in equal parts frightened and embarrassed by his despair.

In the end Aidan had flown up to Colorado himself, forced his way into the chalet and demanded that Brogan see him. It was the first and last time that Brogan would submit to another man's demands. But he knew he needed help – a cool, rational, trustworthy head to do all the things he couldn't. And Aidan was absolutely that guy. Standing there in his cheap suit, his Adam's apple bobbing up and down grotesquely as he exhorted his boss to get a grip, to get mad, then even, then vengeful against the son-of-a-bitch who'd stolen his wife, instead of laying around in bed snivelling like Howard Hughes, Aidan's physical ugliness struck Brogan as forcefully as if he'd never laid eyes on the guy before.

It seemed that had been his problem all along: not seeing things that were right in front of his face. But Aidan's intervention was exactly the jolt he needed. Twenty-four hours later, dressed, shaved and rested, thanks to the prescription knock-out pill Leach had insisted he take, Brogan was boarding his private jet for New York with a single thought on his mind: destroying Danny Meyer.

In the event, it had been almost too easy. He hadn't had

to go through any of the time-consuming intimidation and skulduggery he'd used on Scarlett Drummond Murray in London. Danny's market was New York, Brogan's back yard, a city where a quiet word from Aidan on his behalf had every jeweller, cutter and dealer on the street jumping to heel, dropping Danny from their Rolodexes like a burning turd without a backward glance. Having cut his income supply off at the knees, and effectively frozen Diana's funds, Brogan could sit back and leave the rest to his divorce attorney, another contact of Aidan's, and a master at spinning out disputes for so long that the weaker, poorer party got priced out of the game. Last he heard, Danny and Diana were living in borderline penury somewhere in Brooklyn, contemplating decamping to England. That'd show the bitch what life was like without the added security blanket of his money.

'Any other business? Or are we done here, gentlemen?'

Mickey O'Connor, the CFO, cast his pale, watery eyes nervously around the table. Once considered a dynamo in the diamond business, three years working for Brogan had transformed him into a nervous wreck, albeit a wealthy one. Pale and weak chinned, the shoulders of his suit jacket permanently dusted with dandruff like icing sugar on a chocolate cake, Mickey was a mere shadow of his former vibrant self. Brogan's management style – capriciously alternating praise and scalding public humiliation, the better to keep his execs on their toes – had reduced him to an almost childlike state, scared to open his mouth in his boss's presence. Even something as simple as concluding a board meeting had the potential to turn into an excruciating, emasculating ordeal, and Brogan's face today had given nothing away as to his ever-changing mood.

'Uh-uh.'

'Not from me.'

'Don't think so.'

Happily his colleagues seemed as anxious as he was

to bring this thing to a close and retreat to the safety of their big glass-walled offices, where they could order their secretaries around for a few hours until their balls grew back.

'In that case,' said Mickey, risking a smile, 'meeting adjourned.'

Brogan watched them all file out. He contemplated calling Mickey and a couple of the others back at the last minute, to rake them over the coals for some invented misdemeanour. They'd all gotten off lightly this afternoon. But he had a date with Natalia tonight – to his own surprise as much as anyone's, she'd morphed from casual fuck to bona-fide girlfriend since Diana left him – and he wanted time to work out before he saw her.

Outside it was a grey, nondescript winter's day. The sky was already getting dark, and a stream of toxic drizzle pounded against the floor-to ceiling windows with relentless monotony. For a flicker of an instant, Brogan felt his stomach churning with nerves at the prospect of returning home to the apartment. Natalia had steadfastly refused to move in with him. Her independence was probably the key factor still holding his interest – that and the naked envy in other men's eyes when he walked into a restaurant with her on his arm – but her decision left him stuck in a space haunted with memories of Diana and his marriage.

It'd be OK tonight, though. Freddie, his trainer, would be waiting to distract him. And he'd bring Natalia back for sex after dinner, so he wouldn't have to spend a miserable evening alone.

The last to leave the boardroom, as always, he strolled along the corridor to his own corner office. Outside, Rose, his PA, was taking a rare coffee break, but she hurriedly stuffed the gossip magazine she was reading into a drawer when he approached.

'It's OK,' he laughed. 'You don't have to hide it. You're the one person in this office who's earned a little R&R.'

Nervously, she removed the magazine from the drawer.

'What is this shit, anyway?' Brogan teased her, turning over the copy of *Star* with amused curiosity. '"Brangelina on the Rocks?"' He frowned at the sensational headline. 'Come on, Rosie! You're smarter than that.'

'It's just for fun,' she mumbled, wincing as he flicked through it. For a few pages his wry smile remained fixed. Then abruptly, it vanished, replaced by a knitted brow and a tightening of the lips that she knew spelt trouble.

'Where did you get this?' he demanded. He wasn't teasing now.

'The news-stand downstairs, sir,' she replied meekly. 'In the lobby.'

'I don't want to see this publication anywhere else in this building. Do you understand me?' He was speaking loudly enough now for every head in the office to turn and stare.

Rose, who knew better than to speak when the boss was venting, merely nodded.

'And you can tell that little Mexican fucker, Rico or whatever the fuck his name is, that he just lost his franchise. If that news-stand isn't gone by tomorrow morning, I'm calling immigration on his ass.'

Slamming the door of his office, Brogan drew the blinds so that no one could see in, and opened the magazine again at the page that had so offended him. The picture itself was small, one shot amongst six or seven others in an 'as seen' spread, where readers post in their own snaps of celebrities out and about. Even the caption was harmless enough: 'Celebrity designer and former model Scarlett Drummond Murray enjoys some down time with Diana O'Donnell and friends.'

The snap was of Scarlett at a beach cafe in Santa Monica, laughing alongside Diana. Also at the table, but with only their backs in shot, were Jake and Danny Meyer.

Brogan had seen plenty of pictures of Diana and Danny

together. Both Aidan and his divorce attorney had insisted on continuing to have them followed, and had gone to some lengths to harden Brogan emotionally, forcing him to look at the images and use them to feed his anger. He was also well aware that Scarlett and Jake were now in business together in LA, and that despite his best efforts, Flawless was continuing to thrive. Yet somehow, in all his fevered, jealous imaginings, he hadn't pictured a scenario in which Diana made up a happy foursome with *both* the Meyer brothers and that bitch of a girl.

His own betrayals forgotten, he felt winded with righteous indignation. Wasn't it enough for her to leave him, to run off with that British bastard, humiliating him in front of the entire industry? Did she have to rub salt into the wound as well, by buddying up with a woman she knew was trying to ruin him, to undo everything he'd ever worked for?

But what irked him the most, though he couldn't admit it, even to himself, was how happy Diana looked. Part of him, he now realised, had been nursing a small, desperate hope that if Danny became too poor to support her, she would eventually fall out of this infatuation and return to him. He'd tried to convince himself that he was happy with Natalia, and his newfound freedom. But one glimpse of that picture, of Diana's make-up-less, smiling, carefree face, exposed his so-called happiness for the fantasy that it was.

He wanted his wife back. Wanted it more than he'd ever wanted anything in his life. But he couldn't have her, and she knew it, and now she was laughing at him.

Unable to hurt Diana, he settled for the next best thing. He would destroy the livelihood of the man who'd sold Rose the magazine. He would fire anyone he caught reading it. Picking up the phone, he left a furious message for Aidan:

'Scarlett Drummond Murray. Why the fuck is she still alive?' he barked. 'I'm tired of reading how her shit don't stink, all right? Find me some dirt. On her, her family, that motherfucker Meyer she works with. Don't you fucking call me till you have something I can use.'

Slamming down the receiver, he picked up the magazine and looked at the offending picture one more time, photographing it for his memory. Then he ripped it out, tore it into shreds and dropped it in the trash where soon, he hoped, all four of those smiling sons of bitches would be joining it.

If Brogan could have seen what a shitty day Danny was having, a stone's throw across the water from his office, it might have taken the edge off his anger.

Walking back from the subway, his clothes soaked and feet throbbing with pain and cold after another wasted day pounding the pavements, Danny was as close to despair as his naturally sunny nature allowed.

How had it come to this?

A year ago, he'd been a partner in an established, respected diamond-dealing business, with a good track record and a list of loyal, regular clients as long as his arm. OK, so he'd had a few squabbles with Jake over the simulants. And Tyler Brett had put a dent in their profits that had only recently begun to be repaired with Flawless. They hadn't been making the kind of silly money they had been pulling in during the tech boom of the late nineties, when every nerd with a dot com idea was out buying diamonds for women light years out of their league. But they were doing all right. He'd been living in a gorgeous apartment, driving a flash car, and going out to five-star restaurants whenever the mood took him. Like an idiot, he'd imagined that all he needed to complete his happiness was Diana by his side. Little had he thought that winning Diana would mean losing everything – absolutely *everything* – else.

At first, the idea of battling it out with Brogan seemed almost romantic. He'd long ago resigned himself to the fact that Diana would probably walk away from her marriage with less than she brought into it. Brogan had all his money tied up in a maze of offshore accounts so interminably complicated that no judge would be able to get through it. There were no children, and, officially at least, Diana had taken the fall as being the guilty party in the break-up. What he *hadn't* counted on was the degree to which his own wealth would be depleted. How he would have to watch fifteen years of work unravel terrifyingly quickly, and his assets and savings being sucked into the insatiable vortex of a divorce case that, no matter how little they asked for or how many outrageous concessions they agreed, never seemed to end.

'Spare any change, man?' The wino on the corner accosted him with a beery-breathed stagger. Guiltily, Danny reached into the sodden pocket of his overcoat and pulled out a solitary dollar bill, pressing it into the man's hand without stopping. Plenty of people are worse off than you, he told himself sternly, as a cab splashed filthy water all down his right side. Plenty of people don't *have* a home to go to tonight, never mind a gorgeous, patient, loving woman cooking them spaghetti on a shitty two-ring stove, a woman who had never once complained about what *she'd* lost by following him blindly on this great romantic adventure.

It had taken Diana a long time to emerge from the shadow of her guilt about leaving Brogan. But having gone through the soul-searching and the pain, she'd emerged completely committed to Danny and the new life she'd chosen. It was almost as if, having risked so much, she felt a duty, a burning need to be happy, no matter what arrows life hurled at her.

Ironically, Danny was the one who found things tougher. Try as he might to talk himself round, his day-to-day misery refused to listen to reason. He hated their new apartment. Hated the filthy stairwell leading up to it, hated the street below with all its depressing reminders of poverty: the launderettes and pawn shops, prostitutes, drug dealers. He hated the crappy Ikea furniture, the plastic blinds, the heating that belched out broiled air like a furnace all night so they couldn't sleep, but shut off during the day, forcing Diana into the local Starbucks just for the warmth. Most of all, he hated himself, for having brought her to this godforsaken shit hole – and for constantly snapping at her, as if his inadequacy were somehow her fault.

Diana's family had offered to help out until the divorce settlement came through, but grateful as they were, they'd both rejected that idea. Able-bodied, middle aged-adults didn't take handouts from their parents. And besides, there was every chance that the settlement, if it ever came, would be too small to cover their legal costs, never mind provide excess funds to pay back the Framptons' generosity.

Tonight, vowed Danny, stopping by the liquor store to pick up a cheap bottle of red and a packet of fags – thanks to bloody Brogan he was back on the smokes, nearly a pack a day – they wouldn't argue. He wouldn't spend the entire night moaning about his day, about the miles he'd walked and tens of doors he'd knocked on without making a single sale. Jake had left him a voicemail from South Africa, on the last night of his long trip, excited about the new stones he was bringing back. But Danny wouldn't bitch to Diana about how it didn't matter, how he wouldn't be able to shift them even if they were the most perfect, conflict-free diamonds on earth. He knew that if he didn't stop taking his frustrations out on her, she'd leave him, whatever she might say to the contrary. And right now, he wouldn't blame her. He'd leave himself if someone gave him the option.

After stabbing at the door three or four times, the key slipping around in his wet fingers like a live fish, he finally managed to let himself in, and trudged slowly up the stairs to the apartment. As soon as he opened the door he was hit by a burst of warm air, packing a punch of delicious cooking smells – garlic, onion, paprika. Moments later, Diana's smiling, flushed face appeared round the kitchen door.

'It'll be ready in ten,' she said, globules of homemade tomato sauce dripping from the wooden spoon in her hand onto the peeling linoleum floor. 'I left you the hot water. Go have a shower and then we'll eat.'

Christ, she was beautiful. Even with her hair scraped back, a face full of steam, and that vile butcher's apron on over her jeans and T-shirt, she looked a knockout, a princess as out of place in the apartment's falling-down kitchen as Cinderella, sweeping her ugly step-sisters' floor in rags. She deserved so much better.

'Smells good,' he said, forcing the cheer into his voice.

'I got it from that old recipe book of your mother's. I'm sure it won't be as good as her version,' said Diana, humbly. 'But I figured I'd give it a shot.'

Dumping his clothes in the laundry hamper, he noticed that Diana had emptied it since this morning; unlike him she seemed to positively revel in the novelty of poverty and the hitherto unknown demands of domestic life. He stepped into the shower, and let the steaming jets of water work their magic. He wished Diana hadn't brought up the subject of his mother. That was another thing he felt guilty about. Both Minty and the usually neutral Rudy had formed an immediate, lasting dislike of Diana – Diana whom they'd never met, and who had no idea of the forces of Meyer family hostility ranged against her. The truth was his parents would probably have had a problem with any girl he planned to marry, especially if she wasn't Jewish. But Diana had compounded this sin by being American, already married to someone else, and (as Minty saw it) the root cause of all Danny's financial troubles. In less than a month, the two women would meet for the first time when they flew back to London for Christmas, an event Danny was looking forward to about as much as root canal surgery without anaesthetic.

Ten minutes later, feeling marginally better in some dry clothes, he came back into the living room. His heart melted when he saw the table. Diana had lit candles, the cheap tea lights you could buy in packs of two hundred from Costco, and spread the Formica fold-out diner with a bed sheet, doubled over to make a table cloth. A bunch of pale pink tulips sat jauntily in a plain glass jug, which she'd dressed up with a single piece of dark-blue ribbon, and the white Ikea plates gleamed like moons between the stainless steel knives and forks, guarding them like sentries. His wine was open, the burgundy glass bottle looking particularly warm and welcoming in the candlelight, and a steaming, aromatic clay pot of spaghetti and sauce bubbled merrily in the centre of the table. It was tough to make the flat's single, down-at heel reception room look inviting. But Diana, driven by love and a desperate desire to cheer and comfort him, had managed it. Sitting down, it was all Danny could do not to weep with guilt.

'How'd it go today?' Diana asked, ladling a hefty spoonful of pasta onto his plate. She'd removed the apron, and changed from the jeans and T-shirt into a clinging navy jersey dress that caressed her waist and high, round-apple breasts, sexy without being slutty.

'Good,' he lied, not wanting to ruin the positive atmosphere she'd gone to such trouble creating. 'Better.'

Helping herself to a portion half the size of his, she shook her head when he offered her wine.

'Not for me,' she said, beaming. He'd been so blown away by the little-house-on-the-prairie welcome, he hadn't stopped to notice the way she was staring at him. But he noticed it now: her entire face seemed aglow, as if she were willing him to give her some sort of sign, the answer to a question that she hadn't actually asked.

'What?' He laughed nervously. 'What happened? Do I have spinach in my teeth?'

She shook her head, still beaming.

'Did Brogan sign the papers?' Danny heard himself asking, appalled by the desperate hope in his voice.

'No,' she said calmly. 'Not that.' Then all of a sudden, out of nowhere, she burst into tears. 'I'm pregnant!' she sobbed, laughing and crying at the same time. 'Oh, Danny, please be happy. Please, please tell me you're happy?'

'I'm happy,' he said automatically, pulling her into his arms, partly because it seemed to be expected of him, and partly so that she wouldn't see the panic writ large across his face. They were barely keeping their heads above water as it was. How the hell could they afford a child? 'I'm a bit shocked,' he admitted, 'but of course I'm happy. That's amazing.'

'It's more than amazing.' She pulled out of his embrace so he could see her face, tear-stained but at the same time awash with relief that he shared her joy. 'It's a miracle. Brogan and I have been trying for almost ten years. We've tried everything: IVF, snake oil, hypnosis ... and then you come along and bam! that's it. Maybe this was God's plan all along? Maybe it wasn't right for me to have kids with Brogan, in that atmosphere? Maybe I was supposed to wait for you.'

'Maybe,' said Danny, staring at the rapidly congealing spaghetti in his bowl and wishing he could block out the sound of prison doors clanging shut. For some irrational reason, he remembered a documentary he'd seen about 9/11, where one of the firemen inside the building had described the steady 'thud ... thud ... thud' of the floors above him collapsing on top of one another, certain that when he heard the last thud, he'd be crushed to death, and praying that that death would be quick. He loved Diana. He really did. But recently his life had started sounding like one long series of thuds. And the baby was the loudest of all.

'I saw my gynaecologist today, and he confirmed I'm in the early stages; can you believe it?' she said excitedly.

'Officially we shouldn't tell people till we're past twelve weeks. But I really want to tell my mom, and yours. I can't keep a secret like that all through Christmas. Hey!' Her eyes lit up. 'If it's a girl, we could call her Araminta! After your mom.'

Danny closed his eyes, and tried to find his happy place.

'One step at a time, eh?' he said gently, kissing her. 'One step at a time.'

# Fourteen

Scarlett gazed out of the 747's grimy plastic porthole window and tried to shake the depression creeping over her, mirroring the brooding grey storm clouds outside.

'Thank you for your patience, ladies and gents.' The captain's voice rang out over the speaker system, full of false jollity. 'I'm afraid air traffic have just told us we've got to keep circling for about another ten minutes. Another plane has taken our slot, apparently, but we should be on the ground by half past three, so do bear with us.'

A collective groan rose from the passenger cabin. After eleven hours in an overcrowded plane full of young families returning home for Christmas, the mothers with sick in their hair and kids in various stages of meltdown, nobody was in a particularly patient mood. Scarlett, although in no particular hurry to deal with Heathrow's baggage reclaim hall, also wanted to get off the plane, which had begun to feel stiflingly claustrophobic.

It was the first time she'd been back home in a year, and already it felt like a let-down. If only she'd made it back in the summer, when she was riding high with Flawless, Trade Fair's Siberian campaign was taking off, and things were still new and exhilarating with Magnus. But of course, she'd been too busy to take a break back then. Now, in the winter, when the world had shut up shop for Christmas and she finally had a week to herself, everything seemed to be going wrong.

Well, all right, perhaps not *everything*. The store was still making a solid profit. She'd had a late run of Christmas orders, some of them for complicated, hundred-thousand-dollar or more pieces, which was gratifying (if a little exhausting) right before she took off for the holidays. Working late into the night in her workroom up at Nancy's cottage, with Boxford snoring and farting contentedly at her heels, she'd had little time to brood on the other, less gratifying aspects of her life. But there was nothing like a long-haul flight to provide one with brooding time.

After an encouraging start, Trade Fair's momentum in the US seemed to have stalled. Scarlett had spent months working with Andy Gordon on a joint piece about Brogan O'Donnell's cancer-stricken Siberian workers for NPR. They'd been paid for the work, so they couldn't officially complain, but every week the air time was pushed back, and it now looked like the story wouldn't run at all.

'You mustn't be too disheartened,' Andy told her, over one of their many long midnight chats on Skype. 'This sort of thing is very common in radio. Print media's even worse. You just have to keep flinging mud at the wall and hope that, eventually, some of it sticks.'

But Scarlett's flinging arm was getting tired and Brogan O'Donnell's starched, Ralph Lauren shirt still wasn't looking remotely mud-splattered. In fact, recently he seemed to have started selling himself as the diamond industry's Mr Nice Guy. From the Fox News interview he did a few months ago, you'd have thought he was the next Mahatma Gandhi, not a modern-day version of a tyrannical Victorian factory owner. He and Rupert Murdoch must be golf buddies or something.

Then, last month, she'd had two serious setbacks. *Vanity Fair* cut the piece they'd been planning to run in their February, pre-Oscar issue, showcasing the much talked-about pictures for Trade Fair's new Russian campaign; and Ingrid Olafssen, the Swedish supermodel who'd been on the point of signing on as the face for both Flawless and Trade Fair, suddenly pulled out of her contract. Once again, Brogan O'Donnell's foul stench oozed around both these roadblocks like raw sewage. Apparently, he'd poached Ingrid away from her agency, Elite, for an eye-watering amount of money.

She felt her stomach lurch as, without warning, the captain swung the plane down through the top layer of clouds. They must have been cleared to land at last. Gripping the sides of her seat as the cabin rattled around, she wondered if this was what it felt like for animals on their way to the slaughterhouse – bumping fearfully along in the back of a dark lorry, their fate entirely out of their own hands – and felt a pang of guilt about the turkey sandwich she'd just eaten. Then she thought how hard Jake would have laughed if he'd overheard her train of thought, and looked out of the window again, trying to pinpoint St John's Wood in the dizzying cityscape below.

She hadn't heard from him at all in eighteen days. Not that she was counting or anything. But it was by far the longest they'd gone without speaking since Flawless opened, and she couldn't help but feel faintly bereft.

They hadn't discussed it, but she'd totally assumed that after his Africa trip he'd fly back to LA with the diamonds, and that the two of them would head out to London together. It wasn't a prospect she'd been looking forward to. Having flown with Jake before, she knew how irritating he would be, shamelessly feeling up the prettier stewardesses, burying himself in the latest copy of *Forever* whenever she tried to talk to him about anything serious, falling asleep the moment he slipped his eye-patch on after dinner, and proceeding to snore loudly next to her for the remainder of the flight. And yet now that she'd been spared the ordeal – from Cape Town he'd decided to go straight to Europe, visiting clients in Paris and Madrid before flying on to London – she felt as though he'd somehow let her down. As if a vital piece of her Christmas was missing, and it was all Jake Meyer's fault.

Although the person she was really upset with was

Magnus. With less than a week's notice, the bastard had blithely called to inform her that he'd decided to spend the holidays with his parents in Vail, and wouldn't now be coming to Scotland after all.

'But what am I supposed to do at Drumfernly for ten whole days without you?' wailed Scarlett. 'I only agreed to stay so long because you said you'd be there.'

'Come on, honey. You haven't seen your folks in a year. It'll be fun to catch up,' said Magnus glibly. He seemed to have conveniently blacked out his memories of Caroline, and how much 'fun' she could be.

'*Fun*? Are you out of your mind?' Scarlett pleaded. 'You can't just dump me with them, Magnus. You promised.'

'I know, I know. But my folks are old,' he said, in his best, caring-son voice. 'I'm all they have.'

'Come off it. Your mother's barely sixty,' Scarlett shot back scathingly, 'and your dad climbed Mont Blanc last year. They're hardly in their dotage. Surely they can spare you for one lousy Christmas? Tell them you already made plans.'

But it was obvious she was flogging a dead horse. And, though it pained her to admit it, she was really more annoyed with him for bailing out selfishly at the last minute than she was distraught at the prospect of being denied his company. Certainly his presence at Drumfernly would have made the holiday more bearable. But how much of that was because he could have acted as a buffer between her and her family, and how much was because she actually wanted to be with him, she honestly wasn't sure. Somewhere along the line, the joy seemed to have gone out of their relationship. But right now, with Brogan yapping like a Rottweiler at her heels, she didn't have the mental or emotional energy to try to revive it.

It was a rocky landing. After swaying the 747 to and fro like one of those horrid pirate ship rides at the fairground, the pilot slammed down onto the tarmac with all the grace and subtlety of an elephant on an ice rink. Thank God she'd left Boxie in LA with Nancy. He'd have had a heart attack stuck in the hold, sedatives or no sedatives.

'Well, ladies and gents, here we are at last.' The pilot sounded awfully chipper for someone who'd just narrowly escaped death. 'It's a brisk two degrees Celsius outside, it's pissing with rain, and we've just heard, for those of you that are interested, that Great Britain came last in the Olympic speed skating this afternoon. Yes, that's right, *last*. Behind Samoa. What can I say? Welcome home, and Merry Christmas.'

Cameron auto-locked the doors on his new Porsche from the inside and tried not to panic.

You heard about these things all the time. Wealthy, white professionals being targeted by gangs of black youths, stabbed in the heart for the sake of a mobile phone, or a few lousy quid's worth of cash in their wallets. How much more satisfying a target must he make, broken down in his hundred-thousand-pound car on the outskirts of Canary Wharf, home to all the fat-cat investment bankers that these so-called 'hoodies' hated with such violent passion.

'Go away!' he yelped, as the two tall figures in jogging suits approached his driver's side window. 'Go away or I'll call the police.'

But they kept coming – three of them, he could see now, all with their heads down – moving like snakes along the shadow of the underpass, surrounding the car on all sides.

'Don't hurt me!' he whimpered, cringing down in his seat as one of them tapped on the glass. 'You can have the car. Take whatever you want. Just please don't hurt me. I have a wife and child at home!'

Closing his eyes tight, like a frightened child, the next thing he heard was laughter, raucous laughter, echoing around him in the darkness.

'Get out, you prat,' said a familiar voice. 'It's us.'

'Rob?' The relief was so overwhelming, Cameron thought he might be physically sick. 'Christ alive, you scared me.'

'No kidding!' laughed the voice. Pulling back the hood on his sweatshirt, he revealed himself as Robert Allen, one of Cameron's teammates at Goldman. 'Ten more seconds and you'd have shit your pants, I reckon.'

The two guys with him sneered knowingly. They were also from GS, associates from the Equity Capital Markets desk whom Cameron knew by sight but not by name. Chances were they were called Chip or Chuck or some other suitably American, frat-boy name, he thought bitterly. Certainly they were exactly the type of guy he'd pray *not* to run into whilst cowering behind the wheel like a pussy.

For all his grandstanding to Scarlett and the rest of his family, Cameron was not popular at work, and he knew it. The atmosphere on the trading floor of an investment bank was not dissimilar to public school, or (he imagined) prison. The players might be older and, in theory at least, more mature – but the play itself was the same: an endless game of one-upmanship, with turf wars raging between dominant and less dominant groups. Rob was one of the leaders of the 'cool' group in M&A – the guys who spent their Saturday nights at Soho House, dated well-known actresses or heiresses, and partied on each others' yachts in St Tropez every summer. Primarily American, this group also contained a few of the flashier French traders, and of course the Italians, who were all so uniformly handsome they could never have been anything other than popular.

Cameron, by contrast, was one of the very lowliest members of the 'also-ran' group, a miscellaneous posse of nerds, losers and married guys, most of them British, who pretended to look down on Rob and his ilk as stupid and shallow, but who secretly longed to sleep with coked-up lingerie models half their age and be arrested for speeding at the Gumball rally in Monte Carlo.

'Trouble with the old wheels, eh?' said Chip or Chuck, his white teeth flashing cruelly in the darkness. 'Serves you right for being such a cheapskate. You shoulda sprung for a Ferrari, man.'

'"I got a wife and child"?' mocked Rob. 'Fuck, Drummond, have you got no shame at all?'

'His wife came with a free pump from Ann Summers,' quipped the third guy, not wanting to be out-done by his buddies. 'But where'd he buy a blow-up kid, that's what I'd like to know!'

'Ha ha,' said Cameron, his earlier relief at being out of physical danger draining away as the full magnitude of his humiliation hit home. None of them would let him forget this at work tomorrow morning. 'What are you doing out here anyway, dressed like that? I thought you were muggers.'

'Going for a run,' said Rob, peeling off his sweatshirt to reveal a Nike vest top and an upper body that wouldn't have looked out of place on the front cover of *Men's Health* magazine. 'You should try it some time. Good for the old ticker, you know? I'd say yours could do with a bit of toughening up.'

Vain tosser, thought Cameron, as the three of them began giggling again like schoolboys. But he restrained himself, sticking to polite small talk and laughing off his cowardice as best he could as they helped him push the car to the nearest lay-by. Once there, he waved them off as cheerfully as possible – they were still laughing and sending him up mercilessly as they jogged away, the bastards – and called the AA.

It was only half past four, but the last of the winter sunlight had already disappeared behind the horizon, and the temperature was dropping like a stone. Pulling his cashmere coat more tightly around him against the wind and drizzle, Cameron waited gloomily for rescue, glad of the hustle and bustle of the McDonald's opposite and the weak orange glow from the lamp-posts, that somehow made him feel far safer than he had done alone on the road.

He was well aware that he'd overreacted in front of Rob and the other guys, and that he'd pay for it dearly in the office. But despite being one of nature's cowards, he was pretty sure he wouldn't have been so shaken up if it hadn't been for all the other weird things happening to him lately. It had got to the point where even something as innocent as a car breakdown was starting to feel like part of a conspiracy.

It had started about a month ago, with a break-in at his flat – not in itself such an unusual event. Cameron lived in one of the most expensive parts of Chelsea and anyone watching the house would have known he worked long hours. But the weird thing was that the thieves hadn't taken anything, not even the wad of cash he'd left lying out on the kitchen table for the char lady. The papers on his desk had been disturbed, and his desktop computer was switched off – odd, when he was pretty sure he'd left it on hibernate when he left for work that morning. But other than that, it was as if someone had broken in, looked carefully for something specific, and then left, as far as Cameron could tell, empty handed.

He might have forgotten all about this curious incident had it not been for that night the following week, when he could have sworn a black Fiat was tailing him home from Nobu; and then two days later he saw the same car, driving slowly past Pucci Pizza on the King's Road while he was enjoying his usual Saturday pepperoni garlic crust special. It was only after he contacted the police, and was outraged by their lack of concern, bordering, in his opinion, on derision, that he remembered Scarlett, and her wild accusations about Brogan O'Donnell after Bijoux burned down.

Was there more to her claims than he'd imagined? Was it possible that whoever his little sister had so needlessly irritated last year was now extending their long arm of retribution towards him?

He glanced at the clock on his BlackBerry – five fifteen; where the fuck were the AA? – and then at the calendar. Scarlett should have landed at Heathrow three hours ago. As soon as he got this mess with the car sorted out, he'd call and have it out with her. If she wanted to risk her own skin pursuing some hopeless save-the-nig-nogs campaign, that was up to her. But if she thought she could turn his life upside down with impunity, goddamn it she had another think coming.

After a nightmare two hours at Heathrow – BA had some-how managed to lose her luggage, necessitating an endless round of form filling before she could catch the Tube home – Scarlett finally collapsed through the door of her flat at half past six at night.

Christ, it looked depressing. With hindsight, she really ought to have rented the place out. But when she left for LA in January, she'd still been kidding herself that the move was temporary, and getting a tenant felt uncomfortably like admitting defeat. Instead, she'd arranged for Mrs Minton from downstairs to keep an eye on the place and pop in every now and then to open the windows and vacuum up the worst of the dust. This she had clearly done. The whole flat smelled of wood polish and Shake 'n' Vac, and there was some horrid blue gunk down the loo. She'd even gone out and bought a bunch of lilies from the market, in an effort to make the place a little more welcoming, and changed the sheets on Scarlett's ridiculously big bed. But nothing could quite eradicate the feeling of emptiness that hung in the air as Scarlett wandered from room to room. All the warm, homely atmosphere seemed to have been sucked out along with the carpet dust. From the empty grate in the sitting room, to the bare, disinfected fridge, the entire place seemed to be enveloping Scarlett with a cold reproach, as if to say 'and where the hell have *you* been?'

She was desperate to have a bath, but there was no hot

water, and when she went to turn the boiler on the pilot light was dead as a doornail. It was turning out to be that sort of a day. Mooching into the sitting room she turned on all the lights – perhaps some hundred-watt illumination would lift her mood? – and lit a fire with the last of the Tesco extra-long matches, before grabbing the bedspread and blanket from her bed and dragging them onto the sofa. Deciding to order some takeaway – fish and chips from the Pie Shop should hit the spot – she picked up the phone and was surprised to see the red message light flashing. The answerphone's recorded message told people not to leave voicemail here, but to try her LA number. Maybe it was her parents, calling to welcome her home?

Close, but no cigar. Hitting the play button, she found herself greeted by a torrent of abuse from her brother. It was all a bit confusing, but he seemed to be accusing her of having had him followed or some such nonsense. She caught the name O'Donnell, and the tail end of a typical Cameron rant about Trade Fair and how she was in over her head, but she hit three and deleted the rest of the message before she got to the end. Whatever his problem was, she had no doubt he'd fill her in up at Drumfernly this weekend. She was far too tired to deal with it now.

The second call was from Nancy, sounding happy and excited. She deleted that message too, deciding it was quicker to call straight back and hear the good news, whatever it was, in person.

'Omygoditsyou!' Nancy picked up after one ring, in full-on hyperactive mode. Scarlett must have caught her right after her mid-morning quadruple espresso. 'Thank God. Did you get my message? I have *soooo* much to talk to you about.'

Scarlett, feeling desperately weary, was about to explain that she hadn't heard the message, but had barely drawn breath before Nancy started up again.

'He is gorgeous, he is divine. I don't know where to start!' she squealed. Then, as if registering that Scarlett had not yet spoken, added, 'But how are you, sweetie? How was your flight? Must have been nice not to have to listen to Jake "I put the *me* in Meyer" the whole way.'

'It was,' lied Scarlett. 'The flight was fine.'

'OK, good, so, Che Che,' said Nancy, back on message now that the pleasantries were over.

'Who? asked Scarlett.

'Che Che. The guy I told you about.'

'You slept with a guy called *Che Che*? What is he, a maracas player in a Cuban band?'

'Why do you assume I slept with him?' Nancy feigned outrage. 'We only met last night. What are you saying? That I'm some kind of slut?'

'OK,' said Scarlett, 'so you didn't sleep with the maracas player—'

'He is not a maracas player. And of course I fucking *slept* with him,' laughed Nancy. 'Jesus, are you kidding me? With the body that guy had on him? Not to mention his—'

'All right, all right,' said Scarlett. 'I get the picture.'

'The picture' turned out to be a lot more interesting with Che Che than with Nancy's usual conquests. A black African painter – 'not African American, *real* African' as Nancy told her proudly – he'd fled to the States four years ago as a refugee from Sudan, and made a name for himself on the LA art scene.

'He's totally different from everyone else I've dated,' gushed Nancy. 'God, Scar, I wish I could describe him to you. He has this strength, this presence. I think I'm gonna move in with him.'

'Nance,' Scarlett did her best to sound disapproving. 'You've only known the guy twelve hours.'

'I know,' said Nancy, as if amazed by the situation herself. 'But when you know, you know, right? Like you and Magnus?'

261

'I suppose so,' said Scarlett. She didn't want to think about Magnus.

'Anyway, Boxie adored him on sight,' said Nancy. 'The only fly in the ointment is my parents. You know what I mean. They're not exactly ... enlightened.'

Scarlett smiled at the understatement. Mr and Mrs Lorriman were decent people, but they made George Bush look liberal. They'd almost certainly prefer for their only daughter to be abducted by aliens than for her to bring home a black boyfriend – never mind a Sudanese freedom fighter, or whatever this fellow was.

'I wouldn't worry about that yet,' she said kindly. 'Like I say, I'm sure Che Che's wonderful, but you only just met. Maybe he won't have to meet your parents?'

'He will,' said Nancy, seriously. 'I'm telling you, Scar, you don't get it. He's the one. I'm gonna marry this guy.'

The conversation continued in this vein for another five minutes, with Scarlett finally hanging up when Nancy launched into an impromptu ode to Che Che's 'insanely huge' manhood. That was more than even Scarlett could stand on no sleep and an empty stomach.

Deciding a change of air might do her good, she abandoned the takeaway idea and decided to walk to the Pie Shop instead. The rain had stopped, and it was only a ten-minute stroll down Portobello. Nipping into her bedroom to dig out some winter clothes, she pulled the first two sweaters she found on over her head and, teaming them with a pair of comedy Christmas reindeer gloves and matching hat left over from last year's Christmas stocking, headed downstairs.

Opening the front door, she jumped a mile.

'Jesus! Oh my God, you frightened the life out of me.'

There, swaying on her doorstep, his finger on the buzzer to her flat, was Jake.

'Sorry,' he said, stepping back onto the path into the pool of light thrown by the streetlamp. Only then could Scarlett see that his lip was bleeding and a bruise the size and colour of a small plum had formed above his left cheekbone. 'I didn't mean to scare you. Nice hat, by the way.'

Blushing, she pulled the offending article off her head and stuffed it into her jeans pocket.

'What happened?' she asked. She reached up to touch his bruised face, but he instinctively pulled back.

'Oh, nothing,' he said, unconvincingly. 'I fell out with a bloke in the pub, that's all. Arsenal fan, you know what that lot are like.'

'Hmm,' said Scarlett sceptically. 'I see.'

In fact, he'd run into a guy he'd flogged some dodgy diamonds to years ago, quite by chance – a guy who unfortunately wasn't inclined to let bygones be bygones in the spirit of the season, as Jake suggested, and who had declined his offer of a drink with rather more force than Jake felt was strictly necessary.

'D'you want to come in?' said Scarlett, horrified by how pleased she was to see him. 'I think I have some witch hazel and arnica cream in the bathroom. Although they're probably past their sell-by date.'

'That's all right,' said Jake, smiling drunkenly through the pain in his face. 'So am I.'

He followed her back up the stairs, admiring the tight fit of her jeans on her perfect bottom, and wondering what excuse he could offer for his presence on her doorstep, once she got around to asking.

The truth was, he hadn't been entirely honest with her about his movements after his Sierra Leone trip. His original plan was to go to Paris and see some old clients. But after two weeks of obsessing about Magnus, he decided he couldn't stand it any more, and had to do something either to confirm his doubts or lay them to rest. So he'd flown up to Seattle instead. And after a little digging he had uncovered more than even he had bargained for.

It turned out that not only were Magnus and his wife

not divorced, but three months ago they'd moved back in together – hence the 'romantic' hotel breaks with Scarlett. Worse still, they had a two-year-old son.

'Make yourself at home,' said Scarlett, ushering him through into the sitting room where the fire was still blazing. 'I'll see what I can find for you in the bathroom.'

'I could murder a Scotch, if you've got any,' Jake called after her as she disappeared. The numbing effects of the tequila shots he'd been downing in the pub, before things turned nasty with the ex-client, were starting to wear off, and he suddenly felt in need of Dutch courage. On the flight back to London from Seattle he'd been rubbing his hands with glee at the prospect of finally opening Scarlett's eyes about Shag-nus. But now that he was finally here, the thought of causing her pain seemed a lot less palatable. 'Maybe some food if you've got any?'

'Sorry,' she called back. 'I'm completely out of everything.' He could hear various bottles tumbling out of the medicine cupboard on to the tiled bathroom floor and smiled. For someone used to doing such delicate work with her hands, she could be a terrible klutz. 'There's a takeaway menu by the phone. I'll have fish and chips, and a green salad if they've got it. Otherwise mushy peas.'

Half an hour later, his face smeared in arnica and his lip still stinging from the witch hazel Scarlett had insisted on applying, ignoring his yelps of protest ('Oh for heaven's sake stop whingeing. You're worse than Boxford at the vet's'), Jake was still no nearer to telling her what he'd come there to say. Ensconced next to her on the sofa, eating chunky chips smothered in salt and vinegar, and rambling about his Africa trip – he skipped the part about Dr Katenge's orphanage, scared that she might think he was sucking up – he couldn't seem to work out how to begin. *I went to Seattle to snoop on your boyfriend* made him sound like a stalker. *Magnus has a kid* was too blunt. *I'm hopelessly in love with you and can't stand watching you throw your life away on that lying toe-rag,* was probably too honest at this early stage.

'I got some terrific deals in Jo'burg,' he said instead, chickening out again. 'You're gonna die when you see the stones.'

'I'm assuming you got the certificates of authenticity?' said Scarlett, eyeing him sceptically.

'Yes, Mum,' Jake gave a salute. 'All diamonds present and correct. There's nothing to trouble your conscience, don't worry.'

'What about Danny? Did you bring back anything for him?' asked Scarlett. She didn't want to shatter Jake's good mood by probing further into his business ethics.

Jake shook his head. 'No point. The poor sod can't sell a dollar for ninety cents in New York. Brogan's got him over a barrel.' He gave Scarlett a brief run-down of Danny and Diana's financial woes. 'Plus, and this is top, top secret so you can't breathe a word,' he said, dispatching another chip to its doom in the gloomy recesses of his stomach, 'Diana's pregnant.'

'She is?' Scarlett sounded thrilled. 'Oh, how wonderful! Danny must be over the moon.'

'Not so as you'd notice,' confessed Jake. 'I mean, he loves her. But he's feeling the strain, with business going down the shitter and O'Donnell dragging out the divorce. Then there's Mum.'

Because of Minty's decided dislike of her prospective daughter-in-law, Danny had persuaded Diana to keep schtum about the baby, at least until things cooled down. Even so, the atmosphere at Casa Meyer so far this Christmas could only be described as toxic.

'Really?' Scarlett sounded surprised. 'Your mother seemed so warm and funny when I met her. She was lovely to me.'

'That's because you weren't about to lead me down the aisle,' said Jake.

'I should say not!' Scarlett blurted out.

'It's not personal, with Diana,' Jake explained. 'It's just the way it is in families like ours. You're expected to marry a Jewish girl, ideally one whose mum and dad live down the road.'

Scarlett thought of her own parents, particularly her mother's obsession with her marrying a local laird, and nodded in silent understanding. Perhaps her family and Jake's had more in common than she'd first imagined?

'Listen,' said Jake, finally screwing his courage to the sticking point. 'There's something I need to tell you.'

'Oh?' Scarlett cocked her head and smiled, waiting for him to go on.

'Yeeeeah,' said Jake, reluctantly. 'It's, er ... it's about Magnus.'

Scarlett's shoulders tensed instinctively. If she could steer clear of hot topics, like his dodgy dealing, the least he could do was give it a rest about her relationship.

'What about him?' she sighed, adding, 'Do we really have to do this tonight, Jake?'

'I wish we didn't,' said Jake truthfully. 'Look, I'm no good at this sort of thing, so I'm just gonna come right out and say it: he's been lying to you.'

'Jake, *please*,' Scarlett frowned. 'I honestly don't have the energy—'

'He's living with his wife.'

Scarlett opened her mouth to speak, then closed it again.

Eventually, she stammered, 'Are you sure? How do you know?'

'I went up to Seattle,' said Jake quietly. 'I saw it with my own eyes. I've seen cartons of milk more separated than those two, Scar. They're together.'

He'd been expecting tears, anger, maybe even some hurled chinaware. Instead she looked more puzzled than hurt.

'Why did you go to Seattle? *When* did you go to Seattle, for God's sake?'

'Last week,' he mumbled awkwardly. 'I knew you'd be mad, but it was bugging the hell out of me. You can do so much better than that berk.'

'Hmm,' said Scarlett. 'So you saw Carole.'

'Yes. I saw her.'

'What's she like?'

'Pretty, actually,' said Jake, realising belatedly that perhaps it wasn't the most tactful response. 'I mean, she's not a patch on you. But she's much too good for him, let's put it that way. They have a kid, you know.'

Now he really had her attention.

'A child? No! Are you serious?'

'On my life,' said Jake. 'A little boy. And I'm sorry to have to tell you that they called the poor sod "Taylor".'

To her horror, Scarlett found herself giggling. It really wasn't funny. It was awful! Magnus had been lying through his teeth the whole time they were together. Lying about his wife was one thing, but what sort of psycho hid the fact that he had a child?

And yet weirdly, sitting here with Jake in her old flat, on her old sofa, it didn't seem to matter. What was wrong with her?

'I can't believe you're laughing,' said Jake.

'Nor can I,' said Scarlett. Appallingly, she started to laugh again. Perhaps she was hysterical? 'That is a dreadful name though, isn't it?'

'Shocking,' Jake grinned.

Without thinking, he leaned forward and kissed her, just once and very gently, on the lips. When he pulled away, Scarlett said accusingly: 'Why didn't you call me?'

'Call you?' Jake looked taken aback. 'What d'you mean? When?'

'From Africa,' said Scarlett. 'You never once rang to see how things were going at the store.'

'You never called me either,' shrugged Jake.

Why were they talking about this? She was supposed to be distraught about Magnus. Or annoyed that he'd kissed her without asking. Or ...

'How could I? I didn't know where you were.' Scarlett sounded indignant. 'For all I knew you might have been stuck up a tree on safari somewhere. Your US cell phone didn't work—'

'How d'you know that?' Jake pounced on her unexpected admission like a rattlesnake. 'Did you try to call me?'

'Only once,' fibbed Scarlett, cursing herself for letting it slip. 'And only because I needed your advice on something in the accounts. It wasn't a social call.'

'Oh.' Jake looked crestfallen.

'I thought at least you might have made the effort after the Jimmy Choo party,' pouted Scarlett. 'You never even asked me how it went.'

'How did it go?'

Scarlett looked up. Jake's violet eyes bored into hers in a most disconcerting manner. The sexual tension in the air was so thick she could have swum in it.

'It went very well, thank you,' she said, trying to sound unruffled, but failing miserably.

'I wanted to call,' said Jake. 'But bloody Magnus was there, wasn't he?'

'So?' said Scarlett.

'So I couldn't deal with it, all right? I try not to hate people, but I really hated that fucker. From the very beginning, I hated him.'

'But why?' said Scarlett. 'I mean, I can understand it now. Now you know about the lies and everything. But before?'

Jake swallowed hard. 'Because he had you,' he said softly. 'I hated him because he had you.'

He kissed her again, and this time there was nothing tentative about it. Scarlett felt the urgency in his lips, his arms, his chest, years of frustrated desire rushing at her like a tsunami. But it wasn't Jake's desire that surprised her so much as her own. The rough graze of his stubble on her cheeks and neck felt so good, so right, she wanted to scream with delight. Instinctively her back arched at his touch, her hands grasping hungrily for his hair and back, pulling him closer. He was unhooking the clasp on her bra, and she found herself thinking 'Faster, for God's sake, faster!' Wriggling out of her jeans, she was dimly aware of her own voice, calling his name, begging him to touch her. When he did, slipping two fingers inside her while his thumb gently stroked her clitoris, it felt so wonderful she was terrified she might come on the spot, before she'd so much as touched him.

'Wait!' she gasped, fumbling for the buckle on his belt. But Jake was too quick for her. In one fluid movement he shed his clothes like a snake shedding its skin. Scarlett felt his huge, hard erection press against her belly like an iron bar.

'Please,' she whispered. And he was inside her, possessing her, fucking her with an intensity that she had not known possible.

In that moment, she knew why she had not felt upset about Magnus. The lies he'd told her were terrible, unforgivable. But lies like that only had the power to hurt you if you were in love with someone.

Scarlett was in love with someone. But it wasn't Magnus.

Wrapping her long legs tightly around Jake's back, she realised that it hadn't been Magnus for a very long time.

Jake's lovemaking was a revelation. Scarlett had often wondered in the past (idle curiosity, she used to tell herself) what he might be like in bed. She decided that, while no doubt technically skilled, he was probably a selfish lover. Women had always thrown themselves at him, so he didn't have to try.

Boy, was she ever wrong. For hours on end Jake explored her body, delighting in every inch of her as if he'd never seen a naked woman before. After the desperate hunger of the first time, they both relaxed a little. There was nothing hurried, nothing demanding in Jake's touch, none of Magnus's impatience, or perfunctory, brutish desire. His body was strong, but not over-muscled, his dick big, but not overwhelming. If she had to pick one word to describe their sex it would have been 'playful'. They were both rejoicing in the miraculous unexpectedness of finally being together.

'I feel like Lady Chatterley's lover,' said Jake, rolling on to his back at three in the morning, once they were both too tired to move another inch. Having made love on the sofa, then in the shower, then again twice between the soft, worn sheets of Scarlett's four-poster, sleep was overtaking both of them. 'I've never shagged a posh bird before.'

'Rubbish!' laughed Scarlett. 'What about Izzy Davenport? Or Camilla Manley-Walters?' She reeled off the names of the socialites whose names had been linked with Jake's over the years. 'Or Serena Walsingham? Her family own half of Norfolk.'

'And her sister,' said Jake dreamily, earning himself a thwack on the head with a pillow. 'All right, all right, I may have had a few silver-spooners back in the bad old days. But none of them were real ladies. Not like you.'

'Steady on, Lionel Richie,' said Scarlett, humming 'Three Times a Lady' under her breath. Picking up the pillow, Jake hit her back. 'If it's any consolation, you're my first proper bit of rough too. My diamond in the rough,' she smiled, kissing him.

'Am I?' He looked really pleased. 'Brilliant. 'Course, I always knew you fancied me.'

'Oh, please!' Scarlett rolled her eyes. 'You did not.'

'Clear as daylight, right from the start,' said Jake. 'You

were worried about what everyone else would think, that's all.'

'No I wasn't.'

'Your friend Nancy hates my guts.'

'She's protective of me,' said Scarlett, unable to deny the accusation. What was Nancy going to say when she told her about tonight?

'And somehow I doubt I'm exactly the Mr Right your family had in mind for you,' said Jake.

Again, too true to deny.

'Well, your mother's not going to be thrilled about me either, is she?' asked Scarlett, deftly lobbing the ball back in his court. 'I mean, if she loathes Diana O'Donnell ...'

'I think dishonesty is probably the best policy there,' said Jake.

'You mean you're not going to tell her?' said Scarlett, slightly put out.

'Well, not now,' Jake hedged. 'Eventually, obviously. But there's no rush, is there? I mean, a few hours ago you were with Magnus, remember?'

'Was I?' Scarlett sighed happily. Magnus already felt like a fading memory from her gallery of exes.

Part of her wanted to argue the point about not telling Jake's family. Yes, they'd been together only a matter of hours. But they both knew this was serious, and not some fly-by-night affair. They might as well start as they meant to go on: honestly. But exhaustion was pulling her inexorably towards sleep. They could talk more in the morning.

'I know I've been a shit in the past,' Jake murmured in her ear, his voice ebbing and flowing as Scarlett drifted in and out of consciousness. 'But I can change. I want to change, Scarlett. For you.'

'Change,' she mumbled incoherently.

Three seconds later she was deep, deep asleep.

*

The next morning, Scarlett had to race for the airport to catch her flight to Scotland, leaving Jake to make his reluctant way home to St John's Wood.

Minty, insane with worry when he didn't come home, or even call – 'I don't care how old you are, Jacob Meyer! How *dare* you turn your mobile off?' – switched from anger to horrified dismay when she saw his bruised and battered face.

The whole family was in the sitting room. Jake felt like he'd walked in to a gathering of the Spanish Inquisition – if the Spanish Inquisition used to gather on a motley collection of chintz and World-of-Leather sofas. The walls were papered in a noisy blue floral print, which clashed cheerfully with the yellow and pink upholstery. Knick-knacks from Minty's travels to Israel and America fought for space with Rudy's Spurs memorabilia, and every object appeared to have a white paper doily placed between it and whatever it was standing on.

The room never failed to make Jake smile. It was hideous, but it was home.

'I'm fine, Ma,' he sighed, his attempts at brushing away Minty's fussing, fluttering hands all to no avail. 'Honestly, it's not as bad as it looks. I stayed at a friend's last night, and she cleaned me up pretty good.'

'Pretty *well*, Jake. She cleaned you up pretty *well*,' said his father, shaking his head at his son's poor grammar. He hadn't moved from his lazy chair when Jake walked in, and wouldn't until the strain on his bladder made getting up an absolute necessity. 'Speak English, boy. You're not in bloody America now.'

If this last comment was directed at Diana, for once it missed its mark, as she was deeply engrossed in an article on up-and-coming London artists and didn't even look up.

'She did *not* clean him up pretty well, Rudy,' said Minty furiously. 'Look at him. That lip needed stitches right away. You'll have a scar there now, Jakey, because this so-called "friend" didn't get you to casualty. It was a woman, I suppose?'

'It's no one you know, Ma,' said Jake wearily. 'Give it a rest, eh?'

'Dear oh dear.' Danny, who'd nipped out to the corner store for the paper when Jake came home, walked in to find his brother being dabbed at with a warm flannel on the couch. For the first time in days, he smiled. 'What happened to you? Walk into a door or something?'

'He says it was a pub fight,' said Minty, sceptically. 'Bloody fishy if you ask me. And he won't say where he stayed last night.'

'Trust me, Ma,' grinned Danny, 'you probably don't wanna know.'

'Know what?' asked Diana, looking up from her article at last and reaching her arm out to Danny, who squeezed her hand.

'Mind your own beeswax, Wallace Simpson,' snapped Rudy.

Diana blushed.

'For fuck's sake, Dad, back off,' said Jake. He liked Diana. She didn't deserve the abuse. At the end of the day, all she'd done wrong was fall in love with Danny.

'Don't you tell me to fuck off!' roared Rudy. 'This is my ruddy house!'

'I didn't tell you to fuck off,' said Jake reasonably.

'Jacob, language!' chided Minty, peeling the backing off a Mr Bump plaster that must have been in the medicine cupboard since the nineteen seventies and pressing it painfully onto his cheek.

'All right, enough,' said Jake, his patience finally snapping. Next year he was having Christmas in Cabo bloody San Lucas on his own. Or, if he was lucky, with Scarlett. 'I'm going upstairs to my room to make some calls.'

Up in the bedroom he'd shared with Danny as a kid, surrounded by reminders of his boyhood – Ossie Ardiles's signed Tottenham shirt, the silver cup he'd won for coming second in some poxy cross-country tournament, treasured by Minty because it was the only prize either of the twins had won in their long, less than illustrious school careers; even the Kim Basinger posters were still stuck to the wall – he thought about calling Scarlett, then decided against it. For one thing, she probably wouldn't have reached Drumfernly yet. And for another, it never paid to look too keen. Last night had been amazing, magical in every way. He'd had to pinch himself several times this morning to confirm that it really was Scarlett lying warm and naked beside him, and that the whole thing hadn't been some orgiastic, wish-fulfilment dream brought on by the alcohol, or the beating he'd taken, or both. But who knew where things would go from here? They were different, very different, and while opposites might attract, in his experience they rarely lasted as long-term couples. *Long-term couples* – listen to him! At almost forty years of age, he'd never had a long-term relationship in his life.

Then there was the business to consider: without the steady income stream Flawless had brought them, Solomon Stones would have collapsed completely this year. Jake couldn't afford to fuck that up by making a mess of things with Scarlett romantically.

Not that he was prepared simply to walk away. He'd waited too long for her to do that, and the memory of her glorious, lithe body last night was in no danger of fading. Just thinking about it now was making his cock harden. But for once in his life, he decided to tread cautiously. Danny had already rushed in where wise men feared to tread, and look where that had got him.

No, he wouldn't call. He'd let Scarlett make the first move.

Never had forty-eight hours dragged on for so long.

Two days! Two whole days before she deigned to pick

up the phone! Used to women chasing him, Jake had no idea how to handle this sort of nonchalance. Was she already regretting sleeping with him? Had Magnus called and spun some web of bullshit to win her back?

Going slowly out of his mind in London, he did his best to distract himself by partying up a storm, flitting from the Groucho club to Soho House and the Electric like a deranged social butterfly – anything to avoid the depressing atmosphere at home, and to block out the insistent voice in his head chanting: 'You've lost her, you've lost her, you've lost her,' like a runaway train.

Scarlett, meanwhile, was tied up with problems of her own and had had precious little time to dwell on the fact that Jake hadn't called her. The largest, and most irksome of her problems was Cameron, who was convinced that he was on the point of being 'whacked', as he put it, by a Brogan O'Donnell-employed hit-squad, and who demanded to know what Scarlett intended to do about it.

'This time last year, you were calling *me* far fetched for thinking he was behind what happened at Bijoux,' she reminded him. 'And now you think he's trying to kill *you*? Because you saw the same car twice, and your new Porsche broke down?'

'I don't think you're taking this seriously,' Cameron spluttered. Standing in the kitchen at Drumfernly in tweed plus-fours, like an overweight Bertie Wooster, it was certainly difficult to take him seriously. But Scarlett tried, as he was obviously in a highly agitated state. 'With my connections in international high finance, I'm a far more valuable, important target to these thugs than you are,' he blustered, puffing out his cheeks like a blowfish. 'It'd be big news in the city if anything were to happen to me.'

'But nothing *has* happened to you,' said Scarlett reasonably. 'Don't you think that if Brogan wanted to scare you – or use you to scare me, which is what you seem to be implying – he'd do something a bit more drastic than photograph you eating pizza? I mean, I got threatening letters, poisonings and arson. And I've got about as many connections in international high finance as a Tellytubby.'

'Pucci Pizza was one incident,' said Cameron. 'There have been others.'

Watching him pace back and forth in front of the fridge like Sherlock Holmes Scarlett had to bite her tongue to stop herself from sniggering. All he needed was a checked cape and a pipe.

'I saw the same car lurking in the shadows in Vauxhall the other night. It was late, very late. Maybe three in the morning.'

Scarlett's ears pricked up. She asked the obvious question.

'What on earth were you doing in Vauxhall at three in the morning?'

'I was ... clubbing,' said Cameron. He looked even more agitated now. 'But look, that's not the point. The point is they were after me. They were looking for something.'

Indeed, thought Scarlett. But what?

Her brother might be self-important, and prone to suffering from delusions of grandeur. But he wasn't a complete fool. If he'd seen this car on four separate occasions, as he claimed, then chances were it *was* following him. Could it be Brogan? And if so, why? What was he hoping to discover from Cameron? And how could it help him in his battle against her, Trade Fair, or the Meyers?

All of a sudden a deeply troubling thought gripped her.

'You weren't ... you weren't at a gay club, were you, Cameron?'

Vauxhall was famous for its swinging gay scene. There wasn't much else going on there at three in the morning.

'A gay club?' Cameron arranged his flabby features into an appropriately flabbergasted expression. 'A *gay club*? What on earth would possess you to ask such a ridiculous question?'

'So that's a "no" then?' she pressed him.

'Of course it's a no,' he snapped. 'And stop trying to wriggle off the subject. My question is, are you going to drop this dangerous, ill-conceived campaign of yours or not?'

'Well of course I'm not,' said Scarlett, getting irritated. 'Why should I?'

This last remark sparked a shouting match so loud that the entire castle echoed with it. Before long, inevitably, Caroline arrived, demanding to know what all the fuss was about, and weighing in as usual firmly on Cameron's side.

'But darling,' she turned to Scarlett, 'surely you can see that family safety must come before the needs of a group of complete strangers?'

'It's not that simple, Mummy,' Scarlett sighed.

'Bloody well is,' fumed Cameron.

'These Siberian miners have no one to speak up for them. There's a mountain of evidence linking their cancers to Brogan O'Donnell's mines, but he won't lift a finger to help,' Scarlett explained.

'I dare say. But your brother's life could be at risk!' Enjoying the drama of it all, Caroline's voice was veering towards the hysterical.

'Cameron's life is not at risk,' said Scarlett calmly. 'And nor is mine. Brogan's a bully, and he's capable of some pretty below-the-belt tactics to get what he wants. But he isn't a killer. If he was going to take out a contract on anyone, it'd be Danny, not us.'

'And who, may I ask, is *Danny*?' asked Caroline, turning the name over on her tongue as though it were a revolting pill she was being forced to swallow.

'She means Danny Meyer,' said Cameron. 'He's the ghastly little North London Jew who ran off with O'Donnell's wife.'

'How awful,' shuddered Caroline, apparently forgetting that Brogan O'Donnell was the man responsible for terrorising both her children. 'No wonder the poor man's upset.'

'He's also the twin brother of Scarlett's so-called business partner,' said Cameron nastily, 'a crook called Jake Meyer who fancies himself as a bit of a Jack the Lad. He's notorious in London.'

'Jake is not a crook,' said Scarlett, hotly. 'He may have been a little shady in the past, I grant you—'

'A little shady?' Cameron laughed. 'You've changed your tune. Last Christmas you told me he was the diamond industry's answer to Ronnie Biggs!'

'Yes, well. He's changed,' she blushed. Any fantasy she'd had about floating the concept of Jake as a serious boyfriend to her family melted faster than an ice cube on an Aga hotplate.

'I do hope you're not getting mixed up in anything criminal, poppet.' Hugo, who'd arrived in time to catch the tail end of the conversation, looked concerned.

'Of course not, Daddy,' Scarlett reassured him. 'Brogan O'Donnell's the criminal here, not Jake. But brave Sir Robin,' she nodded scathingly at Cameron, 'would rather see me give up Trade Fair, and see Jake and Danny lose their business, than stand up and fight for what's right.'

That was the first of the many circular, pointless arguments that were to ruin whatever faint hope Scarlett had nurtured of a restful family Christmas. As well as battling Cameron, she'd had the usual mother/daughter conflicts to deal with, the tedious round of local social calls to be endured, and on top of it all, the surprisingly unpleasant task of calling Magnus to put an official end to their relationship.

His first response had been to deny everything.

'Don't be silly, darling,' he said, dismissing Jake's claims in that supremely confident way of his, that in the early days she'd found so masculine and powerful. Now it just seemed patronising. 'I don't know what he thought he saw. But Carole and I are married in name only.'

'Really?' said Scarlett. 'And what about Taylor? Is he your son in name only too?'

Even when faced with irrefutable evidence of a child whose existence he'd hidden from her completely, Magnus managed to try and paint himself as the injured party.

'Jake's always had it in for me,' he complained. 'He only told you all this because he wants to get into your pants himself. That's why he came up here, spying on me.'

'Forget Jake,' said Scarlett. 'You have a son, Magnus. A *son!*'

'I know I have a son,' he snapped. 'And of course I was going to tell you about him when the time was right. That's the irony of all this, you know. I was going to propose to you at New Year, as soon as my partnership's announced. I would have told you all about Taylor then. But oh no, you have to go listening to Jake Meyer's muck spreading. I can't believe you're seriously intending to throw away everything we have together over *this*. After all the love, all the support I've given you.'

Scarlett racked her brains trying to think what 'support' he might be referring to, before the ridiculousness of the situation dawned on her – why was she even talking to him? The guy had a secret family, for Christ's sake. He was a congenital liar, and yet here she was, attempting to defend *her* actions to *him*.

'Look, Magnus, it's over, OK? Let's face it, we haven't exactly been happy together in a long time.'

'Are you sleeping with Jake?'

'What? I ... That's none of your business,' stammered Scarlett, taken aback.

'Oh my God, you are. Do you even realise what a cliché that is?'

By the end of the conversation, she almost felt guilty. Arguing with Magnus was the verbal equivalent of going ten rounds with Mike Tyson. No wonder his law firm were making him a partner.

Afterwards, drained of every last ounce of mental energy, she called Jake.

'How are you?' she asked wearily, pulling a blanket up over her knees. 'How's London?'

She was sitting on the window seat of the library in Drumfernly, looking out over the snowy parkland, dotted with deer and Christmas-card perfect in the twilight. But after the battering she'd just had on the phone she didn't feel remotely peaceful.

'Awful and awful,' came back Jake's miserable response. His plan to play things cool had gone out of the window the moment he heard her voice. 'I miss you like mad. I've been waiting for you to call for days. I thought you'd gone off me.'

'Not yet,' smiled Scarlett. She told him about Magnus's reaction to being caught in the act, and how gruelling their conversation had been.

'Tosser,' said Jake with feeling. 'Well at least it's over now. You never have to talk to him again.'

'That's true,' said Scarlett, brightening.

'If it's any consolation, things are bloody terrible here,' said Jake. 'Mum's gone into nag-overdrive, Dad's drunk day and night, and Diana spends half of every day slumped over the loo with morning sickness, pretending she's got a stomach bug, which of course Ma's interpreting as some sort of sly dig at her cooking. I've been trying to stay out of the house, but there're only so many hours you can spend in clubs on your own without looking like a Norman No Mates.'

'What about Danny?' asked Scarlett, trying to banish a mental picture of Jake alone in a trendy London club, surrounded by marauding women. Whatever he said, she very much doubted he'd spent the last two evenings alone. 'Didn't he come with you?'

'Nah. He's stuck to Diana like glue, trying to protect her from Ma. If the old girl keeps this up, picking on Diana all the time, I doubt Danny'll be back next Christmas. They'll have a kid by then,' he added, almost disbelievingly. It did all seem to have happened terribly fast. 'How're your lot?'

'Dreadful,' said Scarlett with feeling. 'Indescribably bad.'

She told him about Cameron getting spooked by Brogan.

'That's bizarre,' he said. 'Why would he want to put the frighteners on *your* brother? I mean, I can understand his problem with mine.'

'I know,' she said. 'I don't want to feed Cam's paranoia, or my mother's, any more than I have to. But I have to say, it worries me. I'm definitely back in the centre of Brogan's radar screen since Trade Fair started focusing on Yakutia. To lose NPR and *Vanity Fair* within weeks of each other can't be a coincidence.'

'Hmm,' said Jake. 'Are you sure this new campaign of yours is worth it?'

Scarlett sounded put out. 'Not you, too? Of course I'm sure. You were the one who told me I should raise Trade Fair's profile in America, remember?'

'Yeah, I know,' Jake sounded doubtful. 'But that was when you were trying to help the Africans. I mean, don't get me wrong. I feel bad for those Russian guys.'

'The ones dying of cancer, you mean,' Scarlett reminded him tersely.

'Yes, all right, but let's be honest. The shit going down in O'Donnell's mines is hardly on a par with what's going on in Congo or Sierra Leone. No one's starving, or watching their family get chopped up by some heroin-crazed militia. Are they?'

Scarlett felt a knot of anger grow tighter in her chest. This was rich! Jake lecturing *her* on Africa's problems?

'Death is death. Injustice is injustice,' she said sanctimoniously. 'Those Yakutian miners are as deserving of help as anybody else in this industry, suffering at the hands of greedy bastards like Brogan O'Donnell. Besides, what do you know about Sierra Leone? You and Danny are too busy partying on those buying trips of yours to notice the misery on the streets. Since when did you care about anything other than your precious profits?'

'Thanks,' said Jake quietly. 'Thanks a lot.'

He'd been in two minds whether to tell her about his dealings with Dr Katenge last month, but there was no way he was going to open up now. Screw her. Did she think she was the only person in the world with a fucking heart?

'Oh, look, sorry,' said Scarlett. Why was she being so mean to him? He'd made a real effort to change his ways since they teamed up on Flawless. She ought to give him some credit for that, especially now that they were supposedly 'together'. (*Were* they together? They hadn't really talked about it properly. There hadn't been time.)

'I really need your support about Brogan, that's all. I've got my brother, my parents, everybody telling me to walk away. But I made a promise to try to help those men, and I have to honour it.'

'Fine,' said Jake. 'I understand. Just don't make me the enemy, Scarlett. All right?'

'All right,' said Scarlett meekly, hanging up.

If she and Jake *were* going to work as a couple, they were going to have to learn how to communicate. They might have known each other for years, but all they'd ever done was bicker. Not the greatest foundation for true love.

# Fifteen

'You had these results yesterday?'

Brogan had his back turned toward his doctor, and was staring out of the window as he spoke. Below, on Fifth Avenue, a crush of bargain hunters was thronging to the Christmas sales. A human wave of post-Christmas consumerism, like a thick blood clot forcing its way through the arteries of the city, they made him feel sick. Why weren't they at home with their families instead of out shopping, stuffing their greedy arms full of yet more crap they couldn't possibly need?

'Why didn't you call me right away?'

'On Christmas Day?' said the doctor, gently. 'Come on, Brogan.'

'But every day counts, right? Every hour?' Leaning against the cool glass of the window, Brogan evidently didn't trust himself to turn around. As if eye contact with the bearer of such bad news might somehow unleash the fear burning its way through his insides like acid.

'One day won't have made a difference,' said the doctor. 'Trust me on that. Besides, I want Lennox Dubray to do the operation. He's the best there is, and he wouldn't have taken my call on Christmas morning.'

Brogan shook his head and let out a short, joyless laugh. Lung cancer. Fucking *lung* cancer, of all the shitty illnesses in the world. The irony wasn't lost on him – nor, he knew, would it be lost on his enemies – that the great Brogan O'Donnell should be struck down with the very same disease that had crippled his Siberian workforce, and for which he had steadfastly refused to pay the treatment costs.

'I never smoked, you know,' he said, finally composing himself enough to resume his seat opposite the doctor's desk. 'Not even as a kid.'

The doctor shrugged. 'Sometimes it happens that way. It doesn't have to be something you did. Could be genetic. Could be just ... random. I know that's not very comforting.'

'So you're certain they should operate?' said Brogan, cutting to the chase. 'What about chemo?'

'You'll have that too, afterwards. Look, Lennox'll make the final assessment, not me. But if your primary tumour's operable, and I'm ninety per cent sure it is from the CAT scan, I know he'll want to take it out as soon as possible.'

'Which is?'

'Wednesday,' said the doctor. 'Theatre's already booked for nine a.m., pending Dubray's findings this afternoon. They'll need you in pre-op the night before.'

'Fine,' said Brogan brusquely, rising to go. 'I'll clear my schedule for the week.'

The doctor raised an eyebrow. 'You're gonna have to clear it for a lot longer than that, I'm afraid. Even if everything goes well, you're going to be weak for some considerable time. Work is out of the question.'

Crunching his way along the icy sidewalks twenty minutes later, hands thrust deep into the pockets of his Burberry Prorsum overcoat, Brogan turned the words over in his mind: 'You're going to be weak.' He'd spent a lifetime fighting to be strong, to be the fittest, fastest and best, in business and in every aspect of his life. He hated weak. He didn't *accept* weak.

When Diana left him, this time last year, he'd felt weak. Like a shorn Samson railing at the heavens, the strength had poured out of him. He knew it wasn't rational, but it was hard not to link this latest weakness, this cancer, to that earlier blow. As if, if he only had her with him, had her back, he could turn back the clock, drive this shitty tumour out of his body through sheer force of will. Or something.

Thank God Natalia wasn't with him, he thought, turning the corner on to Lexington and walking aimlessly north. She'd offered to come with him to his appointment today – evidently her disaster radar was more accurate than his – but he'd brushed her off, and was glad he had. Having to talk through his feelings with her, or anyone, was the last thing he wanted. In fact, he'd already begun to feel that the relationship had run its course. She was a stunning girl, smart, funny, not in the least bit clingy. Everything he professed to want, in fact. But he'd found the holidays depressing, cooped up in the apartment with her twenty-four seven. They'd decided to stay in New York because Telluride brought back too many unhappy memories of Diana and last Christmas, but with hindsight that had been a mistake. At least in Colorado he could ski and get away on his own. Here he had no excuse not to 'relax' at home, while she pranced around in her new red silk La Perla panties, miming to 'Santa Baby' and getting happy on Cristal.

It should have been sexy but it wasn't, it was sad. Loneliness, and longing for his wife, sank over him like a cloud. And now this. Cancer. He could no more talk to Natalia about it than to a stranger on the subway. The one person he *could* talk to about it was gone.

Diana sat on a damp bench in Regent's Park staring at a mallard duck and his mate as they preened one another lovingly, huddling together against the cold.

'I wish Danny would huddle together with me,' she thought sadly, thinking of the arctic atmosphere back at the house in St John's Wood and looking at her watch. It was after eleven – he'd promised to meet her at ten this morning for a walk, as soon as he'd dropped Minty at his Auntie Bella's place – but something must have happened. Obviously he wasn't coming, not now.

The London Christmas she'd so looked forward to had turned out to be a crushing disappointment. Danny had warned her that his parents had reservations about him marrying outside his religion, but he hadn't prepared her for the caustic levels of rejection doled out by Minty on a daily basis. Nothing Diana did, or said, was right. It was as if she were being held personally responsible for every wrong ever perpetrated by America, Christianity, and wealthy women generally, not to mention blamed for all of Danny's present business troubles.

'He was doing so well last year, before he met you,' Minty sighed pointedly over Christmas lunch. 'Now he can barely afford the plane fare home.'

'Don't exaggerate, Ma,' said Danny, not looking up from his mountain of roast potatoes. 'We're fine.'

'You are not fine, Daniel. Tell him, Rudy,' she turned to her husband. 'Jake told me you said your new apartment is an s-h-one-t hole. Said it wasn't fit for rats and you were the most miserable you've ever been since you moved to New York.'

'*Mum!*' said Jake and Danny in unison.

'I never said that,' Danny turned placatingly to Diana. 'I never said I was miserable.' But of course, she knew he had.

'We're going to move to something a lot better, Mrs Meyer,' she offered meekly. 'As soon as my divorce comes through.'

Minty gave a derisory snort. 'Oh, of course you are. With your husband's money, I suppose. The same husband who's made it his business to try and *ruin* my boys this past year.'

'Ma, that's enough,' said Jake. That was another thing that upset Diana – it always seemed to be Jake leaping to her defence, not Danny. Not that she wasn't grateful for his support. But it was Danny she'd given everything up for, Danny whose child she was now carrying. He might have stuck his neck out on her behalf just once with his awful, poisonous mother.

Then, last night, they'd had a titanic row because Diana, backed into another corner by Minty, had blurted out the news about her pregnancy, something she'd promised Danny she wouldn't do on this trip. In the back of her mind, she'd hoped that perhaps a first grandchild might soften the old witch up, but no such luck. Minty was furious.

'A child? Unmarried? And with her still married to what's-his-face? Are you out of your mind?' she screeched at Danny.

'I do have a name, you know,' said Diana quietly from her seat in the corner of the living room. But mother and son were too busy shouting at each other to notice.

'Lay off, Ma, for God's sake. We will be married,' said Danny. 'Soon.'

'Why? Because she's pregnant?' sobbed Minty.

'No.' Danny clapped a hand to his throbbing head. 'Not because she's pregnant. Because we love each other. The baby was a mistake.'

'A *mistake*?' That was the last straw for Diana. 'A *mistake*? How dare you!'

'Oh, look, you know what I mean. Not a mistake, an accident. It was an accident, all right?'

But Diana was far from all right.

'No child on this earth has ever been more wanted. By me, anyway. But it's great to know how *you* feel so early in the pregnancy. A mistake, indeed. That's just terrific, Danny.'

By the time he'd talked her round, it was past eleven and they retired wearily to bed. Diana longed to make love, but Danny had been drinking all day – no one could accuse the Meyers of stinting on the wine at Christmas – and was far too mentally and physically exhausted to get it up. After a quick peck on the cheek he'd fallen immediately into a deep, dreamless sleep, snoring like a happy pig beside her as she tossed and turned with frustration. Then this morning he'd disappeared with his wretched mother at the crack of dawn – Diana had point-blank refused to join Minty's sister for her annual Boxing Day brunch – promising to meet her in the park by ten.

Standing up slowly, rubbing the minuscule bulge in her belly as she pulled her cardigan more tightly around her, she set off towards the zoo. She might as well walk by herself as sit here, dying of hypothermia. Dr Brennan, her gynae back in New York, was big on the importance of gentle exercise during pregnancy – that and lowering one's stress levels. If only!

Just as she began crunching her way along the gravel path, she felt her phone buzzing to life in her jeans pocket.

'About time,' she muttered crossly, assuming it was Danny calling to apologise for standing her up. How she hated the way he jumped every time Minty said jump. Stabbing the answer button with a gloved finger, she did her best to sound nonchalant.

'What happened?' she said. 'Where have you been?'

'Diana?'

She stopped walking, clutching the new life inside her even more tightly.

'Brogan? Is that you?' To her surprise she found her knees were shaking. Without thinking, she reached out a hand and leaned against an ancient oak tree for support.

'Yeah.' He sounded hesitant, as if he were on the point of hanging up. 'How … er … how are you?'

'Fine,' Diana lied. She'd received a total of three calls from Brogan since she left, all of them rage-filled and threatening. At the time his anger had upset her dreadfully. But now she rather thought she preferred it to this strained civility. Her heart was pounding like a woodpecker on speed, whether from fear, or guilt, or surprise, she didn't know. And yet was there a tiny, hidden part of her that was happy to hear his voice? 'You?'

'Er, well ...' Brogan laughed, a deep, throaty chuckle she hadn't heard in a long time. 'I've been better, I gotta tell you. They just told me I've got cancer.'

Diana's whole bodyweight sank into the tree.

'Oh my God, honey,' she whispered. After fifteen years, the endearments were a hard habit to break. 'I'm so sorry. What—'

'What species?' Brogan interrupted. 'Lung. So there's karma for you.'

Diana was silent for a moment, unsure what to say.

'Have they talked to you about treatment options?' she stammered eventually.

'I literally just saw Doc Franks,' said Brogan. 'Ten minutes ago. I'm still trying to take it in myself. He was talking about an operation to remove the tumour, then maybe chemo. I don't know. I see the specialist tomorrow morning.'

Diana closed her eyes. She could hear the honking of New York traffic in the background, a sound that transported her instantly back home. So he'd only known for a matter of minutes? She must have been his first call.

'Have you talked to Natalia about this?' she heard herself asking. Not that she cared, but it seemed like the appropriate thing to say. After all, they had been a couple for over a year now.

'No,' said Brogan gruffly. 'It's over with me and Natalia.'

'Oh,' said Diana, uselessly. 'I'm sorry.'

'Are you?'

Another long, painful silence fell. This time it was Brogan who broke it.

'I miss you.'

Diana's head was spinning. She'd heard nothing but hate from Brogan for so long, she'd forgotten he was ever capable of tenderness.

'Come home, Diana. I love you. I've always loved you.'

'Please, Brogan, don't. I can't ...' she began, her voice breaking.

'You can. Of course you can,' he pushed her. 'Just get on a plane. I need you now, baby, more than ever. Whatever's happened this past year, we can work it out. That son of a bitch can't possibly love you as much as I do. He can't; it's not possible.'

'I'm pregnant.' The words were out of her mouth before she even knew she'd thought them. She could hear Brogan's intake of breath on the other end of the line. Shit, how could she have told him now, like this? After he'd just phoned to tell her he had cancer, for God's sake. Talk about kicking a man when he's down.

'Oh honey, I'm so sorry, I shouldn't have told you,' she babbled. 'It's not important. I want to hear more about what Doctor Franks said.'

'No, no, it's fine,' said Brogan gently. 'I'm happy for you. How could I not be, after all we went through together? You're going to make a fantastic, fantastic mother.'

She was so taken aback by this unexpected kindness, she burst into tears.

'What?' said Brogan. 'What's the matter? If one of us should be crying right now, I'm pretty sure it ain't you.'

'I know,' Diana sniffed. 'I'm sorry. It's just, you being so sweet about it. I don't know, maybe it's my hormones. And London. Turns out I hate London. Who knew?'

Brogan laughed. 'Me too! Most overrated fucking city in the world. Listen, honey.' He dropped his voice to a whisper. Suddenly he felt so close he could almost touch her. 'I meant what I said about coming home, pregnant or not. Please. Just think about it.'

'Brogan,' she began. But the line had already gone dead.

Ten seconds later, the phone rang again. She picked it up instantly, but it was only Danny, sounding typically harassed.

'Please don't have a go at me,' he began, inauspiciously. 'I've had it up to here today already. The whole family's been giving me grief about leaving Auntie Bella's early, even bloody Jake. I couldn't get away any sooner.'

'Brogan's got lung cancer,' said Diana, breaking his flow.

'Has he? Well it couldn't have happened to a nicer bloke,' said Danny. After spending twenty of the last twenty-four hours being harangued by various of his loved ones, he wasn't in the most compassionate of moods, especially towards the man who'd cut his business off at the knees and who was dragging his heels on the world's most expensive divorce.

'Danny!' Diana sounded shocked. 'That's a terrible thing to say. He sounded so different on the phone. Really vulnerable and—'

'He called you?' The earlier irritation in his voice had been replaced by suspicion.

'Yes. Just now,' said Diana. 'He was on his way home from the doctor's office.'

'Look, I'm not being funny,' said Danny, 'but I really don't give a fuck where he was, or what he's got. He shouldn't be calling you. This is the man who rearranged your face last Christmas, remember? The man who's done everything in his power to make our lives a misery. He didn't care when those poor sods who work for him in Yakutia started dying like a warren full of myxie rabbits. But now he wants *us* to feel sorry for *him*?'

'I'm just telling you he called,' said Diana coolly. Of course she couldn't expect Danny to be thrilled about it. But a little human sympathy didn't seem that much to ask, under the circumstances. They had each other, and the baby. Brogan had nothing but a pile of money and his own loneliness and fear to go home to.

'Did you tell him about the baby?' asked Danny, still wary.

'I did, actually, yes,' said Diana.

'And?'

'And he was sweet about it. He said he thought I'd make a wonderful mother, which was big of him.'

'Oh yeah, huge,' said Danny snidely. 'What is this, the Brogan O'Donnell fucking fan club?'

Diana bit back her irritation. All this rowing was bad for the baby. But surely Danny should be the one apologising to her for his no show, instead of trying to make *her* feel bad for taking a call from a man she'd been married to for half her life, and who might very well be about to die?

'Where are you now?' he asked, softening slightly. He hated fighting with her as much as she did. They seemed to have got into a horrible rut on this vacation.

'Still in the park,' she sighed. 'It's getting kinda cold, though.'

'Go to the nearest gate and I'll pick you up in the car,' he said. 'I'll be there in five minutes, all right?'

'All right,' she nodded. 'Danny?'

'What?'

'You do love me, don't you? I mean, despite your mother and everything. You do still want me and the baby?'

'Of course I do,' he answered briskly. 'What sort of a silly question is that?'

But somehow, as she made her slow, pensive way towards the park gates, Diana wasn't certain she believed him.

# Sixteen

With the Oscars just around the corner, January was the busiest month of the year for jewellers in Los Angeles, and from the moment she arrived back at Flawless, Scarlett's feet barely touched the ground. All her grand plans for reviving Trade Fair were put on hold as she joined the last-minute scramble for celebrity endorsements, churning out exotic necklaces, bracelets and earrings like a one-woman sweat shop.

'I'm not sure what part of this you aren't getting,' Rachel Bilson's agent, a toad of a man with a voice like Jack from *Will & Grace*, only minus all the charm, sneered at her down the phone. 'Rachel's dress *was* gonna be red. But *now* it's gonna be green. So we need to see the exact same pendant with emeralds instead of the rubies. It's not rocket science, sweetie.'

Scarlett tried to explain that, while not rocket science, it would necessitate crafting a second pendant entirely from scratch, a process that with the best will in the world could not be completed before the end of the week, never mind by the end of the afternoon, as the agent was demanding.

'It's not like clicking a different colour on Microsoft Paint,' she said patiently. 'I don't even have that many cut emeralds in stock. I'm afraid she'll have to wait, at least for a few days.'

'No honey,' snapped the toad. 'She won't *have* to do anything. Forget about it. We'll try Neil Lane.'

In the end, thankfully, Rachel had called personally to tell Scarlett she'd be happy to wait, and that she was still interested in buying the original ruby piece too. Like many young actresses, she was actually rather sweet once you managed to prise her out of the grasping talons of her management. But close calls like these were enough to keep Scarlett in a permanent state of nervous tension.

'Are you sure I can't get you anything?' Nancy, dressed for dancing in her new pair of red, seventies flares and a silver top that tied above her midriff, poked her head round the corner of Scarlett's room as she slaved over the finishing touches on a charm bracelet, dangling with scores of miniature Oscar statuettes. 'At least have a bagel. You shouldn't work so late on an empty stomach.'

'I'm fine,' said Scarlett, barely looking up. 'I ate a big lunch. And it's not late. It's not even five thirty.'

'Whatever,' mumbled Nancy under her breath. 'Six cups of black coffee is not lunch.'

Disappearing into the kitchen, she returned five minutes later with a bagel spread thickly with peanut butter and jelly, a banana and a large glass of OJ. Placing these offerings in front of Scarlett, she stood over her like a prison guard, arms folded. 'Eat it,' she said firmly. 'I'm not leaving till you do.'

Giving in to the inevitable, Scarlett put aside her work and took a bite of the bagel. She was surprised to find she was ravenous, and in a few minutes had devoured the entire plate, crumbs and all.

'Thanks,' she said, wiping her mouth on the back of her hand as she gulped down the last of the juice. 'I needed that.'

'I know,' said Nancy. It was amazing how maternal and stern she could look, even whilst dressed as an extra from *Saturday Night Fever*. 'I'm telling you, Scar, I'm this close to reporting you to Anorexics Anonymous. I'm surprised Jake hasn't sliced off his dick on those razor-sharp hip bones of yours.'

Scarlett laughed. It was a relief to hear her finally saying the J word without launching into a stream of (admittedly well-meant) invective. To say Nancy had been horrified by Scarlett and Jake's romance would be an epic understatement.

'JAKE MEYER? JAKE FUCKING MEYER?' she roared, the night Scarlett arrived back in LA and filled her in on what had happened. 'Are you on drugs? Are you completely and utterly out of your mind? You can't be fucking Jake Meyer. You hate Jake Meyer!'

'I thought I did,' said Scarlett, shrugging meekly. 'But it turns out I hate him less than I thought.'

'Boxford!' said Nancy, startling the sleepy spaniel from his comfortable doze on the porch. 'Tell your mistress she's lost the plot. Tell her Jake the snake is bad news.'

'Actually, Boxie's always liked him,' began Scarlett. But Nancy wasn't close to being finished.

'He's a user, a liar, a womaniser,' she counted Jake's minus points off on her fingers. 'He buys contraband diamonds—'

'Not any more,' said Scarlett. 'He's changed.'

'Please!' Nancy scoffed. 'Men like that don't *change*. He's selfish, he's lazy, he's a chauvinist. He probably has every STD known to man, and a bunch that haven't even been discovered yet.'

'I think I might be in love with him,' said Scarlett helplessly.

'*In love?*' Nancy looked like she was about to choke. 'Lord preserve us. And what about Magnus?'

'Ah yes, Magnus. Now that's another story,' said Scarlett. And not without some relish, she related all the gory details of Jake's trip to Seattle.

'*Taylor?*' Nancy frowned disapprovingly. 'I must say, I'd have thought he'd go for something a bit less trailer-trash than that. Poor kid. And poor you. Were you dreadfully shocked? Magnus, eh? Who'd have thunk it?' She shook her head in wonderment. 'He seemed so perfect.'

'Exactly!' said Scarlett. 'But he wasn't. Which surely

goes to show that one should never judge a book by its cover.'

'You mean Jake?' said Nancy, the fires of her indignation only slightly abated by the Magnus digression. 'Just 'cause Magnus was a master of disguise doesn't mean hooking up with Jake's a good idea. God damn it, Scar, I *knew* this would happen. I *knew* he'd worm his way around you eventually.'

Scarlett had tried to explain that there had been no 'worming'. That Jake's absence in Africa had made her heart grow fonder, and that by the time he'd come to her in London, she'd already decided that whatever it was she'd once felt for Magnus, it was a) not love and b) not there any more. But after three weeks Nancy's scepticism remained as rock solid as ever, to the point where Jake had become an almost total non-subject between them.

As a result, Scarlett had only had him stay overnight at the cottage twice since they got back from London, both times on nights she knew Nancy would be staying at Che Che's. The second time, Nancy came home just as Jake was leaving, and Scarlett could have cut the tension with a knife.

'What's her problem?' Jake complained to Scarlett afterwards. 'Is she jealous, or something? 'Cause you're getting shit-hot sex and she's not?'

Scarlett laughed. 'Somehow I doubt that's it,' she said, giving him a conciliatory kiss. 'She just needs a little time to adjust, that's all.'

But privately she'd begun to wonder whether Nancy was ever going to accept the relationship. If she didn't, Scarlett thought sadly, she'd have to start thinking about looking for somewhere else to live, a hassle she could well do without right now.

Technically she supposed she could move in with Jake. But it seemed an awfully big step to take so early on, particularly given the fact that she had yet to set foot inside his apartment. He'd always been a bit secretive about his place. Even last year, before they got together, he'd made excuses not to invite her in on the rare occasions she drove by to pick him up for work or drop him off after a meeting when his car was in the shop. At the time she hadn't given it much thought. But now that they were a couple, his prevaricating seemed somehow more disturbing.

'Trust me, it's a shit hole,' he'd tell her breezily, whenever she suggested they spend the night there instead of the cottage. 'I'd be embarrassed to show it to a princess like you.'

In other circumstances, Scarlett would have turned to Nancy for some girlfriendly advice. As it was, the last thing she wanted to do was sow any more seeds of doubt about Jake into the veritable forest of disapproval that was Nancy's mind.

Once Scarlett had finished her food, Nancy carried her empty plate and glass back into the kitchen.

'Is Che Che taking you dancing tonight?' Scarlett called after her.

'No, sieve-for-brains,' Nancy called back. 'He's coming over here, remember? The three of us were going to get takeout from Chin Chin and brainstorm how to revive your NPR piece. It was your suggestion.'

'Of course. Right,' said Scarlett, who'd completely forgotten, and had promised Jake earlier that they were on for a private night of passion. He'd go mad when she called him to cancel, but it couldn't be helped. Che Che had kindly agreed to get involved with Trade Fair, and had close friends at KCRW, the LA radio station, who might be able to revive the show she and Andy had toiled over for months last year. No way was she going to flake on him. Plus, with his background as a refugee and his rising profile on the LA art scene, he'd have huge credibility as a guest speaker if she could really get him interested in the cause.

'I'm dropping off some flyers for him down in Venice,'

said Nancy, 'then I'll pick up the food and be back by seven, seven thirty latest.'

'You don't think you're a tad overdressed for a leaflet drop and a trip to the takeout?' Scarlett looked questioningly at the *Saturday Night Fever* outfit.

'There's no such thing as overdressed in Venice,' said Nancy firmly. 'Besides, Che Che likes it when I make an effort.'

She'd only known him for five weeks, but Nancy had already gotten into the habit of 'making an effort' for Che Che. Never, in her long career as a party girl, had she adored and admired a lover as much. After so many years being chased, it felt strange to be the one making all the running for a change. But figuring that most of the prizes worth having in life involved a challenge, she threw herself into the task of winning her new boyfriend's heart with the same enthusiasm she brought to her writing, her friendships and everything else that was dear to her.

Tearing west along the freeway in her gleaming yellow Thunderbird – after her second script had been optioned in December, she'd rewarded herself by getting the car resprayed, transforming her loyal banger into a polished work of art – she let the top down, allowing the cool breeze to ruffle her hair and blow it into a sexy, tousled mop.

Scarlett must really be frazzled to have forgotten about tonight's dinner. She'd been on at Nancy for weeks to set up a meeting with Che Che and pin him down on a time. (No easy task, given he had two exhibitions coming up at the end of the month, and a string of social commitments. He barely had enough time to devote to Nancy, never mind to spend a whole evening putting the world to rights with Scarlett.) No doubt Jake fucking Meyer was behind the new, even scattier Scarlett. How *could* she have fallen for that jerk?

Turning off the freeway at Ocean Park, Nancy turned

her thoughts back to her own life. Like Scarlett, she'd endured an unusually stressful family Christmas. Her mom had been struck down with mysterious, debilitating headaches that had hung over the rest of the family like a dark cloud. Lucy Lorriman was an old-school stoic. By the time she got around to calling the doctor or popping a pill, most normal people would have collapsed on the floor in agony, demanding ambulances and morphine. For her to complain of headaches at all, never mind take to her bed with them, something had to be seriously wrong. So far the specialists had all drawn a blank – there was no obvious tumour. But both Nancy and her father remained privately convinced that some frightening, nameless evil lurked behind Lucy's symptoms. And neither of them knew how to handle it.

Making a left on Main Street, then again onto Abbot Kinney, she searched for a parking space amongst the maze of streets that made up downtown Venice. She loved the area, with its quaint streets and canals, its brightly painted nineteen-twenties shacks (built for the poorest of the poor, they now sold for millions), its run-down art galleries and kooky new-age stores: palm readers, tarot specialists, tattooists. There was even a 'spiritual acupuncture temple', whatever the hell that meant – pins with your hymns, presumably, she laughed, picturing her dad's horrified face at the very thought of it.

The Ramenez Gallery, where Che Che's work was being shown, looked as beat up as the rest of the establishments surrounding it, but in fact sold very little under the twenty-thousand-dollar mark. Venice's poverty, like so much of LA, was an affectation. It might be full of artists, and they might be living in attics. But the attics went for the price of a decent family home in Connecticut, and none of the artists was starving. Most of Ramenez's front window was taken up with a single, childish drawing of a sunflower, priced at an astonishing eighty-five-thousand bucks. Not for the first time, Nancy seriously considered chucking in the writing, changing her name to Moonbeam, and flogging some hopeless daub in the name of 'high art'. She'd never say as much to Che Che, but part of her thought his entire line of business was the world's greatest scam.

'Hey, baby.' Sauntering through the gallery door, her hips swaying like a short, blonde Elvis, she made her way over to the front desk, where he was deep in conversation with Rodrigo Ramenez, the gallery owner. 'I got you the flyers.' Dumping a stack of paper bound with a single elastic band down on the desk, she snaked her arm around his waist, simultaneously flashing her most winning, come-up-and-see-me-some-time smile at Rodrigo. It never hurt to stay on the good side of one's lover's boss. 'You nearly ready to go?'

'I need twenty minutes.' Che Che's huge, labourer's hand instinctively slid down over her butt and gave it a squeeze. 'Forty tops.'

Rodrigo caught the gesture – a big black line-backer groping the smallest and cutest cheerleader – and didn't know where to look. The sexual chemistry between these two was so hot it was about to start fucking with his air-con.

'Why don't you order for me, and I'll meet you back at your place?' said Che Che, removing his hand and inspecting the flyers for his exhibition with a critical eye. 'I'll have Singapore Ho Fun, no pork and some noodles, the clear ones. I'll be right behind you,' he added, seeing her hesitation and a sceptical look pass across her pretty, doll-like features.

Nancy thought about it. As always, in his presence, it was a physical wrench to let him go, even for a short time. Plus, if she left him here, talking art and prices with Rodrigo, she ran the risk that he might be hours. On the other hand, she didn't want to be the sort of clingy, nagging girlfriend that hung around, looking at her watch and tut-tutting while he tried to work.

'OK,' she said. 'But please, baby, don't be late. Scarlett's expecting us at seven.'

'I won't.'

He smiled, and Nancy felt her insides melt like chocolate on a hot summer sidewalk. Her parents would come around eventually, once they saw how talented and strong and beautiful he was. Once they saw how happy he made her.

After she left, Rodrigo shook his head at his newest young artist with unfeigned admiration.

'That's quite a girl you've got yourself there.' If he'd been a few years younger, he might have whistled.

'I know it,' said Che Che proudly. He still felt like pinching himself every time he looked at Nancy – and especially when he looked at her from behind, sashaying down the street like a forties siren, wiggling that perfect backside of hers with seemingly limitless confidence. 'I'm a lucky man.'

While Che Che counted his blessings, Jake was sitting in the living room of his apartment with Solomon Stones' latest quarterly accounts spread out in front of him on the coffee table, feeling distinctly less lucky.

'Bollocks. Piss, wank, bollocks,' he mumbled, to no one in particular. The numbers were bloody awful. Even he, with his barely scraped CSE in maths, could tell that. Looking at the situation on paper, in black and white, it was plain that their East Coast business was dead. Not dying, actually dead, kaput, finished, as fully expired as the Monty Python parrot, or the slab of Whole Foods cheddar mouldering in the dairy drawer of his untouched fridge. Brogan had cooked Danny's goose good and proper. In LA, Jake's own sales were up on the previous quarter – thanks to the Flawless connection he'd at last regained some ground against the ubiquitous Tyler Brett. But without the life-saving injection of steady income from

Scarlett's store, Solomon Stones would have been royally fucked.

He tried to tell himself that Flawless's success was a good thing, and that he had a perfect right to his share in it. After all, the store had been his idea in the first place, and he'd played a very active role in getting the business started. But deep down, he knew that the runaway success of their first year was ninety-nine per cent attributable to Scarlett's incredible talents as a designer. And he badly didn't want to feel beholden to Scarlett for anything, least of all his livelihood.

That was the trouble with falling in love with a girl so patently out of your league. It was hard enough keeping your distance, trying to hold on to the upper hand in the relationship. Scarlett was so evidently his superior in looks, breeding, intelligence – basically any measurement you cared to count – the idea that she would soon be out-earning him too was more than Jake's ego could bear. With every glance at the figures, he could feel his dick shrinking. It wasn't a good feeling.

'What the fuck?' The buzzing doorbell disturbed him from his gloomy reverie. At first he ignored it. It was bound to be some bloody hobo selling tea towels, or a bunch of rosy-faced girl scouts trying to foist their disgusting boxes of cookies on him at extortionate 'charidee' prices. But the buzzing soon became so insistent, he was forced to get up and deal with it.

'Who is it?' he barked into the intercom.

'It's me. Rachel.'

Jake gave his memory a perfunctory search, but drew a blank.

'I'm sorry, Rachel who?'

'Rachel *who*?' An intensely irritating, tinkly laugh rang out through the speakerphone. Oh God. Rachel.

'Rachel *Kingman*, silly,' simpered the voice. 'Aren't you gonna buzz me up?'

She pronounced her surname 'King-maaaairn,' in true valley-girl style. Jake felt the hairs on the back of his neck rise. What the hell was she doing here?

There was no part of him that wanted to see Rachel again. The nineteen-year-old daughter of a local property mogul, she'd lured him into bed last year, hypnotising him with her improbably enormous rack and a trust fund almost as big as her sense of entitlement. For months she'd kept him hanging, promising to spend a chunk of money on a diamond necklace for her mother. Of course, it never happened – some fucker of a trustee got wind of Rachel's proposed generosity and cut off her funds faster than a gangrenous leg – after which Jake had struggled for months to get rid of the girl and her narcissistic posse of vacuous girlfriends.

'Actually, Rach, it's not really a good time,' he blustered. 'I'm sort of in the middle of something right now. Some business.'

There was a tense, ten-second silence, in which he could have sworn he heard her pout through the phone. Then valley-voice was back.

'This is business too. I have some money from my godfather. Cash,' she added meaningfully. Even coming from Rachel, this last syllable couldn't help but warm Jake's heart. 'I wanna buy something, Jakey.'

'Something? Something like what?' asked Jake, whose mind was still half focused on the stomach-churning figures he'd been looking at.

'Jesus, I don't know. Diamonds or some shit,' said Rachel, starting to sound irritated herself. She had her pride – not much of it, mind you, but enough to resent being given the brush off so peremptorily, or forced to conduct her conversations through a fucking doorbell. 'Are you gonna let me in, or what?'

Five minutes later, she was ensconced on his couch, crossing and uncrossing her long brown legs like a wannabe

Sharon Stone and gazing at him with ill-concealed lust. In a minuscule plaid skirt and heels, her white shirt unbuttoned to reveal a cleavage to rival the Grand Canyon, and her blonde hair teased into two little-girlish pigtails, she looked like every red-blooded male's schoolgirl fantasy. Unfortunately for her, Jake, who'd already fucked her more times than he'd wanted to last year and found the whole experience depressingly underwhelming, felt nothing at all beyond a mild hope that he might at last be about to make a sale.

'So,' he smiled, pretending not to notice the flash of sheer pink panties she deliberately gave him as she repositioned herself for the third or fourth time. 'Are you still thinking of something for your mom?'

'That bitch?' Rachel snarled. 'Are you kidding me? She's gross. I wouldn't get a gift for that tight-fisted fucking whore if she was dying of cancer. She's the one who turned Daddy against me, siding with Richard fucking Mayhew.'

'Who's Richard Mayhew?' asked Jake. He didn't care, but felt he needed to show some sort of interest if he was to stand any chance of flogging her a rock at long last.

'My trustee,' pouted Rachel, adding caustically, 'She's probably balling the decrepit son-of-a-bitch.'

'Fair enough,' said Jake. 'So we're not shopping for Mommy. So who were you thinking of surprising?'

But Rachel was apparently done with small talk. Vaulting athletically over to Jake's side of the couch, she straddled him, spreading her legs so widely that her tiny skirt rucked up around her waist. 'I don't give a shit, OK?' she whispered hoarsely. 'You can give the diamonds to the fucking homeless shelter for all I care. I miss you, Jakey. Let's make love.'

Arching her back, she lunged towards him like a falcon diving in for the kill.

In fairness to Rachel, a couple of months ago Jake would probably have been a willing victim. Even now, he was unable to stop his dick from twitching in response, like a prehistoric snake emerging from the permafrost into a land of unexpected sunshine. But from the waist up he knew he did *not* want to screw Rachel Kingman. If he fucked things up with Scarlett – which he seriously hoped he didn't – it'd better be over someone a good deal more worthy than a spoilt, over-sexed teen queen with all the class of Anna Nicole Smith on a Vicodin binge.

Just as Rachel's tongue darted into his mouth, the doorbell rang for a second time.

It was bizarre. No one came by the condo. Ever. And yet tonight for some strange reason he was suddenly Mr Popular.

'I'd better get that,' he said, wriggling out from under her with what he hoped came across as a disappointed shrug. 'It might be important.'

Whoever was selling tea towels this time was in luck. If Rachel was about to part with as much cash as he thought, he'd buy the guy's entire inventory and whack a nice little tip on top for his trouble.

'Hurry up,' said Rachel, straightening her skirt and hair, and perfecting her trademark pout while he ran to the door. She didn't appreciate being interrupted mid-seduction. 'I won't wait for ever, you know.'

Sure you will, thought Jake. Danny had christened Rachel 'Boomerang Girl' last year, because she'd been so impossible to get rid of. Which was mean, but not as nasty as her other nickname on the LA party scene – The Cockie Monster. Jake chuckled quietly to himself as he remembered it.

'Hello?' he said, still laughing as he picked up the intercom. 'Who is it?'

'It's me.'

It was hard to tell whose face fell faster, Jake's or Rachel's, as Scarlett's cut-glass English accent rang out through the hall.

'Listen, darling, I'm really sorry but I'm going to have to bail on tonight. Nancy's boyfriend's coming over to help me strategise some stuff for Trade Fair, and I completely forgot about it. Can you buzz me up?'

Panicked, Jake looked from Rachel to the intercom and back again, like a fox trapped between two baying packs of hounds.

'*Business*,' mouthed Rachel. '*Tied up.*'

'Er ... I'm sort of tied up, er, right now,' stammered Jake, wincing at how insincere he sounded.

'What? Well untie yourself,' said Scarlett briskly. 'I've driven all the way down here to see you, so whatever hang-up you've got about letting me see your apartment, you're going to have to get over it. I'm not leaving until you open this door.'

Jake looked at Rachel in desperation.

'Oh, for Christ's sake!' she hissed, getting crossly to her feet. Her amorous mood seemed to have deserted her. 'Just let her in. I know when I'm not wanted.'

There goes another sale, thought Jake wistfully.

'Angel, don't be like that,' he said, forgetting for a moment that he was still on speaker.

'*Angel?*' Scarlett's voice sounded suddenly hollow. 'Who are you talking to? Oh my God. Is someone with you up there?'

'Not any more,' said Rachel, smiling maliciously as she pushed past Jake and spoke directly into the intercom. 'I was just leaving. You're welcome to him, honey.'

'You bitch,' said Jake, elbowing her aside. 'Scar, are you there?'

But he was met by an echoing silence.

'Look, there's nothing going on,' he pleaded into the emptiness. 'Scarlett! Come up and see for yourself. Aw, shit.' Shoving Rachel unceremoniously through the door in front of him, he bolted down the stairs of the building two at a time, through the lobby doors and out into the street. It was rush hour, cars and people everywhere, but he couldn't see hide nor hair of Scarlett.

Spinning around, he turned his fury on Rachel.

'What the hell did you do that for?' he demanded. 'Now she thinks I'm doing the dirty on her.'

Climbing into her Lamborghini with a look of supreme unconcern on her hard, spoiled little face, Rachel shrugged. 'You will be, soon enough,' she said, matter-of-factly. 'I was just saving you both some time.'

And without a backward glance she sped off down Melrose, taking her godfather's precious bundle of cash with her.

Too upset to go straight home – she couldn't face Nancy and her I-told-you-sos, not until she'd got her head together – Scarlett drove mindlessly over Laurel Canyon to Ventura. Once in the valley, she turned into one of the hundreds of Wisteria Lane residential streets and pulled over, shaking and sweating like someone in the last stages of an acute fever.

'He's cheating on me,' she said aloud. Watching her lips move in the rear-view mirror, it was as if they were being spoken by an actor. As if this whole nightmare were some sort of farcical, out-of-body experience. 'He's cheating on me. And it hasn't even been a month.'

As soon as she'd heard the girl's spiteful, taunting voice, she turned and ran, bolting into her car as if she'd just been scalded and driving to nowhere in particular as fast as she could. But now she was regretting her impulsiveness, and wished she'd hung around to find out more. Who was this chick? She wanted to see her face, see what kind of woman had got Jake to fall at the first fucking hurdle. *Bastard*!

Just then her mobile began jumping around on her lap, buzzing like an angry bee. She startled, then assuming it was Jake, picked up and yelled into the receiver.

'Don't call me! Don't you dare call me! I don't want to hear it.'

'Er, OK,' said Nancy. 'I'll just go with the hot and sour shrimp then, shall I?'

'Oh, shit. Sorry. It's you,' said Scarlett. 'I thought you were someone else.'

'Yeah, well, I'm glad I'm not if that's how you were gonna greet them. What's happened? Are you all right?'

No, thought Scarlett. No, I'm not all right. Not remotely. 'Fine,' she said briskly, forcing herself to stop shaking through sheer effort of will. 'I'm just a bit distracted, that's all. Where are you?'

'Chin Chin,' said Nancy. 'I'll be home in five. Che Che's right behind me.'

'Good,' said Scarlett, not entirely convincingly. 'Great.'

'You *are* still on for this meeting, right?' asked Nancy. But it was more of a statement than a question.

'Sure,' said Scarlett. 'Of course.'

Talking shop with two lovebirds was the last thing on God's earth she felt like doing. But she couldn't very well sit here all night, staring at the kerb and fuming about Jake like a madwoman. Besides, a commitment was a commitment. Unlike some people she could mention, Scarlett knew how to keep her word.

'Scarlett? *Scarlett*?' Nancy waved a frustrated hand in front of her friend's face. 'Anybody home?'

'Hmm, I'm sorry?' said Scarlett, blinking. 'What were you saying?'

'*I* wasn't saying anything,' said Nancy patiently. 'Che Che wanted to know whether Andy had pitched the programme to anyone back in London.'

'I just wondered whether it might have been a copyright issue with NPR. They can get a little edgy about editorial exclusivity.'

'Oh. I see,' said Scarlett. She was trying to concentrate, truly she was. She knew that getting the Yakutian miners' story out there was infinitely more important than her relationship with Jake, or rather her ex-relationship ... dickhead, how could he make a fool out of her like that ...

'Scarlett!' Nancy kicked her under the table. 'Wake up! Did Andy show it to the BBC or not?'

'Er, no. At least, I don't think so. He never said anything to me.' Scarlett smiled apologetically to Che Che, who smiled back, a disarming flash of ivory against his jet-black skin. 'In any case, the NPR producer said it was a scheduling issue.'

'Which makes no sense at all, as they commissioned it,' said Che Che.

'Exactly,' nodded Scarlett, wondering if this was the first time Jake had done the dirty on her, or if she'd been one of many all along. 'I do appreciate your help with this, or rather your friend's help,' she said sincerely, standing up to clear away the empty plates. 'I'm sorry I'm a bit distracted.'

A few minutes later, she was so absorbed in scrubbing dried noodle off one of Nancy's chipped rose bowls that she didn't even see Jake striding up the garden path. He was on the porch and through the screen doors before she knew he was there, never mind had a chance to lock him out.

'Hi,' said Nancy, rising to greet him with as much cordiality as she could muster. 'Scarlett didn't mention you'd be coming by. Can I offer you a glass of red?'

Jake's eyes narrowed in confusion. Was this a trick question? But his attention soon swung back to Scarlett, who was staring intently into the sudsy water of the sink, as if suddenly fascinated by the floating remnants of Che Che's Singapore Ho Fun (No Pork).

'We need to talk,' he said, dropping his voice to a whisper as he walked up behind her.

'I'll take that as a "no" to the wine then, shall I?' said Nancy, rolling her eyes at Che Che. Really, if she could make the effort to be polite, the least Jake could do was respond.

'No we don't,' Scarlett hissed back. She could feel her eyes welling up with tears of anger, and bit her lip hard in an effort to bite them back. 'There's nothing to say.'

'It's not what you think,' said Jake. 'There was nothing going on.'

'Please!' Scarlett spun around to face him, a picture of righteous indignation. Suddenly she didn't care if Nancy and Che Che heard or not. They were going to find out sooner or later. 'So if I'd had a hidden camera in that apartment, I wouldn't have seen anything to upset me? Nothing at all?'

Jake hesitated. An image of Rachel straddling him, her head thrown back wantonly, popped up in his mind's eye.

'She was a client. I was trying to make a sale,' he said, trying not to lie outright, and wishing he didn't have to have this conversation in front of an audience, especially an audience as hostile as Nancy. 'Look, can we talk in your bedroom?'

'My *bedroom*? I don't think so,' said Scarlett. He wasn't about to charm her back into the sack that easily.

'Outside then,' pleaded Jake. He looked so desperate, and every bit as miserable as she did. It was hard not to feel a tiny bit sorry for him. 'All I'm asking for is a chance to explain. You owe me that much, at least.'

'Owe you? I don't owe you anything,' said Scarlett firmly. But she was also conscious of Nancy and Che Che's eyes boring into her back. Drying her hands on a tea towel, she followed him out into the garden.

Outside there was a chill in the air, although the night was beautifully clear. Sitting down on a wooden bench at the bottom of the garden, the furthest point from the house, Scarlett leaned back against the wall and gazed heavenwards. She could clearly make out the pole star and Orion's belt. It was difficult for one's problems to seem significant against such an awe-inspiring cosmic backdrop.

'Her name is Rachel,' said Jake, taking a deep breath and deciding to begin at the beginning. 'I wasn't expecting her to show up tonight. Haven't laid eyes on her in almost six months, in fact. But she rang the doorbell unannounced, saying she wanted to buy something from me.'

'What?' asked Scarlett suspiciously.

'She wasn't specific,' said Jake. Then, realising how lame this must sound, added hastily, 'There wasn't time. She just said she'd got some cash and she wanted to do a trade. She'd only been there five minutes when you showed up.'

'Something she seemed pretty pissed off about,' said Scarlett angrily, her voice rising despite herself. 'Look, Jake, I'm not stupid, OK? I obviously interrupted something. *Rachel* admitted as much over the speakerphone.'

'You didn't interrupt anything,' insisted Jake, grabbing her hand and willing her to believe him. Perhaps this was karma, payback for all the times he *had* been fooling around and gotten away with it. Now here he was, innocent as a lamb, and about to lose the one girl he'd ever really cared for over nothing. If it was karma, it seemed a high price to pay. 'She's a spoiled little bitch, OK? She came on to me, I told her I wasn't interested, and she got shirty.'

Scarlett rolled her eyes disbelievingly. '*She* came on to *you*?'

'It's the truth!' said Jake. 'She only made out something was going on to you because she was jealous.'

Looking down at the lights of Hollywood twinkling in the valley below like a tacky, sequinned carpet, Scarlett felt awash with conflicting emotions. She wanted to believe him, wanted it so desperately that she feared it must be clouding her judgement. Even if, by some miracle, he *was* telling the truth and nothing had happened – how could she know that it wasn't simply because she'd interrupted them before he had a chance to give in?

'How old is she?' she asked, apropos of nothing.

'Nineteen,' said Jake, closing his eyes and waiting for

the inevitable shit storm to hit him. But Scarlett seemed remarkably calm.

'I see. And have you slept with her in the past?'

Another long silence. Why did she have to keep asking questions that forced him either to lie or to dig his own grave?

'Yes,' he said eventually. 'Last year a few times. We were never an item, though.'

'But she's been to your apartment before, right?'

'Well, yes, but . . .'

'Unlike me,' said Scarlett pointedly. Suddenly the tears that had been threatening to overwhelm her all evening made an appearance. 'I'm tired of being your dirty little secret, Jake,' she sniffed. 'You don't act like my boyfriend in public, you don't let me stay at your place. I mean, what the hell am I supposed to think? Are we a couple, or not?'

'Of course we are. Of course we're a couple,' said Jake. He was about to add 'I love you,' but changed his mind at the last minute, opening and closing his mouth like an accused criminal being silenced by an invisible attorney.

'So what's it all about?' sobbed Scarlett. 'Why do you have to be so . . . so *sly*?'

He hated to see her cry. Without thinking, he pulled her into his arms and held her. Too tired to fight any more, Scarlett let him. But she still wanted an explanation.

Now it was Jake's turn to look away for inspiration. What was he supposed to tell her? Clearly the truth – that he was used to having his own space; that he would need somewhere Scarlett-free to retreat to and lick his wounds once she finally realised how much better she could do than him and left him; that flirting with female customers was an integral part of his business, and he couldn't *afford* to appear too completely attached in public – was not an option. But no suitable white lie was leaping to mind either.

'Look, I know I'm not perfect,' he said eventually,

skirting the issue as deftly as he could. 'But I'm trying, babe, I really am. I'm trying to be what you want. Can't you just—'

'Just what?' asked Scarlett, drying her tears.

'Wait?'

He looked so hopeful, like a little boy asking his mother for a birthday present, knowing that what he wants is too expensive.

'Be patient? And trust me? I swear to you, on my life: I did not cheat on you with Rachel.'

His face in the moonlight was so unearthly handsome, Scarlett wished she had a fraction of Che Che's gift for sketching. With his long, straight nose, hypnotic amethyst eyes and thick pieces of blonde hair falling forwards, some as far down as his cheekbones, she wondered how on earth she'd resisted him sexually for so long. Magnus seemed like the palest of pale shadows by comparison.

She believed what he said about Rachel. She didn't know why, but it felt true. Even so, the fragility of their relationship, whatever this thing was that they had together, had been brought home to her with renewed force tonight. It was time to face some home truths:

She would never be able to escape Jake's past. Not while they lived in LA.

Beautiful, predatory girls would continue to consider him fair game.

He would continue to flirt with them, in the name of business.

And even if he did remain faithful to her, there would be a part of him that he continued to hold back. His fetish about the apartment was almost certainly the tip of a much bigger, much more worrying iceberg. He was hers, but not hers. And that might never change.

'Don't give up on me yet,' he whispered, reading her mind. But it was the unbearable slowness of his touch as his hand stroked her inner thigh, and not his psychic powers, that had her resolve crumbling like flaky pastry.

'All right,' she sighed, opening her lips to receive his kiss. Relief that she wasn't about to lose him mingled with the desire sweeping through her body like radiation. Her hands reached up around the back of his neck.

'Can we go inside now?' His voice was gruff and urgent between kisses. His breath felt warm against her ear, and she could feel and hear his excitement, greater even than her own.

Scarlett just about managed a nod. Clasping his hand tightly, she followed him back up the path toward the house.

But as soon as they stepped through the porch doors, she let go of him.

'What happened?'

Nancy, slumped against the wall like a rag-doll, was shaking and white as a sheet. Scarlett rushed to her side and shot an accusatory glance at Che Che, until she saw the concern writ large on his face too.

'Her father just called,' he said. 'Her mom's been diagnosed with a brain tumour.'

'Inoperable,' said Nancy weakly. 'They told her it was inoperable. We should have forced her to get a second opinion at Christmas. Now it's too late.'

'You mustn't blame yourself.' Sinking to her knees, Scarlett flung her arms around her friend. Jake and Che Che looked on awkwardly, both wanting to help, but neither knowing how. 'Besides, maybe there is something they can do, with radiation or whatever. Or maybe the doctor made a mistake? I mean, they're not always infallible, right?'

'I have to go back to New York,' said Nancy, staring straight ahead like a zombie.

'We'll go together,' said Che Che, stepping forward, relieved to have found a role at last. 'I'll cancel my exhibition. We can fly in the morning.'

'No,' said Nancy, not even looking up. 'Dad won't want anyone who isn't family. I appreciate the offer, but I have to do this on my own.'

Scarlett was totally focused on Nancy. Only Jake saw the way Che Che recoiled, stung by her rejection. Perhaps all was not as blissful in that love affair as Scarlett made out?

'OK,' said Che Che, with a fixed, rigor mortis smile. 'Well, at least let me book your tickets. I'll go online and do it right now.'

'Thanks,' said Nancy absently. In her mind she was already at her mother's bedside. She just prayed that by the time she actually got there, it wouldn't already be too late.

# Seventeen

Earlier that same day, in New York, Danny sat across the desk from his divorce attorney, a jovial bear of a man who rejoiced in the improbable name of Wentworth Chambers, trying to keep a lid on his despair.

'Don't look so worried,' said Wentworth kindly. 'She's only fifteen minutes late. That's seconds in female-time. It's kinda like dog years, only the other way around.'

Danny smiled weakly. 'Yeah.'

'We can always go ahead without her, you know. It's only a progress meeting.'

'I know,' said Danny, privately thinking how odd it was to call something a 'progress' meeting when the only direction they were going was backwards. 'But at the end of the day this is her divorce, not mine. She should be here.'

He was well aware that all was not well with Diana. Or rather, that all was not well between Diana and him. They loved each other – that wasn't the problem. But the combined pressure of their dire financial situation, the ongoing divorce, the pregnancy and his family's hostility was pushing their so-called romance to breaking point. She'd complained the other day that it had been months since she'd seen him laugh, and she was right. He was turning into a card-carrying misery-guts. But recently life seemed to have transformed into one back-breaking burden after another. If he couldn't make her happy when it was just the two of them, how on earth was he supposed to provide for a child?

The biggest thorn in his side, however, continued to be Brogan. Not content with destroying his business and refusing to give Diana a divorce, now he was playing the sympathy card, to devastatingly good effect. Last night Danny had slept on the couch in high dudgeon, after Diana floated the idea of visiting Brogan in hospital.

'Those cancer wards are terrible places,' she said, putting the finishing touches to an embroidered muslin for the baby. 'I remember when my Aunt Maud was in one. The entire floor smelled of death.' She shuddered. 'But at least she had us. Brogan has no close friends, no family to comfort him.'

'Well whose fault is that?' said Danny, incredulous. 'He doesn't have any friends because he's an arsehole, Di. Besides, he won't be on a cancer ward. He'll be in some private suite that probably costs more per night than a year's rent on this dump. Which, by the way, we are only living in because your darling husband is continuing to rob us blind.'

'I know, but—'

'But nothing,' Danny snapped. 'You're not going to see him and that's final.'

Well, the 'firm hand' approach had turned out to be an error, hadn't it? Jesus, she'd flown at him like a banshee, a one-woman ball of fury powered by pregnancy hormones. How dare he speak to her like that! He called Brogan a bully, but was he, Danny, any better? He didn't own her … In the end he'd given up trying to apologise – why did he always have to be in the wrong, anyway? – and skulked off to the couch. When he woke up this morning, with a crick in his neck worthy of a hospital bed of its own, Diana had already gone out. She knew about today's meeting with Wentworth. Clearly finishing up her damn divorce wasn't top of her priority list this morning.

'Why don't I give you a brief summary of where things stand?' said the lawyer, sensing Danny's darkening mood. 'You can fill Diana in later. There is *some* good news you know, Mr Meyer.'

'Has he died?' asked Danny, deadpan.

'Not yet.' Wentworth grinned so wickedly, even Danny had to laugh. 'But you never know your luck. In the meantime, it seems he's decided not to contest Diana's latest financial statements.'

'Which means?'

'We could be back to arbitration as soon as next month,' said Wentworth brightly.

'*Arbitration?*' Danny seemed less thrilled by this prospect than the lawyer. 'What, again? When do we get to *court* is what I wanna know. When can we finish this thing?'

Wentworth gave him a puzzled frown.

'We can go to court as soon as you like. Didn't Diana tell you?'

Danny looked blank. 'Tell me what?'

'Brogan agreed to sign the papers before the holidays,' said Wentworth, somewhat awkwardly. 'It's Diana who's been holding off. She wanted to go back to round-table discussions.'

'She wanted what?' Now it was Danny's turn to look puzzled. 'But ... why? That doesn't make any sense.'

Wentworth shrugged. 'She told me she wanted to make some changes to her financial statements. Very minor points, but they seemed important to her.'

Danny said nothing. He didn't have to.

Diana was having second thoughts about going through with it. All these delays were just excuses. She'd changed her mind, and been too scared to tell him.

'I think,' said Wentworth gently, 'this is something that you and she need to discuss between yourselves. I can help, but only if you both agree on what you want. I wouldn't want to charge you for wasted hours.'

'No,' said Danny bleakly, getting up to leave. 'Thank you. I appreciate everything you've done.'

'Talk to her,' Wentworth counselled him. 'Divorce is never an easy thing, even when it's the right thing.'

But Danny's head was pounding so loudly, he could barely hear him.

Diana watched the numbers climb on the red elevator LCD – 5, 6, 7 – and felt her stomach lurch with each additional floor.

Danny had been right about the private room. The duty nurse downstairs informed her that Brogan was on the fourteenth floor (the penthouse, naturally) in a suite of rooms usually reserved for visiting royalty, major hospital donors and their families, or Hollywood stars. But a cancer hospital was still a cancer hospital. However upscale, the walls still dripped with pain. Even the smooth, chrome elevator seemed to echo with sadness and fear as Diana made her slow, nervous way up through the heart of the building.

What was she doing here, really? Was she proving a point to Danny, or herself? Was this about making her own choices? About compassion for a man she'd once loved? Or was it something much less noble than that? An escape, perhaps, from the doubts and uncertainties besetting her on all sides. She wanted so desperately to make a new start with Danny, to raise their child together, to leave the past behind. And yet the past kept calling to her, tugging at her heart strings, playing on her guilt. And all the while Dan seemed so utterly, utterly unhappy. If this was true love, all she could say was that it wasn't everything it was cracked up to be.

'Mrs O'Donnell?'

The elevator doors opened. Diana stepped out into what looked for all the world like a hotel lobby. Certainly the uniformed man who greeted her looked more like a concierge than an oncology nurse.

'That's right,' she whispered. She didn't know why, but hospitals always gave her the urge to whisper. 'Is he, erm ... is he well enough for a visit?'

'Oh yes,' the man smiled. 'He's wide awake. And expecting you. Please, follow me.'

She walked in to a room flooded with sunlight. In front of the window was a huge vase of sweetly scented freesias, perched on an antique walnut table. Adjacent to this was a desk, another gorgeous piece of furniture and quite decidedly not hospital standard-issue, on top of which lay Brogan's laptop, open at the Bloomberg pages. His BlackBerry flashed green beside it while it charged, and papers and memos littered the remaining available surface. Clearly he'd been up and working already this morning.

'I see some things never change,' she said, walking over to the bed where he sat propped up with pillows, a Wall Street Journal spread across his lap. 'You should be resting. Keeping your strength up, remember?'

'I am,' he grinned, making no attempt to hide his delight at seeing her. 'I had a lie-in till six. You look wonderful.'

'I look fat,' said Diana, blushing and patting the small mound of her pregnant belly awkwardly. For some reason she felt crippled with nerves, seeing him again. To her relief, he didn't yet *look* like a cancer patient. He still had his hair, and apart from minor weight loss looked much the same as she remembered. Even so, she struggled to meet his eye.

'Not at all. You're glowing. Pregnancy suits you.'

'Thank you.'

She jumped at the sound of the door closing as the concierge/nurse left the room.

'It's all right,' said Brogan. 'You're quite safe. I'm in no condition to do anyone any harm.'

'It's not that,' she mumbled. 'It's … odd, that's all. Me being here. I didn't know if you'd want to see me. You know, under the circumstances.'

'What circumstances are those?' said Brogan. 'Me dying, or you being knocked up with another man's child?'

Diana looked up, horrified.

'Stop it. You're not dying,' she said seriously, before

noticing the wry smile on his face. 'Oh, for God's sake, Brogan, don't joke!'

'Why not?' Laughing openly now, he reached for her hand and pulled her closer to the bed. 'Things can't get much worse, can they? Does Danny Boy know you're here?'

Diana hesitated. She should have told him to mind his own business – she didn't want to talk about Danny – but the way he was stroking the inside of her wrist was distracting, and she couldn't seem to find the words.

'He doesn't, does he?' Brogan couldn't keep the triumph out of his voice.

'I didn't want to worry him,' she said lamely, belatedly withdrawing her hand. 'He has a lot on his plate right now.'

'Does he? My heart bleeds,' sneered Brogan. 'So, tell me. Why *did* you come?'

'I ...' Diana stumbled. It was the question she'd been asking herself all morning. Looking into Brogan's eyes, his gaze so searing, so unrelenting, she was painfully aware that she still didn't have a satisfactory answer. 'It seemed like the right thing to do,' she said eventually. 'I still ... I care about you, all right? We were married a long time.'

'We're still married,' said Brogan.

He wasn't about to let her off the hook now. Clearly, all was not well between her and Meyer. Just when he'd been about to give up hope of a reconciliation, his cancer had opened up a window, the slimmest crack, a glimpse of daylight, a chance to win her back. If it was the last thing he did – and at this point, it very well might be – he intended to wedge his fingers into that tiny gap and pull and pull until he could drag her through it.

'You know what I think?' he said, seizing on her silence. 'I think you still love me.'

'Please,' she whispered. 'Don't.'

'That's why you held up the divorce,' he pressed on

mercilessly. 'That's why you came here today, behind lover boy's back.'

'It wasn't behind his back,' she said. 'It wasn't like that. You're twisting things.'

'Bullshit,' said Brogan. 'I'm calling a spade a spade. You think it's too late but it isn't.'

'It is.' Up to this point she'd been staring firmly at her shoes, but now she looked up at him, her expression pleading, her eyes brimming with tears. 'The baby ...' she began.

'*I'll* bring up the baby,' said Brogan. 'You think I wouldn't love any child of yours? Christ, honey, I pushed you into all this; I know that now. I don't blame you. But you can't stay with this guy just because you're pregnant. You don't love him.'

'I *do*,' she insisted, sobbing. 'I *do* love him.'

'Not like you love me.' Reaching forward, he put a hand on the back of her neck and pressed his lips against hers. For a moment she resisted, her back and shoulders stiff, her mouth unyielding, rigid with shock. But then to his joy and surprise, she started to kiss him back, a desperate, longing, searching kiss, fuelled by guilt, by need, by the embers of the early passion they'd once shared, back before life became so complicated.

Releasing her at last, he whispered in her ear. 'Come back to me. Come back to me, my darling. Please. I need you now more than ever.'

Diana opened her mouth to speak, but no sound emerged. Instead she shook her head, turned and ran from the room, not stopping until she reached the elevator. Frenziedly hammering on the 'close doors' button, she felt her heart race so fast it made her nauseous.

What had she done?

What in God's name had she just done?

Back at their apartment later that evening, Danny poured

322

himself his third whisky and stared mindlessly at the TV screen. How the fuck had *Antiques Roadshow* transformed itself into one of the most successful global formats for a TV show? Who wanted to watch a bunch of greedy OAPs salivating over a Renaissance harpsichord stand?

After leaving Wentworth's office this morning, he'd spent the rest of the day mooching aimlessly around the city, intermittently calling Diana's mobile, which had remained resolutely switched off, and going round and round in circles in his head. He knew he ought to talk to Jake about quitting Solomon Stones – for months now he'd been nothing but a drain on their joint finances, and with a baby on the way he had to start thinking about finding himself some sort of paid employment – but he hadn't the courage nor the energy to start that conversation today. Besides, until he knew where he stood with Diana – where he *really* stood – he couldn't focus on anything else. He loved her so fucking much. How had everything gone so pear shaped? How had he played it all so badly?

When she finally walked through the door at eight o'clock, wet and tired, he was torn between relief at seeing her and anger about what Wentworth had told him this morning. What the hell was she playing at, stalling the divorce? And where had she been all day?

'I tried to call you,' he said grumpily, without either standing up or switching off the TV. 'About a hundred times.'

'My phone was off,' said Diana, hanging up her wet coat and sinking down into the tatty armchair opposite him. His eyes had the frozen, glazed look of the slightly drunk. Looking at him, she felt overwhelmingly depressed.

'You don't say,' he said bitterly. 'I'd ask you where you've been, but then again you'll probably only lie to me, so what's the point?'

'What do you mean?' she said, stung by his aggression. 'I don't lie to you.'

'Not much,' he laughed bleakly. 'I had an interesting meeting with your divorce lawyer this morning. He told me Brogan agreed to sign the papers weeks ago. Funny you never mentioning that, while I've been working my tits off trying to keep our heads above water.'

'I'm sorry.' Diana looked shamefaced. 'I know I should have told you. I needed time to think.'

'About what?' said Danny. 'About how long you planned to string me along?'

All he wanted to do was take her and kiss her and make love to her. But it all got muddled up inside and came spewing out as anger. She was only a few feet away, and yet the distance between them in that moment felt like an ocean, unswimmable, unbridgeable, hopeless.

'I went to see Brogan today,' said Diana, fiddling nervously with the ring she'd bought from him the night they met. Pregnancy had swollen her fingers so much she now wore it on a chain around her neck.

'What a surprise,' said Danny. On the screen in front of him a chubby middle-aged woman was handing over a revolting gold and pink vase to one of the show's 'experts'. He kept his eyes glued to her paisley-clad bosom as he spoke, unwilling or unable to show Diana the crushing pain he felt inside. 'How was he?'

'All right. Better than I expected,' she said, adding so quietly that at first he could barely hear her, 'He kissed me.'

Danny felt the bile rising up in his throat, but said nothing. It was like sleepwalking through a nightmare, knowing that you couldn't wake up.

'I kissed him back,' whispered Diana. 'I'm sorry.'

She wasn't sure why she was telling him. Perhaps because, at this point, there seemed nothing to lose by being honest. What did she want him to do? Yell at her? Forgive her? Cry? She didn't know. Any sort of reaction would be better than this blankness, this hopeless, comatose stare that he hid behind whenever the going got rough.

'Aren't you going to say anything?' she asked, once the silence became too deafening to bear.

'Like what?' Finally, wearily, Danny picked up the remote and switched off the TV. 'If you want to go back to him, go. I'm not gonna stop you.'

Diana's eyes brimmed with tears. 'You don't love me any more, do you?'

'Jesus Christ!' Jumping to his feet, Danny threw his empty whisky glass on the floor, shattering it into thousands of shards of crystal. '*You're* the one creeping around with your ex behind my back! *You're* the one who's been lying through her teeth about the divorce since fucking Christmas. *I* don't love *you*? Look in the fucking mirror, Di.'

'You've been miserable as sin ever since I told you I was pregnant!' she shouted back at him. In a weird sort of way it was a relief to be fighting openly at last.

'It was a shock,' admitted Danny. 'It may have escaped your notice, but we're barely scraping by as a couple. How are we supposed to afford this baby? Have you ever thought about that?'

'Don't be so ridiculous,' said Diana. 'People have babies all over the world, people with nothing. All you seem to care about is money, money, money.'

'Oh really? As opposed to your magnanimous ex?' Danny's eyes widened. 'Brogan's giving it all away to charity, is he? Converted on the road to the radiology unit?'

'Shut up!' shouted Diana. 'At least he wants this baby! It isn't even his, but he wants it more than you do.'

As soon as the words were out of her mouth, she regretted them. Danny's face darkened, and a muscle in his jaw began to twitch.

'I'm sorry,' she said. 'I shouldn't have said that.'

'It's fine.' Walking past her towards the door, he slipped on his bomber jacket. All the energy, all the spirit had gone from his voice. It was like he'd given up.

'Where are you going?' asked Diana, panicked.

'Out.'

'But you can't. Danny, you can't just run away. We have to talk about this.'

He looked back with a sad half-smile.

'There's nothing left to say, is there? I tried, Di, I really did. But I can't do this on my own. I just … I can't.'

Diana waited until the apartment door had swung closed behind him and the last thud of his footsteps had faded away. Then she walked numbly into the bedroom, pulled her suitcase out of the battered old wardrobe, and started to pack.

# Eighteen

Three weeks later, Jake sat opposite Danny in a corner booth at Cohen's Deli in the East Village, warming his chilblained hands over a cup of steaming chicken broth.

'I don't know how you stand this cold,' he complained, shaking his head as the door of the restaurant opened briefly, allowing a flurry of snow and biting wind to blast towards their table. 'New York in February makes London feel like St bloody Tropez.'

Danny shrugged. 'You get used to it.'

Since Diana had moved out, he'd barely had the energy to get out of bed in the mornings, never mind respond to Jake's brotherly banter. She'd returned not to Brogan – not yet, anyway – but to her parents' house in East Hampton, where Danny had seen her once, the day of her twenty-week ultrasound scan. How excruciating that had been, standing beside her like a spare part, staring at the grainy monitor. Although the technician claimed that the blobs represented a healthy growing foetus, Danny could make out nothing but a series of grey blobs. But the truth was he hadn't come to see the baby. It was Diana who haunted his dreams, whose face filled his waking moments, a daily, hourly vision of regret. He'd come hoping to talk to her, to try to make things right. But of course, once he got there, he had no idea where to begin. Her elderly parents, understandably frosty towards him, had refused to leave the two of them alone for a second until they left for the hospital. But even there, he'd some-how managed to let three whole hours slip through his fingers like sand, feigning a polite indifference that he was very far from feeling, too frightened even to hold Diana's hand.

Only Jake understood how hard her defection had hit him, and that was more through twin-tuition than any direct communication on Danny's part. He'd flown to New York ostensibly to discuss restructuring the business – Danny seemed intent on getting out of Solomon Stones, much against Jake's wishes – but the truth was he was worried about his brother.

For Danny's sake, he was glad he'd come, but leaving LA had been a wrench. After the misunderstanding with Rachel, he'd been treading on eggshells with Scarlett, trying to win back her already fragile trust. It wasn't easy. Women in LA loved to gossip, especially the bored, rich, nothing-better-to-do-with-their-lives girls that shopped at Flawless. Scarlett was forever being told that Jake had been seen with such and such a woman – invariably clients – and that the pair of them had looked 'very friendly'. He did his best to put her mind at rest. But he was also starting to resent being forced to defend himself on a daily basis. What did she want from him, blood? Didn't she understand that he had to make a living? And that this was how his living was made?

It didn't help that with the Oscars days away, Trade Fair was now right back at the front of her agenda and Scarlett was working like a dog, which meant they had less time together than ever. Honestly, Jake could strangle that fucker Che Che. Why couldn't he just have written a cheque like any normal person, and been done with it, instead of stirring her up about those bloody Russian miners again? This of course meant more time for the malicious gossips to poison the well, and sow doubt in her mind with their innuendos and shit-stirring. It was all highly taxing.

Obviously his love-life woes were as nothing compared to poor Danny's. But he couldn't help thinking that this was supposed to be the 'honeymoon period' of his and

Scarlett's relationship. So far their first two months as a couple had been rockier than Grand fucking Rapids.

'So,' said Danny, desultorily prodding his matzo ball with a fork. 'About dissolving the partnership ...'

Jake held up a hand to interrupt him.

'Look, we agreed. No rash decisions.'

'I'd hardly call it rash,' said Danny. 'You've been carrying me for over a year now. And things are gonna get worse before they get better. It's me Brogan's after. As long as I'm part of Solomon Stones, he'll be on our backs.'

'But he knows ... you and Diana?' Jake tried to choose his words carefully.

'That we're separated? I'm sure he does. Those two are thick as thieves these days,' said Danny, unable to conceal the bitterness in his voice. 'It doesn't matter, though. As far as he's concerned, I stole Diana from him, and he's never gonna forgive me for that. If I pull out of the business, you and Scarlett might just have a chance.'

'But that's crazy,' protested Jake. 'The guy's got cancer. He won't have the energy to pursue some personal vendetta.'

'I wouldn't bet on it,' said Danny. 'Look at the way he hounded Scarlett, the lengths he went to.'

'That was different,' said Jake.

'Yeah,' agreed Danny. 'This is worse. He hates me far, far more than he ever hated Scarlett. And he's so powerful now, he doesn't need to waste his energy. He has a legion of minions to do his dirty work for him. Have you seen OMC's latest press release?'

'The Sgaarstadt mine, you mean? Yeah, I saw it,' Jake nodded grimly.

Since the New Year, some sick God seemed to have been pouring Miracle-gro on O'Donnell Mining Corp's profits. Already the fastest-growing business in the sector globally, and by far the most profitable player in Russia, at this rate it wouldn't be long before the unthinkable happened and Brogan emerged as a viable competitor to the once-invincible Cuypers. The only question was whether he would beat his illness and live long enough to enjoy such a triumph.

'Forget Brogan for a minute,' said Jake, still unwilling to cut Danny loose. 'You've spent half your life building this business.'

Danny shrugged again. 'I don't care,' he said bleakly. 'I want out. I want to start again.'

'Start again doing what?' asked Jake. 'What are you going to do? Open a fucking garden centre? Diamonds is what we do, bruv. It's who we are.'

'It's not who I am,' said Danny. 'Not any more.'

'Well, what about the baby then?' asked Jake, clutching at straws. 'Don't you want to leave something for your son?'

'My son.' Danny repeated the words softly, as if puzzled by their meaning.

'Yes, your son,' said Jake. 'Diana might have slung her hook, but that baby's still yours.'

'Brogan wants her back, you know,' said Danny, staring into space. 'Her and the baby. He wants them to raise it together.'

'And you're gonna let that happen, are you?' Jake could feel his temper rising. Heartbreak was all very well, but Danny had to snap out of this life-sapping apathy and fast if he wanted to protect his child. 'You're gonna let that maniac, that *rapist,* bring up your kid?'

'It's not up to me, is it?' said Danny, his voice breaking with emotion. 'Diana and I never married. She holds all the cards here. She can do what she wants and I can't stop her.'

'All right.' Reaching across the table, Jake put a hand on his shoulder. 'It's all right, mate. We'll think of something.'

He knew what it was like to feel powerless when it

came to the woman you loved. He'd been begging Scarlett for weeks to drop this NPR thing about Brogan's Russian miners, but she was having none of it. Half the KGB old guard worked for O'Donnell these days, and those guys brought new meaning to the word 'ruthless'.

Since meeting Dr Katenge and becoming involved with the Freetown orphans, he'd become much more sympathetic to Trade Fair and what Scarlett was trying to achieve – although he was too stubborn to admit this change of heart, and had yet to mention the trip either to her or to Danny. But he hated the idea of her putting herself in harm's way, and hated even more his inability to prevent it.

For her part, Scarlett longed for his support with Trade Fair, for encouragement, a pat on the back. Dismissing his fears about her safety as melodramatic and ridiculous, and his concern for the business as selfish, she felt let down by his reticence.

'You're being a total coward,' she'd chastised him a few days ago, before he came out here to see Danny. 'Brogan turns up the heat half a notch, and you want me to drop the whole thing and run for the hills. And for what? So you and I can keep our nice little earner going in Beverly Hills, and I can have more nights free for dinner and sex?'

'Well, what's so wrong with dinner and sex?' Jake had replied angrily. 'You put yourself out enough to keep the home fires burning with Magnus, flying off to bleeding Seattle left, right, and centre. I'm five minutes down the road. Why am I always last on your list?'

Scarlett saw his negativity about reviving Trade Fair as another betrayal. What she couldn't see was how little *she* was supporting *him*. How her constant, nagging doubts about his commitment, and her devotion to her work and her cause, were pushing him further away with every passing day.

Jake clung to the hope that perhaps after the Oscars

things would improve. Scarlett would have more time for him, and the almost constant rows and misunderstandings might stop. He certainly hoped so, especially if the alternative was joining Danny at the Heartbreak Hotel.

'I'll tell you what we'll do for now,' he said, wrenching his mind back to Danny and their immediate problems. 'You sell me an option on your share of Solomon Stones.'

'An option?'

'Yeah, you know. The right to buy you out. It means you can't sell to anyone else for the next six months.'

'I know what an option *is*,' said Danny. 'I'm just wondering why on earth you'd wanna do that. No one else is gonna buy me out. It's pointless.'

'No it's not,' said Jake firmly. 'It'll give you some cash now, which you need. It'll save me being saddled with some weirdo partner I don't want. And it'll give you a bit of breathing space to come to your senses and change your mind.'

'I'm not going to change my mind,' said Danny.

'Course you will,' Jake grinned. 'Just as soon as you discover what the rest of us already know.'

'And what's that?' asked Danny.

'That you're completely crap at everything else,' said Jake cheerfully. 'In the meantime, give me the names of your lily-livered, defecting customers – I only want the sexy ones, obviously – and I'll stick around for a few days, see if I can't tempt them back into the old Solomon Stones fold.'

Danny laughed.

'It won't do any good,' he said. 'But you're welcome to try. Of course, Scarlett won't be best pleased if she catches you at it.'

'Scarlett's never best pleased, no matter what I do,' said Jake with feeling. 'Besides, I'm not planning on doing the dirty on her. Just switching on a bit of the old Meyer charm, that's all.'

'And what she doesn't know won't hurt her, right?' said Danny.

'Exactly,' said Jake. 'Exactly.'

The next morning, Scarlett lay sprawled on an outdoor massage table at Shutters beside Nancy, losing herself in the delicious sensation of the two-handed Hawaiian massage and listening to the soft lapping of the waves against the shore. It was the first time she'd felt relaxed in … actually, she couldn't even remember the last time she'd felt relaxed, not properly. If only Nancy were here under happier circumstances, today's spa mini-break would have been utterly perfect.

'When I left the house yesterday, she was out cold,' Nancy was saying. She'd vowed not to talk about her mom today – to allow herself a few hours of mental release – but in the event she found it impossible not to. There was nothing else in her head. 'She looks so peaceful on the morphine. I've half a mind to try and get hold of some myself.'

'Get some for me while you're at it,' said Scarlett drowsily. 'Although actually, this massage is almost as good. How're you feeling?'

'Good,' said Nancy, unconvincingly. Try as she might, she couldn't let go, not even under the expert fingers of the Shutters masseuses. 'Fine. It's awful the way your mind works though. As I got in the cab to JFK, part of me was thinking, what if she doesn't wake up? Or what if she wakes up just one more time, sees I'm not there and then, you know, that's it? By the time I get back on Monday she's gone, and I never got to say goodbye?'

Her voice began to falter. Reaching out a bare arm, Scarlett touched her gently on the shoulder.

'The doctor said she was stable,' she said, reassuringly. 'I'm sure it won't happen like that. But you know what, even if it did, your mum knows how much you love her.

You've had a lifetime to prove that to her. She wouldn't have wanted you to miss the Paramount meeting. You've worked for this for years.'

'Yeah, well,' Nancy laughed wryly. 'She might not have wanted me to miss it. But I know someone who did.'

Che Che, who was already secretly put out by Nancy's refusal to let him help during her mom's illness, was furious about her latest project. A treatment she'd written years ago, a black comedy about an African refugee moving to a New York housing project, had been optioned by Paramount Studios, who were about to move it into the development phase. In an almost unheard-of vote of confidence in Nancy as a writer, they'd floated the idea of having her work on the project full time as a 'creative advisor', alongside their own in-house screenwriters. Not only would this mean big bucks if the movie ever saw the light of day, but it would earn her a much-coveted 'co-creator' credit – an incredible accomplishment for a jobbing writer like herself with zero studio experience.

Unfortunately, Che Che had got a bee in his bonnet about the story from day one.

'It's patronising. It's stereotypical. It's crass,' he railed at her on the phone when she'd called from New York to break the good news.

'Well, duh, of course it is,' she joked. 'It's a Hollywood movie. I never said it was gonna be Dr Zhivago.'

'I'm serious,' thundered Che Che. 'It's utterly disrespect-ful, to me and to everyone else who suffered like my family and I did.'

'Jesus, lighten up, would you?' said Nancy, crossly. After a long, gruelling day keeping vigil at her mother's deathbed, she could do without a moral lecture from her boyfriend. 'It's a comedy.'

'Oh yeah, hilarious,' seethed Che Che. 'And why exactly are African refugees considered funny? Because we're black?'

334

'Whaaaat?' said Nancy. 'What on earth has that got to do with anything?'

'I don't see Paramount making a whole bunch of comedies about the Holocaust, do you? Ben Stiller in *Gas the Parents*? That ain't gonna get optioned any time soon.'

On one level, of course, she could see he had a point. But he of all people should know she was no racist. And besides, the script wasn't disrespectful. It was warm and funny, and having a big studio bite at it was the single best thing ever to have happened in her career. She couldn't understand why he was being such a jerk about it.

'If you loved me, you'd be happy for me,' she heard herself saying, fighting back the tears in her father's study.

'If you loved *me*, you'd tell Paramount you've changed your mind and throw the damn thing in the trash where it belongs,' snapped Che Che. At which point Nancy hung up on him. The pair of them hadn't spoken since.

'He'll come round,' said Scarlett, who had heard about the argument from both Che Che and Nancy. Though firmly on Nancy's side, she didn't want to alienate Che Che completely. Thanks to him NPR had reinstated her interview on next month's playlist, and she very much hoped his interest in Trade Fair would morph into a long-term commitment. Not only was he respected as an artist and an activist across the US – she'd had no idea his profile was so high in artsy, intellectual circles – but he was a tough guy for the likes of Brogan and the cartels to discredit. For one thing, he wasn't in the business, so couldn't be accused of having any axe to grind, unlike her. For another, he was a direct eye witness to atrocities paid for with diamond dollars, and an articulate spokesman for the African oppressed. And for a third thing, as un-PC as it might be to say it, he was black. No one wanted to be the first white man to cast aspersions on the black survivor's integrity.

Not that any of that excused him being such a dick to Nancy. But at the end of the day that was their shit to work out. If it was meant to be, they'd find their way back to one another eventually.

'I couldn't care less if he comes round or not,' lied Nancy, turning over on her massage table so the masseuses could focus on her feet and head. The sky above her was so blue, it looked like it had been ripped out of the pages of a travel magazine. 'Anyway, I screwed things up so badly yesterday, he'll probably get his wish. They're bound to drop the whole idea now.'

Having flown back to LA specifically for the meeting, she'd ended up breaking down in tears in front of an entire panel of studio execs and had to take a full ten minutes out of the room to compose herself. The combined stress of her mom's illness, her dad's unspoken but omnipresent unhappiness, and Che Che's complete lack of understanding proved too much for her, and at the first remotely challenging question, she'd folded like a pack of cards.

'Michael Landry must be pissing himself,' she said bitterly, remembering the look of shocked surprise on the Head of New Project Development's face when she'd fled the room in tears. 'He's probably biking the script over to Sacha Gervasi as we speak.'

'I'm sure he's not,' said Scarlett kindly. 'They said they wanted to see you again, right? Once you're back in LA for good?'

'Once my mom dies, you mean?' said Nancy. 'Yeah, they did say that. And of course I'm gonna be in a *way* better emotional state then.'

'Sorry,' said Scarlett. 'I didn't mean to put my foot in it.'

'No, no. I'm sorry,' said Nancy, wincing as one masseuse ground her knuckle into a sore spot on her neck. 'I shouldn't be so caustic. You're the one person keeping me sane right now. I appreciate it, more than you know. By the way, do you know that guy?'

Scarlett turned over, willing herself out of her relaxation-induced coma.

'Which guy?' she mumbled. 'Where?'

'There,' said Nancy, sitting up and pointing at a pale-skinned man on the beach patio in front of them, who suddenly seemed intent on his coffee and newspaper. 'He's been staring at you for the last minute. Really staring.'

'Has he?'

Aware he was being pointed at, the man got up, dropped a note on the table and scurried away, disappearing into the main lobby of the hotel. In the brief instant before he disappeared from view, Scarlett shivered, as if a ghost had walked across her grave.

'I don't know him,' she said. 'At least … I may have seen his face before somewhere. I can't be sure.'

Memories of London, and being hounded by Brogan's paid shadows, flooded back to her, accompanied by sound bites of Cameron's moaning over Christmas: *This is serious, Scarlett. They're out to get me,* and Jake's never-ending warnings to her about 'meddling in Russia', as he put it.

'It's probably nothing,' she said, trying not to give in to paranoia. The NPR programme still hadn't aired. Which meant as far as Brogan was concerned, Trade Fair was still dead in the water. It couldn't be him.

'Maybe Jake's paid a PI to follow you. Check you aren't up to no good while he's out of town?' joked Nancy. 'He's always struck me as the jealous type.'

'Now that I *very* much doubt,' said Scarlett, a tinge of sadness creeping into her voice as she sank back onto the table. 'If he's thinking about me at all right now, I'd be surprised. You know what the last thing he said was, before he got on the plane?'

'What?' asked Nancy.

'"Maybe a break will do us both good."'

'Ouch,' Nancy winced. 'Trouble in paradise?'

'Don't sound so hopeful,' teased Scarlett.

'Seriously,' said Nancy. 'Is something wrong? You can

tell me, really. I promise I won't judge. Or say "I told you so" more than twice.'

Deciding to throw caution to the wind – she had nothing to lose at this point, and she'd missed Nancy's sisterly counsel these last few weeks more than she could have imagined – Scarlett decided to tell her everything: the whole drama with Rachel, the never-ending rumours about other girls, and the constant sniping over Trade Fair and her work commitments that neither of them seemed able to stop.

'I think he resents my success,' she blurted, at the end of a long, tortured monologue about their problems.

'Probably.' Nancy shrugged. 'But you know, you always knew he was a macho guy. The fact he needs to make his own money and have his own business be a success shouldn't come as a surprise to you.'

'It doesn't,' said Scarlett, somewhat wrong-footed by Nancy's unexpected support for Jake. 'But he's so inconsistent. One minute he's telling me not to antagonise Brogan because it might impact on Flawless – as if the store and our profits are all he cares about – but when I do something to *help* the business, like hooking another sponsor for the Oscars, he acts all "so what?" about it. Almost like I'm showing off, or something. I can't win.'

She could feel her earlier, euphoric calm evaporating, replaced by a familiar feeling of stress creeping into her chest and shoulder muscles.

'And then there's the girls,' she added wearily.

'All right, so let's look at everything piece by piece,' said Nancy. 'Do you think he's cheating on you?'

Scarlett paused. 'Not *technically* cheating, no. Not yet. But—'

'But nothing,' said Nancy. 'The man's a natural born flirt. If you're not gonna let him look, you might as well chop off his cojones right now and put 'em in a jar on your mantel.'

'Thanks for that,' said Scarlett, sarcastically. 'That's a lovely image.'

'OK, so second thing. This radio interview you wanna do about the Russian miners.'

Scarlett looked at her grudgingly, waiting for her to explain why Jake's unsupportive behaviour on that score was suddenly OK too. Since when had Nancy become the president of the Jake Meyer fan club?

'He has three beefs with that, as I understand it. He's scared Brogan O'Donnell might hurt you. He's scared he might hurt the business. And he resents the fact that you spend more time at work and with Che Che than with him.'

'Right,' said Scarlett.

Nancy gave her a puzzled smile. 'Remind me again. What part of that did you find so unreasonable?'

'Oh, look, if you're not going to take this seriously ...' said Scarlett, crossly. 'I thought you hated Jake?'

Nancy shrugged. 'I'm trying not to hate anyone these days. Call it a late New Year's resolution. Life's too short.' Her eyes were welling up again, and Scarlett immediately felt guilty for picking a fight. What was she doing burdening Nancy with her love-life problems anyway? They didn't amount to much, compared to what she was going through.

'I thought he was wrong for you,' said Nancy, pulling herself together. 'As a matter of fact, I still think he's wrong for you. But let me ask you this. Do you love the guy?'

Scarlett was silent for a moment. Not because she needed time to consider her answer. But because it was hard, for some reason, to speak that answer out loud.

'Yes,' she nodded miserably. 'I'm completely mad about him. That's the problem.'

'That is indeed the problem,' agreed Nancy. Taking Scarlett's hand she squeezed her fingers so tightly it hurt. 'You really want my advice?'

'I do,' said Scarlett, deadly serious.

'Don't throw it away over nothing,' said Nancy. 'Real love doesn't come around that often. My parents have been together thirty years, but Dad keeps telling me how it's gone by in a blink.'

Thirty years, thought Scarlett wistfully. There were days when she and Jake could barely seem to manage thirty minutes.

'I don't know,' she said. 'Danny and Diana seemed so in love, so right for each other, but they're breaking up.'

'With a baby on the way,' added Nancy.

'And you and Che Che . . .'

'I know,' said Nancy. 'I'm a fine one to talk, right?'

'I didn't mean that. It's just that things aren't supposed to be so hard right at the beginning. Are they?'

Nancy laughed. 'I don't know. With Jake Meyer, I'd have said "probably". But what do I know? Other people's relationships always shock the shit out of me.'

Scarlett closed her eyes and tried to recapture the peace she'd felt only moments ago, but it was useless. Damn Jake stupid Meyer. Even on the other side of the country, he was managing to ruin her day.

# Nineteen

Oscar week in LA began with a heatwave. While most of the East Coast shivered with chattering teeth beneath a fresh dump of February snow, Southern California basked smugly in ninety-degree temperatures. As if nature itself were putting on its game face for the most important event in the movie-industry year, the sky shone cartoon-blue, palm trees swayed gracefully in the lightest of breezes, and the blooms in the permanently irrigated gardens and parks turned their heads delightedly towards the unexpected sun, competing with one another in gaudy display.

Even those not in 'the business', never mind involved in the Oscars themselves, were swept up in a sort of city-wide fever, as if royalty were about to pay them a visit – which in a sense, of course, they were. Suddenly it became impossible to book a table at any of the decent restaurants. Staff manning the reservations desks at the big hotels threw back their heads and laughed maniacally when asked about availability. Even the illegal Mexican immigrants, the poorest of LA's poor, looked happier than usual as the influx of stars and their entourages, tourists and press meant that every business in town was taking on extra staff: valets, bus boys, gardeners, kitchen hands. Nail salons and beauty parlours were booked solid, and star-sightings in the coffee shops and boulevards of West Hollywood were at an all-time high, much to the excitement of locals and tourists alike. Suddenly it wasn't just Tara Reid or that Greek kid that used to go out with Paris Hilton hanging around outside Kitson. The A-list were in town: Brad and Ange, Tom and Katie, Johnny Depp, even Nicole Kidman, Botox-taut and translucent under a big floppy sun-hat, like a cave-monkey thrust unwillingly into the light of day.

Scarlett had been here for last year's Oscars, but as a newbie on the jewellery scene had not experienced the full force of the pre-awards buzz. This year, however, she was right in the eye of the storm. Teaming up with Jimmy Choo again, she'd signed up as a co-sponsor of E! Entertainment's coverage of the event. In practice this meant providing Maria Menounos, Nancy O'Dell and a bevy of other presenters with Flawless diamonds and accessories, as well as allowing the channel's film crews to follow her wherever she went in Oscar week. Two days ago the store had been transformed into a temporary reality-TV studio, with four camera guys and a full sound and light crew pitching camp behind the counter, in the hope of catching some of Scarlett's celebrity clients coming and going. In fact, ninety per cent of the pre-Oscars' traffic was assistants, agents, managers, and managers' assistants, most of whom were mightily pissed off to find a camera being thrust in their face the moment they walked in the door. But as Tamara Mellon told Scarlett, 'You need the publicity more than you need to keep the PAs sweet, babe. If they ask you to swallow a camera, do it.'

Perry, needless to say, was in his element, lapping up the attention like a love-starved kitten. Scarlett's feelings were more mixed. On the one hand it was a thrill knowing that her designs were going to be worn on camera in front of millions worldwide. On the other hand, she could have happily stepped out of the limelight herself. All the hoo-ha reminded her of her modelling days, which she'd never truly enjoyed, and she lacked Tamara's natural flair for publicity and glamour. Deep down, a part of her also felt guilty for being swept along by something as shallow as an awards ceremony, when there was so much serious work to be done with Trade Fair. Thanks to Che Che's string-pulling she expected the NPR report on Yakutia to come out any day now. Although irritatingly the producers at E! had stipulated a strict 'no politics' rule, and insisted she keep all on-air comments related to Flawless, her designs and her A-list clientele, so she couldn't use the coverage to plug Trade Fair.

With so much going on, it was almost a blessing to have Jake in New York, distracted with Danny and his problems. She missed him of course, but they'd been rowing so much about her workload before he left, he'd only have been resentful if he were here, hanging around the store while she multi-tasked. He had yet to congratulate her on landing the E! job, and the NPR thing had become a no-go area. She could only pray it wouldn't kick-start their problems all over again when it finally aired. Oh God, why was it all so complicated?

Four days before the awards she managed to snatch a precious hour in the afternoon to slip upstairs to her 'office' at Flawless, a souped-up cupboard above the store. Wading through a backlog of emails, an unexpected pang of homesickness prompted her to open one from her mother. Unfortunately, instead of being news of Drumfernly and the comforting sameness of the comings and goings in Buckie, it turned out to be a rambling rant about Cameron. Apparently his house had been broken into while he was at work, and his PC stolen. From Caroline's hysterical tone, one could be forgiven for assuming that a world banking collapse was now imminent, but Scarlett was too tired to plough through all the details.

Pinching her cheeks to keep awake, she clicked instead onto two overdue invoices and paid them online, before her phone buzzed on the desk with an IM from Jake.

'Just landed,' he wrote. 'Lots to tell. Meet me at Chaya for supper?'

Scarlett bit her lip. Despite everything, she was longing to see him. Nancy's advice at the spa, about not letting him go for nothing, had really struck a chord and she'd determined that once he got back to LA she'd start making more of an effort, to make time for him, and to trust him. But she hadn't expected him back until tomorrow. As a result, she'd already accepted an invitation to dinner with some of the team from E! tonight.

'Hi, darling. Stuck in work thing till eleven,' she texted back. 'Can I meet you after?'

Two minutes passed. Gnawing nervously on the end of a pencil, Scarlett stared at the blank screen. When no message came back, she typed in another.

'Love you. Really happy you're home.'

The second she sent it, she received Jake's response.

'Don't bother,' it read, tersely. 'Going to bed.'

'Shit,' said Scarlett aloud, banging her fist down on the desk so hard it hurt and sending a pile of papers fluttering to the floor like feathers. Why did everything have to go wrong in minute one? Why must he take everything so personally? Picking up her phone, she called his mobile number, but he'd switched it off, obviously in a huff.

'This is Jake Meyer. Leave a message.' Even the recording of his deep, North London growl made her stomach churn. It was too long since they'd made love. She couldn't bear it if she had to sleep alone again tonight.

'Darling, it's me,' she said, her voice as conciliatory as she could make it. 'Please don't be angry. I wasn't expecting you tonight, and I can't let these people down, especially not this week. Call me when you get this, OK?'

'Knock knock.' Perry stuck his frazzled, overworked head round the door. 'Sorry to disturb, boss,' he sighed, 'but I need you downstairs. Janice Dickinson's finger's swollen up and they need you to resize the ring. Her PA's on the couch, hyperventilating.'

'OK,' said Scarlett, switching off her computer and forcing Jake's disappointed face from her thoughts. 'Give her a herbal tea or something. I'll be right down.'

★

Jake swung his rented Porsche Boxster into the garage at his apartment building, screeching to a halt in his reserved resident's space. He'd had to give up the Maserati last month – a client had fallen in love with it and offered him an amount of money so crazy that he couldn't in all conscience refuse to sell. The little white Porsche, with its girlie curves and jaunty chrome hub caps was a feeble replacement, but it was all the dealer had had in his price range (for appearances' sake, he had to drive a relatively high-end convertible) and Jake loathed it with a vengeance. As a symbol of his recent emasculation, it couldn't have been better. He might as well cut his balls off and hang them from the rear-view mirror, like a pair of fluffy dice.

Dragging his case into the elevator, he pressed the button for the fourth floor morosely. He still couldn't believe Scarlett had blown him off like that. After two weeks apart, she couldn't even be arsed to bail on a stupid work dinner to see him. Accustomed to being pursued by eager, cock-hungry women, it was an unpleasant shock to find himself consistently at the bottom of a woman's priority list. Especially given that he'd spent the last two weeks manfully resisting temptation, in the form of Danny's sexually frustrated Hampton housewife clients, in an effort to stay true to Scarlett.

Struggling into his apartment, he was even more annoyed to see evidence of her invasion of his life mocking him from every room. Her toothbrush stuck jauntily out of the mug in the bathroom beside his own; photographs of her family nestled on his mantelpiece – inbred toffs the lot of them; even her black cashmere shawl hung from the peg on the back of his front door as if it had a perfect right to be there. After the whole Rachel thing, he'd been forced, against his better judgement, to give her a key to his apartment and to allow semi-regular sleepovers. Not that he didn't enjoy her company, not to mention the more frequent sex. But it was another level on which he seemed to have relinquished control of his life. He was rapidly turning into a fully fledged Guy Ritchie, laughably playing the alpha male when the whole world knew it was his missus who *really* called the shots.

Dumping his suitcase in the bedroom, he went straight to the wet bar (marvellous invention, wet-bars; he couldn't think why they hadn't taken off in England) and poured himself three fingers of Jack Daniels, filling the remainder of the glass with three giant cubes of ice. The angrily flashing answerphone could wait a few more minutes for his attention. Peeling off his grey cashmere sweater – it had been arctic in New York when he boarded the plane – he sat down on the couch, closed his eyes, and willed himself to relax.

Ironically, he'd been in a great mood earlier today, looking forward to surprising Scarlett with an early homecoming and releasing the pent-up sexual energy he'd accumulated during the past week in the Hamptons. Unfortunately Danny was right about his clients. Jake had turned up the charm to code red, but no one was biting. They'd all been knobbled by Brogan's pet dealers, suddenly able to offer them O'Donnell-sourced stones at ludicrously knock-down prices. Not that he hadn't enjoyed himself trying to get the leggy investment bankers' wives to change their minds.

'Whatever happened to loyalty?' he'd pleaded with Kathy Miller only last night, his right hand idly caressing the back of her neck as he passed her a Singapore sling with his left. They were seated in the darkest, most discreet corner of Giorgio's Restaurant, one of Danny's all-time favourite haunts in his pre-Diana days and a notorious rendezvous for illicit, adulterous liaisons. 'You've been buying from my brother exclusively for years.'

Kathy shrugged. At thirty-four she was older than most of the East Hampton Hotties, but with her mocha-tanned skin and full, pouty lips she could out-smoulder her younger rivals in a heartbeat. Her husband, Edmund Miller, ran Citigroup. Known as the Silver Fox amongst the other Wall Street wives, Ed was unique amongst the handful of big hitters who ran US banking in being genuinely good looking. Kathy had landed the most desirable shark in the Wall Street ocean, but she wasn't above casting her nets about for any smaller, tasty fry that might swim her way.

'Danny brought me the best diamonds for years,' she said, without rancour. 'But this new guy has the same quality stones at half the price. Business is business, Jake. What can I tell you?'

Taking a solitary ice cube from her drink, she dragged it lasciviously along her full lower lip, before reaching forwards and slipping it into his mouth. Christ, she was fuckable, and as up-for-it as a bitch in heat. Scarlett would never know ...

'Don't get me wrong. I adore your brother,' she drawled, her fingers now snaking their way up the inside of Jake's corduroy Ralph Lauren trousers, and getting dangerously close to his rapidly hardening groin. 'But he'd have done the same to me, if he'd found a more valuable buyer.'

Jake, who couldn't deny this, swallowed hard and laid his hand over hers, to stop it creeping up any higher.

'Of course, if he ever wanted to see me ... socially,' Kathy played with the word, toying with it like the ice cube, 'he'd be more than welcome.'

'I'll pass that on,' said Jake, about ready to weep with frustration.

'And what about you?' Kathy picked up his ringless left hand. 'You're single, aren't you? Or do you only sleep with women you know are gonna buy from you?'

In a black Ballantyne polo neck and Donna Karan slacks, she didn't have an ounce of flesh on display. Yet somehow she was far more desirable, more wanton, than any of the LA bimbettes he was used to seducing in the line of duty.

'Mrs Miller, on my mother's life,' he said, raising her

hand to his lips, 'I can think of nothing I'd rather do than take you to bed, with or without a sale. But I'm afraid I'm spoken for at the moment. At least, I hope I am,' he added, thinking nervously of Scarlett alone in LA without him.

Kathy sat back, taking another long sip of her drink.

'Faithful, and not even married,' she smiled. 'Whoever she is, I hope she appreciates it.'

'Me too,' said Jake, who couldn't help thinking that the last time he'd spoken to Scarlett she'd seemed less than a hundred per cent appreciative of his devotion. 'Me too.'

It was partly this encounter with Kathy Miller that had prompted him to fly home early. Clearly he wasn't going to get Danny his clients back, and there didn't seem much point hanging around, hurling himself headlong into the path of temptation for nothing. He'd been so horny when he boarded the plane this morning, it was all he could do not to drag one of the Jet Blue stewardesses into the bogs for a quick blow job. But no, once again he'd saved himself for Scarlett. And for what? To be blown off, brushed aside like some irritating fly, so she could spend the night yukking it up with a bunch of fat suits from E! fucking Entertainment? What the hell was he doing?

The bourbon was ambrosial, but it wasn't working. Opening his eyes, he reached across the side table for the answerphone and began playing his messages.

As it turned out there were only four, and three of those were from utility companies, cold calling to try and get him to switch providers. The fourth, however, was a surprise.

'This is a message for Scarlett Drummond Murray.' An elderly, clipped, aristocratic woman's voice rang out through the apartment. It was the sort of voice that made you sit up and listen. Jake did. 'Scarlett, it's Aunt Agnes. I've tried all your other numbers and can't seem to get hold of you. Anyway, darling, I'm in Los Angeles. I've been touring the Redwood Forests with my friend Beattie and we're flying home tomorrow, but I'm around tonight on the off chance that you are. Not to worry if not. I'm sure you're *frightfully* busy.' She pronounced it freight-flee, which made Jake chuckle. 'But do call at the Peninsula if you get this before supper time.'

She left a room number in the same, clearly enunciated tones, and rang off.

Aunt Agnes, eh? How funny. Scarlett had spoken to him many times about her eccentric aunt from South Africa, her stories always steeped in a sort of whimsical nostalgia that fascinated him, perhaps because there was no one in his own childhood who remotely related to the character Scarlett described. On a whim, he picked up the phone and rang the hotel.

'Agnes Headington please. Room 220.'

Within seconds he was put through.

'Hello?'

For a second, Jake was tongue-tied. What on earth had he called to say?

'Hi. Is this Aunt Agnes ... er, I mean, Miss Headington?' he stammered.

'Yeeees.' Her tone was a combination of amusement and suspicion, as if she feared she might be being Punk'd. 'Who is this?'

'My name's Jake, Jake Meyer. I'm your niece's boyf—'

'I know very well who you are,' the old woman interrupted regally. 'How do you do?'

'I'm very well. Thank you,' said Jake, feeling about ten. 'Listen, I'm sorry to disturb you. I just got your message and I thought I ought to let you know that unfortunately Scarlett has a business dinner tonight.'

'Ah.' Aunt Agnes sounded disappointed. 'Well, it's kind of you to call and tell me.'

'I know she would have wanted to see you,' said Jake. 'You could try her mobile again if you want to reach her. She normally keeps it switched on at work.'

'No, no, I won't disturb her if she's working,' said Aunt

Agnes briskly. 'But what about you, Jake? Do you have dinner plans?'

Well, this was a curve ball. Tired after his journey and still pissed at Scarlett, the last thing he felt like doing was spending the evening babysitting her octogenarian aunt.

'I ... well ... not exactly,' he said lamely, unable to conjure up a suitable excuse on the spot.

'Marvellous,' said Aunt Agnes. 'You can pick me up in an hour.' Click.

'What? Hang on,' grumbled Jake, but he was already speaking to a dial tone. 'I don't believe it,' he mumbled to himself, hanging up. He'd now been dissed by two Drummond Murray women in the space of an hour. Aunt Agnes was clearly mad as a box of frogs, but age had evidently not withered her feistiness, nor her bulldozer-like determination to get her own way. No wonder she and Scarlett were so close. Standing up, he looked grumpily at his watch. At least it was only five thirty. With any luck he could eat, drop the old girl home and be back in bed himself by nine.

Still, what a pain in the ass. That'd teach him to play the Good Samaritan. Next time Scarlett could return her own stupid calls.

Strolling into the Peninsula an hour later in a dark suit and tie, he felt a profound and mildly depressing sense of déjà vu. He'd lost count of how many deals he'd closed here over afternoon tea in the lobby, while the hotel's famous harpist serenaded his unsuspecting clients, lulling them into a false sense of security over a silver tray of crustless cucumber sandwiches. Though it was arguably the most luxurious hotel in the city, he'd always found the faux-British touches faintly absurd – 'tea' at four, served by English waiters, all doing their very best impression of Jeeves; Wedgwood china, 'English muffins' for breakfast – the Yanks lapped it all up. For Jake though, the Peninsula's charm lay in its lush, landscaped gardens, and the light-flooded villa rooms with their huge, white California Kings, the most comfortable beds in the world. Casting his mind back, he wondered how many of the rooms he'd had sex in, but lost count at four, distracted by a posse of six teenage hotties loitering outside the bar in their designer mini-skirts and heels, checking him out while they waited for someone more famous to hit on them. Judging by the gaggles of security men milling around in the lobby, there must be a lot of Oscar nominees renting suites here for the week. No doubt the girls were hoping for a celebrity notch on their bedposts.

'I'm meeting a guest.' He smiled at the receptionist, a pretty girl in her early thirties with a long, shiny ponytail. 'A Miss Headington, room 202. You wouldn't call up for me, would you, sweetheart?'

'You must be Mr Meyer,' the girl smiled back. 'Miss Headington is waiting for you in our restaurant. Would you like me to direct you there?'

'No thanks,' said Jake, his heart sinking. He knew the Belvedere Restaurant well, and also knew its prices. Somehow he doubted Aunt Agnes was a feminist believer in picking up her own tab.

Walking back to the heated, covered patio at the rear of the hotel, through the signature yellow and white tables, Jake could feel the thickness of the air, heavy from the heat of the day and the mingled perfumes of wealthy women diners, crammed into the small space like diamond-encrusted sardines.

Aunt Agnes wasn't hard to spot. Sitting alone and bolt upright at a centre table, reading glasses perched precariously on the bridge of her long, slightly hooked nose as she perused the menu, she was the oldest person in the restaurant by at least two decades. In a tweed jacket and high-necked white shirt, with her long grey hair piled up into a bun, she could have been a Victorian schoolma'am, were it not for the whopping diamond and pearl ring on the middle finger of her right hand, and the distinctly mischievous twinkle in her watery blue eyes when she rose to greet Jake.

'You're on time.' She smiled, shaking him by the hand with that extra-tight old-person's grip, the kind that could whip off a jam jar lid in 0.2 nanoseconds. 'Scarlett told me you were always late for everything.'

Despite himself, Jake laughed as he sat down. 'Did she now? I'll have to have words with her about that later.'

'Sparkling or still?'

Jeeves appeared, bearing a silver tray and two bottles, one of Evian and one of Perrier.

'Not for me, thank you, I'll stick with Scotch,' said Aunt Agnes, raising a glass tumbler of amber liquid, much to Jake's delight. Perhaps tonight wouldn't be a total washout after all. 'But if you'd like some ... ?'

'Still, please. Something tells me I'd better pace myself. No offence, Miss Headington, but I've got a feeling you could drink me under the table in a heartbeat.'

Dinner, to Jake's surprise and delight, was the most fun he'd had in ages. Aunt Agnes turned out to be a riot, with more chutzpah at eighty than most people mustered in a lifetime, and a sense of comic timing that was second to none. He found himself roaring with laughter, clutching his stomach at her farcical tales of life in apartheid South Africa, like the time she had to convince police that her maid was an undercover British agent so she'd be allowed into an all-white compound, or the time she hid an entire family of nine in her chimpanzee sanctuary, and used the squawking apes to scare the security services off the scent. Reading between the lines, it was clear she'd witnessed plenty of tragedy too. But she had the sort of grim humour that Jake knew well, common to long-term expats in Africa where life is so fragile and brutal, yet at the same time so uniquely beautiful and blessed. He could see in an instant why she'd left such a deep and lasting impression on Scarlett.

'I've not yet met Scarlett's family,' he told her, as they both tucked in to plates of melt-in-your-mouth Beef Wellington, 'other than the brother, for about three seconds.'

'Three seconds too long, I should think,' said Aunt Agnes, quick as a flash. 'Appalling little creep.'

'I was going to say that none of them sound much like you, from Scar's descriptions,' said Jake.

'They aren't,' said Aunt Agnes, 'thank God. I'm the black sheep, you see. Ran off to Africa with my first husband Johnny at eighteen and never looked back.'

'What happened to Johnny?'

'No idea,' she said cheerfully. 'Last I heard of him he was in Rhodesia, on the run from some rather unpleasant chaps over a gambling debt. He was a bit of a bad hat, old Johnny. Terribly good looking, but the morals of an alley cat. Luckily in those days you could get marriages annulled for a few pounds. I married again when I was twenty-two, to a lovely man who died the day after my fortieth birthday. Then I was on my own for fifteen years, which is when I started the sanctuary. Scarlett was born at the end of that time. Then came Headington.' She gave a little shudder. 'He's dead now too.'

'I'm sorry,' said Jake.

'Don't be,' said Aunt Agnes, dabbing daintily at her mouth with a napkin. 'He was ghastly. Had the most appalling bad breath.'

'Right,' chuckled Jake. 'So now you're young, free and single, will you stay in Africa?' Refilling her wine glass – they'd moved from single malt whisky straight to a bottle of super-Tuscan, which Aunt Agnes was polishing off at an impressive rate.

'Of course,' she looked puzzled. 'Why ever not?'

'I don't know,' he shrugged. 'Don't you miss home?'

'Home? You mean Drumfernly?' she laughed. 'Good God no. Scotland's terribly dreary, you know. It never really felt like home to me, even as a child. My brother Hugo, Scarlett's father, is a nice enough old stick.' Jake smiled inwardly at this description of a brother ten years her junior. 'But I'd rather shoot myself than live his life, walled up in that freezing castle like Rapunzel, never going further than Aberdeen for entertainment. People think Scarlett grew up in a fairytale, but I can assure you she didn't. Living on that estate, it's immurement.'

'Right,' said Jake, who didn't know what immurement was, but assumed it was something negative.

'As for that mother of hers,' Aunt Agnes shook her head. 'Horrific, small minded ...'

She shared a few, caustically funny anecdotes about Caroline that left Jake in no doubt of their mutual enmity.

'Cameron's just like her, a whining, wheedling little social climber. Honestly, it's a miracle that Scarlett's turned out as wonderfully as she has.'

Obviously this was Jake's cue to say some nice things about Scarlett. Instead he sat morosely, pushing his beef around the plate like a guard prodding a reluctant prisoner. The silence seemed to last for an age, but Aunt Agnes knew better than to break it. At last her patience was rewarded.

'I do love her, you know,' said Jake quietly. 'It's just, everything's so ... fucked. At the moment.'

'Fucked?' Aunt Agnes raised an eyebrow.

'Sorry,' Jake blushed. ''Scuse my French. I meant difficult. Things are difficult with Scarlett and me.'

'In what way?'

He told her, as briefly and politely as he could, about the arguing over everything from Flawless to Trade Fair. He touched on Scarlett's jealousy about his supposed 'other women'. Finally, he mentioned Brogan O'Donnell and his malevolent influence on both their lives.

'He destroyed Scarlett's last business in London – he could have killed her in that fire – but she refuses to drop this bollocks about his Siberian miners and their stupid healthcare.'

'Is it "bollocks", as you put it?' asked Aunt Agnes gently. 'I read the latest Trade Fair newsletter; Scarlett emails these things to me. It sounded as though the man had behaved very shabbily.'

'He has,' admitted Jake. 'So all right, no, it's not exactly bollocks.'

'And presumably you've always known that Scarlett feels passionately about these things?'

'Yes,' he conceded, grudgingly. 'Yes, I have. But … it's more complicated than that.'

Aunt Agnes gave him a look as if to say, 'Really?' but said nothing. Eventually Jake elaborated.

'He's dangerous,' he said. 'Maybe subconsciously Scarlett thinks that because he's got cancer, he won't be bothered to hit back at her this time. But I'm telling you, he will. He's vengeful, vengeful to the fucking bone. He's already broken up my brother's relationship with the only woman he's ever really loved.'

Aunt Agnes, who'd heard the Danny and Diana saga from Scarlett and read about it in the gossip columns, thought privately that there were worse crimes in life than trying to win back one's own wife, but decided not to share this insight with Jake.

'I've warned Scarlett till I'm blue in the face that she's putting her life, not to mention her business – our business – at risk over this. I mean, why can't she stick to Africa? It's not as if there isn't enough injustice there to keep her busy. All the mine owners there are bent as nine bob notes.'

'So what is it that upsets you exactly?' asked Aunt Agnes, seeing straight to the heart of the matter. 'The fact that Scarlett might be endangering herself? Or the fact that she chooses not to take your advice?'

Jake closed his eyes and rubbed his temples hard, as if searching for the answer in the deepest recesses of his mind. 'God, I dunno,' he sighed. 'Both, I suppose. It does piss me off that she doesn't need me. She's so fucking independent.'

'You know, young man, you really *must* make more of an effort with your language,' chided Aunt Agnes.

'Sorry,' said Jake again. 'But at the same time, I love her, you know? I don't want to wake up one morning and get a call from Cedars-Sinai telling me Scar's in the ICU with a Russian bullet lodged in her skull.'

'Indeed not.' Aunt Agnes shivered.

'And I don't want Flawless to go under either. Scarlett acts like I've no say in the matter, but I'm a partner in that store. Brogan could put us out of business like *that* if he wanted to.' He clicked his fingers for emphasis. 'He's already decimated my and Danny's business. Wiped us out on the East Coast like a couple of fucking ... like a couple of bugs,' he corrected himself.

'I see,' said Aunt Agnes, nodding quietly to herself.

She hadn't known what to expect of Jake. Hugo and Caroline both spoke of him in the most disparaging terms, but then they'd always been crashing snobs; quite apart from which she knew from Scarlett that neither of them had in fact met the man, which she couldn't help but feel detracted somewhat fatally from their credibility as witnesses. Scarlett's evidence – that Jake was simultaneously the most wonderful and the most infuriating man on the face of the earth – was also not to be trusted. The girl was plainly head over heels in love and couldn't be expected to know her own mind, let alone anyone else's. When Jake had called tonight, she'd seized the unexpected opportunity to size him up for herself.

Overall, she liked what she saw. He was blunt and, it seemed to her, honest, despite having what was clearly a well-earned reputation as a bit of a Lothario. More importantly, he seemed to be genuinely in love with Scarlett. Agnes was excessively fond of her niece and, unlike her brother and sister-in-law, viewed deep, passionate love as a prerequisite for a happy marriage. Jake could give her that, even if right now it was all he could give her, with his business on the ropes. That in itself need not be a problem. Agnes was a wealthy woman, with no children of her own. She'd be quite prepared to help out financially, should Scarlett and her husband ever need it. Besides, Jake was obviously rampantly ambitious, not to mention a natural salesman. Men like that had a habit of bouncing back from adversity, in her experience. They also had a habit of clinging pathetically to their macho pride. For such a smart boy, Jake seemed to be doing a first-class job of screwing up his relationship. Had she been forty years younger she'd have reached across the table and throttled him till he saw sense. As it was, she decided to treat him to a few choice words of elderly aunt advice.

'You're a fool, Mr Meyer. A first-class fool,' she said bluntly.

Jake looked thoroughly miserable, but didn't contradict this assessment.

'The truth is, Aunt Agnes, I'm not really cut out for relationships. I'm not the man Scarlett needs, and she's started to figure that out for herself.'

'Nonsense.' The old woman put her knife and fork together and pushed her plate away crossly. 'Everyone's cut out for relationships. Relationships are life, for heavens' sake. What else is there?'

Jake shrugged. 'Random shagging?'

'Unsatisfying,' said Aunt Agnes firmly, 'as you well know.'

In her certainty, she reminded him of an older Doctor Katenge. Both were strong women, moral forces to be reckoned with. Scarlett had a streak of that in her, but she also had a vulnerability that her aunt entirely lacked. Agnes Headington was about as vulnerable as a prop forward on steroids.

'So what do you suggest?' he asked meekly. 'I can't force Scarlett to listen to me.'

'Exactly,' said Aunt Agnes, 'so stop trying. Brogan O'Donnell is a thoroughly unpleasant little man. I'm proud my niece has the courage to stand up to him and so should you be. You want to control her behaviour because that's what you're used to doing with women—'

'Steady on,' said Jake defensively. 'You don't know that.'

'And because you feel threatened by Scarlett's success.'

'I'm not *threatened*!' said Jake indignantly, and entirely unconvincingly.

'Stop focusing on Scarlett's behaviour and change your own,' said Aunt Agnes. 'If your brother's side of the business has suffered because of this Brogan chap, work doubly hard on the West Coast market. You clearly hate the fact that you're being "carried" by Flawless, as you put it. So pull your finger out and start turning your own business around.'

'Yes, well, I'd love to, but I'm afraid it's not that easy,' said Jake petulantly. He was starting to feel cross himself now.

'Nothing worth achieving ever is,' said Aunt Agnes, 'and that goes for romance as well as your career. Now, listen.' She clapped her hands imperiously to get his attention, which seemed to be focused somewhere in the region of his shoelaces. 'What you do from here is up to you.'

'Thanks very much,' he said wryly.

'But I think it would be best if you "forgot" to tell Scarlett about this evening, our meeting like this.'

'Why?' Jake quipped. 'You think she might be jealous?'

'Don't be cheeky,' snapped Aunt Agnes. Once again Jake found himself blushing like a naughty little boy. 'It's you I'm thinking of, young man, not myself. Scarlett loves me dearly, but she wouldn't appreciate my meddling in her affairs any more than she appreciates it from you.'

'Ah, but you still do it, don't you?' said Jake, thrilled to have found a break in the old bat's logic at last. 'You meddle because you love her. Like me.'

Aunt Agnes smiled, her earlier good humour apparently completely restored.

'My dear boy, I'm nothing like you. The secret of a good meddler is not to get caught out. Now.' Fixing her glasses more firmly in place, she scanned the room for their waiter. 'I suggest you get the bill. It's getting late.'

'You suggest *I* get the bill,' muttered Jake under his breath. 'Un-fucking-believable!' But the truth was he was more than happy to pay. Despite her rudeness, or perhaps because of it, he liked her a lot. This evening, on many levels, had been a learning experience and education rarely came cheap.

Driving home along Beverly twenty minutes later, beneath a perfect full moon, he thought over Aunt Agnes's advice and contemplated calling Scarlett then and there, to apologise for his childishness before. But realising he was drunk and would almost certainly fuck it up, he thought better of it and decided to wait until morning. She wasn't going anywhere after all, at least, not tonight.

Tomorrow he'd make a fresh start.

# Twenty

At around nine in the morning on Oscars day, the strip of Hollywood Boulevard extending a quarter of a mile on either side of the Pantages Theater was closed to the public. By nine thirty, trucks full of metal crash barriers were being unloaded onto the sidewalk by overweight black men with sunglasses and earpieces. Roll after roll of red carpet was laid along the sidewalk, next to the hundred-metre stretch of road set aside for the stars' limos, and a separate area was fenced off for the press.

No Angelino with a modicum of sense tried to get to, through or around Hollywood Boulevard on Oscars night, unless they happened to be one of the favoured few attending the ceremony. And even the favoured few had been known to feel less than favoured when, with less than a half hour to go until doors closed, they found themselves stuck in a line of limos as long as the Great Wall of China, with everybody beeping at everybody else and nobody moving so much as a millimetre further toward the 'drop zone'.

This year, Jake and Scarlett fell into the latter category.

'This is just complete bollocks,' said Jake, for the third time in as many minutes. 'It's worse than last year. They have twelve months to prepare, and still they can't organise a piss-up in a fucking brewery.'

'How much further to the theatre?' asked Scarlett, looking anxiously at her watch, a rose gold and diamond evening piece she'd designed herself. 'Could we get out and walk, do you think?'

'I could,' said Jake, glancing across at her sky-high heels and skintight, gunmetal-grey dress, a vintage Hervé Léger.

'But you won't go far in that get-up. Not unless I give you a fireman's lift.'

He smiled, and Scarlett smiled back, relieved at this tiny flicker of camaraderie between them. Things had been desperately tense since he got back from New York. Jake had apologised after that awful first night, when she'd been stuck in that stupid dinner with the E! people – the exec producer turned out to be a lecherous old goat with permanently open, wet lips like Gordon Brown, and had spent the entire evening trying to goose her – and the next day they'd had truly fabulous make-up sex. But the thawing of relations proved to be short-lived. Two days ago, the NPR programme on the O'Donnell miners in Yakutia finally aired, and all Jake's good resolutions seemed to evaporate.

Perhaps she was stupid even to have hoped for his support. He'd made his feelings on the subject pretty plain since Christmas, after all. She could hardly claim to be surprised. But still, part of her had thought that when he actually heard it, he might see things her way. Andy Gordon, her friend from the BBC, had done a spectacular job pulling together all the evidence, and presenting it far more calmly and dispassionately than she would ever have been able to. In fact, she'd been worried when she heard her own interviews that she might have come across as too hysterical, too emotive. She'd been audibly close to tears at one point, recounting the story of a mother from Yakutsk who'd lost two of her sons to cancer in the past eighteen months, both of them O'Donnell miners. She'd written to Brogan O'Donnell directly to ask for help towards the funeral costs, but he hadn't even bothered to reply.

'Oh God, I sound awful,' she winced, listening to her voice crack as she sat on Jake's couch with a portable HD radio in her lap. 'D'you think Andy'll be furious? I promised to stay rational and detached.'

'Why're you asking me?' growled Jake, without glancing up from his Nintendo DS Lite. 'If you gave a crap about my opinion, you wouldn't have done the show in the first place.'

He knew he was being childish. That he was throwing all Aunt Agnes's good advice out the window, sabotaging things again. But it was like being in the throes of relationship Tourette's. He couldn't seem to control himself.

'Oh for God's sake, grow up!' snapped Scarlett. She knew she shouldn't rise to his moodiness, but she was running on empty after weeks of almost no sleep and her self-control had deserted her. 'Sitting there sulking like a little boy with your stupid computer game. Maybe if you listened to these people's stories instead of wallowing in self-pity you'd understand why I *can't* just let it go.'

'And maybe if you stopped lobbying so hard for your bloody sainthood,' he shot back at her, 'you'd be a bit more fun to be around.'

'I'm trying to do some good,' said Scarlett. 'Then again, why should I expect you to understand that?'

'Just because I don't bang on about things on the radio, doesn't mean I don't do my bit,' said Jake.

'Oh really? Like what?' demanded Scarlett.

Jake bit his lip. It would have been so easy to tell her about Dr Katenge and the work he'd been doing behind the scenes with the orphans in Sierra Leone. But some perverse desire for control, a need to have one, simple, good thing that he kept just for himself, held him back. Instead he jumped back on the offensive.

'Listen, Mother Teresa. You may *think* you're doing good with this crap, but let's just see what happens, shall we? You think the radio listeners of America are going to go into bat for these guys?' He gave a short, derisive laugh. '*You're* the one who should grow up. And don't come crying to me when Brogan and his thugs come knocking at our door again.'

'Don't worry,' Scarlett yelled after him as he stormed

out of the apartment, 'I won't. I can take care of myself, you know. Dickhead,' she added, under her breath.

But for all her fighting talk, the argument had left her deeply and lastingly depressed. Jake had come home a few hours later, bearing roses and apologies, both of which she'd accepted graciously. But she left for work the next morning with a heavy heart. There were only so many times you could paper over the cracks in a relationship. She and Jake were running out of chances, and they both knew it.

Thankfully, she'd spent the last forty-eight hours in such an all-consuming work frenzy she'd had little time to dwell on personal problems. She'd even put Boxford in kennels so that she could concentrate. Aware that the Oscars was her first big chance to establish herself as a serious player in the LA jewellery market, and that other people, such as Perry and Jake, were depending on her to succeed, she felt the weight of responsibility like a grand piano on her back.

Tonight, finally, was make or break time. If she could just get through her hour in front of the cameras – a billion people worldwide would be watching – everything else would be fine. She could enjoy the ceremony and the Elton John after-party with Jake ... just as long as she didn't fuck up in front of *the entire world*. Oh, God!

'Seriously, I think we should walk,' she said, looking anxiously at the solid line of cars in front of them. 'If you carry me to Vine, I can probably hobble from there. The film crew were expecting us forty minutes ago.'

Jake looked at his own watch, a Patek Philippe he'd bought the day after flogging that three-carat lump of GGG to Al Brookstein. Christ, that felt like a lifetime ago.

'All right,' he said. 'You're on.'

Jumping out into the street he ran round to the other side of the car, opened Scarlett's door for her and scooped her up into his arms. They'd shared a bed every night this week, but only when he picked her up did he fully appreciate how much weight she'd lost recently. The stress of work, plus all their arguments, must have affected her more than he'd realised. He'd lifted heavier eight-year-olds.

'You need to get some more meat on your bones, sweetheart,' he said guiltily. 'Bloody sexy dress though.'

'Thanks.'

Scarlett positively glowed with happiness. It felt like aeons since he'd complimented her. Pressed against his chest, breathing in his aftershave, her hands clasped around his neck like a fairytale damsel in distress, she felt a surge of desire for him gush through her body like a blood transfusion. His strength, his warmth, his confidence, all the things that had drawn her to him in the first place, were suddenly there again. Her nervousness about the night ahead began to melt. So what if she'd never presented before? How hard could it be, really? She was going to the Oscars – the Oscars! – on the arm of the sexiest man in the world. Jake Meyer loved her and she loved him back. In that instant, nothing else mattered.

Fifty yards from the red carpet line, Jake set her down on the sidewalk.

'Think you can make it from here?'

'Uh huh,' she nodded. 'Just don't walk too fast. And hold on to me. These shoes are like stilts.'

After a brief flashing of paperwork at the various security checkpoints (Jake was also frisked, airport-style, for a weapon) they were ushered through banks of slavering paparazzi, all of whom ignored them utterly.

'Look at 'em. They're like wolves that have just been fed,' whispered Jake, nodding at Will and Jada Smith, who'd arrived immediately ahead of them to a barrage of flash bulbs.

'I know,' Scarlett giggled. 'I feel like I could strip naked and no one would lift a camera.'

'Don't bet on it,' said Jake, patting her bottom.

Scarlett smiled as once again joy and relief washed over her. It was OK. They were going to be OK.

Seconds later she saw Christian, the E! cameraman, signalling frantically for her to come over.

'Shit, that's me. I've got to go,' she said, kissing Jake perfunctorily as he waved to another old friend. He seemed to know a lot more people here than she'd expected. 'Wish me luck.' But he'd already wandered off towards his buddy, out of earshot above the din of partygoers, and Christian had the look of a man in no mood to wait.

'Where've you been?' he snapped, thrusting an earpiece and microphone into Scarlett's hand. 'Coverage started fifteen minutes ago. Lara's been winging it solo.'

'Sorry,' mumbled Scarlett, fiddling with the wires. 'The traffic was insane. We couldn't move.'

'OK OK. To camera two,' yelled Christian. 'Annette and Warren are coming over. Scarlett, ask her about the necklace.'

Talk about a baptism of fire. For the next twenty minutes, Scarlett wilted in the combined heat of the afternoon sun and the TV lights as she rattled off an on-camera commentary about various stars' choice of jewellery.

'That's Marcia Cross in a gorgeous black-pearl choker,' she heard herself saying, hoping she didn't sound like quite as much of a QVC saleswoman as she feared. 'I have no idea who made that, but the pearls are Tahitian, and it looks like her ring ... yes, it's vintage Cartier. Full marks, Marcia.

'And here's Lindsay Lohan in Neil Lane. Wow. Those diamonds must weigh more than she does. Not my style, but she's young enough to carry it off.

'Goodness gracious, is that Clive Owen? He's gone very Puff Daddy on the cufflinks, hasn't he? I dread to think who made those. We'll have to ask him.'

The plan had been for her to do the interviews alongside Tamara Mellon, who'd pontificate about the shoes and clutches while Scarlett dealt with the diamonds. But Tamara must have still been stuck in the never-ending limo queue, and Scarlett found herself acting as expert sidekick to Pat O'Brien instead, marvelling at his ability not to sweat in a tuxedo and six-inch-thick make-up, not to mention the heat. She wanted to ask him if he still got nervous at these things, but their camera breaks were so short there was barely time to reapply powder and take a sip of water before being plunged back into the maelstrom.

Jake, meanwhile, was happily prowling around, soaking up the sunshine and attention, when he found himself being pulled aside by a skinny, insistent female arm.

'You don't write. You don't call.'

It was Julia Brookstein, pouting at him reproachfully in a micro silver chainmail minidress. Her honey-blonde hair had been cut short and dyed platinum, a look Jake normally hated, but on Julia oddly it worked, emphasising her wide mouth and ridiculously leggy figure. She looked like a sexy first mate from the Starship Enterprise.

'Your husband wants to have me kneecapped,' he said, glancing round nervously for Al as he kissed her on both cheeks.

'Oh, he so *doesn't*.' Julia waved her hand dismissively. 'He was over that months ago. It's a great pendant, even if it is a fake.'

Jake laughed. 'Thanks.'

'In any case,' said Julia, slipping a hand blatantly under the waistband of his pants, 'he's my ex-husband now. Well, almost.'

'No. Really?' said Jake, removing her hand from his groin as tactfully and subtly as he could before Scarlett saw and blew a gasket. How could the Brooksteins be getting a divorce, and he not know about it? Not so long ago he was plugged into the heartbeat of this town like a human fucking pacemaker. Evidently he was no longer an insider. 'You left Al?'

Julia shrugged.

'We kinda left each other. Oh, don't look so po-faced,

Jacob, it's all very amicable. He wants to marry his girl-friend; I wanna buy a bunch of horses and move to Malibu. Plus it'll be nice to have my freedom, you know?'

She took another step closer to him, a predatory gleam in her eye.

'As I recall, darling, you were never terribly literal about your marriage vows. How much freedom do you want?'

'More,' Julia grinned. She was very close now. Jake could feel the heat of her magnificent body radiating against him. 'Al's been real decent. I get the beach house, eight in cash, the cars and all my diamonds. Oh, and the kids,' she added as an afterthought. 'I'm a woman of means now. You know, I'd treat you a whole lot nicer than your British Sugarmommy does.'

She glanced over at Scarlett, who was nervously thrusting a microphone towards Kirsten Dunst.

Jake's eyes followed her gaze, and he realised with a pang how beautiful Scarlett really was. With her piled-up dark hair, freckled nose, and her long, slender body shrink-wrapped in that ludicrously sexy dark-grey dress, she looked both innocent and sophisticated, like a teenager at her first grown-up dance, or a little girl preening around in her big sister's wardrobe. He wanted to fuck her and protect her all at once. To march over to all the idiots standing around her and let them know that she was his, only his. He wanted to take her away, back to England, to safety and sanity. Back home.

All these thoughts were compressed into a single second. The next second, his mind had whiplashed back to Julia's comment.

'What do you mean, Sugarmommy?' he asked, frown-ing. 'Scarlett's my girlfriend, and my business partner. She doesn't bankroll me, you know.'

Julia raised a perfectly plucked eyebrow. 'OK baby. If you say so.'

'I do say so.' Jake was getting angry now. 'Why? Who says different?'

'No one,' laughed Julia. 'I mean, no one specific. There's no need to be so touchy.'

Jake could smell her perfume, Prada, mingled with the sweet mint of the candy in her mouth. Unbidden, an image of her naked and climaxing, a glistening pink stone nestled between her perfectly smooth labia, popped into his head, like an errant porno-shot slipped accidentally into his mental slide projector. Weirdly, he wasn't aroused but revolted. With an effort, he blacked it out.

'It's no secret that Solomon Stones isn't what it used to be,' she went on, rubbing salt in the wound. 'We all have bad years, Jake. There's no shame in it.'

'The business is fine,' he said brusquely. 'I'm fine.'

'Sure you are.' Julia's voice was soft and soothing. 'Look, honey, you're taking this all wrong. I wasn't criticising. You got yourself a piece of Flawless, and good for you. That girl's going places.' She looked over at Scarlett again. 'Grab onto her coat-tails for dear life if you want to. I would, in your shoes. All I'm saying is, you don't *have* to save yourself for Anorexic Annie like some kind of monk. You're not married, Jake. You *do* have other options.'

'Well, thank you for reminding me, Julia,' said Jake, his face like stone. 'But it just so happens I'm not a flank steak, up for sale to the highest bidder. Nor am I in the business of hanging on to women's coat-tails.'

'Hey, come on,' she pouted. 'Don't be like that, Jakey.'

But he was already making an angry beeline for Scarlett.

Scarlett looked pleadingly at Christian. 'Are we done yet?'

Conscious that her face was flushed, her foundation running and she had to get to a loo before this year's compère, Eddie Izzard, took the stage (some perverse God had decided to make her period arrive this morning, the

368

one day in the entire year that she least wanted to have to worry about a leaky Tampax), she was desperate to call it a day.

'I need to find Jake and get to our seats.'

'All right,' said the cameraman grudgingly, handing her a much-needed chilled bottle of Evian. 'You go have fun. Tamara's here now; she can take over. By the way, if you're looking for lover boy he's headed our way.'

Scarlett glanced up and caught her breath. She'd spent the last twenty minutes talking to some of the best-looking, most eligible men in the world, but none of them could hold a candle to Jake for pure, unadulterated sex appeal. Even in a tuxedo, with his thick blonde hair combed and his silk bow tie in place, there was something animal about him – a primal ball of pheromones, wrapped in an Armani jacket.

'Hey,' she beamed, kissing him on the mouth as soon as he reached her. 'Sorry that took so long, but the boss here says I'm free to go. Have you been having fun?'

'Having fun?' Jake snapped. 'You make me sound like a fucking nine-year-old at Chessington World of Adventures.'

'Sorry.' Scarlett looked baffled. 'I didn't mean ... I wasn't trying to be patronising.'

She ought to be used to his mood swings by now. But she'd really thought that tonight would be OK, after he'd been so sweet and flirty in the car, complimenting her dress and everything. Perhaps if she ignored his bad temper, he'd get over whatever it was and switch back into Good-Boyfriend mode.

'I think I did OK at the presenting,' she said, smiling at him nervously for approval. 'Almost everybody they wanted gave me an interview. Jen Aniston was really sweet.'

Jake laughed mockingly. '*Jen* Aniston? What are you, best friends all of a sudden?'

'Why are you being so mean?' Despite herself, Scarlett

found she was biting back tears. What the hell had she done wrong now?

'Sorry,' said Jake, who clearly wasn't, 'but have you heard yourself lately? I thought you despised the whole Hollywood scene?'

'Oh for heavens' sake. You're starting to sound like Magnus,' she said. 'I don't despise anyone. Except perhaps Brogan O'Donnell.' Jake rolled his eyes. 'It's true I'm not a sceney person, but this is work. And besides, it's the Oscars. Aren't I entitled to be a little excited?'

'You call this work?' said Jake. 'Fawning over a bunch of actors like the coach of the Olympic arse-licking team? And here I was thinking you designed jewellery for a living.'

'That's not fair.' Scarlett felt her disappointment harden into anger. 'Why am I the enemy again, Jake? What happened?'

'Nothing happened,' he grunted.

What could he say? That he'd just woken up to the fact that, while he'd been away comforting his brother, and hanging out in Africa trying to be the good, noble man she wanted him to be, he'd turned into a Hollywood laughing stock. That women like Julia, women who'd once perceived him as an alpha male, a success story, now thought of him as a jumped-up gigolo? As Scarlett's plaything, clinging on to her and Flawless's success like a festering fucking toadstool on a damp tree.

'Tons of stars were wearing our stuff,' said Scarlett making one, last, valiant effort to salvage their happy evening. 'Rhianna took the drop earrings in the end. Anna Kournikova wore the yin-yang pendant and we even got Enrique in the topaz cufflinks, which he was really cute about on camera. Nicole Richie went for the snake cuff.'

'*Your* stuff,' said Jake. He wasn't even looking at her. 'They were wearing your stuff, not mine.'

'Yes, but ...'

'I'm just your lowly diamond dealer, remember?' He

kicked the ground morosely. Suddenly Scarlett became aware that they were being watched – that perhaps the red carpet at the Oscars was not the best place for a lover's tiff.

'I probably won't even be that for much longer.'

'You know what? Fine,' snapped Scarlett. She was tired of pandering to his constant neediness. He wanted to push her away? He'd just succeeded. 'If you don't want to be here, why don't you just piss off?' She turned on her heel. 'Go on. Go home. Feel sorry for yourself. I'm past caring.'

Sweeping regally into the theatre alone, her head held high, she steeled herself not to look back.

Jake, bitterly ashamed of himself, watched her go.

From behind she looked powerful and supremely confident, a pewter Amazon in that dress. As she disappeared into the throng, he felt smaller and more pathetic than he could ever remember. With a heart full of ashes and a mouth as dry as dust, he turned in the other direction and walked away.

Aunt Agnes was wrong.

She didn't need him. Not in the least.

Had he followed her into the powder room sixty seconds later and seen Scarlett bent double over the wash basin, sobbing her heart out, he might have felt differently.

Cried out, she splashed cold water on her face, dabbed away the worst of the mascara smears with a paper towel, and looked in the mirror.

'That's it,' she told her reflection, ignoring the sidelong glances from actresses perfecting their make-up beside her. 'No more. It's over.'

It was funny the way relationships ended. How some of them exploded in a ball of passionate fury and others, like with Magnus, faded away with a whimper. With Jake, it had been different again: a growing realisation that, love or no love, they couldn't live together. They were the classic opposites attracting. But Jake's anger, his resentment, the whole professional jealousy thing that had got so utterly out of hand – it was no way to live, or to love.

She'd go home to Vado Drive tonight, alone. And tomorrow she'd drive over to Jake's and clear her stuff out of his apartment.

She doubted there'd be any drama. Deep down, she knew, he felt the same way she did – that it simply wasn't working. All the rows must have taken it out of him, too. Besides, they had a good reason to keep things civil. Whatever he might say in the self-pitying heat of the moment, Scarlett *did* need Jake at Flawless. The diamonds he brought her were second to none. She couldn't hope to find another supplier half as good, never mind one who understood promotion and branding in the jewellery business as well and instinctively as Jake did.

For all her bravado, secretly she shared Jake's fears about Brogan. He might well set his sights on her again after this NPR business, and try to damage Flawless. Judging by how effectively he'd eviscerated Solomon Stones, not to mention the lengths he'd gone to – burning down Bijoux – the last time she strayed onto his radar screen, it was not a threat to be taken lightly. And it wasn't something she wanted to face alone. Professionally, she needed Jake more than ever – and for obvious reasons, he felt the same way. Maturity had never been his strong point. But she felt confident that even *he* would see the need to maintain a viable working relationship. Who knew? Maybe, once the dust had settled and the broken hearts begun to heal, they might even salvage a friendship from this unholy mess.

The rest of the evening was torture, on so many levels. Scarlett was an Oscars virgin, and no one had warned her how interminably long the ceremony itself would be: hour after hour dragging by with nothing to do but think about Jake and how she'd lost him, staring into space throughout the wooden links, the forced laughter, the endless nominations for categories nobody but the friends and family of those involved gave a shit about: wardrobe co-ordination, sound editing, light engineering, the list went on and on. And on. It was like School Speech Day at St Clements, except four times as long, with no pee breaks, the world's most uncomfortable dress on and a heart that was crumbling inside her chest like a stale Wensleydale cheese.

By two a.m., when she staggered up the porch steps of Nancy's cottage, she felt as drained and spent as a sun-withered flower. Somehow she'd managed to keep a professional smile glued to her face at Elton John's star-studded Aids Foundation party, and schmoozed everyone she was supposed to. But boy, was it a blessed relief to be out of there at last!

The night was calm and clear when she got home, and she lingered on the porch for a while, sinking down onto the love-seat and pulling off her agonising stilettos at last. Too tired to think any more, she rubbed the balls of her feet and stared up at the night sky, taking comfort in the blanket of stars twinkling above her in their agelessness. She imagined those same stars over Scotland, and London, Africa and Siberia. What time was it in Yakutsk, she wondered? Were Brogan's miners out there, gazing up at the heavens like she was right now, bracing themselves for another day's gruelling labour in his mines, hacking away at an open cast pit, the cancer in their lungs multiplying with every breath? What right had she to be unhappy, compared to those men?

The ringing of the house phone brought her back to reality. In the silence of the night it sounded supernaturally loud, like an air-raid siren or a fire alarm. Jumping to her feet, she scrambled inside and picked up after five rings.

'Scarlett?'

The voice on the other end of the line was so choked

with tears, it took a second for her to register that it was Nancy.

'Yes, Nance, it's me.' She tried her best to sound comforting. 'What's happened, darling? What's the matter?'

A long intake of breath.

'Mom died. A couple of hours ago.'

'Oh, Nancy.' Scarlett winced. There was nothing to say, but unspoken sympathy hung in the two thousand miles of air between them.

'Can you come to New York?'

Scarlett didn't hesitate.

'Of course. As soon as you want me.'

'Can you come tomorrow? I hate to ask, but Che Che and I broke up officially last night ...' Tears broke the flow again. 'I can't face the thought of doing the funeral alone.'

Scarlett made quiet, shushing noises, like a mother calming her newborn. Of course she'd be there. She'd throw some things in a bag right now and catch the first plane out in the morning.

The morning. It was already the morning. She hadn't slept, yet she felt like she was in the middle of some nightmarish dream.

'Just hold it together, Nance, OK?' she said, grateful for the chance to put thoughts of Jake aside entirely for a few hours. 'I'm on my way.'

# Twenty-one

The Cathedral of St John the Divine, on the corner of Amsterdam and 112th Street, is the home of the American Episcopal Church, and the largest neo-gothic edifice in the world.

Built in the 1880s at the height of the second great wave of immigration into New York City, its architects conceived it as a 'house of prayer for all nations', a bricks-and-mortar symbol of America's status as the ultimate ethnic melting pot. Anyone visiting the church for the first time on the day of Lucy Lorriman's funeral, however, would have seen precious little of this much-vaunted diversity.

Nancy's mother's funeral was old-school to its Ivy League core. Every face in the congregation was white, protestant and Republican. The dress code was traditional, with mourners wearing black, not miscellaneous 'dark colours'. Women covered their heads, carried prayer books and kept jewellery and make-up to a minimum. Children stood rigid-backed and silent beside their parents, their scrubbed faces a picture of forced solemnity. The whole occasion reminded Scarlett of home, and the stiff, joyless church services she'd been forced to attend in Buckie as a child. 'Remember, young lady, you're a Drummond Murray,' her mother would warn her sternly before they went inside. 'People will be watching you. Behave yourself.'

People were watching her now, too. Standing in the front row with the family, clasping Nancy's hand, she felt the stares of the six-hundred-strong congregation burning into her back like blow-torches and developed an irrational terror that she might fart, or get the hiccups, or in some other way let the side down. Of course, immediately afterwards she felt guilty for allowing her thoughts to turn to such frivolous things when Nancy's mother's coffin lay not ten feet in front of them, a gruesomely gleaming slab of polished wood on a solid gold plinth.

She remembered Mrs Lorriman well from her and Nancy's schooldays as a warm, doting mother, always quick to see the funny side of her daughter's outrageously naughty behaviour (unlike Caroline). On the rare occasions when Nancy's parents flew in for speech days or other important school occasions, Lucy always went out of her way to include Scarlett in the Lorriman family plans, which were inevitably far more glamorous and exciting than the Drummond Murrays'. Nancy's speech-day picnics involved Fortnum & Mason game pies, mountains of smoked salmon, and as much champagne as one could drink to wash down the cream cakes and strawberries for pudding. Dear Mrs Cullen's Tupperware pots of coronation chicken, washed down with Panda cola and a packet of Mr Kipling's French Fancies didn't stand a chance by comparison.

Envious of the Lorrimans' fortune, and Lucy's close bond with her daughter, Caroline Drummond Murray looked down her nose at Nancy's mother for being vulgar and nouveau. In fact, the Lorrimans were anything but vulgar. They did, however, wear their wealth unapologetically, enjoying the finer things in life unencumbered by innate British embarrassment, and they brought their daughter up to do the same. It never occurred to Nancy to apologise for her parents' new Bentley, or for the fact that she always flew first class, any more than it occurred to her to boast about those things. Unlike Scarlett, whose brother Cameron was going to get Drumfernly, Nancy stood to inherit her family's entire fortune one day, but she never made a big deal about it.

Glancing to her right now, at the stricken profile of

Nancy's father, Scarlett wondered if that day might not come sooner than her friend expected. Morty Lorriman must have aged twenty years since she'd last seen him two years ago, on the fateful trip to New York when she'd first laid eyes on Brogan O'Donnell. At Tiffany. The same night she'd had that humdinger of a fight with Jake.

Oh God, Jake. Would she ever be properly over him? She'd been in New York two weeks now, so she hadn't seen him in person since Oscar night, but he seemed to have absorbed by osmosis the fact that their relationship was over. When she rang the next day, to tell him about Nancy's mother and that she was leaving town for a while, he'd been polite and sympathetic. But he'd already begun referring to 'us' in the past tense. He'd even offered to deliver Scarlett's things back to the cottage without being asked.

In one way she was relieved, to be spared the official break-up talk and pointless post-mortem. She also wouldn't now have to go to his apartment and collect her stuff in person, thus avoiding any possibility of a relapse. However mad she got at him, she did have an uncanny ability to find herself giving in to temptation the moment he laid a hand on her arm, or so much as glanced towards the bedroom.

But in another way, it hurt to see him letting her go so easily. If he was heartbroken, he was doing a damn good job of hiding it.

'Here you go, Scarlett honey.' Morty handed her a hymn book, which she took with guilty thanks. Poor man. The illness that had killed Lucy had clearly ravaged him too, turning his salt-and-pepper hair a uniform, saintly white, and draining the blood from his cheeks.

'This is the last hymn.' Nancy's voice in her ear startled her. 'We're all going to the Plaza afterwards, for the reception. There's space for you in the family car.'

'Oh, no, sweetie, really, I wouldn't want to impose,' Scarlett whispered back. 'Your dad might want to talk to you privately.'

'That's what I'm afraid of,' said Nancy, looking in her father's direction and seeing the same, haggard, defeated old man that Scarlett had just been pitying. 'He's right on the edge. If I give him a window, I'm scared the floodgates'll open and he'll break down completely. And what do I say if he asks about the movie?'

Paramount had called last week, just days after her mom had passed away, and confirmed Nancy's position as creative advisor on her comedy script. It meant big bucks, her first really big credit ... and a full-time, paid position in LA. Though he hadn't spelt it out in so many words, her dad had dropped numerous hints over the past few weeks about how much he needed her home in New York, and how lonely he was without her. So far she hadn't had the strength to tell him about Paramount's offer, but she couldn't put it off for ever.

'He won't ask,' said Scarlett. 'Not today.'

'I guess not,' said Nancy. 'But ride with me all the same, will you?'


As it turned out, the three of them drove the few blocks across town to the Plaza in almost total silence. Father and daughter gazed blankly out of their respective, blackened windows, while Scarlett sat between them, making intermittent small-talk with the driver about the beauty of the service and the flowers, and the unseasonable spring chill that had seized New York. It wasn't until they got to the hotel, and Nancy was finished with receiving line duties, that she was able to whisk her friend off to an upstairs Ladies room for a private chat, their first real conversation of the day.

'D'you want to give us a minute?' Nancy glared at the uniformed Puerto Rican maid, hovering over the washbasins with towels and soap like a superfluous human dispensing machine. 'I need to talk to my friend alone.'

'Sorry,' the maid shrugged. 'I not allowed to leave my station. Hotel policy.'

Pulling out a fifty from her purse, Nancy pressed it into the woman's hand.

'I'll explain to your manager if you get into trouble,' she insisted, manhandling her out of the door. Hanging the 'restrooms closed for cleaning' sign up outside, she locked herself and Scarlett in.

'Probably thinks we're doing drugs,' she said, forcing a smile as she collapsed into the attendant's chair. 'Either that or we're two sex-crazed lesbian goths who like to fuck each other in toilets.'

Scarlett leaned back against the wall. 'You OK?'

'Not really.' Nancy ran her hand through her hair. 'There's been so much to do, and I've had to do it all. Dad can't butter his own toast in the morning. I think he's still in shock. I'm so fucking tired, I can barely speak.'

'Of course you are,' said Scarlett sympathetically.

'And I know it's ridiculous, but I miss Che Che. I do.'

'Why is that ridiculous?'

Nancy shrugged. 'I don't know. Because we were only together a few months, and for the last third of that time he was a complete, selfish, self-righteous jerk?'

'I could say the same about Jake,' said Scarlett. 'Unfortunately it doesn't make breaking up any easier.'

'He called this morning. Offered me his "condolences".' Nancy's brow knitted into a contemptuous frown. 'I swear to God, Scar, he sounded like a freakin' funeral director or a shitty greetings card or something. *Condolences*? Who uses a word like that? It's like saying the weather is "clement", or my new girlfriend is really "personable". Asshole. Why couldn't he just say he's sorry? Why couldn't he tell me he loves me?'

She was looking up now, her jaw jutting forwards defiantly, a pint-sized ball of righteous indignation. Tinier than ever in her fitted black Dolce & Gabbana skirt-suit and vintage Izzy Blow pillbox hat – the grief and stress diet had taken pounds off her naturally curvy frame – she might almost have appeared fragile, if she hadn't been so mad.

'Men aren't always the best in these sorts of situations,' said Scarlett, vaguely. 'Jake's got all the tact of a Sherman tank in a butterfly house.'

'Do you think I'm a bad daughter?'

Nancy's anger seemed to have vanished as quickly as it had appeared, and her voice sounded querulous. To her dismay, Scarlett saw that she was crying.

'What? No, not at all. Why on earth would I think that?'

'Because my mom just died, and here I am crying about some stupid *guy*.' She spat out the word angrily. 'Because I'm abandoning my dad when he needs me most, just to take a job.'

'You're not abandoning him,' said Scarlett firmly. 'You're getting on with your own life, which is exactly what your mom would have wanted you to do. Your dad'll want it too, once he gets through this initial period of shock. Besides, it isn't just *a* job. It's your big break, babe. If you didn't go back, I'd kill you.'

Nancy smiled and blew her nose noisily on one of the maid's linen napkins.

'D'you ever see him still? For Trade Fair stuff?'

Apparently they were back to Che Che again.

'Not really,' said Scarlett. In fact she had seen him a couple of times before she came out to New York, but she didn't see the point in rubbing salt in Nancy's wounds by admitting it. She'd even taken him out for lunch in Oscar week to thank him for bringing the NPR programme back from the dead, and spent most of the meal pleading with him to swallow his pride and get back together with Nancy. The whole thing was so stupid. Any fool could see the two of them belonged together. But he was stubborn as a mule – as stubborn as Nancy herself – and hadn't given an inch. He reminded Scarlett of a Yeats poem she'd learned at school, something about too long a sacrifice making a stone of the heart. She liked Che Che and admired his principles. But surely only a heart of stone could fail to be moved by Nancy's sorrow and need right now?

'Probably just as well,' sniffed Nancy, pulling herself together. 'I feel bad I haven't asked about you and Jake. I know you must be hurting too.'

'Nah,' lied Scarlett, 'not really. It was a mutual decision, and it's for the best. We're still gonna work together. We can still be friends.'

Nancy gave her a 'yeah, right,' look that said it all.

'I'm serious,' said Scarlett. 'I mean, we're both adults. Why shouldn't we stay friends?'

'Firstly, only one of you is an adult,' said Nancy. 'And secondly, correct me if I'm wrong, but I don't remember you ever being friends in the first place. First you hated each other. Then all of a sudden you loved each other. And now ...'

'Now, we drive each other crazy,' said Scarlett.

'Yeah, well,' smiled Nancy, 'at least you've been consistent in that.'


Across town later that evening Diana stared out of a grimy cab window and pulled her cashmere wrap more tightly around her shoulders. For once the little life inside her had stopped wriggling. Asleep, she assured herself, although the hideous fear that her longed-for baby might die in the womb never quite left her. Every kick was a relief and a joy, even the ones that kept her awake at three in the morning, tortured with back pain and nausea.

Outside a blustery March night was in full swing. Even from the warm confines of the cab she could see how bitingly cold the wind was. She wondered, yet again, about Danny – where he was, who he was with tonight, whether he thought about her and the baby at all. Contact between them had dwindled lately, and was now mostly restricted to one, regular weekly call after her ObGyn appointment, a progress report on the baby's health. Diana found each of these calls torturous. Longing to reach out to him, missing him like a physical pain, she had no idea how to break through the cold, businesslike tone with which he spoke to her. Rarely did he confide any information about his own life. When he'd taken a job as a lowly shop-floor salesman in a West Village jewellery boutique, Diana heard about it not from Danny, but through a mutual friend. Similarly, he never once asked after *her*, as opposed to the baby. It didn't occur to her that perhaps the pain of separation was too great for him to bear; that it was all he could do to make it to the end of those desperate conversations without breaking down in tears. All she saw was a frostiness that at times seemed to border on hatred. She had no idea how things would play out once the baby was born, what role if any he would play as a father. But she tried not to think about it. Having read in countless magazines that stress could harm one's foetus and even cause lasting learning difficulties, she was determined to keep her life as calm and comfortable as possible.

It was this desire, this need for calm that had brought her back, slowly, into Brogan's life. Certainly guilt was a key factor in her decision to start visiting him regularly. What kind of person would she be to turn down a dying man's tearful request for reconciliation? A man who, whatever wrongs he may have done her, she'd loved once with all her heart?

But other forces were at work too. Living with her parents, a lifeline when she'd first split with Danny, had rapidly turned into an unhealthy situation. While she lived under their roof, they felt entirely free to bombard her with unwanted advice, about the baby, Danny, her divorce, everything. The ceaseless background noise of criticism was making it very hard to maintain the Zen-like inner peace that her unborn child apparently needed, if it wasn't to run amok with a machine gun in the high school cafeteria the moment it turned thirteen.

When Brogan first suggested she move back in to the marital apartment, Diana rejected the idea out of hand. Their divorce might be on perma-hold, but the truth was she was still in love with Danny. She needed time to grieve for that relationship before she could even think of beginning another. As for going back to Brogan, every shred of logic and reason that had survived the onslaught of her pregnancy hormones argued against it. She'd been unhappy with him for so many years, quite apart from the issue of his violent, unpredictable temper. Their marriage, as it had been, was no environment in which to raise a child, whatever lingering affection she might feel for him now he was sick.

And then, of course, there was the cancer itself. The operation to remove his primary tumour had been successful, and since then the army of specialists caring for him had declared his response to chemo to be 'satisfactory to good', whatever that meant. Brogan still referred to himself in conversation as 'dying', but whether that was the reality, or a cynical attempt to maintain her sympathy levels and attention, Diana didn't know.

What she *did* know was that his need for her, emotionally, was real. Unlike Danny, Brogan bombarded her with calls, sometimes as often as fifteen times a day. His solicitousness for her health and happiness bordered on the obsessive – it was almost as if he needed to focus on her, to distract himself from his illness and to keep his spirits up, something the doctors had told her could be vital for his recovery. On a more practical level, with Brogan hospitalised four weeks out of five (every four weeks he had a break from chemo, to recuperate and regain some strength), she would have the apartment almost entirely to herself. In the end the lure of regaining her privacy and getting away from her parents proved too much. She'd accepted his offer and moved back in.

So far, despite her misgivings, she had to admit the arrangement had worked out well. Brogan was once again picking up all her bills, quietly making sure she was taken care of. She visited him daily in the hospital, visits that he let her know meant everything to him, although he was careful not to push her on the subject of their getting back together. There'd be time enough for that once he was well – whatever he might say to Diana, in his own mind Brogan never doubted his recovery – and after the baby was born. For now, he was happy to have her home again and, though she might not have realised yet, back under his control.

'You can pull over here,' she told the cabbie, as they approached Minx, the new 'hot' Asian restaurant in the West Village. Released from hospital this morning, Brogan had insisted he was well enough to eat out, and arranged to meet Diana for dinner. He carefully hadn't termed it a date, although clearly that was what he believed it to be. In a masterstroke of tact, he had even checked himself into the Plaza for the week with his nurse instead of coming home to the apartment, because he 'wouldn't want to invade Diana's space'.

Diana was duly impressed. Putting others' needs before his own was certainly something only the 'new' Brogan would do. He kept telling her that the cancer had changed him, but it was actions like this that spoke so much louder than words.

Winching herself out of the taxi – she was only six months gone but already felt comically huge and ungainly – she paid the driver and, with a smile at the windswept doorman, hurried inside the warm restaurant.

'Do you have a reservation? Name?' the frazzled Asian hostess barked at her crossly. In a crotch-skimming mini-dress and silver go-go boots, the girl looked like she'd just walked off the set of an Austin Powers movie. Diana felt fatter and frumpier than ever.

'I'm meeting a friend,' she said. 'His name is O'Donnell.'

Immediately the girl replaced her scowl with a smile as broad as it was fake.

'Of course,' she beamed. 'Welcome to Minx, Mrs O'Donnell. If you'd like to follow me, your husband's already at the table.'

'How the hell do you do it?' Brogan, with the aid of a cane, got to his feet as Diana approached his corner table, the best in the house. 'Six months pregnant and you're the most beautiful girl in here by a country mile.'

'Those drugs must have affected your eyesight,' she smiled, kissing him gently on the cheek as she took her seat. It was an effort to hide her shock at his appearance. She'd seen him every day in the hospital, but somehow out in the real world, in a suit rather than a medical gown, his bald head, taut, green-grey skin and wasted frame looked a thousand times more pronounced. 'I'm a whale.'

'You're a goddess,' he insisted. 'Can I get you something to drink?'

'Cranberry juice, please. And let's order food right away.'

'Yes, ma'am,' laughed Brogan. 'Never come between a pregnant lady and a meal, right?'

It was bizarre, sitting down to dinner together at a swanky restaurant. As if the last two years – Danny, the baby, the cancer, the divorce – had never happened. But the atmosphere was buzzing, the food ambrosial, and to Diana's surprise she soon found herself relaxing and even, dare she say it, enjoying herself.

'I hope it wasn't too much for you,' said Brogan, his voice full of concern as she stifled a yawn. 'Coming out so late.'

'Hey, I'm only pregnant,' she joked. 'You're the one

with cancer. I'm sure the doctors said you were meant to be resting this week.'

'They said "relaxing",' said Brogan. 'This is relaxing. I do have to catch up on a little work later, though. Once you're safely tucked up in bed.'

'Work?' Diana raised an eyebrow. 'Please tell me you're kidding.'

'Darling, you know me. If I can't work, I might as well be dead,' he said cheerfully. 'Aidan's meeting me here at eleven for a drink, and to run through some stuff. It shouldn't take long.'

Diana wrinkled her nose in distaste. 'Aidan Leach? You still use that guy?'

'He's a great lawyer.'

'He makes my flesh crawl,' she said, shuddering to emphasise the point.

'He makes a lot of people's flesh crawl,' said Brogan. 'That's part of what makes him a good lawyer. He's been very loyal to me.'

'I'm not sure it's loyalty if you have to pay for it,' said Diana bluntly. 'I wish you'd get rid of him.'

Brogan looked at her quizzically. 'Really? I'm surprised you care.'

Realising she'd given something away, Diana blushed, and tried to backtrack.

'It's not … I mean, it's your life, and your business. I don't like him, that's all I'm saying. I never have.'

But it was too late. Brogan was already wrapping up her flash of concern in silk, like a spider stashing away its paralysed prey for a future meal. It was tiny moments like these – admissions of a continued involvement in his life – that sustained him through not only the chemo, but the slings and arrows being fired at him from all sides professionally.

He'd listened to Scarlett's NPR programme from his hospital bed, eaten alive by rage. How dare they broadcast such a biased, bullshit piece of propaganda? This was one of many items on the agenda for his meeting with Aidan later. Brogan might be down, but any enemies unwise enough to consider him 'out' were about to receive a rude wake-up call.

Diana had also heard the show. Moved to tears by some of the miners' stories, she'd begged Brogan to intervene, something he'd promised solemnly to do.

'Believe me, honey, I felt terrible too when I heard those interviews,' he said. And it was true, he *had* felt terrible. Just for very different reasons. 'I intend to take urgent action, sweetheart. You can depend on that.'

Diana had taken this as another sign of his improved, reformed character. Struck down with a serious illness himself, he could at last begin to appreciate what those poor, desperate men were going through.

Suddenly shattered, Diana waved away the dessert menu, and asked the waiter for their check.

'Don't be silly,' said Brogan, as she reached beneath the table for her purse. 'The day I let a woman split the check is the day they carry me off in a wooden box.'

'OK,' she said reluctantly. 'Well, thank you.'

'Not at all,' said Brogan gallantly, getting up to help her out of her seat. He was so weak, it was an effort to pull back the chair, but he managed it, handing her her shawl as he bid her goodnight.

On the way out, she ran into Aidan, straightening his tie anxiously on the street outside.

'Diana.' He pressed his sweaty cheek against hers. 'Long time no see. How are you? How was dinner? Great place, no?'

'Dinner was fine,' she answered frostily.

'So I hear you moved back in. Things didn't work out with Danny Meyer, huh?'

Every word was laced with spite. Diana could feel her upper lip curl with revulsion.

'I don't believe that's any of your business,' she said curtly.

'Hey, look, I wasn't being funny,' said Aidan, feigning innocence. 'I'm just happy to see you and Mr O'D are working things out. He's always loved you, you know.'

'For your information, Brogan and I are friends – nothing more. I'd appreciate it if you kept your misinformed comments about my private life to yourself.'

Aidan waited until she'd hailed a cab and sped away, before muttering 'stuck-up bitch,' to her retreating tail lights. Brogan must be out of his mind to want her back. Who took a fat, middle-aged, holier than thou cow, six months gone with another man's kid, over the stream of nubile hotties offering themselves up on a plate at Premiere?

Aidan had other reasons not to want Diana and Brogan to patch things up, not least the fact that she clearly loathed him, and could easily undo the close working and personal relationship with Brogan he'd tried so hard to build this past year. Finally, after years of loyal service, his boss was starting to show him the respect he deserved. Cosy dinners with Diana did not bode well for that. He'd have to figure out a way to make himself completely indispensable before she sunk her claws into Brogan any deeper.

'Hi, boss.' Marching purposefully over to Brogan's table, he sat down and ordered himself a dirty martini and a sashimi salad before getting down to business. 'I ran into Diana outside. I hope I didn't offend her.'

'So do I,' said Brogan, frowning deeply. 'What the fuck did you say?'

'Nothing!' Aidan looked hurt. 'Jesus. I asked her if she'd enjoyed her dinner.'

'That's it?'

'That's it. I don't know what it is. I've always had the feeling she doesn't like me, that's all.'

'Sure she likes you,' lied Brogan. 'Stop being so paranoid. So, tell me. Where are we?'

'With what? Where d'you want me to start?'

'Yakutsk. That fucking radio show. What's the latest?'

'It's all in hand,' said Aidan smoothly.

'Meaning?'

'I'm dealing with the little Scottish piece of shit who wrote it – ask me no questions and all that. And I'm working with Fleishman-Hillard here and Freud's in London to try and limit the negative press.'

'Has there been much?' said Brogan. He still got all the major international papers delivered to his hospital bed every morning, but recently he'd been too weak to read more than a fraction of the business pages.

'Some,' said Aidan. 'It aired on BBC Radio Four in the UK, and on the World Service, which was unfortunate. But Matthew Freud's been quick to play the 'heartless media kicking a sick man when he's down' card. And Fleishman-Hillard got a great quote in the *Wall Street Journal*, about the allegations being completely unfounded, with not a shred of medical evidence to link these cancer cases to conditions in our mines.'

'I should think so. There *isn't* a shred of evidence,' said Brogan, coughing heavily into his napkin.

'As many people responded negatively towards the BBC and Trade Fair as have taken a pop at us,' said Aidan, hoping to calm him down. He wasn't well enough to get mad about this shit. 'On the other hand, it *has* raised awareness. Sooner or later we're going to have to be seen to be doing something to address the problems over there.'

'Hmm,' Brogan grunted. 'As it happens I've already got something in mind. And what about the Drummond Murray girl? I'll be honest with you, Aidan, that kid is starting to seriously irritate me. She doesn't know when to quit.'

'We have to be careful about going after her directly,' said Aidan. 'There were rumours after we took care of things in London, which we don't want to stir up again.

Plus now she's closely linked with the Meyer brothers, who everyone knows aren't top of your Christmas card list, as well as making herself the voice of fucking Siberia. Much as I'd love to run her off the road or have Fleishman-Hillard start a whispering campaign, it'd be too easy to trace that shit back to us.'

'So what are you saying?' asked Brogan. 'We let her get away with it?'

'Come on, boss,' Aidan frowned, 'this is me you're talking to. Of course she doesn't get away with it. We have to play things a little smarter, that's all. Come at this laterally.'

Brogan looked unconvinced. 'You have something in mind?'

'As a matter of fact, I do.' Aidan's face brightened. 'A little tidbit for the British papers. Take a look.'

Reaching into his briefcase, he pulled out three black-and-white photographs and pushed them across the table.

'Jesus,' Brogan whistled, wrinkling his nose in distaste. 'I just ate, man.'

'I know,' Aidan chuckled. 'Pretty hardcore, aren't they?'

'Who is it?' asked Brogan.

'Cameron Drummond Murray,' Aidan replied. 'Scarlett's brother, and heir to the family estate. He works at Goldman in London.'

A malicious smile spread across Brogan's face. 'Not for much longer he doesn't.'

'So you want me to run with this?' said Aidan. 'You're sure?'

'Never surer,' said Brogan. 'Just for fuck's sake make sure you don't leave my fingerprints. And if Diana hears a word of any of this ...'

'She won't,' said Aidan confidently. 'You focus on getting well and back in that boardroom. Everything else you can leave to me.'

# Twenty-two

Scarlett stood in the front display window at Flawless, gazing out on a gorgeous, sunlit April day.

'Sweetie, I don't mean to annoy,' said Perry, who was kneeling at her feet trying to artfully wrap another strand of fake moss around a papier mâché tree trunk, 'but do you think you could possibly, like, get back to work? I know you're the boss and all, but I can't get the Forest of Arden finished with you standing in my shady glade.'

With Scarlett in New York for the best part of a month and Jake distracted with Solomon Stones and his brother's personal problems, Perry had enjoyed free rein at Flawless. Scarlett had been back for ten days now, but she was still mentally elsewhere, and had been more than happy to leave the thorny subject of their spring storefront up to him. He'd decided to go to town with a *Midsummer Night's Dream* theme, with diamond jewellery nestling in miniature lichened valleys, peered over by tiny porcelain faeries. If he did say so himself, it looked awesome. Or it would if Scarlett would only get out from under his feet and let him finish.

'Sorry,' she said, swinging a gazelle-like leg over his shoulders as she stepped over him back onto the shop floor. In a ribbed American Apparel vest and skintight J brands, she looked skinnier than ever, something Perry put down to heartbreak since her split with Jake. 'It's book-keeping day today. I've been putting it off.'

'I don't blame you,' said Perry. 'Those figures make my head swim. But if you want cheering up, check out the last entry in the sales ledger.'

Scarlett walked over to the big brown leather book in which she still hand-wrote every sale.

'I don't believe it,' she said, delighted. 'You sold the dagger necklace. And *both* of the diamond and ruby eternity rings.'

'Uh huh,' Perry nodded airily, removing a silver tack from between his teeth and pressing it firmly into the papier mâché bark. 'Last night, right after you went home, to a little Asian dude. He only came up to my knees, and he couldn't speak a word of English, but he took one look at the rings, whispered something to his ladyfriend, and started nodding and pointing like a maniac. They were in and out in five minutes, then they came back half an hour later and bought the necklace too. I'd love to say it was my brilliant salesmanship that clinched it, but all I did was nod when he pointed to the American Express sign and say "That'll do nicely, thank you," so I'm afraid the credit's all yours.'

'Rubbish. You're a star,' said Scarlett, blowing him a kiss. 'Honestly Perry, I don't know how to thank you. You've saved my arse these last few weeks.'

'Yeah, well, you know,' he shrugged. 'A pay rise is always an option, hint hint.'

Scarlett blushed. 'Of course, of course. God, I'm sorry, Perry, you're well overdue for a pay review. I've really been off the ball lately, what with Nancy and Trade Fair and ... things.'

'I know,' he said kindly. 'I'm not going anywhere, sweetie, don't worry.'

Scarlett sighed. That was it. She couldn't put it off any longer. She'd have to sit down with Jake. Perry's pay rise was only one of a zillion pressing business matters she'd been avoiding dealing with since she'd got back, afraid of how she'd react when she saw him in person. It was over six weeks since the Oscars, and despite numerous cordial emails and texts, and even the odd stilted phone call, she still hadn't laid eyes on him since that night.

'I think I might run out for coffee,' she said when, after a few minutes, she realised she'd been staring at the same page of figures on her PC screen without taking anything in. 'D'you want something?'

'I'll have a skinny blueberry muffin, if you're going,' said Perry, standing back and admiring his now-finished handiwork. 'And for God's sake, get a full-fat one for yourself. If those ribs get any more visible the only guys that'll want to date you'll be palaeontologists.'

Strolling down Rodeo a few moments later with the sun on her face and a warm, almost summery breeze in her hair, Scarlett made a conscious effort to count her blessings. She was healthy. It was a gorgeous day. No one in her family had just died; she had a bunch of great friends (albeit on the other side of the Atlantic) and her business, touch wood, was still thriving. Having waited with bated breath for weeks after the NPR programme aired, expecting Brogan to retaliate, she'd finally begun to relax. Other than the few defensive comments his spokespeople had made in the press, he'd been silent as the grave. Whether it was his cancer, or the reconciliation with Diana that had done it, she didn't know – like everyone else in the business, Scarlett had heard on the grapevine that Brogan's wife had moved back in with him; poor Danny must be crushed – but something seemed to have muted Brogan's thirst for revenge.

Walking into the coffee shop with a familiar feeling of guilt – she really ought to support small local businesses and not huge multinationals like Starbucks – she was pondering whether or not she could stomach an entire, human-head-sized muffin when her phone rang.

'Hello?' she answered.

'Scarlett, it's Che Che.' It was weeks since she'd heard from Nancy's ex. She'd started to wonder whether he'd ever get back in contact, but decided not to chase him. If he wanted to stay involved with Trade Fair, he'd let her know eventually.

'How are you?' she said warmly. 'I was hoping you might call.'

'I'm guessing from your tone that you haven't heard,' he said. Only then did Scarlett realise how deathly serious his voice sounded. Something must be wrong.

'Heard what?' she said, trying not to sound panicked. 'It isn't Nancy, is it? Has something happened?'

Though still sharing a house up at Vado Drive, the girls' conflicting work schedules meant that Scarlett and Nancy had barely seen one another all week.

'It's not Nancy,' said Che Che bleakly. 'It's Andy Gordon. He's been killed.'

For a horribly long moment, Scarlett was silent. She'd heard what he said, but she couldn't seem to get her brain to register its meaning.

'He was found last night outside a block of flats in Moscow,' said Che Che, filling the dead air himself. 'Shot through the back of the neck. Executed, apparently.'

Scarlett felt the nausea rise up within her, and put a hand over her mouth to stop herself from vomiting.

'Excuse me, ma'am. Can I help you?'

She'd reached the front of the line, and the pissy-looking barista was hassling her for an order. Looking at her blankly, Scarlett backed away, sinking down onto the nearest available chair.

'What was he doing in Moscow?' she heard herself croak. Her throat was suddenly dry as dust.

'I have no idea,' said Che Che. 'It's the lead story on BBC news right now. You should try and get to a TV; they may be reporting more.'

'Do they know who did it?' she whispered, still struggling to take it all in. A snapshot of Andy's face beneath his shock of red hair, smiling his wry, I've-got-a-secret smile flashed through her mind. He was only her age, for Christ's sake. How could he be dead? 'Do they have any leads at all?'

Che Che let out a cynical laugh. 'Not officially, no. This is Russia. Shootings like this are a daily occurrence over there. But it doesn't take Einstein to figure out who wanted him dead.'

Too stunned to speak, Scarlett stared straight ahead of her, willing this not to be true. Was Brogan really capable of such extreme retribution?

'Listen, I'm sorry,' said Che Che eventually. 'I know you knew the guy personally. But you mustn't blame yourself.'

'Mustn't I?' Her words came out in a strangled sob. 'Why on earth not? If I hadn't pushed him to do the exposé—'

'You didn't,' said Che Che firmly. 'He was neck-deep in all this long before you came along. He's been on O'Donnell's hit-list for years, and he knew the risks he was taking.'

'I don't think he expected to die,' whispered Scarlett. 'Do you?'

Che Che didn't answer the question. Instead he tried to get her to focus on more practical considerations, such as protecting herself.

'I don't mean to be melodramatic,' he said, 'but you need to look seriously at your security, Scarlett.'

'What security?'

'Exactly. You and Nancy are a pair of sitting ducks up at that cottage on your own.'

'It's our home,' said Scarlett, her old defiance surfacing through the layers of shock and fear. 'Why should we leave? Besides, where would you have us go? Didn't you say Andy was shot on the street?'

'In broad daylight, yes,' said Che Che. 'But that was Moscow. This is LA. You'd be a lot safer in a hotel.'

'I'm not living in a bloody hotel.' Scarlett's response was immediate. 'I can't think of anything worse, and I know Nance will feel the same. No way.'

Che Che, who knew better than to argue, sighed heavily.

'Then at least get some protection installed, will you? An alarm, a dog. And I don't mean Boxford, I mean a serious guard dog. Armed security would be the best option.'

'OK,' said Scarlett after a long pause. 'I'll think about it.'

She could hear the genuine concern in his voice, for both her and Nancy, and was grateful for it, although fear for her own safety was the last thing on her mind right now. All she could think about was Andy, and the tragedy of what had already happened, a tragedy for which, no matter what Che Che or anybody said, she couldn't help but feel at least partly responsible.

Staggering out of Starbucks in a daze, she had no idea where to go. It seemed ridiculous to head back to work, as if nothing had happened. But nor did she want to go home alone, knowing Nancy would be at work at the studio till probably gone midnight. She should let Nancy know what had happened, of course, although that would mean driving over to Paramount – Nancy never answered the phone when she was writing – and she wasn't sure she trusted herself to get behind the wheel. Turning a corner, it occurred to her that Jake's apartment was only about six blocks away, an eminently walkable distance. He probably wouldn't be in either. But at least it was somewhere to go, and in that moment what she needed most was a plan. One shouldn't be alone at times like these. Jake might not be the ideal shoulder to cry on, but he was better than nothing.

'Ma, please. No. No, I don't think he needs you to fly over. Ma, have you been listening to a word I've said?'

Still in the boxer shorts and grey Labatt's T-shirt he'd worn to bed, Jake lay back on the leather couch in his living room with the phone pressed to his ear, rubbing his throbbing temples. He had a hundred and one business calls to make today, to clients (the few he had left) creditors (still plenty of those) and, if he could only work up the balls to do it, to Scarlett, to discuss the new order of diamonds for Flawless's summer collection. But getting Minty off the phone was proving even more difficult than usual.

'I don't know why you ask my advice about Dan if you're not going to listen to it,' he said, exasperation oozing from every pore. 'Yes, he's down. No, he's not suicidal. He needs some space ... I don't know, Ma, you'll have to ask him. Of course he cares about the baby ... Jesus Christ, woman, how would I know what he's eating? He's not wasting away, if that's what you mean. No, in all honesty, I doubt your homemade chicken soup *is* what he needs. There are one or two Jewish delis in New York you know, Ma ...'

The conversation continued in this vein for several more minutes until he finally snapped and, cutting Minty off mid-sentence, hung up the phone.

Christ. If they had an Olympic team for talking the hind legs off a donkey, his mother would be the coach. He knew she was worried about Danny – they all were – but her repeated threats to fly to New York and 'take care of him' weren't helping matters. Jake suspected her surge of maternal devotion was at least partly rooted in guilt. She hadn't exactly made Diana feel welcome at Christmas, and had certainly done her bit to add to the pressures they were under as a couple.

With Danny cutting himself off from everyone, including his well-meaning parents, the only outlet Minty had for her fears and concerns was Jake, who was starting to feel like the world's worst-paid agony uncle. Thank God he'd never told his mother about him and Scarlett. He didn't think he could have stood the daily calls from home, post-morteming his love-life. As it was he was already regretting the schoolboy error he'd made last week, when he accidentally mentioned the name of a Jewish girl, Ruth, whom he'd been casually dating since he and Scar called it quits.

'What's her family like? Have you been over for Shabbat yet? She's not one of those scrawny little things you go for, is she Jacob? It's not good for a woman's fertility to get too thin. No, don't sigh. You need to think about those things at your age.'

Oh my God, it was incessant. She'd be booking the fucking Rabbi next.

Groaning, he shoved the phone under the couch cushion so he wouldn't hear it ring and stumbled into the bathroom. Yet again he'd had far too much to drink last night and made a cock of himself in front of some girl. Dealing with the pain of losing Scarlett the only way he knew how – by shagging for England and drinking like an Irishman at a funeral – he was finding the work days tougher and tougher to get through.

Catching sight of his green, unshaven face in the mirror, he winced. The ad-men at Alka-Seltzer had a fucking nerve. 'Plop, plop, fizz, fizz, oh, what a relief it is' my arse. It hadn't felt like much of a relief at seven this morning, slumped in front of the porcelain goddess for an hour straight when he woke up, spewing his guts out. Afterwards he'd crawled back to bed and slept for another two hours, only to be wrenched back to consciousness by the insistent, shrill ringing of the telephone at half nine. He felt like a barnacle being chiselled off the bottom of a trawler. Except that in this case the chisel was Minty's strident, motherly voice, aimed directly at the point in Jake's cranium that acted as the nerve centre for a headache so throbbingly violent, he half expected it to interfere with the local phone network.

After a hot shower, two more Alka-Seltzer and an aggressive encounter with some cinnamon mouthwash, he began to feel vaguely human again. Grabbing his dressing gown, he wandered into the kitchen and had just finished putting on a pot of coffee when the doorbell rang.

'Go the fuck away,' he muttered, before picking up the entryphone. 'Yes?'

'It's Scarlett. Can I come in?'

'Of course. Shit, yes, of course. Always,' he babbled,

buzzing her up. What the fuck was wrong with him? His heart was beating like a hundred-metre sprinter's just at the sound of her voice. What was he, twelve?

But all thoughts about his lack of cool evaporated the moment he saw her. She looked whiter than he did, and stood in the doorway of his apartment, shaking like a whippet.

'Sit down,' he said, shoving her into an armchair in the living room and returning moments later with a tumbler of Scotch. 'Drink this.'

'It's half past eleven in the morning,' said Scarlett, fingering the glass.

'Stop arguing. Drink.'

Still passive with shock, she threw the honey-coloured liquid down her throat. It burned like battery acid, but it did have the desired effect of sharpening her senses.

'Thanks,' she said, once she'd finished coughing. 'I think I needed that.'

'So?' Jake eased himself back down onto the couch facing her, and tried not to think about how much he wanted to rip her skintight jeans off and make love to her, preferably for the next hundred years or so. 'What's the matter? You look like you've seen a ghost.'

For the first time since Che Che had called and told her, Scarlett found herself starting to cry.

'Andy Gordon,' she sobbed. 'The chap I was doing the radio show with.'

'I remember,' said Jake. How could he forget? Their constant squabbling about Andy's NPR programme had been the straw that broke the camel's back of their already fragile relationship. It wasn't a name that brought back happy memories.

'He's been murdered,' said Scarlett.

'Fuck,' said Jake. He hadn't expected that.

'Shot dead in Moscow in the middle of the day.' Scarlett started shaking again. 'Oh God, Jake, you were right, you were right. We should have left Brogan alone!'

'Hey, hey,' he said gently. Getting up, he took her hand and led her over to the couch. 'You couldn't have foreseen this. You mustn't blame yourself.'

'That's what Che Che said,' sniffed Scarlett. 'But who else should I blame?'

'Well, that's the next thing I was gonna say,' said Jake, who really didn't want to hear about fucking Che Che's opinions. 'Do you know for sure it was O'Donnell?'

Scarlett looked at him disbelievingly.

'He hasn't signed a confession, no. But surely ... I mean, don't you think it was him?'

'Possibly,' said Jake. 'I dunno, though. Murder?'

If the circumstances hadn't been so grim, Scarlett would have laughed. 'Is this the same Jake Meyer that screamed blue murder at me for months about how dangerous Brogan was? "Vengeful and psychotic" – wasn't that what you said?'

'I know,' Jake frowned. 'I know. But part of that was me trying to scare you off. I mean, I thought he'd do *something*. I thought he'd come after Flawless, or trash you in the press. I know he torched Bijoux and everything, but having a man shot? Organising that from his bed in the cancer ward? And not just a man, a journalist, a BBC journalist? I don't know. I can't see it. It doesn't ring true.'

Scarlett pressed her cheek against the soft towelling of his dressing gown and closed her eyes. She wanted to believe that what he was saying was true. That he wasn't just trying to make her feel better. Although the sad truth was that simply being here with him made her feel better. His body, his presence, the smell of soap and mouthwash and man was more than comforting. It was intoxicating. She'd missed him so much.

'Even so,' he continued, stroking her hair, 'you need to get some protection.'

'Che Che said that too,' she whispered.

'Scarlett, I'm not being funny, but I don't give a monkey's

cock what bloody Che Che thinks, all right?' Jake snapped. 'If it weren't for him you wouldn't have stirred up all this shit with Andy in the first place.'

Scarlett sat up. 'But you just said this wasn't my fault! That it might not even have *been* Brogan.'

'It's not your fault,' he said, grabbing her hand and staring at it, too scared to meet her eye. 'Look, just ignore me, all right? I'm being a jealous prick.'

Feeling the rough warmth of his palm laid over hers, Scarlett found herself instinctively stroking it with her thumb. It was a tiny movement, barely noticeable. But it sent jolts of electricity through Jake so violent he felt like he'd been scalded.

'Sorry,' she said, feeling him startle.

'It's fine,' he said, forcing a smile as he stood up. 'I'll make us some coffee, and we can talk about what to do.'

Standing in the kitchen a few seconds later, mindlessly filling the kettle with water, he gave himself a stern talking to:

*No, you wanker, you should not take her to bed just because you want to, and she probably wants to, and because it might make her feel safe for an hour or so. Nothing's changed. She needs a decent, honest, steady bloke. That's not you, it never will be you; you never—*

'I think it's full.'

Scarlett, appearing at his shoulder, pointed to the overflowing spout of the kettle as it spewed wasted water into the sink.

'Oh, yeah, right,' he mumbled, turning off the tap and plonking the kettle awkwardly back on its stand. 'Sorry. Miles away.'

'It also works better when you turn it on,' said Scarlett, flicking the switch. 'Is everything OK?'

Before he had a chance to answer, her phone rang.

'You've got to change that ring tone,' said Jake, shaking

his head as a tinny version of Madonna's 'Lucky Star' echoed round the room.

'I like it,' said Scarlett, flashing him a sweet, defiant smile that made his knees go weak. 'Oh, hi, Mum.' The smile evaporated. 'Listen, you've actually caught me at a rotten time. Could I possibly call you back?'

Jake watched as she held the receiver away from her ear, while Caroline unleashed a hysterical torrent of abuse at Minty-esque decibel levels. What was it with the mothers this morning?

'Hang up,' he mouthed to Scarlett, making slashing motions across his throat with his index finger. 'Tell her to piss off.'

But Scarlett waved him away. Slowly piecing together stray words as Caroline shot them out like shrapnel, she began to get a sense of what was happening. Leaning back against the kitchen counter, she forced herself to breathe deeply.

'And where is he now?' she asked, once she was finally able to get a word in edgeways. 'At the Maudsley? I see. But you haven't seen him yourself yet? OK, OK, Mum, calm down. It doesn't help when you yell. Is Daddy there? Can I speak to him?'

Jake made a pot of PG Tips while this one-sided conversation continued for a few more minutes. When she finally hung up, looking almost as drained as she had when she'd first arrived, he handed her a mug of heavily sweetened tea, and waited for her to fill him in.

'It's my brother,' she told him with forced calmness. 'He seems to have suffered some sort of breakdown or … I don't know what you'd call it exactly. Some poor woman motorist found him crawling along a lay-by off the A25 on his hands and knees, babbling about Binky.'

'Binky?'

'A dog we had when we were kids. Cameron didn't

know his own name, and couldn't tell this woman or the police how he got there.'

'I'd call that a breakdown,' said Jake. 'So what happened?'

'He's been sectioned and taken to a psychiatric facility in South London.' Scarlett put her head in her hands. She was too spent from the news of Andy's death to even think about crying over Cameron. All she felt in that moment was overwhelming tiredness, offset by a sense of the ridiculous. How had her life turned into a bad soap-opera episode in the space of a few short hours?

'Wow. They chucked him in a loony bin, eh? I guess he's not faking it then,' said Jake, employing all of his world-famous tact.

'My parents haven't seen him yet. They want me to fly home and take over. "Make some sense of it all," as my father put it.'

'How are you supposed to do that?' said Jake, who realised with sudden certainty that he didn't want her to go home. Even with things as strained and weird as they were between them, he needed to know they were at least in the same city. 'If he's flipped his lid there's not a lot you can do about it.'

'Probably not,' sighed Scarlett. 'But I have to go. He is my brother, after all. Something must have triggered all this.'

'What about Flawless?' said Jake, clutching at straws. 'You were gone all last month with Nancy. You can't just up sticks again. What about the summer collection?'

'I meant to talk to you about that. And Perry. He needs a pay rise,' said Scarlett, aware as the words came out how pathetically unimportant they were in comparison to Andy's death, never mind whatever bizarre crisis may have befallen Cameron.

'Exactly,' said Jake. 'You're needed here.'

*I need you*, he added in his head. *Please don't go.*

'I'm sorry,' she said, taking a big gulp of the tea he'd made her. 'Hopefully I won't be away for long. If need be I can email you the designs so you know what to order. But I don't have a choice, Jake. I have to go.'

# Twenty-three

It was strange coming from Los Angeles's seventy-five-degree sunshine, and plunging directly into the bitter, grey chill of a London 'spring'. Stranger still was checking into a hotel. This was Scarlett's home city, but after only two years away she found herself feeling increasingly like a tourist.

The Mitre was an ex-pub in the so-called 'posh' end of Denmark Hill. Caroline had insisted that they stay somewhere very close to the hospital, and this was the best option Scarlett had been able to find online at such short notice. In fairness to the smiley, Jamaican management, some effort had been made to brighten the place up. Scarlett could still smell the glue from beneath the newly laid carpets, and someone had been inspired to paint the reception area downstairs a jaunty, Postman-Pat's-van red. But after a long, sleepless flight, during which she saw an agonisingly brief BBC report on Andy's death before the in-flight entertainment 'glitch' proved terminal, it was still a depressing place to unpack. Through the lace curtains on her bedroom window she could see the belching traffic crawling its way through rush hour, past a string of desultory-looking fish 'n' chip shops, pawnbrokers and arcades. The double glazing provided some noise insulation, thank God, but nothing could insulate her from the charmless sprawl that was South London on a rainy Wednesday afternoon. Nor from the knowledge that, in less than an hour, she was supposed to be at the Maudsley trying to get some sense out of a brother who apparently didn't know who he was, and was highly unlikely to recognise her.

Caroline and Hugo were still in transit. Their flight had been delayed and she wasn't expecting to see them at the hotel till late, one tiny blessing in an otherwise hellish day. It meant that she would be able to have her first meeting with Cameron alone, minus her mother's hysteria. She'd already spoken by phone to the psychiatrist handling his case, who assured her that these sorts of personality collapses were often temporary, a response to some specific, unbearable stress event – the death of a child was the example he gave her – and that there was every chance Cameron would return to his normal self as abruptly and completely as he'd broken down. Scarlett hadn't mentioned that Cameron's 'normal self' was not necessarily something she, or anyone who knew him, *wanted* to be restored. But she'd taken on board his advice about being patient, and not showing panic in front of the patient.

Peeling off her dirty travel clothes, she ran herself a lukewarm bath and after a quick scrub changed into jeans, Ugg boots and several layers of thick Gap sweaters before braving the bitter cold. The kind, fat landlady downstairs had given her directions to the Maudsley, which was only a short walk away. With any luck the fresh air would help wake her up and clear her head before she saw Cameron.

A grand, red-brick Edwardian building, the Maudsley was built as a mental hospital at the turn of the twentieth century, but had none of the Dickensian gloominess of its Victorian predecessors. Fronted by a graciously curving driveway and well-kept lawns, the front doors opened into a hallway filled with light and colour, with children's pictures adorning the walls and fresh flowers in a large vase on the reception desk.

'Hi.' Scarlett smiled nervously at the staff nurse. 'I'm here to see one of Dr Garfi's patients, Cameron Drummond Murray. I'm his sister.'

'I see,' the nurse smiled back. 'And do you have your appointment card with you?'

Scarlett pulled the small, handwritten psychiatrist's note from her pocket and handed it over. As Dr Garfi had explained, no one was allowed access to patients without written permission from the case doctor, or without a medical professional present at all times. Mental illness almost always had the potential to turn violent, and hospitals like this one had to err on the side of caution.

'Lovely,' said the nurse. 'You need the Lucan Suite, room six. It's on the third floor; the lifts are straight along the corridor at the end there.'

A few minutes later, Scarlett knocked tentatively on the half-open door of Cameron's room.

'Come in, come in. You must be Scarlett.' A short, Persian man with a Saddam Hussein moustache and a beaming smile stood up to greet her. 'I'm Uzai Garfi. A pleasure to meet you.'

'Hi,' said Scarlett, shaking his hand warmly. Behind him, on the bed, she saw Cameron, but his face was turned away from her towards the wall. 'I wasn't sure you were going to be here.'

'I won't get in your way,' he assured her. 'I'll be waiting outside so you have some time alone.'

'Oh, that's OK,' said Scarlett hurriedly. 'You don't have to leave.'

'You're not in any danger, my dear, I can assure you,' said Dr Garfi, lowering his voice. 'And he may well be more responsive if I'm not here. It's very early days, as we discussed on the phone, but so far he's been highly reluctant to talk at all, to me at least. Which is not uncommon,' he added. 'The majority of new patients view their psychiatrists with suspicion at first. Anyway, I'm right outside the door if you need me.'

Once he'd gone, Scarlett peeled off her outer two

sweaters, dumped her handbag on an armchair, and walked over to the bed.

'Cam?' She laid a hand gently on his shoulder. 'Cameron, it's me, Scarlett.'

Slowly, he rolled over and looked at her. The odd thing was that, if it hadn't been for the hospital gown and the fact that they were here, in this room, he wouldn't have seemed any different. The neatly parted, investment banker hair, the slight hint of fat-cat double chin, the pale, permanently moistened lips ... all he needed was a suit, tie and his trademark superior sneer and he might be on his way to work at Canary Wharf right now. For a second she jumped as he pulled one arm out from under the covers and reached up to touch her face. Then she watched his bottom lip quiver and his eyes well up, and a wash of genuine sympathy came over her.

'Hi,' he said, so quietly she had to bend lower to hear him. 'Thanks for coming.'

'So you ... you know who I am?' she asked. She felt stupid asking the question, but after everything she'd been told it was something of a surprise to find him so lucid.

'Yes,' he nodded. 'I know I lost it pretty badly before. I don't ... I can't remember everything. How long have I been here?'

'Not long. A few days,' said Scarlett, squeezing his hand reassuringly. 'They found you out in Surrey by the roadside somewhere, in a pretty bad way. What happened, Cam?'

She immediately regretted being so blunt. Letting go of her hand, Cameron started to cry and shiver, his eyes darting all around the room as if searching for some half-expected intruder.

'Hey, hey, it's OK,' she said softly. 'You don't need to answer that.'

'I don't know ...' he began shakily. 'I don't know what I was doing in Surrey. The car ... I can't remember that part. What day is it today?'

'Wednesday,' said Scarlett. 'Honestly, Cam, you mustn't worry about the details. It'll all come back with time. Dr Garfi says that—'

'Fuck Dr Garfi,' hissed Cameron, a flash of his old self breaking through the mental fog. 'Listen to me, Scarlett. We only have four days left. In four days, they'll know. Everyone'll know! You have to protect Mummy.'

Shit, thought Scarlett. His lucidity was obviously a lot more fragile and sporadic than she'd first thought.

'Shhh,' she said, stroking his forehead. 'It's all going to be fine. Mummy's fine.'

'No, Scar, listen to me.' His voice was getting louder and increasingly urgent. 'They're going to publish on Sunday. Last weekend, that's when they called me, asking for a comment. They've got pictures!'

'Who, darling? Who's got pictures?' she asked, humouring him.

'The *News of the World*,' he whispered, tears streaming down his face. 'Those bastards are outing me. They picked up on the story in a local paper and are threatening to go to town on it: "Scarlett Drummond's brother outed!" I'm finished, finished at the bank, finished at Drumfernly. What's Dad going to say? Oh God. It's over! I want to die!'

Reeling, Scarlett sank down into the nearest available chair. Was this true? Or was it the psychosis talking? Suddenly her suspicions of last year, about Cameron's sexuality, came flooding back to her. If he was gay and had been living a lie all this time, well that was exactly the sort of thing that gave people breakdowns, wasn't it? And Dr Garfi had spoken about a specific, traumatic event. A call from a national newspaper that had hold of incriminating pictures, pictures that could overturn and destroy your entire life? It was certainly pretty traumatic, if it had happened.

'So, you're gay?' she asked at last, as kindly and unthreateningly as she could. 'Is that what you're saying?'

He stared at her blankly for a moment, then retreated

back under the covers, curling up into a foetal ball and turning back to the wall.

'Cameron, come on, don't,' she pleaded. 'It doesn't matter.'

But whatever protective shell he'd emerged from on first seeing her was now firmly back in place. It wasn't even as if he was ignoring her, more that he no longer seemed able to hear. He'd shut down his senses.

After a few, long minutes of silence, Scarlett walked sadly into the corridor.

'I heard voices. He spoke to you.' Dr Garfi sounded delighted. 'Well done, my dear, that's quite a leap forward.'

'Thanks,' said Scarlett, 'but I'm not sure it is. He disappeared on me again.'

'Like I said,' said the doctor, 'it takes time. Is there anything you feel I ought to know? Anything that might help his recovery?'

Scarlett thought for a moment. Her initial instinct was to repeat everything Cameron had just told her. But the memory of the panic in his eyes held her back. What he feared most appeared to be exposure – that, and the impact all this might have on their parents. Would he want his doctor to know? If not, did she have the right to tell him? Moral considerations aside, she still wasn't sure that everything Cameron had told her wasn't a figment of his increasingly paranoid imagination. She ought at least to get the facts straight before she opened such an enormous can of worms.

'Not really,' she hedged. 'He knew who I was, and who he was. He seemed pleased to see me, which is kind of unusual for us. We're not exactly close.'

'All right, well, we'll leave him to rest for tonight,' said the doctor. 'I'll write you another slip for tomorrow, and one for your parents too. They are still coming?'

Scarlett rolled her eyes. 'Unfortunately, yes. I'll be seeing them later tonight.'

'Right. I'll see you all here tomorrow afternoon then,' said Dr Garfi brightly. 'Try and get some sleep, my dear. You look exhausted.'

Miraculously, despite her jet lag, Scarlett did get some sleep, and felt almost human when she came down to breakfast the following morning.

'Darling.'

Her parents were already in the dining room and half-way through their bacon and eggs when she walked in. Hugo, looking every one of his seventy-two years, stood up to greet his daughter.

'Hello, Daddy,' said Scarlett, kissing him on both cheeks before stooping down to do the same to her mother. 'What time did you get in in the end?'

'Late,' said Caroline. Immaculately dressed and made up as always, in a crisp white shirt and cashmere cardigan, her hair scraped meticulously up in her trademark tight bun, she nevertheless looked tired and drawn. The strain of the last few days had taken quite a toll on her. 'Did you see him?'

Sitting down and pouring herself a coffee from the stain-less steel pot on the table, Scarlett nodded.

'And?' said Caroline impatiently. 'For God's sake, Scarlett, how was he?'

'OK,' she said. 'Better than I expected. You'll see for yourself this afternoon.'

'Was he able to shed any light on, you know, what happened?' asked her father.

Steeling herself, Scarlett took a deep breath. 'Yes,' she said. 'But you're not going to like it.'

As straightforwardly and dispassionately as she could, she told them both what Cameron had told her last night. Hugo sat rigid backed, listening intently throughout. Caroline, by contrast, squirmed and twitched in her seat, as if Scarlett were pouring itching powder down her back. Finally she could bear it no longer.

'It's nonsense, absolute nonsense!' she exploded. 'Clearly he's unwell; he doesn't know what he's saying.'

'That's very possible,' agreed Scarlett. 'There's one simple way to find out, of course. We should call the paper this morning, find out if there's any truth to it.'

'Absolutely not,' said Caroline, her lips tightening in resolution.

'But Mummy,' Scarlett reasoned, 'we must. That way we'll know for sure.'

'We already know for sure,' said her mother. 'Cameron is not a homosexual. The very suggestion is ludicrous.'

'Darling.' Hugo reached across the table for her hand. 'It's no good sticking our heads in the sand. If these oiks have pictures, and if they intend to publish those pictures, we need to be prepared. It may not be too late for some sort of injunction. I could talk to my lawyer—'

'No!' Caroline snatched her hand away. 'What's wrong with you both? Has my entire family gone mad? They do not have pictures. Because my son is not gay. He's confused; he's rambling.'

'You know, I'm not entirely surprised.' Hugo turned to Scarlett. 'I've often wondered if he might be a bit that way inclined.'

Scarlett was amazed, both that her father had had the sensitivity to notice such a thing, and by the fact that he seemed remarkably unfazed by it.

'Really?'

'Yah,' mused Hugo. 'We had quite a number of them at Harrow, you know. Terribly nice chaps, mostly.'

Caroline looked as if she were about to spontaneously combust.

'Listen, Mummy,' said Scarlett, who felt sorry for her, despite everything. Cam had always been her golden child. Accepting this would mean reconstructing her entire world view, never an easy thing to do. 'You may be right. This might be nothing but rambling.'

'Of course I'm right.'

'But it may also be connected with me. With my charity campaign.'

Caroline frowned, confused. 'What do you mean?'

Scarlett told them about the radio programme she'd been involved with, reigniting Trade Fair and her efforts to bring Brogan O'Donnell to some form of justice. When she mentioned Andy Gordon's death, Hugo jumped in.

'The fellow from the BBC? Yes, of course, we know all about it.' Caroline looked blank. 'Yes, darling,' said Hugo, 'you remember, the young man, the Scot. It's been all over the news. I had no idea you knew him, Scarlett.'

'We worked together,' she said, 'recently. He was a lovely man, funny and terribly brave.'

'I still don't see what this has to do with Cameron,' snapped Caroline.

'Maybe nothing,' said Scarlett. 'But it's not inconceivable that Brogan's the one behind these pictures. If they exist,' she added hastily. 'Cam's been complaining for a while about being followed. To be honest, I never took him too seriously. But since Andy's death, and now this ...'

'You mean you believe this O'Donnell creature might be using your brother as a way to get at you?' said Hugo slowly.

Scarlett shrugged miserably. 'It's possible. It's possible he's the one who had Andy killed. I don't know.'

'You selfish, selfish, stupid girl.' Caroline, unable to control herself any longer, unleashed all her pent-up rage at Scarlett, relieved to have found a scapegoat for her own unhappiness. 'I warned you years ago to drop this nonsense. So did Cameron. I remember that conversation at Drumfernly as if it were yesterday.'

'I remember it too,' said Scarlett meekly.

'But would you listen? Oh, no! Far be it from Miss Know-It-All to consider anyone else but herself and her precious *cause*.'

413

'Dearest, steady on,' mumbled Hugo. But Caroline was far from finished.

'You've ruined your brother's life, not to mention mine. You've gone and got that poor man from the BBC murdered.'

'Caroline!' said Hugo. 'Really.'

'It's all right, Dad,' said Scarlett. 'Let her finish.'

'I *am* finished,' seethed Caroline, flinging her napkin down on the table. 'Finished with *you*. If Cameron doesn't recover ... if these filthy journalists print their lies about him ... I will never forgive you, Scarlett. Never.'

Scarlett watched in silence as she left the table and stormed back upstairs to her and Hugo's bedroom. Only once she'd gone did she allow the tears to flow.

'Poppet, you mustn't cry,' said Hugo, pulling out the neatly folded linen handkerchief he always kept in his breast pocket and handing it to her. 'This business with Cameron has been a lot for Mummy to take in. You know how she dotes on him. It's hardly your fault the lad's a whoopsie.'

Despite herself, Scarlett laughed. The alternative was collapsing into a heap, and she couldn't afford to do that. One nervous breakdown in the family was more than enough to be getting on with.

'I don't know what to do, Daddy,' she told him, honestly. 'I don't know where to begin putting any of this right.'

'Well,' said Hugo, wiping his mouth with his napkin and pushing his chair back thoughtfully. 'First things first. I'll go with Mummy to the Maudsley. You call this newspaper and see what you can find out. In the meantime I'll put in a call to Kevin Fahey, my solicitor, and suss out the lie of the land.'

'All right,' said Scarlett. She'd never seen her father in decisive mode before, but she couldn't have been more grateful to discover this side to his character now. It was a relief not to have everything falling on her own, overloaded shoulders.

'At some stage,' Hugo went on, 'we need to have a little chat about Drumfernly.'

'We do?' Scarlett looked perplexed.

'I'm afraid so,' said Hugo. 'Of course it's far too early to make any long-term judgements yet. But if your brother should remain ... shall we say, mentally incapacitated? I'll need you to take over the estate.'

'But it's entailed,' said Scarlett, her heart thumping with panic. At some point, when all this was over, she wanted her life back. The thought of being manacled to Drumfernly was too awful to contemplate. 'It would go to cousin Ronan, wouldn't it, if Cameron couldn't inherit?'

'Over my dead body,' said Hugo, deadly seriously. 'That house is not going to the junior branch of the family, not after four hundred years. I won't allow it.'

Scarlett's heart sank, but she said nothing.

'I'm not sure how we'd work it,' said Hugo. 'I need to talk to Kevin about that too. Perhaps Cameron would inherit, but you would act as his agent throughout his lifetime. Then it could pass to your sons. Anyway, as I say, we're getting ahead of ourselves. One step at a time, eh?'

'Hmm,' Scarlett nodded, wishing she had Jake or Nancy or even Boxie here to talk to. 'One step at a time.'

Two weeks later, Danny Meyer sat opposite his boss at Gemology, the trendy West Village jewellery store where he'd been working for the past two months, and tried to picture him naked, taking a dump.

It was a trick he and Jake had learned at school, whenever authority figures like teachers or prefects had a go at them. Picture the guy naked, having a crap. It helped to mentally level the playing field. Over the years Danny had found it worked equally well in adult life, with anyone who tried to lord it over him. With a petty-minded megalomaniac like Todd, his current boss, it was proving particularly effective.

'What are you smirking at?' Todd looked positively furious, his pink, baby face reddening exponentially as Danny smiled back at him across the desk. 'This is not a joke, Daniel. You are *this close* to getting fired.'

'I've told you. It's Danny,' said Danny. 'No one calls me Daniel. And I can't see what you're getting so hot and bothered about. Customers appreciate honesty in a salesman.'

'Don't be facile,' snapped Todd. 'No one appreciates being told they're too fat to wear a choker.'

'Her saggy neck folds were hanging over the pearls like fucking foreskin,' said Danny bluntly. 'No one should shell out a hundred grand on a necklace they can't even see for double chins. It's grotesque.'

'Your job, Daniel, is to make sales. To make our clients feel good *so they buy something*. What part of that concept do you find so hard to grasp?'

Danny stared over Todd's bald head out of the window. What the fuck was he even doing here? He'd taken the Gemology job in desperation, after every half-decent outfit in town had turned him down, fearful of making an enemy of Brogan O'Donnell. He tried to remind himself that he was working to survive and to provide for his child, that there was no shame in it. But recently that rationale had begun to look as hollow as everything else in his life. Brogan and Diana were back together, living, as far as he knew, as man and wife. What use would the baby have for his feeble paycheque? Brogan might be a card-carrying cunt, but he could provide a far better life for the kid than Danny could dream of doing, and he knew it.

He'd thought about fighting for joint custody once the kid was born. He no longer doubted but that it would be a fight if he chose to go that route, and his lawyer had stressed how important it would be for him to show he was in regular work and could provide a stable, loving environment. Jake and Minty, needless to say, were very gung-ho about this idea. But Danny himself wasn't so sure. Loving he could do, but stable? He still woke up crying most days which, let's face it, wasn't exactly normal for a grown man. And though he hadn't voiced the fear to anyone, even Jake, he worried that the child might remind him too much of Diana. That if he played an active part in its life, he was effectively giving up all hope of ever getting over her, of ever being happy again.

'Am I boring you?'

Todd's mean, wide-set eyes glared at him from behind thick-lensed, horn-rimmed glasses. He reminded Danny a bit of Himmler, although he definitely had no balls at all, so perhaps Goebbels was a better analogy.

'Daniel!'

'It's Danny,' said Danny, sighing heavily, 'and quite frankly, Todd, yes, you are boring me. So I suggest you stick your stinking job where the monkey stuck his nuts, and we'll call it quits, shall we? I can see myself out.'

Strolling through the leafy streets of the West Village half an hour later, he already felt lighter, as if someone had unstrapped a backpack full of rocks and lifted it gently from his shoulders. He knew he was being irresponsible. It had taken him for ever to land that job, and he still had a stack of bills to pay higher than the Eiffel Tower. This was no time to be skipping about feeling pleased with himself. And yet it was impossible not to savour the taste of freedom just a little bit. He'd felt like a rat in a cage almost since the day Diana had moved in with him, knowing that Brogan would coil himself around their lives like a cobra and not let go till he got her back. Then came the pregnancy, another closing door. Then the break-up, Diana going back to Brogan, the collapse of his business. One by one he'd watched the separate pillars of his life being flicked out from under him like matchsticks.

But today, as of right now, there was nothing left to fall. He had nothing, not one thing left for O'Donnell or anyone else to take. He could up sticks and move to Malawi if he felt like it. Not a single tie bound him to anything, a thought that ought to have been depressing, but for some reason felt gloriously liberating instead.

'Hey, man. Your usual?'

Turning on a whim into Agostino's, his favourite local coffee shop and usual Sunday-morning hangout, he returned the smile of Permanently Cheerful Toni, the world's most upbeat barista, and ordered a hot chocolate with extra whipped cream and sprinkles. Simple childhood pleasures were the only ones he could readily afford these days. Sinking down into one of the capacious leather sofas, he took a long, luxuriant sip, and wondered idly what his twin brother was up to right now.

Two and a half thousand miles away, Jake turned out to be in a considerably less Zen-like frame of mind than Danny.

'No don't, don't buy it. Not till you've seen the ring I've got you, Lexi.' Pacing the shop floor at Flawless, phone in hand, the volume of his voice was rising in direct proportion to his stress levels. 'Please tell me you haven't already done the deal? *Alexis!*' he shook his head in frustration. 'Why?'

Alarmed by the shouting, a customer who'd been browsing idly through the higher-end necklace display case decided to try her luck elsewhere, scurrying out of the store with a silent wave at Perry.

'Jake!' Perry hissed crossly once she'd gone. 'Do you have to do that here? You're scaring away business.'

'Fuck, fuck, FUCK,' said Jake, hanging up and banging his fist down on the counter so hard that the credit card machine jumped. 'Why are rich women so unutterably stupid?'

Perry rolled his eyes. He still adored Jake, but in the two weeks since Scarlett had been gone, he was starting to see what it was she'd found so impossible to live with. Everything had to revolve around him.

'What's happened now?'

'Lexi Bennett, one of my so-called loyal clients, has gone and paid cash, *cash*, for an eternity ring from Tyler fucking Brett. I swear to God, that man must have clones. He's everywhere.'

'All the more reason not to frighten off the trade from this place, I'd have thought,' said Perry sanctimoniously. 'There's no point you being here, standing in for Scarlett, if you're going to spend every waking moment working on Solomon Stones.'

It was fair criticism, and Jake knew it, but apparently his temper didn't.

'And what exactly do you suggest, Liberace?' he snapped, casting a disdainful look at Perry's appliquéd sequin jacket. 'I've got Scarlett on my case day and night, begging me to be here. Although what the fuck it is she expects me to do, I've no idea.'

Run the business, maybe? thought Perry, but he kept his thoughts to himself. He'd only just been given a whopping pay rise, and didn't want to rock the boat too much.

'Meanwhile that cunt Brett is waltzing off with what's left of my clients,' fumed Jake, 'and I've got you giving me a flea in my ear because you can't keep customers in the bloody store for five minutes at a stretch. I mean, you're the fucking manager, Perry. And Scarlett's the designer. As you rightly say, I shouldn't even fucking be here.'

Perry waited a few moments for the self-righteousness storm to pass before speaking again.

'Would you like me to answer the question now?' he said archly, pretending to polish the walnut countertop with a little felt cloth.

'What question?' said Jake.

'The, "what exactly do I suggest?" question,' said Perry. 'Because as it happens, I do have one or two ideas.'

'Be my guest,' said Jake, throwing himself grumpily down into one of the customer armchairs with all the surly gracelessness of a spoiled sixteen-year-old. 'God knows I'm fresh out of ideas myself. Unless you were thinking of flying to Scotland, kidnapping Scarlett and getting her bony arse back here pronto.'

Perry smiled. He missed Scarlett, perhaps not as much as Jake, but acutely nonetheless, from both a business and a personal perspective. If he could have beamed her back to LA, he certainly would have, but as it looked like she'd be stranded in Blighty for the foreseeable future, his mind was turning to more practical solutions.

'If your friend Mr Brett has clones chatting up your clients,' he said, 'perhaps it's time you called on your own clone for assistance.'

'English please,' muttered Jake. 'What are you on about?'

'Your brother?' said Perry slowly. Honestly. Getting through to Jake in one of his moods was like trying to teach calculus to a chimpanzee: slow going. 'Super-twin? The one you always used to say could sell ice to Eskimos. Didn't you tell me he was between jobs at the moment, and miserable as sin in New York?'

'He's got a job,' said Jake. 'But he is miserable.'

Ridiculous. Why hadn't he thought of this? It was so obvious. Danny should move out to LA and take on Tyler Brett while he stepped into the breach at Flawless.

'So call him,' said Perry. 'By the sounds of it he hasn't got much to lose. Nor will you have soon, if you carry on haemorrhaging customers the way you are right now.'

'Thanks for the vote of confidence,' grumbled Jake, but he was cross only because he knew Perry was right. All he'd been thinking about was Scarlett, and how much he wished she were back. But the truth was she wasn't coming back, at least not any time soon, and in the way that *he* wanted, probably not ever. In the meantime, having Danny here

could make all the difference, emotionally as well as professionally. They'd be a team again, just the two of them. The
Meyer boys, back in action. Why the hell not?

Perry had returned to his pretend polishing, and had the
good sense not even to look up, never mind smile trium-
phantly, when he heard Jake punch out the numbers of his
next call.

'Dan? Yeah, hi mate, it's me. Listen. I've got a proposition for you.'

It might have pleased Jake to know that, while he was
reaching out for brotherly support, desperate for Scarlett's
return, she was equally desperate to reclaim her life in Los
Angeles.

Sitting in Hugo's office in Drumfernly, surrounded by
mounds upon mounds of unfiled estate paperwork, she
barely glanced at the dramatic, blood-red sun, oozing out
the last of its light over the pine forest outside her window.
Now that spring was finally here, and the days had at last
begun to lengthen, there was enough beauty in this part
of Scotland to sustain even the most depressed of souls.
But Scarlett, for once, was oblivious. All she could see was
the Herculean task ahead of her – the task of securing the
estate's future. Everything else, not least her own hopes
and dreams, had slipped from her grasp like so many grains
of sand.

It was only two weeks since she'd landed in London, but
already it felt like years. Flawless, Jake and her American life
had started to take on an almost dreamlike quality, utterly
divorced from the 'reality' she now found herself living,
cooped up in Drumfernly with no reprieve, no escape, no
parole in sight.

So much had happened since those first, awful days at
the Mitre. On the face of it, much of the news had been
good. The *News of the World*, to everyone's relief and astonishment, seemed to have decided not to run the story after

all. This was particularly bizarre, given Scarlett's deeply unproductive conversation with the deputy editor two Thursdays ago, when he'd basically confirmed to her that yes, they were going to press, yes, they had pictures, and no, nothing she could do or say would change those two facts, although she was welcome to make a quote on behalf of the family. At which point Scarlett had given him a quote that no family newspaper would be able to print without exceeding the legal limit for asterisks, and the phone call had screeched to an abrupt, terminal halt.

Sunday morning had found the entire Drummond Murray family rushing to the newsagent at the crack of dawn, poised for the worst and fully expecting to be locked in a crisis meeting with Hugo's lawyer at ten a.m., only to discover that the dreaded exposé never appeared. Another week passed, another Sunday, and still nothing. No one from the news desk would talk to Scarlett, and a phone call from the lawyer had failed to shed any further light on the reasons behind this editorial volte-face.

But there it was. No story.

Unfortunately, not even this great good fortune meant an end to the family's problems. Despite his early flashes of lucidity, Cameron remained seriously unwell. Taking Dr Garfi's advice, Scarlett and her parents had flown back home to Scotland, and were not scheduled back in London for more visits until next month at the earliest.

'I think it's harder for him to work through these identity problems in front of those people closest to him,' the doctor had informed them tactfully; a statement Scarlett interpreted correctly to mean that their mother's visible disappointment was an added pressure that Cameron's fragile psyche couldn't bear. Caroline had swung from total denial to a gushing 'acceptance' of her son's sexuality that was equally cloying.

'It doesn't surprise me in the least,' she insisted, repudiating her earlier attitude in an about-face so shameless it would have made Bill Clinton blush. 'So many truly brilliant men are, you know. Think of Oscar Wilde.'

Scarlett tried to think of any human being on earth who had less in common with Oscar Wilde than Cameron, without question the dullest, least witty conversationalist in the whole of Banffshire (a county that sported numerous, Olympic-level bores), but failed utterly. Not that she was about to point this out to her mother. Like her father, she hoped Caroline's fag-hag phase would eventually mellow, once she'd got over the initial shock, and she could focus like the rest of them on the *real* issue, which wasn't Cameron's sexuality, but his mental instability.

He would never go back to banking. That much was certain. At this point it was questionable whether, and at what point, he'd be well enough to live independently again at all. All of which left Drumfernly's future hanging in the balance, and Scarlett's own life plunged into a permanent state of hold.

'Poppet, good gracious, are you still in here?' Hugo, back from another day's salmon fishing (the important things in life must go on, after all), wandered into the study to find her slumped, Bob Cratchit-like, over one of last year's ledgers. 'Come and have a G&T.'

'I can't, Daddy,' she sighed heavily. Accounts had never been her strong suit, but even she could see that Drumfernly had been allowed to slip into an appalling degree of debt. Whatever skill Cameron had as a banker, he clearly hadn't been applying it to his inheritance. As for the so-called estate manager, the man deserved to be shot, or at the very least fired. 'It's all such a mess.'

'I dare say it is, darling,' said Hugo, blithely unconcerned. 'But it's been a mess for long enough now that your burning the midnight oil is unlikely to sort it out. Not in your first week on the job, anyway.'

'All right,' said Scarlett, stretching as she got to her feet, and thinking fondly that Hugo would have made a marvellous captain of the Titanic, passing out the gin and tonics while his passengers sank into an icy grave. 'I could use a drink. But I need to get back to it after supper, for an hour or so at least.'

She was still clinging to the hope that, if she worked hard and efficiently, she might be able to sort things out enough to leave the rest to a new estate manager and get back to California by midsummer. So far she'd done nothing to look into Andy's death, a thought that shamed her deeply. Nor had she followed up on the momentum they'd gained from the radio programme and pursued next steps for the Yakutian miners, those poor, desperate men that Andy had given his life for. As for her own professional obliga-tions, she still hadn't finished the designs Jake needed for Flawless, or responded to about a thousand unread emails from Perry. Even Nancy's calls had gone unreturned. Poor Boxford had probably forgotten who she was by now. Sometimes she felt she was in danger of forgetting who she was herself.

Following Hugo into the Great Hall, where Mrs Cullen had laid out the usual silver salver of pre-dinner drinks, Scarlett warmed her bottom in front of the roaring log fire while her father fixed their drinks.

'Hugo. There you are.' Caroline, gliding in to the room in a tight tweed pencil skirt and tan cashmere sweater – how Scarlett longed for half her mother's elegance – looked hap-pier than she had done in weeks. 'I've been hunting for you everywhere. *Marvellous* news.'

'Really? What's that, my love?' said Hugo, absent-mindedly handing the gin and tonic he'd made for Scarlett to his wife.

'They've lifted Cameron's compulsory detainment order.'

'His what-do-you-call-it-now?' said Hugo.

'It means he's no longer sectioned under the Mental Health Act. He's free to leave the Maudsley if he wants

to and come home.' Caroline beamed. 'Isn't that wonderful?'

Scarlett shot her father a worried glance. If Cam had
improved enough not to be held against his will, that was
obviously good news. But bringing him back to Drumfernly
surely had disaster written all over it. Caroline was convinced she could 'cure' him with homemade rice pudding
and lots of bracing country walks. She didn't want to admit
how deep his problems ran.

'It is wonderful,' said Hugo cautiously. 'We mustn't
rush things though, darling. Let's talk to Dr Garfi in the
morning and see what he advises.'

Caroline's eyes narrowed.

'Dr *Garfi*?' She made it sound as though the very idea
of asking Cameron's psychiatrist was ludicrous, as if Hugo
had suggested they consult with Dr Pepper.

'He is Cam's doctor,' said Scarlett gently.

'And I'm his mother,' snapped Caroline. 'I think my
thirty-two years of experience trump your little Persian
friend's thirty-four minutes, don't you?'

'It's not a competition, Mummy,' said Scarlett. 'We have
to think of what's best for Cameron.'

'I am thinking of what's best for Cameron,' retorted
Caroline crossly. 'I always have. And don't think I can't see
what you're up to, young lady. You might be able to pull
the wool over your father's eyes, but you don't fool me.
Not for a second.'

'What are you talking about?' Scarlett frowned. She
tried to make allowances for her mother's mood swings.
She was, after all, grieving for the healthy, high-flying,
straight son she'd 'lost', and she was still angry at Scarlett
for, as she saw it, unleashing the hounds of hell upon all of
them with her ill-considered Trade Fair campaign. But it
was hard to keep her temper sometimes, when she'd left so
much behind to come and sort out Cameron's mess. Did
her mother think she *wanted* to be here?

'You're after your brother's inheritance,' said Caroline bluntly.

'*What*?' said Scarlett.

Choking on his gin, Hugo tried to defend her from such a wild accusation, but his words dissolved into a violent coughing fit.

'As soon as you heard he was ill, you swooped in like a vulture. Do you think I don't have eyes, Scarlett? Do you think I don't see you huddled away with Daddy and the lawyers day and night?'

Dumbstruck with indignation, Scarlett could do nothing but shake her head.

'Well now he's better, and surprise surprise, you want to stop him coming home, stop him muscling in on your little scheme before it all comes to fruition.' The vitriol in her mother's voice was quite astonishing. As though all the years of pent-up envy and disappointment, all the strains in their relationship had been waiting for this moment to be unleashed.

'He is not "better",' said Scarlett, with a calmness she was far from feeling. 'Nor will screaming at me, or Daddy, or Dr Garfi make him better.'

Caroline opened her mouth to answer back, but Scarlett was too quick for her.

'I came back to England because you and Daddy *begged* me to,' she said. 'For the record, the last thing on God's earth I want is to inherit Drumfernly.'

'Ha!' Caroline snorted.

'The reason I'm cooped up with the lawyers all day,' said Scarlett, ignoring her, 'is that I'm trying to save at least part of this place from going under. If someone doesn't turn the estate around, and quickly, there won't *be* any inheritance. Not for Cameron, not for anybody.'

Hugo, having at last got his breath back, moved himself physically between the two women.

'Now, come on,' he pleaded. 'We're all under a lot

of strain, but there's no need for all this. The one thing Cameron doesn't need is for the rest of us to fall apart. Hmm?'

Caroline and Scarlett glared at one another, but neither of them said a word. In the end, it was Scarlett who broke the impasse.

'I'm going to go for a run,' she said, addressing herself exclusively to her father. 'I need a bit of fresh air, to clear my head. And you and Mummy should talk.'

'Fine, fine, jolly good,' said Hugo. 'We'll see you at supper then.'

Watching her stalk off, head held high, those long, gangly legs of hers apparently moving with a life of their own, he felt a combined pang of love and apprehension. With Scarlett and her mother at loggerheads, and now the possibility of Cameron coming home, they were in for a rocky few months. He needed Scarlett here, now more than ever. But at the same time he felt guilty for trapping her. Something was clearly on her mind. There was a sadness about her these days that he knew instinctively went beyond family problems, and the rough trot she was having with her mother.

Had he been born in a different culture, at a different time, he might have sat her down and asked her what was troubling her.

As it was, he merely raised a mildly disapproving eyebrow at his wife and settled down in his favourite leather armchair to enjoy his long-awaited drink.

# Twenty-four

Diana lay on the carpeted floor in Brogan's apartment – technically she supposed it was still their apartment, now the divorce was on hold – and pulled her left knee up to her chest, mimicking the woman on the antenatal workout video. She still hadn't figured out for sure whether the blonde, preternaturally smiley aerobics instructor was actually pregnant or whether she in fact had a small, perfectly rounded prosthesis strapped to a set of six-pack abs under her Nike shirt. Either way the woman looked fitter, slimmer and bendier than anyone had a right to seven months into their pregnancy. If she said 'Good jaaarb!' one more time in her upbeat, Disney-chipmunk voice, Diana would be sorely tempted to rip the flatscreen off the wall.

'And stretch it out. That's right! Really feel that stretch in your lower back,' she cooed.

Christ, it hurt. Morning sickness she'd been expecting, but no one had warned her about the back pain that kept her awake now, night after night. She remembered joking about it with Danny in her first trimester, back when even the throwing up made her happy, proof that the child she'd longed for for so long was finally a reality.

'Just wait,' he used to tease her. 'When you're big and fat with varicose veins and a back like an old woman's, you'll be moaning with the best of 'em: "Bloody baby! It's all your fault, baby! You've ruined my body, you little shit!"'

'I will *not*,' she insisted, pretending to be offended, but unable to stop herself grinning. 'Every second of this pregnancy will be a joy. Just you see if it isn't, Danny Meyer.'

They'd been so happy then. It was only five months ago,

but now here she was alone, moaning as predicted ... just not to him.

Feeling the black clouds descending again, she heaved herself to her feet and clicked off the DVD. Was there such a thing as antenatal depression? Waddling back into the guest bedroom, she opened the top drawer of the dresser and, pulling out a family-sized bar of Cadbury's chocolate – another vice that Danny had got her hooked on – began chomping through it. She'd decamped to the guest suite the moment she moved back in. The idea of sleeping in the former marital bed was just *too* weird, even in a domestic arrangement as fucked up and unorthodox as this one. Although she was ashamed to admit she'd lied about this subject to Brogan. Weak and shuddering with pain in the midst of another gruelling session of chemo, he'd told her how he thought of her every night, asleep in 'their' bed, and how much comfort that image brought him. She simply couldn't bring herself to disillusion him, not then, and the time had never been exactly right since.

Other potentially troublesome subjects, such as what she planned to do after the baby's birth, their divorce, and where Danny fitted into her future, if anywhere, they avoided completely under a sort of taboo. So much needed to be said and done and dealt with. But until Brogan recovered or – the alternative that nobody mentioned aloud – died, nothing could be settled. In his current state of physical and emotional need, Diana looked on him as a child. He cried out to the strongest of all her instincts, the maternal, and she was physically incapable of not answering that call.

Polishing off the last few squares of chocolate (sod eating for two; she seemed to be eating for about two hundred) she glanced at her watch. Five past ten. She was due at the hospital at noon and had a million and one baby errands to run before then, including quietly returning the custom-made Versace nursery suite that Brogan had ordered and had fitted as a 'surprise' for her last week.

That had been a bad day. Coming home from yoga to find that not only did Brogan clearly assume she would be raising her baby here, in his apartment, but that he figured she would wish her only child to wake up every morning in a gold-leaf-covered crib emblazoned with the O'Donnell 'crest' (as invented by Brogan in 1986, showing a lion proudly rearing above a cut diamond) in polished black jet, and tucked snugly beneath cashmere leopard-print blankets that wouldn't have looked out of place in a Vegas strip joint.

On the other hand, it was one more gift than Danny had sent for the baby. At least in his own, deeply misguided way, Brogan appeared to be trying.

Stripping off her sweat pants and tank top, she was standing in her panties, idly cupping her swollen breasts in her hands and wondering if they were capable of getting any bigger, when the telephone rang.

Surprised – no one ever rang her at the flat – she reached over to the bedside table and picked up.

'Diana O'Donnell.'

'Ah, Mrs O.D. Aidan here. I was wondering if I could prevail upon you for a favour.'

Diana watched as the hairs on her forearms stood to attention, instantly alerted by his creepiness. Not so long ago, she remembered, he was in to all that ridiculous 'street talk'. Now, apparently, he thought he was a British butler from 1908. *Prevail upon you* indeed. Pretentious idiot.

'What is it, Aidan?' she said curtly. 'I'm kinda snowed this morning to be frank with you.'

'This shouldn't take a second,' he oiled. 'I'd come over there myself and pick it up, but I didn't want to invade your privacy. I know you're probably big into the nesting by this point, right? Getting the kid's room ready and all that? I figured you wouldn't want to be disturbed by the likes of me crashing around.'

'What do you want?' said Diana frostily.

430

'It's nothing important. Just a couple of documents I thought you could bring to the hospital with you when you come. Addendums to your husband's will.'

He knew she hated it when he referred to Brogan as her husband, as if they were still together as a couple, but she was hardly in a position to correct him. It was, after all, the literal truth.

'I believe there should be hard copies in the filing cabinet under "Estate Planning",' said Aidan. 'If I give you the dates of each letter they should be easy enough to find. Both are addressed to his trustees in Cayman.'

'That cabinet's locked,' said Diana. 'If you want the key, you're going to have to ask Brogan where it is. I haven't the foggiest.'

'Dammit. Of course.'

She could hear his irritation crackle down the phone line. So much for it being nothing important.

'How comfortable are you on a computer?' he asked, regaining his composure. 'Do you know your way around email?'

'Yeeees,' said Diana. Patronising little shit. Who did he think he was talking to? 'And I can tie my own shoelaces too. Look, Aidan, I really am running late. But if you tell me where the files are, I'll print them off and bring them with me, OK?'

Scribbling down what he told her on the back of a receipt, she at last got him off the phone and hurried into the shower. Drying and dressing as fast as she could in her current, inflated condition – the putting on of socks had become a struggle of seriously comic proportions – she slipped into Brogan's office and fired up the PC.

Grumbling at Aidan for forcing her to play secretary, although she supposed it was preferable to having him drop by the apartment, she clicked onto Brogan's Outlook. His password – Eleanor, her middle name – hadn't changed since they broke up, which she found oddly gratifying, and she was soon swimming about in a sea of unread messages. Typing in the keywords Aidan had given her – *estate, addendum* and *trustee* – she was about to hit 'find' when a message entitled 'Cameron Drummond Murray' caught her attention.

Wasn't Drummond Murray Scarlett's last name?

With a lurching in her stomach that probably owed more to fear than guilt (she'd have made a terrible spy) Diana clicked open the email. It was from Aidan, dated only a month ago.

*See attached,* he wrote. *Already on their way to the London Sundays. If this doesn't distract that bitch, nothing will.*

For some reason Diana felt nervous, as if someone were about to tap her on the shoulder any moment and demand to know what she was doing snooping through Brogan's inbox. Which was ridiculous, as she was alone in her own apartment. But she still glanced anxiously about her before opening the three attached JPEGs.

The first picture was such a shock she gasped aloud. A slightly podgy young man whom she recognised instantly as Scarlett's brother – despite his ugliness and Scarlett's striking beauty there was an obvious family resemblance in the eyes and nose, and the shape of the face – was on all fours, naked from the waist down, his mouth opened wide in a contorted 'o' that could have expressed pain or pleasure or both. The male figure behind him was hazy. It looked like they were both in some sort of dungeon. But his role in the proceedings was brutally obvious.

Picture two was tamer, and showed Cameron fully dressed, in a business suit, kissing a topless male companion full on the mouth. This time they were in a gay bar and the 'love interest' appeared to be some kind of dancer. Horrified, but compelled by curiosity, Diana clicked on the third image and immediately wished she hadn't. Despite the deep shadows and the graininess of the low-res picture, it still looked like something Hieronymus Bosch might have painted. Bodies piled writhing on top of one another, with Cameron's face clearly visible in the midst of it all, eyes wide and wild with sexual excitement.

Feeling sick and degraded, as if she were somehow complicit in these awful photographs, she closed the files and sat back in the office chair, breathing deeply to calm herself.

Brogan had promised her that he'd changed. That the days of his vendettas were past. He'd even gone as far as to indicate that he understood Scarlett's passion on behalf of his mine workers, that since getting cancer himself he regretted having been so hardline about paying for their healthcare. And yet here he was, apparently preparing to ruin an innocent young man's life in the grossest, most intrusive way imaginable, simply to score some sort of sick 'point' against his sister.

Heart pounding, she scrolled further up the list of mails, hunting for Brogan's response. Sure enough, one day later, there it was.

*Good. Maybe the little pervert'll do the decent thing and top himself. Let me know when it runs.*

Oh God. Oh God, oh God, oh God. What was she doing here? How had she let this man, with all his hatred and intolerance and cruelty, back into her life?

She followed the thread into the following week, forcing herself to read the spiteful camaraderie between Brogan and Aidan as events began to unfold, right through to Brogan's thwarted, splenetic fury when the paper changed its mind and declined to print the pictures after all. She was horrified by how regularly her own name cropped up in their online back and forth, with Brogan consistently referring to their future together as though it were a certainty. *Once I'm well,* he wrote, on one particular note that made her blood run cold, *Diana and I will want to try again for more kids of our own. I don't want any of this stress still hanging over our heads then. Whatever you do, you have to do it now.*

Did he really think they were going to have children together? That after everything, he would come home and they would simply pick up where they left off? Surely, she hadn't encouraged him …

*By the way.* Her eyes were drawn to the postscript he'd written at the end of his last mail. *You can go ahead and make the offer on the new site in Canada. Take this email as a formal instruction. If Miss Drummond Murray wanted to make a difference in Siberia, she's made one. Those fuckers all hate me so much, let's see how much better they like going back to work for the state. I want out of Yakutia. The sooner the better.*

Diana caught her breath.

He was going to close the mine. He was going to turn those men and their families out on the street.

At once, her mind flew back to their conversation at his bedside a few weeks ago, after the radio programme came out. What had he said to her again? 'I intend to take urgent action.' Naturally she'd assumed he meant action to help the men whose lungs had been destroyed by conditions in his diamond mines. It hadn't crossed her mind that 'action' might mean shutting them down. Robbing them of their livelihoods and any last shred of hope for medical care and a better life.

How could he?

And all because he was pissed at Scarlett Drummond Murray, for letting the world know the truth?

He hadn't changed at all. And nor, it seemed, had she. She was still the same, blind, trusting, forgiving fool she'd always been. Danny had warned her about what he called her 'misplaced compassion' and where it might lead. And he'd been right. She remembered how passionately she'd insisted that compassion could never be misplaced. That it could never do harm, that Danny was just jealous. But if it blinded you to the harm being done to others, then weren't you, in fact, complicit in that harm? Perhaps, if she'd opened her eyes sooner, she could have stopped what

434

had happened to Scarlett's family? Perhaps she could still stop what was about to happen in Yakutia?

In a daze, she returned to the letters Aidan had asked her to look for and printed them out. Stuffing them into her purse along with the nursery goods receipt, she ran out of the door, fleeing the apartment and its awful revelations as if it were on fire.

She still had no idea what she intended to do. All she knew was that she had to get out of there. And that even if it meant sleeping on the streets, she would never, ever go back.

'So when you say "remission"?' Brogan quizzed his doctor, 'what does that mean exactly? Does that mean "gone" or "gone for now"?'

'It means that, today, your levels of cancer cells are falling rather than rising,' said the doctor. A superstar from Harvard Medical School, Dr Mike Cannons learned early on that Brogan O'Donnell was a man with whom one should always be direct. Soft-soaping never failed to exacerbate his irritation, however bad the news may be. Happily today, he was bringing his patient the best news possible.

'It means this thing is in retreat,' he grinned. 'It means you've won.'

'The battle or the war?' asked Brogan.

The doctor shrugged. 'That depends how you look at it.'

'And how do *you* look at it, Dr Cannons?'

'If the war is life versus death, then we all lose the war,' said the doctor, philosophically. 'You may die of cancer. You may die of something else. But you will die. So I would say you've won the battle. But you know, that's pretty good news,' he chuckled. 'Not many men your age survive lung cancer. Not many people survive it, period. You are *in remission*, Mr O'Donnell. Be happy!'

'I am happy, doc,' said Brogan, truthfully. He'd never

been one for cartwheels, or big, outward displays of emotion. But he wanted his life back so badly he could taste it. To be healthy again would be wonderful. To be back in his own home, back at work, and most of all to be back with Diana – that would be better still. Everything came back to Diana in the end.

'How soon can I check out of this dump?'

'Not so fast,' said the doctor. 'Now that you're off the chemo, you can go home for an extended visit very soon, perhaps even tomorrow.'

'How about today?'

'Tomorrow,' said the doctor firmly. 'After that I'd like you back in for more tests, and for some intensive rehab. Physio, all of that good stuff. You don't want to fall at the final hurdle by rushing back to work too soon.' Clocking Brogan's sceptical frown he added, 'Stress is a factor in almost all recurrent cancers, you know. That's not mumbo jumbo, it's proven medical fact.'

'I'll tell you what's a fact,' said Brogan. 'This place stresses me out a whole lot more than work. I need to get out of here.'

Once Dr Cannons had left, he lay back on the pillow and closed his eyes, luxuriating in the deep pleasure of knowing that, at last, his nightmare was coming to an end. He was in remission. Diana had left Danny, and was already living back at home. It would only be a matter of time before they were together again, properly, as man and wife. She'd have another child, *his* child, and in the meantime he'd raise her baby with Danny as his own.

Perhaps strangely for such a jealous, competitive man, Brogan genuinely wasn't concerned about Diana's baby not being his. It was the child that had brought her back to him. Had she not been pregnant, and in need of help, he doubted she would ever have moved back in. For him, that was reason enough to love it.

Despite the petty disappointments of the last month

– he'd been irritated when the British newspapers baulked at printing the Cameron Drummond Murray pictures – thanks to Aidan things were looking good on the business front too. Often, when a CEO is absent for an extended period, the stock price suffers, especially when the CEO is as involved and as closely identified with the company as Brogan was with O'Donnell Mining Corp. But OMC shares were at a record high. The market had reacted very favourably to his move into Canada, not least because he'd bought his new diamond mines at an astonishingly low price.

Trade Fair had been neutralised for the foreseeable future, with Scarlett neck deep in family problems on the other side of the Atlantic. Better yet, by gratifying coincidence, the whining little turd from the BBC who had produced her radio programme had been murdered. Clearly, Brogan was not the guy's only enemy.

Opening his eyes, he turned his head wearily to look at the clock on the wall. Ten to twelve. Diana should be here in a few minutes. He might be in remission, but he was still exhausted, and his heavy eyelids were already flickering shut when the two men entered.

'Brogan O'Donnell?'

Wearing a black suit and thin black tie, his pinched, weasel face betraying no emotion, the guy must be either an undertaker or a cop. In either case, Brogan figured, he had the wrong room.

'Last time I checked,' he said drily. 'Who are you?'

'I'm Special Agent Brown and this is my colleague, Agent Da Luca. FBI.'

They flashed their badges so quickly that they could have been from the gas company for all Brogan knew.

'I see,' he said, coughing weakly. 'And how can I help you gentlemen?'

'Mr O'Donnell, I am placing you under arrest,' said the weasel, pulling a pair of handcuffs out of his inside jacket pocket. 'You have the right to remain silent. Anything you say—'

'Wait a minute,' said Brogan, interrupting him. 'For one thing, you don't need those,' he looked at the handcuffs. 'I couldn't run, even if I wanted to.'

Agent Brown looked at the various drips and monitors to which Brogan was connected, and grudgingly put the handcuffs back in his pocket.

'Am I allowed to know what I'm being arrested for?'

At that moment, Diana walked in. Still looking ashen from the shock of what she'd read this morning, her face had set into a mask of determination.

Brogan noticed the change immediately.

'Hello, darling,' he said, concerned. 'Is something wrong?'

Reaching into her purse, Diana pulled out the will documents Aidan had asked her to deliver and pressed them into his hand.

'I'm moving out,' she said.

'Murder,' said Agent Brown. 'I'm arresting you on suspicion of murder.'

'Why?' Gripping tightly on to Diana's hand, Brogan ignored the agent. 'What's happened? Whatever it is, I'm sure we can work it out.'

'I saw the pictures,' she said, wrenching her hand free.

'What pictures?'

'*The* pictures!' she snapped. 'Of Cameron Drummond Murray. Or are you and Leach sexually blackmailing some other poor bastard this week?'

'Now listen,' said Brogan, panicked. 'I can explain.'

'Oh, I'm sure you can! You always can,' Diana laughed bitterly. 'Just like you can explain your plans to close down the Yakutian mine.'

'That was a business decision,' said Brogan. 'I wouldn't expect you to understand.'

'No,' said Diana, 'but you *do* expect me to have another

438

child with you. Nice of you to discuss that with Aidan before discussing it with me! And to think I really believed you this time. I truly believed you'd changed.'

'I *have* changed!' Brogan's voice was rising. 'Please, Di, don't leave me now. Don't do this. At least hear my side of the story.'

'I'm sorry to interrupt this touching moment,' said Agent Brown, not looking remotely sorry. 'But I'm afraid I really *must* arrest you on suspicion of the murder of Andrew Gordon. You have the right to an attorney—'

'Oh, for Christ's sake shut the fuck up,' snapped Brogan. 'I know my rights. You sound like a bad episode of *Law and Order*. I had nothing to do with the murder of that journalist, although I will say that it couldn't have happened to a nicer guy. You can quote me on that, Agent Brown.'

Diana, who had been on the point of leaving, was now rooted to the spot, staring at Brogan wide eyed.

'Oh my God,' she whispered. 'You didn't ... you wouldn't?'

'Of course I didn't!' shouted Brogan, hoarsely. What little energy he had was deserting him. 'Diana, I had nothing to do with this! Nothing! Surely you believe me?'

Wrapping both arms protectively over her pregnant belly, she shook her head sadly.

'I don't know,' she said, her eyes brimming with tears. 'I don't know what to believe any more. All I know is that it's over between us, Brogan. It is. For good, this time.'

Walking down the corridor moments later, blinded by tears, she bumped in to Dr Cannons. With his thick, reddish blonde hair and bright blue eyes, he looked like the promise of youth embodied in human form: strong, capable, good. To Diana he might have been a creature from another planet.

'It's incredible news, isn't it?' he said, mistaking her tears for tears of joy. 'He's in full remission. You'll have him home in the morning.'

But Diana merely looked at him sadly, and walked away.

# Twenty-five

July in Los Angeles was even hotter than usual, with temperatures in the valley regularly topping the hundred-degree mark. At the beach, where the Pacific breezes took the edge off the punishing sun, tourists fought for space with the locals, crowding into cafes and restaurants like bees into a too-small hive. Young girls rollerbladed along the boardwalks, flashing their washboard stomachs and bronze limbs in shorts and bikini tops, while the tired fathers pushing their kids on the beachside swings pretended not to be checking them out. Everywhere you looked kids were laughing, couples kissing. Life seemed to blossom here in the summer sunshine.

Danny Meyer missed New York.

'Those diamonds look incredible against your skin.' He was holding one of Scarlett's most detailed and expensive necklaces against the smooth, cafe au lait throat of Kiki Gillette, one of Jake's clients who had recently begun buying from Tyler Brett. For once, he wasn't bullshitting. Kiki's skin was flawless, and the necklace lit her up magically.

'I love it,' she said wistfully, admiring herself in the mirror. 'I do love it. It's just the price, you know?'

'You should have it,' said Danny. 'We can work something out.'

They were standing in the living room of Kiki's glass-fronted beach house, one of the largest, grandest properties on Malibu's exclusive Colony. Over Danny's right shoulder, an unbroken view of the Pacific, sparkling as if sprinkled with celestial diamond dust, stretched to the horizon beneath a cloudless sky. In front of him was Kiki, a twenty-nine-year-old former aerobics instructor turned producer's wife, staring at her reflection in an antique Venetian silver mirror. Her perfectly toned behind, giftwrapped in skintight Paige denim, brushed against Danny's groin as he held the necklace around her throat, so close that he couldn't help but breathe in her perfume and warmth. But he felt nothing.

Was he crazy to be missing home? It was weird, but not until he'd moved out to LA to help Jake claw back some of their business, had he realised that somewhere along the line, New York had become home. He'd always be a North London boy at heart. But it was the noise and dirt of Manhattan, the greasy hot dogs, the insanely aggressive cab drivers that he longed for, standing in this beautiful house with the beautiful woman and the beautiful view.

That and his darling Diana.

'What kind of a deal do you think you could do me?'

Kiki turned around to face him. The naughty twinkle in her eye, combined with her giveaway body language – the subtle forward thrust of the hips and arching of the lower back – left Danny in no doubt that she would happily jump into bed with him if he asked. But his libido seemed to have gone into hibernation.

'I'll have to talk to Jake, of course,' he said, smiling whilst taking a step back from her, 'but I reckon we could let you have it at cost.'

Jake was going to string him up by the balls. He kept telling him not to cut deals, but Danny knew that they were never going to steal a march on Tyler Brett if they didn't get creative with their pricing, at least in the beginning.

'You can't send me out on to the battle field then tell me I can't use my gun,' he insisted, the last time Jake had chewed him out for closing a deal at a loss. 'Have you seen Brett's prices lately?'

Jake had seen them. Ever since he'd partnered up with a new supplier in Zaire, Tyler Brett had been flogging diamonds to the likes of Kiki Gillette for about the same amount as Swarovski charged for their fucking crystals. Jake and Danny's stones were higher quality, and Scarlett's workmanship was second to none. But the differential was insanely huge. In the end, unless the Meyer brothers could score a similar deal, and pass on economies of scale to their clients, there was no way they'd be able to compete.

In the short term, however, with Scarlett stuck in Scotland and Jake stuck at Flawless, and in the absence of the massive injection of cash they would need to make such a deal, it was Danny's job to try and turn the tide of defections that had been overwhelming his brother. And that meant cutting prices.

'I'll tell you what.' Kiki smiled. She was disappointed that Jake's equally gorgeous brother clearly wasn't going to sleep with her – Danny was rough, but only Jake, it seemed, was ready – but it was a long time since she'd coveted something as much as she did this necklace. 'If you can let me hold on to it for a few days, so I can try to convince my husband, I think we may end up having a deal.'

Danny hesitated. They weren't insured to leave valuable pieces like this one with clients. Besides, the necklace was officially the property of Flawless, not Solomon Stones. If this chick damaged it or lost it, he'd be personally liable to the tune of almost a quarter of a million dollars.

'OK,' he said, forcing the fear out of his voice. First rule of salesmanship: never sound like you're desperate. 'That's not a problem. How about I drop by on Friday and we can talk some more then?'

'Sounds good.' Kiki looked at him mischievously. 'Of course, I'm home alone most afternoons. So if you needed to drive out and, you know, check on the merchandise before Friday, you'd be more than welcome.'

I bet I would, thought Danny, baffled yet again by the fact that he didn't seem to fancy this stunning girl. He wondered if the current, comatose state of his dick was going to become permanent – if this was it for him and sex – and wasn't sure whether to hope that it was or it wasn't.

'Thanks,' he smiled sheepishly. 'I might do that.'

But Kiki Gillette knew perfectly well that he wouldn't.

A few minutes later Danny was back behind the wheel of Jake's car, cruising aimlessly along Pacific Coast Highway. Jake had loaned Danny the girly white Porsche for making house calls, figuring that he could easily walk to and from Flawless and that the business could ill afford a second set of wheels. Danny agreed, although he hated the car even more than Jake did. What kind of a prize prat must he look, running around town in a Barbie-mobile? If any of his mates from London or New York saw him in it he'd never live it down.

He was due to meet Jake for a late lunch at three in Beverly Hills. But it was still only one o'clock, and he had no more clients to see that day. Turning left on a whim up Topanga Canyon, he followed the winding hairpin road as it climbed the sides of a deep, mud-sided ravine. He was only a few minutes from the highway, yet he felt like he'd stumbled into the Wild West. On either side of him the steep hills were covered with boulders and the occasional hardy fir tree. As he drove further up the canyon, rustic wooden huts and caravans began appearing in clusters by the roadside, eventually morphing into the 'town' of Topanga itself: a tiny commercial square consisting mostly of antique shops and yoga studios, with one raw food cafe, a tarot reader and a couple of other similarly hippy themed stores.

Pulling into the half-empty parking lot, he got out of the car. The sound of wind chimes was almost deafening. Suddenly hungry – he'd been so keyed up about the Kiki Gillette meeting, he'd been unable to eat breakfast – he strolled up to the raw food cafe, but quickly thought better of it. Smoked tofu and mung bean salad? Jesus Christ. He'd rather starve.

With nothing better to do, he wandered into the real estate agency on the far north-east corner of the square.

'Can I help you?'

The woman behind the desk wore a dark suit and trendy black glasses. She was in her mid-thirties, and looked corporate and completely out of place in this hick little backwater.

'Probably not. I was just passing,' said Danny. 'I guess I was curious to see what sort of property you had for sale up here.' He picked up a glossy brochure from the desk and began flipping idly through it.

'What's your price range?'

Zero, thought Danny.

'Up to five hundred thousand,' he heard himself saying.

The woman's face brightened. 'We actually have a lot of one- and two-bedroom places on our books right now in the mid fours.' Tapping something into her computer, she smiled at Danny warmly as the colour printer behind her began spitting out property details like bullets.

'Here.' Before he could protest, she picked up the sheaf of particulars and thrust them into his hand along with her business card. 'Take these with you. They should give you a feel for what's out there.'

Two minutes later, Danny was sitting on a bench in the sunshine, reading over the advertisements.

*Stunning duplex, prime Topanga! 360-degree canyon views!* proclaimed one, underneath a picture of a dilapidated, rotting wooden shack that looked like it had been lifted from the set of *The Texas Chainsaw Massacre* piece by piece. *$499,995. Must see.*

Must see a fucking psychiatrist at that price, thought Danny.

*Rustic charmer* read the next ad. *Perfect writer's retreat!* That one was at least pretty, but barely big enough for a typewriter, never mind the human being that went with it. At three hundred and eighty-five thousand it was about the same price per square foot as East Hampton. Ridiculous.

A couple of minutes later, however, he found himself staring at a picture of a farmhouse and inexplicably grinning from ear to ear. It was whitewashed, wooden, he guessed a relic from the 1920s or perhaps even earlier. Perched on top of a precipitous wooded escarpment, it looked like a cross between Hansel and Gretel's cottage and the Amityville house of horror.

The copy was short, to the point, and easy on the exclamation marks.

*Teardown, upper Topanga. 2-acre lot, partially flat. $465,000.*

Scrunching the rest of the advertisements into a ball and dumping them in the nearest bin, Danny carefully folded the picture of the farmhouse and put it in his pocket. He had no idea why. He didn't have four dollars, never mind four hundred and sixty-five thousand. The place would cost a fortune to renovate – if, by some miracle, he were ever to buy it he wouldn't dream of tearing it down. And anyway, who lived in Topanga, in a farmhouse, by themselves? Serial killers, that was who. Certainly not a sad, single, homesick New Yorker.

Climbing back into Jake's ridiculous car, Danny fired up the engine and headed back towards civilisation.

At Urth Cafe on Melrose, Jake sipped his iced water anxiously.

It was unlike Danny to be late. He knew he'd been out to Malibu to see Kiki Gillette this morning, and prayed fervently that he'd been able to woo her back to the Solomon Stones fold. A few years ago, old man Gillette had been good for a minimum fifty grand's worth of business. Kiki's custom alone could mean the difference between surviving another year and going under.

He'd put three calls in to Danny's cell, but it went straight to message, meaning he'd either switched it off or had no reception, a common problem in the Malibu

Colony. With any luck he'd been sealing the deal with Kiki in the marital bed, which would explain his unexpected no-show. Jake hoped so, for Danny's sake as much as his own. His brother could use some cheering up. If memory served, Kiki Gillette had always left Jake with a smile on his face ...

'Sorry I'm late.' Danny was all smiles as he weaved his way through the tables of gossiping women towards his brother. 'I lost track of time a bit, I'm afraid. Have you ordered?'

'Not yet.' Jake grabbed a passing waiter. 'Two cob salads and two Cokes please, one diet, one regular. So.' He grinned at Danny. 'How was Kiki?'

'She was fine,' said Danny, absently. 'Have you ever been up to Topanga?'

Jake frowned. 'Not for years. What's Topanga got to do with anything?'

'Nothing,' said Danny. 'I thought it was charming, that's all. I went up there for a drive this morning and—'

'Hold on.' Jake's frown deepened. 'I thought you'd spent the morning in bed with Kiki Gillette?'

'What made you think that?' Danny looked puzzled. Their Cokes arrived and he took a long, cooling sip of his.

'You were late,' said Jake simply. 'You're never late. So you didn't sleep with Kiki?'

'No!' Danny laughed. 'Jesus, don't look so crestfallen. I'm ninety per cent sure I've reeled her back in. I had to leave the daisy-chain necklace with her.'

'You *what*?' Jake spluttered, sending coca cola bubbles up his nose. 'For fuck's sake, Dan. We're not insured!'

'I know,' said Danny. 'It was a calculated risk.'

'Scarlett'll go ballistic.'

'Only if we tell her,' said Danny reasonably. 'Anyway, I think Kiki's gonna buy it. I offered it to her at cost,' he added, in an almost inaudible mumble.

Jake felt his chest tightening.

447

'Sorry, bruv, I think I must have misheard you. You didn't just say "cost", did you?'

Their cob salads arrived.

'You can't make an omelette without breaking a few eggs,' Danny said cheerfully. 'Do you want the Gillettes back on our customer list or don't you?'

Jake did. Desperately. He just wondered how he was going to explain yet another at-cost sale to Scarlett. She'd been gone for almost three months now, stuck in Scotland at her parents' castle like Rapunzel. Now that he had Danny here to work on Solomon Stones, he was finally able to focus all his attention on Flawless. The combination of Jake's sales skills and Perry's expertise had been enough to keep business ticking over. But the store desperately needed new designs, not to mention Scarlett's physical presence, the missing ingredient that gave Flawless its magic and that had made the store's first year such a runaway success. Jake wasn't the only one pining for Scarlett. Her customers missed her too.

'What do you reckon to this?' Danny pulled the picture of the decrepit Topanga farmhouse out of his jeans pocket.

'Looks like the house that the spooky-old-man-bad-guy from Scooby Doo would live in,' said Jake.

'It does, doesn't it?' Danny's eyes lit up.

'That wasn't a compliment,' said Jake. 'What are you doing looking at houses anyway? You haven't got any savings and you hate LA.'

Danny shrugged and put the picture away.

'I know,' he said. 'I was just looking. Topanga's cute.'

'It's a fucking hippy commune,' said Jake, shovelling down the remains of his salad. Ever since they were boys, Jake had attacked every meal as if he might never eat again. Danny was barely halfway through his own plate. 'Listen, I should get back to the store. When do you think you might close the deal with Kiki?'

448

'Friday, I hope,' said Danny. 'She wanted a couple of days to work on her old man.'

'You should have let her work on you,' said Jake, getting to his feet and dropping his napkin on the table. 'I assume she was willing?'

'Very,' said Danny. 'I just wasn't in the mood.'

Jake shook his head pityingly. 'You should get yourself to a doctor, mate. Score a few little blue pills.'

'Fuck off!' said Danny. 'I don't need Viagra.' I need Diana, he thought. But he didn't say anything.

'If you say so,' said Jake. 'By the way, I'm meeting Ruth for a drink after work tonight, so I probably won't get home till nine-ish.'

'Oh?' Danny raised an eyebrow. That was two dates in one week. 'Are things getting more serious with you two?'

'Maybe,' Jake shrugged. 'We'll see.'

He liked Ruth. She was sexy, with her sleek, dark bob, tiny waist and mischievous smile. He liked the fact that she was physically very different from Scarlett, petite and curvy versus Scarlett's willowy and ethereal. She was smart and funny, and she had her own life – she ran a thriving veterinary practice in Hancock Park – that had nothing to do with the jaded, starry West Hollywood 'scene'.

He knew he was still in love with Scarlett. But love hadn't been enough to keep them together, and now she was further away from him than ever. He wasn't ready to throw in the towel yet, like Danny seemed to have done. Sex was not an activity that Jake had ever considered optional.

It was only after Jake had left that Danny realised he'd stuck him with the bill.

Again.

'Cheeky bastard,' he muttered under his breath.

By the time Danny pulled in to the driveway of Jake's apartment, it was almost six. After finishing his lunch at a leisurely pace, some masochistic impulse had prompted him to walk down Robertson and look in the windows of the various baby stores. Diana's baby – his baby – was due in a matter of weeks. He wanted to start by buying the baby something practical; maybe a stroller? But he realised with a pang that he wasn't even sure what hospital the baby would be born in, and so had no idea where the gift should be shipped. Besides which, Brogan would probably already have got the kid a gold-plated Bugaboo.

Along with the rest of the world, he'd heard about Brogan's arrest. After spectacularly charging him with the murder of Scarlett's journalist friend in Russia, the FBI had dropped the charges a week later for lack of evidence, although if press reports were to be believed he was still under an injunction not to leave Manhattan. Someone, Danny suspected, had been paid off, but he went out of his way not to watch the news reports on the case, in case he accidentally caught a shot of Diana leaving Brogan's building. He had reached the point where the only way he could function was to cut himself off from her completely. No phone calls, no pictures, no nothing. His hope was that by the time the baby arrived, he'd have pulled himself together enough to face her.

So far, it wasn't looking good.

Depressed beyond words – the success of his morning had already faded into memory – he bought a couple of unisex onesies in Kitson Kids and two bibs, a blue one that said 'Brad Spit' and a pink one with 'Drool Barrymore' across the front in gold lettering, before heading back to the apartment.

Taking the stairs instead of the lift, because he missed walking, he felt tired and out of breath as he turned the corner that led to Jake's front door.

'Hi.'

Danny's heart stopped. Diana, red-eyed from crying and looking beyond adorable with a pair of denim dungarees stretched over her enormous baby bump, was sitting cross-legged in front of the door.

'Hi.' He barely trusted himself to breathe, let alone speak. As if the slightest movement on his part might shatter the wonderful mirage in front of him.

'I know I should have called,' said Diana. 'But I didn't know what to say. I thought, you know, when I saw you ... it might come to me.'

'And has it?' Danny felt faint.

Diana shook her head and started to cry. 'I expect you hate me.'

'*Hate* you?' Dropping his shopping bags, he got to his knees and attempted to put his arms around her, which wasn't easy. 'Jesus Christ, Di. I love you. I'm sorry for everything. I've missed you so fucking much.'

They clung to each other, weak with relief. It was a few minutes before Danny recovered sufficiently to help Diana to her feet and lead her inside to Jake's tatty leather couch.

'You don't have a bag,' he said, suddenly panicked. 'Oh God. You are staying, aren't you?'

She nodded, wiping away tears with the back of her hand.

'For ever, if you'll have me. Have us.' Looking down at her spherical belly, she smiled shyly. 'I thought about bringing some things with me when I left my parents, but in the end I thought that whatever happens, I need to make a fresh start. So I drove to JFK and caught the first flight out here. All I brought was a credit card.'

'Don't worry about it,' said Danny, kissing her. 'I've already got the baby covered.' Reaching into the Kitson bags, he produced the clothes and the bibs. 'Oh, and I've found us a house.'

He pulled out the now heavily crumpled picture of the farmhouse and showed it to her. She beamed.

'Of course, there is one teeny problem,' he said, stroking her hair.

'What?' she whispered.

'I'm flat broke.'

Reaching out her hand, Diana stroked his face, fixing him with her most earnest gaze. 'I don't care,' she said. 'I never did care about the money. Please, let's not fight about that ever again. We have each other. That's all that matters.'

'So, you said that you came here from your parents' place,' said Danny, once they'd finished kissing again. 'I thought you and Brogan ...'

'It's a long story,' said Diana. 'Why don't we go to bed, and I'll tell you all about it later?'

'Sure, of course, of course. You must be shattered,' said Danny, still floating on a cloud of happiness unlike anything he'd ever known.

'Actually, that wasn't what I meant.'

Diana gave him a meaningful look. In a single, glorious instant, his libido came out of hibernation. He grinned from ear to ear.

'Really? I mean, wouldn't that hurt the baby?'

Diana laughed. 'Uh uh. Of course, if you don't feel like doing it with a huge great elephant like me.'

'Are you kidding me?' said Danny, who had already pulled her to her feet and was dragging her towards the bedroom. 'You are the sexiest woman that ever lived.'

And he meant it.


When Jake got home a couple of hours later, he walked in to find the two of them naked and ecstatic, coiled in one another's arms.

'Bloody hell,' he said, blushing and making a hasty retreat to the living room. 'Sorry. I didn't know you had, er ... I wasn't expecting ...'

'You can come in,' yelled Danny from the bedroom. He'd pulled the covers up over both of them, but had not unwound himself from Diana's body. He couldn't. 'We're decent.'

'Right,' said Jake, tentatively poking his head back around the door. 'So does this mean you two are back on?'

'It does,' said Diana. 'I hope it won't put you out too much if I stay here for a week or so. Just until Danny and I get ourselves sorted again.'

'Put me out?' Jake laughed. 'Listen, if you hadn't come back I'd have thrown him out on his ear. You have no idea what a miserable sod he's been since you left. Speaking of which, how is that horrible ex husband of yours?'

'Horrible,' Diana shuddered. 'You were both right. I should never have let him back into my life. But I felt so sorry for him, with the cancer and everything. And he really seemed to have changed.'

'All right, new house rule,' said Danny, placing a loving hand across Diana's mouth. 'We don't talk about money, or the lack of it. And we don't ever, EVER, mention Brogan O'Donnell. Not ever. Deal?'

'Deal,' said Jake and Diana in unison.

'Right,' said Jake, rubbing his hands together happily. No one was more pleased to see a smile on Danny's face than he was. 'Who'd like a lovely post coital cup o' tea?'

# Twenty-six

Scarlett gazed at the computer screen and rubbed her eyes blearily.

Six hundred and forty-two unread messages. Good Lord. She needed a PA. That, and about a year and a half's sleep. And possibly a month-long trip to Shivah Som or somewhere similarly warm and sybaritic, ideally with Nancy. There was a time when she wouldn't have thought it possible for her to miss LA. But a wet, grey summer day chained to her father's desk at Drumfernly had got her longing for sunshine, flip flops and skinny chai lattes like a bona fide valley girl.

Cameron had finally moved back home, which was both good and bad from Scarlett's perspective. Good because it got Caroline off her back and gave her something to focus on other than her daughter's failings. And bad because it was immediately apparent, to everyone other than Caroline, that Cam's life was never going to be the same again. Still on antidepressant drugs and suffering from chronic bouts of insomnia, he spoke as if he were permanently stoned. Certainly the listless, broken individual that spent his days shuffling round the castle in tracksuit trousers bore little resemblance to his mother's gay-son fantasies of a happy-go-lucky, Graham Norton-esque shopping partner with whom she could while away her twilight years.

Scrolling past the latest two emails from the estate's accountant – both of them marked with ominous red exclamation marks – Scarlett opened the latest missive from Jake, updating her on the most recent figures from Flawless.

The numbers weren't bad, but the email still left her depressed. She hated the way that she and Jake communicated now. The business-speak, the politeness. No one reading their correspondence would ever have guessed that they were friends, never mind that they were once lovers. Scarlett was frightened by how much she missed him.

Just as she was about to turn back to the accountant's messages, a new email arrived from Nancy. Smiling for the first time all afternoon, Scarlett clicked it open.

*Greetings from sunny Hollywood!* it began. *Your dreadful dog has just crapped all over the floor, having gorged himself on the pinkberry I stupidly left out on the coffee table. I'm afraid I'm going to have to have him put down.*

Scarlett laughed. Nancy was so full of shit. She loved Boxie almost as much as Scarlett did.

*You'll be pleased to hear that the movie is going great. Djimon Hounsou is totally fucking awesome as Keke – I told you he'd been cast, right? He's also hung like King Kong, but that's beside the point. Lucky Kimora Lee Simmons is all I can say …*

The note continued in this vein for quite some time, and Scarlett could feel her spirits lifting with every line. Reading Nancy's emails was like getting a monthly download from *Entertainment Tonight*, only funnier and filthier. For a few minutes Drumfernly and her family problems seemed a million miles away.

*I saw Jake Meyer the other day,* she wrote, towards the end of the email. *He was having dinner at Asia de Cuba with his new girlfriend, and he actually said 'hi' to me.*

Despite herself, Scarlett felt her chest tightening.

Jake had a girlfriend? Obviously she knew he was dating. But the mental picture she'd created for herself involved him out on the scene like a Labrador in heat with a different chick on his arm every night. Somehow that didn't hurt as much as the idea he might be serious with someone.

*You'll be pleased to hear the girl is a hobbit,* said Nancy loyally. *She must only come up to his knees, and she's nothing like as pretty as you are. Still, in a way I guess it's good that he's not shacked up with a full-on bimbo. Who knows, maybe he's maturing at last?*

The rest of the letter was filled with general news. The FBI had released Brogan O'Donnell, but arrested his lawyer, Aidan Leach, for the murder of Andy Gordon, which Scarlett already knew. Apparently Brogan's odious henchman had acted alone, on his own initiative. Scarlett wasn't sure she bought it, but she was pleased that this time a murder prosecution would go ahead. Clearly the FBI felt they had their man. Andy had been such a good, funny, sweet person, the least he deserved was some justice. According to Nancy, the case was dropping off the radar in the States in terms of press interest. All people seemed to care about was what colour wig Britney was wearing, and how loopy she was on a week-to-week basis. Dull little events like murders and conspiracy in the diamond business no longer sold magazines, apparently.

She mentioned in passing that Diana O'Donnell was now back together with Danny Meyer – something else that Scarlett already knew, courtesy of Perry (Jake hadn't bothered to mention it) – and that their baby was due any day. Overdue, in fact. *Diana looks like a snake that swallowed a beach ball,* as Nancy put it.

*I haven't heard from Che Che in months,* she finished, introducing the subject of her ex apparently out of nowhere. *Last I heard he was backpacking in Chile, working on some new video installation or something. But you probably know more than I do.*

Scarlett could sense the pain behind that last, throwaway line. Clearly the misery of Nancy's break-up with Che Che was still raw. She wished she had some news of him to tell her friend, but the truth was she hadn't heard from him herself. Not since the week of Andy's death, the same week that she'd heard about Cameron and flown back home, the same week that had seen her entire life put on hold, apparently for ever ...

'Scarlett, darling?'

Hugo's kindly, vaguely anxious face appeared in the doorway.

'There's someone here to see you.'

'Well, is it important, Daddy?' Scarlett began. 'Because I've hardly started on the estate work and I—'

'Yes, it is important. Vitally important.' Scarlett's face lit up. There, behind her father, stood Aunt Agnes, grinning from ear to ear. 'So get your skinny little bottom up out of that chair and come and give an old woman a hug.'

Scarlett did as she was told, and soon found herself encircled in her elderly aunt's crushingly tight embrace. Greyer and perhaps slightly thinner than Scarlett remembered her, Agnes was otherwise unchanged. She had the same clear, defiant blue eyes she'd always had, the same upright, queenly bearing. Still, it felt strange seeing her here, at Drumfernly, standing next to Hugo who, in his crumpled tweeds and slippers, could hardly have looked less like this grand woman's brother had he been as black as Linford Christie.

'What are you doing here?' asked Scarlett. 'Did Daddy know you were coming?'

'Of course not,' said Agnes brusquely. 'You know as well as I do that your father can't keep a secret. Besides,' linking arms with Scarlett, she led her through into the Great Hall, with a waddling Hugo following in their wake, 'if your mother had realised I was coming she'd have started sending the cooks into Buckie for arsenic weeks ago.'

'Nonsense,' lied Hugo. 'Caroline'll be delighted you're here, Agnes.'

'We don't have cooks any more, Aunt A,' Scarlett giggled. 'I'm afraid those days are long gone. We have Mrs Cullen.'

'Good gracious. Is she still going?' Aunt Agnes looked surprised.

'Agnes, she's twenty years younger than I am,' said Hugo reproachfully.

'In any case, if things continue as they have been we won't even be able to afford her for much longer,' said Scarlett, pouring her aunt a dry sherry before sitting down with her on the tatty old Knowle sofa. 'Then you'll be reduced to Mummy's cooking. Or mine.'

'You're an excellent cook,' said Aunt Agnes loyally, patting her niece's knee. 'I do want to talk to you however – to both of you,' she looked at Hugo, whose worried frown was deepening by the minute, 'about the estate finances.'

'Ah darling, there you are.' Hugo made a brave attempt at a smile as his wife walked in, followed by a mutely shuffling Cameron. 'Look who's here! It's Agnes.'

'Yes, I can see that, Hugo,' said Caroline tersely. Not a fan of unexpected guests in general, she particularly loathed her sister-in-law, who she knew looked down on her socially, not to mention bitched about her with Scarlett. The one good thing to be said about Agnes was that she'd had the good sense to move to Africa donkey's years ago, and that she very rarely inflicted herself on them up at Drumfernly. As usual, however, her timing for this particular visit could not have been worse, what with Cameron still so unwell and relations between her and Scarlett even more strained than usual. Caroline wondered what the old bag wanted.

'What brings you over to Scotland?' she asked stiffly. 'Will you be staying long?'

'Don't worry,' said Agnes cheerfully. 'I'm as anxious to fly back to sunnier climes as you are to be shot of me.'

'Agnes, honestly, do stop being difficult,' mumbled Hugo. Caroline, pointedly, didn't bother to correct her.

'I came to talk to Hugo and Scarlett about some business matters. I'll be here three days at most. Hello, Cameron.'

She smiled at the silent, brooding figure half hiding himself behind Caroline, trying not to betray how shocked she was by the change in him. Agnes had never liked her nephew. But the sneering, arrogant, malicious young man she had known was nowhere to be seen in this rather pathetic, sullen individual. He must have put himself through hell, simply to avoid admitting his sexuality. What a waste! A waste and a shame. She wondered if Caroline felt guilty about all the favouritism she'd shown Cameron over the years: the cloying, adoring love that had not only driven her daughter away from her, but had obviously left the boy feeling that to be himself was never an option.

'How are you? Pleased to be home, I expect.'

Cameron looked at her blankly.

'It's all right darling,' said Caroline, kissing him softly on the cheek. 'You go on into the kitchen and have that hot chocolate. I'll find the cards and be through in a minute.'

Once Cameron had left, Agnes said apologetically, 'I'm sorry. I didn't realise he was still so fragile.'

'He isn't fragile,' Caroline snapped. 'He's fine. He was shocked to see you, that's all. We all are.' Fetching a pack of cards from the bridge table in the corner, she turned to follow her son. 'I suppose I'd better go and ask Mrs Cullen to make you up a bed. You know it wouldn't have killed you to call ahead, Agnes. I understand that Drumfernly is your home. But arrangements do have to be made, you know.'

'Oh dear,' said Agnes, after she'd gone. 'I honestly didn't mean to cause any trouble, Hugo.'

'Yes, well.' Scarlett's father sounded unconvinced. He loved his sister, but a troublemaker she had *always* been. 'Perhaps you should go upstairs and change. Have a little nap or what have you. I'll smooth things over with Caroline.'

'A *nap*?' She sounded suitably disgusted. 'I'm not old, you know. No, if you have a pair of wellies I can borrow

I think I'd like to go for a walk around the grounds with Scarlett.'

She pronounced the word 'grinds' which made Scarlett smile. She really was a relic from a lost era. Having her at Drumfernly automatically brought some of the house's magic back to life.

'Come on then.' Scarlett got to her feet. 'I'd better find you a parka as well. It looks like it's going to piss down.'

Striding through the wet bracken half an hour later, invigorated by the whipping wind and the ubiquitous smell of the pines, Aunt Agnes listened while Scarlett talked. And talked. About Drumfernly, Cameron and the apparently insurmountable problems that had kept her a virtual prisoner on the estate since the spring.

'I assume you've spoken to your father about all of this?' said the old woman, once they reached the top of the hill that bordered the castle's north side, and Scarlett finally paused for breath.

'I tried to,' said Scarlett. 'At the beginning. But I don't think he realises how serious the situation is. We're already remortgaged to the hilt. Daddy's answer to everything is to flog another painting or a piece of furniture, but there isn't an endless supply. The whole concept of sustainability is a closed book to him.'

'And your mother?'

Scarlett laughed.

'Mummy? Are you kidding? Mummy wouldn't know how to balance a cheque book if world peace depended on it. Daddy tells her things are fine, and she believes him. Anyway, I wouldn't want to worry her with money problems. She puts on a brave face, but this whole nightmare with Cameron has crushed her. One more setback and she'll be the next Drummond Murray carted off in a straitjacket.'

'Yes. I do see,' said Aunt Agnes, leaning on Hugo's

mahogany walking stick for support as they picked their way down the bumpy field on the other side of the ridge. Above them, bruise-grey clouds were gathering. The entire sky felt heavy with foreboding, low and close and oppressive. 'Awfully difficult for you, though. Shouldering it all alone.'

Scarlett smiled bravely. 'Yes, well, you know. It could be worse. At least I'm not going through the hell that Cameron's had to cope with.'

'Or *not* cope with,' said Aunt Agnes.

'I just thank God that the *News of the World* never ran those pictures. I have no idea why they changed their minds, but can you imagine if they'd run it? I honestly think he'd have killed himself. Mummy too, in all probability.'

'I paid them.'

She said it so quietly, without breaking stride, that at first Scarlett thought she must have misheard.

'I'm sorry?'

'I paid them. The newspaper. I bought them off,' said Aunt Agnes matter of factly.

Scarlett stopped in her tracks.

'How much?'

Aunt Agnes turned around. 'Darling, do stop dawdling; the heavens are about to open. For a substantial sum, as it happens. But I think it was money well spent, don't you?'

'But ... but ...' Scarlett hurried down the hill after her aunt, who was still walking. 'Daddy doesn't know, does he?'

'No,' said Aunt Agnes. 'And we must keep it that way. I wouldn't want your father to feel under any obligation. Something needed to be done and I had the means to do it. Between you and me, Scarlett, I'm considerably wealthier than your father realises. Divorce has been kind to me, and I've been lucky enough to make a number of good investments over the years. South African property's done frightfully well, you know.'

461

Scarlett didn't know. Not for the first time, she felt in awe of her favourite aunt's ability to surprise them all, even in her eighties.

'All of which brings me to the real reason I'm here.'

They'd reached the bottom of the field now, where a rickety wooden bridge crossed a thin, crystal-clear stream. Aunt Agnes eased herself gingerly down on to the step of the stile that led to the bridge, pausing for a few minutes of well-earned rest.

'This situation can't go on, Scarlett.'

'What situation?' Hopping over the fence in one easy, long-legged bound, Scarlett sat down cross-legged on the bridge, looking up at her aunt. With her flushed, make-up-free face, and tendrils of her dark hair blowing around in the wind, she looked as fresh and innocent as a teenager.

'*This* situation. You, staying here, sorting out Hugo's problems for him,' said Aunt Agnes.

'But there's no one else to do it,' Scarlett shrugged. 'I have to.'

'Fiddlesticks,' said Aunt Agnes firmly. 'What you have to do is get yourself back to Los Angeles and marry Jake.'

Scarlett was so shocked she laughed out loud.

'What on earth makes you think I should do that?'

'Because you're in love with him,' said Aunt Agnes simply. 'And he's in love with you.'

Scarlett looked away: at the silver water, dancing over the rocks below her; at the brooding, stormy sky above; anything rather than looking Aunt Agnes in the eye.

'It's more complicated than that,' she mumbled. 'You've never met Jake. If you had, if you knew him, you'd understand.'

'As a matter of fact, I have met him,' said Aunt Agnes. And she told Scarlett about their dinner at the Peninsula back in February. Scarlett listened, open-mouthed, as Aunt Agnes recounted their conversation, including the part where Jake had admitted he loved her. 'We've kept in contact since, you know. The internet is a quite marvellous invention; I'm something of a whiz at it nowadays.'

'I'm sure you are,' mumbled Scarlett, still trying to take in the idea that Jake and Aunt Agnes were apparently secret BFFs. Was there *no* woman Jake Meyer couldn't charm?

'Even if he did love me,' said Scarlett eventually, 'we broke up for a reason. We're too different. I don't want to make myself out as some sort of saint, but you know Jake really doesn't care about anyone but himself. He always loathed my work with Trade Fair.'

'You're quite wrong,' said Aunt Agnes bluntly. 'He may have behaved as if he loathed it. But I can assure you he was very proud of you, and your charity work had a profound influence on him. Did you know about his involvement with the orphanage in Freetown?'

Scarlett couldn't have looked more disbelieving if she'd just been told a UFO had landed on Buckie town hall.

'Jake? No, you must be mistaken. Trust me, African orphans are not on his radar.'

'He read the books you gave him about Sierra Leone last year,' Aunt Agnes continued doggedly. 'After he went out there, he started sending money to a wonderful woman by the name of Dr Katenge. I know this for a fact, Scarlett, because he managed to persuade me to make a donation. Nothing particularly large, mind you,' she added, humbly. 'But the point is, he's not the unremittingly selfish individual you appear to have convinced yourself that he is.'

'But if …' Scarlett shook her head, trying to make sense of it all. 'If he was doing good work in Sierra Leone, I mean, why didn't he tell me?'

'For heaven's sake, child, how should I know? That's the sort of question you need to be asking him. Male pride, I shouldn't wonder. I'm not saying Jake doesn't have his faults. But I can't abide to see two young people so obviously in love with one another making such an almighty hash of things.'

She sounded really quite cross.

'He's not in love with me,' Scarlett insisted, miserably. 'He's seeing someone else in LA.'

'Well of course he is,' said Aunt Agnes, not unkindly. 'You left him, darling. Locked yourself away up here like some sort of damsel in distress. You can't expect him to come and rescue you.'

'I don't expect anything of the kind!' said Scarlett indignantly.

'Good.' Aunt Agnes smiled. 'Because we women have got to learn to start rescuing ourselves. Now I'd like a straight answer to a straight question. Do you love Jake Meyer?'

Scarlett bit her lip and nodded helplessly.

'But I can't—'

'No buts.' Aunt Agnes was firm. 'Like I told you, darling, not to put too fine a point on it, I'm rich, and I have no children of my own. You've always been like a daughter to me, Scarlett.' Her eyes welled up with tears, and Scarlett found her own following suit. 'I'll have a talk with Hugo. We'll appoint some decent accountants and a full-time business manager to do what needs to be done at Drumfernly.' Pulling her shawl more tightly across her bony shoulders, Aunt Agnes shivered. 'I wouldn't want to live here, but it's my childhood home, and I have no intention of allowing Hugo to let this place slip through his lazy, incompetent male fingers.'

Scarlett sat silently for a moment. Could it really be that easy? Could she simply walk away from Drumfernly, fly back to LA and her old life? Pick up with Flawless where she left off? Perhaps even work things out with Jake? Aunt Agnes made it sound so straightforward. Predetermined, almost. But of course it wasn't. What if Jake really was in love with this girl, as Nancy's letter had suggested? What was she supposed to do, waltz in and demand that he break up with her, on the basis of one, probably drunken, conver-

464

sation that he'd had with Scarlett's aunt half a year ago?

'I know you're frightened,' said Aunt Agnes, reading her mind. Climbing down onto the bridge herself, she helped Scarlett to her feet. 'But look at it this way, darling. What's the worst that can happen?'

He'll reject me, thought Scarlett. Oh God. I can't bear it.

'You need to know if it was meant to be with Jake,' said Aunt Agnes. 'And if not, you need to get back to work and to your own life. You can't hide away up here for ever.'

'I'm not hiding. I'm helping, or trying to,' said Scarlett.

But even as she said the words, she knew they were a lie.

She knew that she would go back home.

# Twenty-seven

'Oh God. Oh Jesus. That's not normal. I don't know what that is but it can*not* be normal. For fuck's sake, will one of you help her? Where's the fucking doctor?'

Danny Meyer's panicked screams could be heard the entire length of the St John's Hospital maternity suite.

The midwife smiled.

'It's perfectly normal, Mr Meyer,' she said. 'That's the baby's head. He's crowning. Won't be long now.'

'He?' Danny's ears pricked up. 'Can you tell the sex?'

'Not from the top of the head, no,' said the midwife patiently. Diana had requested a midwife-only birth. In the midwife's opinion, it was a pity she hadn't banished the father as well as the doctors. Men were worse than useless, especially with their first child. 'Why don't you put the cool cloth on Mom's forehead?' she suggested gently. 'Everything's under control down here.'

Danny, who had never felt less 'under control' in his life, did as he was told, reluctantly. As much as the horror movie between Diana's legs scared the shit out of him, it was better than having to watch the pain on her face as she desperately tried to breathe and focus her way through the final stages of what had been a long, hard labour.

'Can't you knock her out?' he pleaded, dabbing at her head with the wet cloth while she moaned a low, animal sound that frightened him.

'No,' Diana panted, shaking her head violently. 'No drugs.'

'There's nothing we could do now anyway,' said the

midwife. 'The head's almost out. One more push, Diana. Come on! All you've got now.'

Diana clenched her teeth and focused all her energy on the pain deep within her. Danny found himself yelling out in sympathy, a long, sustained *aaaagh*!

'That's it, that's it!' the midwife cried excitedly. 'The head's out. The next contraction and you can hold your baby!'

Danny glanced down at the business end of things, and was greeted by the surreal sight of his child's face blinking up at him, its body still inside its mother. He wasn't sure which of the two of them looked more shocked. Then, before he knew what was happening, Diana let out a final, piercing cry, and with a grotesque, slithering sound, the baby's body and legs shot out. Seconds later, it was lying, still bloody, in Diana's arms.

'Oh, he's lovely! He's so, so lovely!' she breathed, kissing the child's vernix-covered head. All the pain of the past fourteen hours seemed to have evaporated in an instant.

'It's a boy?' Danny stood motionless at the bedside, still in shock.

'Yes, Mr Meyer,' laughed the midwife. 'The penis is usually considered a bit of a giveaway.'

'He looks like you.' Diana smiled up at him, cradling her baby joyously. Danny didn't think he'd ever seen anything quite so beautiful in his entire life.

'He's covered in slime,' said Danny. 'And he looks Chinese. His eyes are all scrunchy. Are you sure he's mine?'

Diana would have been offended, were it not for the delight written all over Danny's face.

'Blimey,' he said, examining his firstborn more closely. 'Check out the size of his tackle! Maybe he is mine.'

'That's hormonal,' said the midwife, deftly monitoring the baby's vital signs without removing him from his mother. 'Both sexes can be born with excessively swollen genitals. It'll go down in a day or two.'

'No it won't, love,' said Danny proudly. 'He's a Meyer.'

Outside in the waiting room, Jake stood up and walked to the window. Seventeen floors below he could see the steady stream of afternoon traffic clogging up Wilshire Boulevard, like jostling red and white blood cells pumping through a vein.

'Sit down, babe. You're making me nervous.'

Ruth, his girlfriend, had insisted on coming with him to the hospital. Perched like a small bird in one of the suede armchairs St John's provided for family and friends – no plastic chairs nailed to the floor here, like you got in London maternity wards – she was reading *Elle* with a calm bordering on ennui that Jake couldn't help but find irritating.

Diana could be haemorrhaging to death in there for all they knew. If the yells and shouts were anything to go by, Danny could be too. How could she sit there, cool as a cucumber, reading about shoes and fucking handbags?

'I can't sit down,' he said testily. 'I need something to do.'

'Why don't you call your mother?' suggested Ruth. 'She's texted me six times in the last ten minutes asking for news. You know she's going out of her mind with worry.'

She meant the advice kindly. In fact, Jake reminded himself, the only reason Ruth was here at all was to support him, to try to do the right, expected, girlfriendly thing. But still he felt his hackles rising. In the short time they'd been dating, Minty had all but adopted Ruth as the daughter she never had, and the love-fest appeared to be mutual. Making an effort with his family was one thing. But all the texting, and the long, gossipy phone calls were beginning to make him feel trapped. Next thing Ruth'd be changing her ringtone to 'Here Comes the Bride'. It was all too much too soon.

Not that she wasn't lovely. Everyone adored her, even Danny, who'd become such a huge Scarlett fan he'd been almost as upset about Jake's break up as Jake himself.

468

Jake looked at Ruth now, her eyes flitting between Minty's latest note on the BlackBerry and the magazine in her hands. With her slender legs crossed and her shiny, perfectly blow-dried hair swinging from side to side as she moved her head, she looked polished and professional. Even the white lab coat – she'd come straight from the surgery – seemed to fit her petite figure perfectly. Without wanting to, Jake found himself dredging up a mental picture of Scarlett in that mad, multicoloured threadbare sweater she used to wear. He imagined her gesticulating wildly, making some impassioned point (wasn't she always?) with her long, unbrushed hair escaping from its elastic band like seaweed, and he missed her like a physical pain.

'Honey?' She looked at him quizzically, proffering her phone. 'Your mom?'

'Hmm?' Jake came reluctantly back to reality. 'Oh, no, just text her back and say we're still waiting. Once she starts rabbiting on I'll never be able to get rid of her.'

At that moment a flushed, visibly elated Danny burst through the double doors.

'It's a boy!' he beamed. 'Zachariah Daniel Meyer. Zac. He is the absolute fucking business, bruv.' He flung his arms around Jake, lifting him up in an almighty, triumphant bear hug.

'How's Diana?' asked Ruth. She waited for the twins to finish hugging before kissing Danny warmly on the cheek. 'Can we see them both?'

'In a minute, yeah,' said Danny. 'They're just getting cleaned up. Diana was amazing. Amazing! I can't believe she went through all of that, without so much as a paracetamol.'

'Nor can I,' said Ruth with feeling. 'When I have a kid they can knock me out cold. Twenty thousand bucks for one night and no doctor? That's more than painful enough if you ask me.'

Jake grinned, and suddenly remembered everything he liked about her.

'Congratulations,' he said, returning Danny's smile. 'I'll nip down to the gift shop and get her some flowers.'

'Don't bother,' said Danny. 'She only has eyes for the baby. She won't even register.'

'That's OK,' said Jake, who suddenly felt an unaccountable need to be by himself and get some air. 'I ought to stretch my legs anyway. You two go on in. I'll be up in a few minutes.'

Outside, the sun was just beginning its descent into the horizon, and a rainbow of blues, reds, pinks and purples oozed into the late-afternoon sky. The day was so clear you could see the ocean glinting at the end of Santa Monica Boulevard, some twenty-three blocks away. Had it not been for the roaring traffic, belching out petrol fumes, the palm-lined street would have looked positively beautiful.

As it was, Jake barely noticed his surroundings, nor the deafening rush-hour sound track as he wandered towards the flower shop on the corner, lost in his own thoughts.

He had a nephew.

Danny had a son.

He knew he ought to feel delighted, and he did, for Danny. Danny who, a few short months ago, had felt that the best of his life had already passed, that love and happiness and success had all slipped permanently through his fingers. Jake doubted there was another human being on earth this evening that felt quite so completely happy as his brother. The thought made him smile.

But at the same time, Danny becoming a father threw his own life into harsh relief. Ruth was a terrific girl. Terrific. But he didn't love her. If he'd been under any illusions about that, they'd shattered with resounding clarity in that waiting room a few moments ago. He would have to break up with her, now, before her expectations really became set in stone. The thought of hurting yet another woman twisted his insides like a gallstone. When the fuck was he going to bring a girl some happiness? When was he going to find happiness himself? Become a father? Settle down?

He tried to picture himself with a wife on his arm and a child on his knee, and realised for the first time in his life that he wanted to be in that picture. He did. He wanted what Danny had. So why did he keep screwing things up for himself?

Maybe what he'd told Aunt Agnes had been the truth. He wasn't cut out for relationships. He might fantasize about becoming a father, but he entirely lacked the skill, or the genetic make-up, or whatever it was he needed to turn that dream into a reality.

He'd been thinking for a while now about getting away. Maybe, if Scarlett ever came back from bloody Scotland and took over the reins at Flawless, he could take a six-month sabbatical? Perhaps go back to Freetown and work with Dr Katenge. Do something useful for a change.

Opening the door to the flower store, the mingled scent of freesias, stocks and lilies was so overpowering it made him feel nauseous.

'I'll be right with you,' the girl at the counter shouted. 'I'm just finishing up here.'

She was serving another customer, a girl, handing her an enormous bouquet of white roses. The girl had her back to Jake, so he couldn't get a good look at her, although he did glance admiringly at her ridiculously long legs in a pair of faded corduroy True Religions.

'Oh, no, no. I don't need the plastic wrap. Just leave them natural.'

Her voice echoed around the empty store. Jake felt his stomach flip like a tossed coin. He'd know that sing-song, posh English accent anywhere. The most beautiful sound in the world.

'That'll be sixty dollars and fifty-five cents please,' the shop girl was saying. Scarlett fumbled in her trouser pockets, dropping notes and change everywhere in her usual, scatterbrained way.

'Here. Let me.'

Inside, his heart was racing, but Jake's voice rang out clear and strong. Scarlett spun around, blushing to the roots of her gorgeous, mahogany hair.

'Oh. Gosh. You're not supposed ... what are you doing here?' she stammered.

'That's my line,' said Jake. 'I thought you were in Scotland.'

For ten of the longest seconds in history, they stared at one another, neither knowing what to say next. Then, to Jake's surprise, he felt his legs carry him forwards and his arms opening. The next thing he knew, Scarlett had fallen into them with the exhausted relief of a marathon runner finally crossing the finish line.

The kiss went on for so long the shop girl started to worry they were going to rip each other's clothes off there and then, and began to cough loudly from behind the counter.

Taking the hint, Jake pulled away, still clasping both Scarlett's hands in his.

'How did you know I was here?'

'Perry told me,' said Scarlett. 'I went straight to the store and he said Diana was in labour and you'd taken off. The flowers were for Diana,' she added lamely.

'Good.' Jake grinned. 'White roses don't really float my boat. I've always been more of a blow-job man.'

'Jake!' Scarlett blushed and giggled.

'Oh, Scarlett,' he said, suddenly serious. 'I've been such a prat. I know we've got a lot to talk about, and we can't just pick up where we left off. You're probably thinking I'm the same old Jake Meyer and it'll never work out, not in the long run. But I've changed, I really have. Since Danny became a father—'

Now it was Scarlett's turn to grin. 'And when was that, exactly?'

'About forty minutes ago,' said Jake. 'Look, I know it's complicated. We need to take things slowly. But I love you; I fucking love you so much, and—'

'Jake?'

Ruth, looking small and bewildered in her white lab coat, suddenly appeared in the flower shop doorway. Diana had been too exhausted for a long visit, so she'd decided to come and find him and suggest they came back in the morning.

But one look at the two figures in front of her told her that wasn't going to happen.

'You must be Scarlett.'

'That's right.'

Smiling bravely, Ruth marched over and shook her rival's hand. Deep in her heart, she had always known there was a piece missing in Jake's love for her. And now here she was, shaking the missing piece's hand.

Watching her, Jake had never felt smaller. Ruth was twice the man he'd ever be.

'Scarlett just arrived,' he mumbled awkwardly. 'I wasn't expecting her. I mean, I didn't know—'

Ruth held up her hand. She was already using every ounce of her pride and strength to hold it together. If Jake started apologising, she knew the tears would flow.

'Please, don't. I understand.' She was looking at Scarlett, unwilling or unable to meet Jake's eye. 'I wish you both the best.'

'Ruth!' Jake called after her. But she had already bolted out of the door and was half-walking, half-running down the street.

'I'm so sorry,' said Scarlett, sincerely. 'It was selfish of me. I should never have come. Your life's moved on, and here I come like the ghost of Christmas past, hurting everybody and—'

He stopped her with a kiss. The cashier started coughing again. The poor girl sounded like she had advanced TB.

'My life started the day I met you,' said Jake, 'and it stopped the day you left. Promise you'll never leave me again. Never.'

Scarlett nodded fervently.

He was right; they had a lot to talk about.

But she knew she would never, ever leave him again.

# Twenty-eight

Topanga was the perfect setting for a Christmas wedding.

Thanks to good old Aunt Agnes – or Saint Agnes, as the Meyer brothers had rechristened her – and her timely investment in Solomon Stones, Danny had bought the 1920s farmhouse he had fallen in love with over the summer and spent the past few months refurbishing it. Diana broke down in tears the day that she and Zac moved in – Danny had insisted that they finish the works first so as not to expose the baby to any dust, and he wanted their first family home to be perfect before his darling girl saw it. And in Diana's eyes, it truly was.

'Oh my God. It's a fairytale,' she sobbed, gazing in wonder at the freshly planted cottage gardens, and the gleaming new whitewash on the façade. 'I feel like Snow White.'

Inside it was even more charming, with not so much as a hint of Danny's bachelor taste in evidence. The old pine floors were simply stripped, the walls painted in strong, bright colours, offset by clean, white Shaker furniture, and all the original features, like the wood-burning stove in the kitchen, had been salvaged and lovingly restored. Best of all was Zac's nursery, a charming, higgledy-piggledy room in the attic, where Scarlett had covered the walls with a mural of an enchanted forest.

'It's an early wedding present,' she told the delighted Diana. 'It's been ages since I did any painting, so I really had fun with it. You don't think Zac'll be frightened, do you? It is a bit spooky in parts.'

'It's magical,' enthused Diana. 'He'll love it. It's like a dream. The whole house is.'

The guests who filed down the garden path into the huge marquee at the bottom of the hillside thought so too.

'It's a little piece of England, isn't it?' Nancy was saying to Isobel, one of Scarlett's model girlfriends from Notting Hill. 'Don't you feel like you're back home?'

'Well, yes, apart from the fact it's eighty degrees and blue skies in the middle of December,' laughed Isobel. 'And the whole double wedding thing is frightfully Hollywood. I don't think Scarlett's mother is a bit amused.'

'No,' Nancy frowned. 'Perhaps not. Then again, when is she ever?'

Caroline, clinging on to Hugo's arm for dear life as he led her to her seat at the front of the marquee, radiated icy disapproval in a vintage Hardy Amies suit and hat. Half of the guests seemed to have dressed for a barbecue, in cheap sundresses and flip flops. Two of them, she noted with horror, were actually barefoot! The whole ghastly, hippy set-up was a far cry from the church wedding at Drumfernly that she'd always dreamed of for her daughter. But then again Scarlett had always been wilful, always *insisted* on going her own way. If only cursed Agnes hadn't encouraged her, they wouldn't be here, sharing their daughter's wedding day with a gaggle of North London Jews and eccentric Californians. They'd be safely at home, ensconced in the sanity of Drumfernly.

Then again, as Hugo had gently reminded her, if it hadn't been for Agnes they wouldn't have Drumfernly to go home to.

In an upstairs guest bedroom, Scarlett and Diana were alone together, helping one another with the last-minute adjustments to their veils.

'This is exquisite,' sighed Scarlett, pinning Diana's 1930s pearl tiara firmly in place. 'Is it your something old?'

'Old, and borrowed. It's my mother's,' said Diana. So soon after Zac's birth she'd lost every ounce of her baby-weight and then some, and looked tiny and childlike in her fitted, Monique Lhuillier gown. 'Brogan very sweetly sent me a silver cross of *his* mother's to be my something old, but Danny wouldn't hear of it.'

'I should think not,' said Scarlett.

'He said Brogan was something old, and should mind his own business,' giggled Diana. 'I guess I see his point.'

Brogan had written her a long letter when her engagement was announced, congratulating her on that and on Zac's birth. Danny had been dismissive and distrustful, understandably, but Diana could tell from his tone that this time Brogan had genuinely changed. Aidan Leach's conviction for the murder of the journalist, Scarlett's friend, had shaken him deeply, and he finally seemed to be taking a long, hard look at his own life. For Diana, knowing that she had Brogan's blessing closed the circle of her happiness. And even Danny had softened towards him slightly when, a week after the baby was born, he finally agreed to make Diana a fair, even generous settlement.

'What about you?' Diana smiled at Scarlett, smoothing down her antique veil. 'Did you do the whole borrowed and blue thing too?'

'Of course,' said Scarlett. 'Just about everything's old – the veil, the dress. Only my shoes are new.' She poked a bejewelled Jimmy Choo sandal out from under the hem of her grandmother's lace wedding gown and wiggled her pedicured toes happily. 'My engagement ring's blue.'

'I *love* that sapphire,' enthused Diana.

'And I borrowed this from Nancy.' Hitching up her skirts, she revealed a sexy lace garter belt with appliquéd skulls and crossbones all over it. 'She felt the outfit needed a touch of rock 'n' roll.'

In the corner of the room, Zac gurgled happily on his sheepskin playmat.

'You and Jake'll be next,' said Diana, catching Scarlett's adoring glance in her son's direction.

'One thing at a time,' laughed Scarlett. 'Jake's only just grown up himself, remember.'

Downstairs in the study, Danny did his best to calm his brother's nerves.

'What if she backs out?' Pacing the tiny, wood-panelled room like a caged leopard, Jake looked as green as the newly irrigated farmhouse lawn. 'What if she takes one look at me in there and comes to her senses?'

'She's had ages to come to her senses,' said Danny, handing him a lit cigarette. 'If she was going to do it, it would have happened by now.'

'Her family hate me,' said Jake, inhaling deeply.

Danny shrugged. 'Diana's family hate me. So what? You're not marrying the parents.'

'But what if her dad gives her a last-minute pep talk?'

'He won't.'

'Or one of her Lord Snooty ex-boyfriends stands up when they say "If anyone knows of any reason why these two may not be joined in holy matrimony," and she listens to him, and—'

'Jake.' Danny put a firm hand on his twin brother's shoulder. 'This isn't a church service, remember? We don't have that bit.'

Jake looked faintly mollified.

'Thank God for that. How long till kick off?'

Danny consulted his watch. 'Twenty minutes.'

Jake groaned. So long?

'I think I need a brandy. Make it a double.'

Most of the guests had filed into the marquee by now, and were milling around talking and laughing and enjoying the canapés and champagne before taking their seats.

Nancy had secured herself a good corner vantage point from which to observe the throng, and was thoroughly enjoying a good bitch with Perry.

478

'Look at Julia Brookstein's skirt!' she whispered, knocking back another big slug of bubbly. 'It's so short you can see her lipo scars from here.'

'Mmm,' Perry agreed. 'Greta Saltzman's ageing so much better. Although the caramel highlights were a mistake. What do you think they're talking about?'

'The size of Jake's cock, I expect, and how much they're going to miss it,' said Nancy.

'D'you think they *will* miss it?' Perry asked archly. 'Do you think our boy has fidelity in him?'

Nancy scowled. 'He's not my boy. And he'd damned well better have. If he plays around on Scarlett, I'll personally sever the infamous Meyer meat with a rusty hacksaw and that's a promise.'

'Ouch!' Perry winced. 'Must you be so graphic, sweetie? Ooo, who's that?' His sharp eyes zeroed in on an impossibly chiselled man in a formal tuxedo jacket who was making his way to the front row.

'Some wannabe from Santa Monica Boulevard,' said Nancy. 'Apparently Scarlett's brother picked him up in a gay bar last night and brought him along.'

'Nooo!' Perry looked suitably shocked. 'I thought the brother was out to lunch? And still stuck halfway in the closet?'

Nancy shrugged. 'Me too. I guess LA is helping him find himself.'

On the other side of the marquee, Minty Meyer adjusted her canary yellow coat dress and matching hat and smiled through gritted teeth at Caroline Drummond Murray, who was staring resolutely in front of her, doing a good impression of someone waiting for root canal surgery.

'Look at Lady Muck over there. Who does she think she is?' Minty hissed at her husband. Happily drunk beside her, he was admiring the endless pairs of silicone breasts as they filed respectfully past him. 'Rudy Meyer, are you listening to me?'

'Of course, dear,' he nodded dutifully, wondering how long a write-your-own-vows-service-for-four was likely to take, and how soon it would be before someone fed him something more substantial than a caviar blini.

Just then Danny sauntered in, beaming from ear to ear, with a wriggling Zac in his arms.

'You couldn't take His Majesty for me, could you, Mum?' he said, handing the bundle to an instantly ecstatic Minty. 'The au pair girl was supposed to get him off Di hours ago, but apparently she was last seen disappearing into the woods with a handsome Englishman and hasn't been heard of since.'

'Just as long as it wasn't your brother,' muttered Rudy. 'When are we getting started?'

'Any minute,' Danny assured him. 'The fathers are on their way up to get the girls now.'

Right on cue, the string quartet picked up their bows (they were also barefoot, much to Caroline's chagrin, and the viola player had visibly dirty toenails!). The last remaining stragglers took their seats to the strains of Handel's *Messiah* while Danny made his way to the dais, a simple, white wooden circle with what looked like a maypole in the middle of it, smothered in Scarlett's favourite Michaelmas daisies. He was joined a few moments later by a still-green Jake, as nervous as Danny was relaxed.

Scores of his stunning exes stared up at him, trying to catch his eye, but Jake's attention was focused rigidly on the marquee's entrance.

'Where is she?' His jaw was so tight, he looked like he was in the early stages of rigor mortis.

'For fuck's sake, mate, she's *coming*,' laughed Danny. 'Try and enjoy yourself. With any luck, this'll be the only wedding you ever have.'

Christ, I hope so, thought Jake. Much more of this and they'll have to take me away in a straitjacket.

But the moment Scarlett walked through the double

doors, walking four abreast with Diana and their respective fathers, his nerves melted away like butter in the sunshine. Glowing as if lit from within, her glorious mane of hair snaking down her back beneath the antique veil, he had never seen her look happier, or more lovely.

'Pinch me,' he whispered to Danny.

'Sorry,' his brother sighed. 'I'm too busy pinching myself.'

Diana, a blonde vision in her simple, clinging dress, was laughing aloud, smiling and waving to her friends like a teenager as she skipped up the aisle towards him.

'I can't believe it. Neither of the girls is wearing diamonds,' Aunt Agnes grumbled to her neighbour, adding proudly: 'I'm a partner in Solomon Stones now, you know. I shall be having words with both the grooms later. Imagine passing up such a glorious opportunity for some free advertising.'

'I don't think they entirely passed it up,' the woman whispered back. For there, trotting along sedately behind the wedding party, was Boxford, his collar dripping with Trade Fair diamonds.

'For heaven's sake,' mumbled Caroline sourly to Cameron. 'Can you believe what Scarlett's done to that *ridiculous* dog?'

But Cameron was too busy gazing into the eyes of his handsome American actor friend to notice.

Scarlett approached the dais.

'I love you,' said Jake, gripping her hand so tightly he nearly broke a finger as Hugo returned to his seat.

'That's a coincidence,' she grinned back at him. 'I think I might love you too.'

'Oh my God, I'm gonna bawl,' sighed Nancy, rummaging in vain through her Marc Jacobs purse for a handkerchief.

'Please don't,' whispered a male voice from the row behind her. 'You'll smudge all your make-up. I was kinda hoping *I* could do that later.'

Che Che's smile was so white and broad, it looked as if it might leap out of his face at any moment. Nancy opened her mouth to speak, but he held a finger up to her lips.

'Later, OK?' he said gently. 'Let's let the happy couples make it official first.'

'I don't forgive you, you know,' said Nancy, desperately trying to sound cross, which was hard when one's mouth insisted on pinging up at the corners. 'I'm not sure if I even like you any more.'

'That's OK,' said Che Che, deadpan. 'I'm taking you down to the woods after this to fuck your brains out. You'll like me again after that, I promise.'

'*Really!*' The elderly Scottish man to Nancy's left huffed indignantly.

Young people today had no respect.

The wedding party rumbled on long into the night. Danny and Diana both seemed happy to party till dawn, while little Zac, exhausted from the day's commotion, slept soundly in his bassinet under a table, oblivious to the deafening rumble of music and laughter around him.

At around midnight, Jake finally managed to prise Scarlett away from her drunk and emotional girlfriends and persuade her to sneak off with him into the night. They had a room booked at the Malibu Inn, and he'd been waiting all night – all his life, really – to get her back there. Alone.

'But surely we're bringing Boxie?' she pleaded as he bundled her into the car, a vintage Alfa Romeo that was his newest pride and joy.

'No way,' said Jake firmly. Seeing her crestfallen face, he added, 'Trust me, you wouldn't want him to have to witness what I'm about to do to you. Nancy'll take care of him.'

The short drive along PCH was magical. The road was silent at this time of night, and all Scarlett could hear was the low rumble of the engine merged with softly lapping Pacific waves.

'Don't you feel even the teensiest bit guilty?' she asked, when they finally pulled in to the hotel parking lot.

'About what?'

Jumping out of the car, Jake hurried round to Scarlett's side and opened the door for her.

'Rushing off without saying goodbye to anybody,' she said, carefully gathering up the train of her dress.

'Not remotely,' said Jake. 'It's our wedding. Now where do you think you're going?'

'What do you mean?' Scarlett gave him a puzzled look as she swung her long legs out of the car.

'Oh no you don't,' said Jake, and scooping her up into his arms, he carried her like a fireman across the parking lot towards their private, beach-side bungalow. 'I'm carrying you across the threshold.'

Scarlett laughed, thinking for the thousandth time how unbearably handsome he looked in his wedding suit, with the moon's shadows dancing across the strong lines of his face.

'I never knew you were so traditional, Mr Meyer.'

'You'd better believe it, Mrs Meyer. I'll have you barefoot and pregnant in the kitchen before you can say stay-at-home mother.'

Scarlett frowned at him knowingly.

'I hope that's a joke! Besides, I thought we agreed we were adopting children? You promised we'd talk to Dr Katenge about it.' Her face was suddenly serious again, and he saw the earnest, passionate moral crusader who'd infuriated and entranced him in equal measure since the day they'd first met.

'There are so many needy children in the world, Jake, and we have so much. The least we can do is—'

He stopped her with a kiss.

'For God's sake, Scarlett. *Shut up.*'

And for once in her life, Scarlett did.